Advance Praise for *Babylon*

"The extraordinary true story of the exile of the Jews in Babylon and their miraculous return seventy years later. The tale is personal and powerful, passing through the experiences of several generations. Some served in the palace, some made their homes in the city of Babylon, and others inhabited the deserted farms of the exiles. Insightful, colorful, and fascinating."

–**Margaret George**, *New York Times* bestselling author of *Helen of Troy, The Memoirs of Cleopatra, The Confessions of Young Nero, The Splendor Before the Dark*, and many others

"*Babylon* brings one of the most exciting Biblical eras to life in realistic, almost cinematic detail. You'll meet Biblical prophets, get caught up in palace intrigue, and witness the devastation of ancient warfare. You'll also fall in love with many compelling characters, especially Sarah and Chava, who leap right from the page into your heart. A thrilling and gripping read!"

–**Lori Banov Kaufmann**, National Jewish Book Award– winner and 2021 Christy Award finalist of *Rebel Daughter*

"Michelle Cameron brings the ancient world to life in a heart-wrenching story you won't want to put down. Beautifully written, with imagery so vivid you'll feel like you're actually there."

–**Michelle Moran**, *USA Today* and international bestselling author of *Nefertiti, Cleopatra's Daughter, The Heretic Queen*, and many others

"*Babylon* vividly evokes hanging gardens, exile, and a too-neglected but powerfully significant period of our cultural history. Michelle Cameron has written a unique and memorable historical tale, rich with Biblical and historical acuity, well-developed characters, vivid changes of milieu, themes of exile and adaptation, and wonderful ironic twists. Informative, entertaining, and evocative, *Babylon* is a book you'll remember."

–**Mitchell James Kaplan**, award-winning author of *Rhapsody, Into the Unbounded Night*, and *By Fire, By Water*

Babylon

Michelle Cameron

WICKED SON

A WICKED SON BOOK
An Imprint of Post Hill Press
ISBN: 978-1-63758-761-4
ISBN (eBook): 978-1-63758-762-1

Babylon:
A Novel of Jewish Captivity
© 2023 by Michelle Cameron
All Rights Reserved

Cover Design by Hampton Lamoureux
Map and Family Trees Design by Elizabeth Schlossberg

Post Hill Press
New York • Nashville
WickedSonBooks.com

Published in the United States of America
1 2 3 4 5 6 7 8 9 10

For Sondra, who encouraged my words to flow
and whose memory is a blessing

Forced March of the Judean Captives
from Jerusalem to Babylon

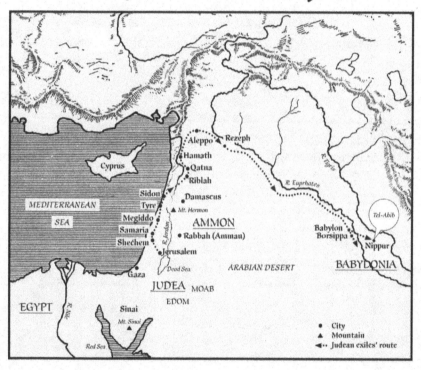

Sarah's Family

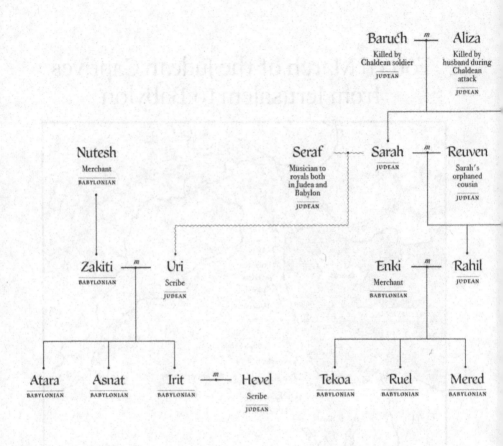

Baruch — *m* — **Aliza**
Killed by Chaldean soldier
JUDEAN

Killed by husband during Chaldean attack
JUDEAN

Nutesh
Merchant
BABYLONIAN

Seraf
Musician to royals both in Judea and Babylon
JUDEAN

Sarah — *m* — **Reuven**
JUDEAN

Sarah's orphaned cousin
JUDEAN

Zakiti — *m* — **Uri**
BABYLONIAN

Scribe
JUDEAN

Enki — *m* — **Rahil**
Merchant
BABYLONIAN

JUDEAN

Atara
BABYLONIAN

Asnat
BABYLONIAN

Irit — *m* — **Hevel**
BABYLONIAN

Scribe
JUDEAN

Tekoa
BABYLONIAN

Ruel
BABYLONIAN

Mered
BABYLONIAN

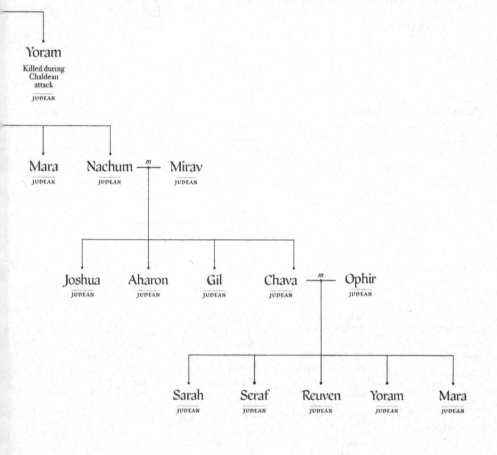

Yoram
Killed during
Chaldean
attack
JUDEAN

Mara
JUDEAN

Nachum —*m*— Mirav
JUDEAN   JUDEAN

Joshua
JUDEAN

Aharon
JUDEAN

Gil
JUDEAN

Chava —*m*— Ophir
JUDEAN   JUDEAN

Sarah
JUDEAN

Seraf
JUDEAN

Reuven
JUDEAN

Yoram
JUDEAN

Mara
JUDEAN

····· Adopted
~~ Couple out of wedlock

Babylonian Royal Family

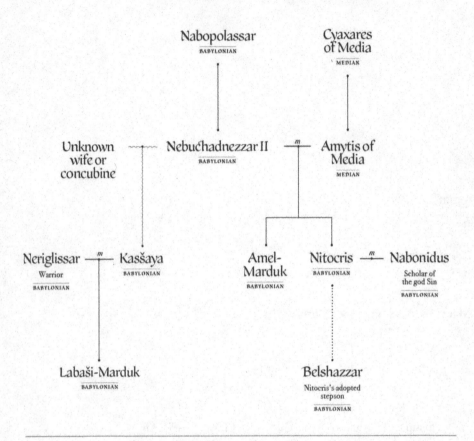

Nabopolassar
BABYLONIAN

Cyaxares of Media
MEDIAN

Unknown wife or concubine

Nebuchadnezzar II
BABYLONIAN

m

Amytis of Media
MEDIAN

Neriglissar
Warrior
BABYLONIAN

m

Kasšaya
BABYLONIAN

Amel-Marduk
BABYLONIAN

Nitocris
BABYLONIAN

m

Nabonidus
Scholar of the god Sin
BABYLONIAN

Labaši-Marduk
BABYLONIAN

Belshazzar
Nitocris's adopted stepson
BABYLONIAN

Judean Prophets:

Ezekiel
son of Buzi

Jeremiah
fled to Egypt

Ezra
fellow scribe to Uri

Second Isaiah

Judeans serving the Royal Court:

Daniel
called Belteshazzar by the Babylonians, seer

Azariah
called Abed-nego by the Babylonians, Daniel's friend

Seraf's fellow musicians:

  Tekoa
  flute player

  Rivai
  harpist

  Oreb
  multi-talented musican

Serving the Royal Court:

Belshazzar
courtier who betrays Kasšaya

Nebuzaradan
Captain of the Guard, conqueror of Judea

Melzar
master of eunuchs

Geb
Egyptian slave, manager of Kasšaya's perfumery

Ibi-Sin
physician's apprentice

Silili
Labaši-Marduk's wet nurse

Cilci
mute nursery slave from Cilicia

Amittai's Family

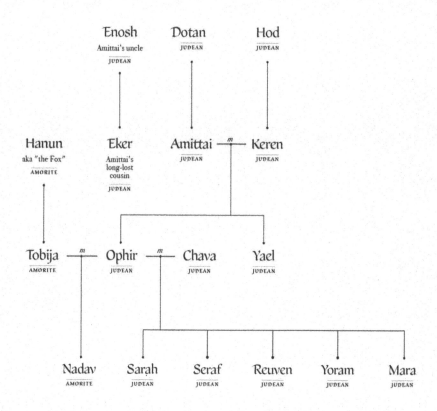

Enosh
Amittai's uncle
JUDEAN

Dotan
JUDEAN

Hod
JUDEAN

Hanun
aka "the Fox"
AMORITE

Eker
Amittai's
long-lost
cousin
JUDEAN

Amittai — m — Keren
JUDEAN   JUDEAN

Tobija — m — Ophir — m — Chava
AMORITE   JUDEAN   JUDEAN

Yael
JUDEAN

Nadav
AMORITE

Sarah
JUDEAN

Seraf
JUDEAN

Reuven
JUDEAN

Yoram
JUDEAN

Mara
JUDEAN

Babylonian/Judean Scribes:

Kur
Babylonian
master of
the scribes

Agga
Babylonian scribe
turned priest

**Baruch ben
Neriah**
head of Judean
scribes

Returning Judeans:

Beula
Judean merchant's
daughter

Uziel
goldsmith's son

**Jeshua
ben Jozadak**
called Sheshbazzar
in Babylon,
Temple High Priest

Zerubbabel
Judean prince
appointed governor
by Cyrus

Manasseh
first-born son of
High Priest

Nehemia
rebuilt the walls
of Jerusalem

**Hanani and
Hananiah**
protectors of the city
of Jerusalem

····· Adopted
～～ Couple out of wedlock

PART ONE

The Captives

586 BCE–Year 1 of the Exile

1

Sarah Under Siege

SARAH STOOD AT THE WINDOW of the family farm outside of Jerusalem, staring across the hills into the confusion of the city. Flames and smoke rose from Mount Moriah. But it couldn't be—

"Papa," Sarah choked out.

"How many times have I said to stay away from that window?" Baruch, her father, pushed her aside to stand in front of the window himself. "God help us," he gasped.

Flames were shooting up from the Temple Mount. Solomon's Temple—God's Temple—was burning. "How could they?" she whispered.

Her father wheeled on her. "They're idolators; that's how. Placed on this Earth for no other purpose but evil."

It was inconceivable. Why hadn't God stopped them? Sarah could almost smell the rich scent of the cedar and fir walls that lined the Temple as they smoldered in flame. Even at this distance, she saw the Chaldean forces gleefully loading carts with the gold and silver ornaments of the Lord, seizing them as war loot to enrich the coffers of the Babylonians. How could anyone destroy such beauty?

Her father irritably brushed aside her comment, his hand smacking the air.

Unable to bear it, she looked in another direction. Beyond the Temple Mount, outside the city, soldiers raced back and forth on the solid earthen banks they'd built up over the past weeks to attack Jerusalem's sacred stone walls. They made Sarah think of wasps buzzing angrily in date palms, swarming about her head as she collected ripe fruit. She watched, helpless, as the enemy cast heavy stones from giant catapults while shower after shower of arrows fell upon the city. The air was acrid with the smell of dust and smoke and of oil bubbling on Judean fires, sent scalding down the walls to repel the attackers.

"We'll see an end to this before nightfall," her father said, his voice heavy with resignation.

They had not seen daylight for many days. The skies were dark and angry, brooding, as if God Himself wished to add to the assault's fury. The prophets had warned them, Father had growled just last night. Jeremiah had warned them. Still Sarah prayed, trying to ignore the tumult surrounding her. It was no use. God was angry with His people, the prophets proclaimed, and had sent the bold Babylonian conquerors to punish them. Sarah believed them.

After all, Sarah's God was always angry. Just like her father. She often confused the two.

"What will they do to us?" moaned Aliza, Sarah's mother.

Mother sat on her stool near the hearth, having gathered her household treasures around her. In her lap was a pile of hand-worked linen, which she stroked compulsively.

"Aliza," Baruch chided her, turning from the window, his face bleak. "With death lurking in every corner, why do you cling to that old cloth?"

But Sarah knew why. Her mother's life was confined to the solidly built rooms and terraced fields of the sprawling white stone farmhouse. She needed to clasp something solid, gain comfort from softness she could touch and caress. As her father turned away, Mother snuck the cloth to her cheek, hand shaking. Sarah knelt by her stool, laying her head in her mother's lap to both give and take comfort. Aliza's trembling fingers moved from the cloth to Sarah's hair.

It would not be long now, Sarah thought, her heartbeat rising in panic.

The servants, suspecting the worst, had fled the farm yesterday, leaving their rakes in the field and dinner half cooked. Only old Dina remained, too brittle and cloudy eyed to contemplate escape. The handmaid sat blinking in a corner of the room, her wrinkled face working in silent terror.

Sarah pictured the soldiers marching up the hillside in orderly rows, breastplates glinting in the sun. The family would huddle in a corner while the greedy troops seized her mother's shining metal mirrors and soft goatskin rugs. They would round up the sheep and goats now bleating piteously in the pen behind the house. But then Sarah willed them to move on. After all, there was no reason for them to lay good farmland to waste.

But even if they burned this season's crop in the field, Sarah thought, that would surely be the worst of it. Her father's fears of death and destruction were groundless. They had to be. Sarah could not imagine life beyond the family farm, this safe, familiar place where she had lived every day of her young life.

"Shouldn't Reuven and Yoram have returned?" Mother's voice quavered.

Baruch cast her a withering glare. "They should never have gone," he growled. "You should not have let them."

Aliza shrank back. Sarah wanted to protest that her father had been the one to let them go. But saying so would only bring Father's ever-simmering anger down upon her head.

Sarah's seventeen-year-old brother, Yoram, and her orphaned cousin, Reuven, a year younger, had disappeared down the hillside an hour ago, eager to see what was happening in the city.

"Let me come with you!" Sarah had called, anxious to escape the house and its fears.

But her father had grabbed her by the forearm and pulled her back.

"You stay under my eye, girl," he insisted. "I'd kill you before letting you become some soldier's plaything. Stay with your mother."

Sarah pulled against her father's iron grasp, despite knowing her resistance would only infuriate him further. He had always kept a close watch over her as her black curls, green eyes and full lips garnered admiration from the neighbors for her beauty. But this past year, with the emergence of new curves and as men looked her up and down, their glances appreciative, lingering on her chest and hips, her father's dominance had become unbearable.

"I'll dress like a child," she'd said, straining against her father's strong grip. "The soldiers will leave me alone then."

But Baruch dug his fingers into her arm and shook his head. "The Chaldean soldiers who fight for Babylon don't care how old you are," he snapped. "They lie with animals and children younger than five if lust takes them. They are animals themselves."

Aliza moaned again now, rocking back and forth on her stool. "You'll protect us, Baruch, won't you? You won't let them harm us?"

Her father curved his hand around the hilt of the sharp dagger he had slipped into his girdle that morning and nodded. "No fear, Aliza."

Sarah felt sick, dizzy. How could her father protect them against a company of soldiers? The thought was ludicrous.

The door banged open, and Reuven burst into the room. His face was dark with soot. Loud cries from the city poured in, sharp and piercing. Sarah looked past him, watching for Yoram.

Reuven panted, his voice reedy with panic. "The soldiers are through the gates! Look! You can see the flames and the smoke!"

Aliza shrieked, her mouth working in fear. Baruch clamped a heavy hand on her shoulder. "Quiet, woman!" he hissed. "Reuven, where is Yoram?"

Reuven opened his mouth, but no sound emerged. A moment passed. Two. They spun to face him, Sarah's heart battering through her chest.

"Dead," Reuven finally moaned. "Killed as we fled the soldiers. I was running a few steps ahead. I turned back but he was already... I couldn't help...." The boy doubled over, shoulders shaking with hard sobs.

Sarah covered her mouth with both hands. Her bossy, strong, handsome brother could not possibly be dead. She jerked her head to one side, trying to dislodge the image of Yoram being hacked to death by a sword or stabbed by a dagger.

"No!" Aliza's sharp-edged shriek sliced through Sarah's anguish. "Not my Yoram! Not my boy!"

The light dimmed from Baruch's eyes. He stepped out of his sandals, took hold of the cloth at his neck, and with one harsh rip, tore a strip over his heart. Barefoot, he sagged into a seat.

Sarah didn't know what to do. She put her arms around her mother, but Aliza pushed her away, keening in misery. Aliza drew her stool up to the table where she had piled her treasures. She pushed the rugs and linen to one side, lying with a cheek flattened on the table's surface, howling for her lost child.

Sarah didn't dare touch her father, who sat hunched in his chair, eyes unblinking, staring into space. "We've lost everything, Aliza," he muttered. "Everything."

I'm here, Sarah wanted to tell them. *I'm still here*. But she knew she was not enough, could never be enough. Yoram, the son of the house, had always been the one her parents' hopes and dreams were centered on. She—like every other daughter of Judea—was only on loan until they arranged her marriage.

Then Sarah noticed Reuven's bloody footsteps. His face was bruised, his leg deeply scratched. She grabbed one of her mother's treasured cloths from the table and swiped at the blood dripping down his leg.

"A bit of stone chipped off one of their catapults," Reuven muttered. "A piece is still buried in my leg."

"Yes, I feel it," Sarah said, probing the skin.

"Can you dig it out?" Reuven asked.

"Let me try," said Dina, rising painfully and shuffling forward.

Sarah let the maidservant move closer.

The cries from the city grew louder. Through the open door, Sarah heard the twang of swords and shields meeting, the heavy marching of boots. It couldn't be long now. Dina pushed on the wound, making Reuven cry out. The caustic scent of rising smoke choked them all, sputtering coughs mixing with their tears. The city was burning, her cousin had said. She'd seen the Temple burning. Mixed with the heavy odor of smoldering was another smell, something metallic and bitter.

"So many wounded lie among the dead," Reuven stammered, wincing as the handmaid's half-blind groping drove the shard deeper into his leg. "People sprawled in the streets, crying and moaning. The soldiers are burning everything." He thrust the maidservant away roughly and turned toward Baruch. "We must leave the city!"

"There is only one safe place," said Father, drawing himself upright. His broad shoulders filled the space with purpose. He curved his thick fingers around his dagger hilt and extracted it, almost tenderly, from its sheath. Sarah drew a sharp breath, fear panging in her throat.

"Aliza," Baruch said, stepping over to her wailing mother, "I have always loved you." He forced her to rise from her stool and hugged her to him. He plunged the dagger through a soft break in her ribs, thrusting it deep inside her body as her eyes bulged whitely from their sockets.

Mother jerked at the force of the blow, releasing one final shattering gasp of pain. Sarah heard the scream ringing in her ears before she realized that the cry had flown, unbidden, from her own throat. Baruch's arms tightened as he embraced his wife one last time. He eased her back to her seat. Aliza sprawled onto the table, hair falling unbound from its headdress, one arm swinging unnaturally. Sarah stood rooted to the ground, trembling. Baruch pulled his dagger from her mother's body. Sarah stared at the red wet blade.

"Sarah." Father beckoned to her.

Sarah's limbs turned to water. She could neither move toward her father nor turn and flee his deadly embrace.

"No!" she protested, her voice echoing in her ears. Her will to survive, all the spirit of her young, unlived life, reared up inside her. *No,* she thought, a rush of terror and denial drumming through her. *I won't die! I won't!*

"Tell your cousin it is the only way," Baruch said to Reuven, who stared at his dead aunt, his lower lip quivering. "God may have abandoned us, but we must trust in the world to come."

Reuven opened his mouth. But before he could speak, Baruch's face crumpled. He fell heavily to his knees, collapsing. His weapon dropped from his grip, clattering on the stone floor.

Dazed, Sarah saw a dagger sticking out of his back.

A soldier, his blue tunic covered with dust and stained by blood, rose behind her father. The soldier put a foot on her father's back and, reaching down, yanked his dagger out with a practiced pull. A squad of ten soldiers crowded into the room behind him. Everything turned cloudy and moved much too slowly to be real. Despite knowing Aliza could not protect her, Sarah instinctively moved behind her mother's chair.

The lead soldier grinned at them. "I take you hostage in the name of General Sangar Nebo for the greater glory of Nebuchadnezzar, King of Kings," he proclaimed, his sing-song voice sounding as though he had repeated this pronouncement many times that day.

The men behind him swooped on the treasures her mother had piled up.

"Pretty," cooed one of the men, rubbing a scarf of lamb's wool embroidered with beads against his cheek. "The whores of Alexandria will like this!"

Another pranced with her mother's favorite shawl draped on his head, stepping around her dead body as he galloped about the room. "Oh, Nebbie, what have you brought me from the wars?" he mimicked in a high, falsetto voice.

Suddenly one of them noticed her crouching behind her mother's body and nudged the other. "I like that too." He whistled.

"Come here, girl." The lead soldier dropped the clay pot he was holding, letting it smash on the floor.

Sarah shut her eyes. *They can't hurt me if I don't see them.* But it was nothing more than a child's thought, and she opened them again as the soldier's rough hand yanked her to her feet.

"Leave her alone!" Reuven cried, his voice wobbling with fear, snatching Baruch's dagger from the floor. The weapon wavered in his young grasp.

As the soldiers laughed, one of them grabbed him from behind, twisting the dagger out of his hand, holding him tightly. Reuven struggled against the restraining arms.

"Someone want this one?" the soldier asked.

"No!" Reuven cried, his broad face blazing.

Sarah gasped in shock. What could he mean? She knew what they wanted from her—a farmer's daughter, she had seen animals couple many times before. It was what her father had always warned her against, the reason he had forbidden her to go to the well alone once she'd turned fourteen, probably why he'd wanted to kill her before the soldiers got here. But Reuven? What could they possibly want with another man?

Dina, forgotten in her corner, limped forward.

"Move, crone!" A soldier thrust her aside.

"Dina, stay back!" Sarah cried. "They'll kill you!"

"That old bag of bones?" the soldier sneered. "She'll be dead soon enough anyway."

The old woman staggered off, groping her way to the back door. The men ignored her. She slid through, leaving the two youngsters to their fate.

The man still gripping Sarah's arm pulled her to the ground, kneeling beside her, fingers curving about her breast, crushing it. Her mother's hand swayed, lifeless, above her. If she reached out, she might have touched her father's prone corpse. She squeezed her eyes shut once more, trying to escape inside her own darkness.

"Now, as for you...." the soldier said, his voice laced with lust. A trumpet blast startled him. "Marduk damn it," he muttered.

Yet another soldier entered the room, armor clanking as he strode inside. "The captain's calling for us," he shouted.

Sarah wanted to sob in sudden relief, but the day was far from over. Pulled to her feet, she was half-pushed, half-carried out of the house. The soldier who still held Reuven forced him outside behind her. The others followed, belt pouches bulging with loot.

"Light it!" one of the commanders cried. Someone brought a torch of flaming straw and set the house and the barn afire.

Sarah could barely see through the film of grief misting her eyes. The scorch of the burning barn was a fever on her skin. Her ears filled with the bleating of the animals tethered to the farthest fence. She stood, shaking and numb, as flames devoured the farm where her family had lived for generations. And then the soldiers led them away.

2

Amel-Marduk's Dream

"YOU WISHED TO SEE ME, Great King?"

Nebuchadnezzar waved Daniel inside the room where he sat on an immense gold throne, flanked by marble statues of the god Marduk and his wife, Sarpanit, and topped by Marduk's snarling dragon, Mušḫuššu. Daniel walked upon the intricate mosaic of the Babylonian Empire sprawled across the entire floor, taking care not to tread on the small area signifying Judea, his homeland. He prostrated himself before the king.

"Belteshazzar," Nebuchadnezzar said, using the name Daniel had been given upon arriving in Babylon as a stripling of thirteen nearly four years ago, when Judea had first fallen to the Chaldeans, and Judean nobles were taken captive. "I wish to consult you on a matter of grave importance."

"Another dream, Majesty?" Daniel controlled his face, fearing that his apprehension would communicate itself through his features. Nebuchadnezzar's recountings of his dreams were always fraught with danger. More than once, the king had threatened death to any magician who could not tell him what they augured. He menaced the seers with dreadful deaths: being torn apart by wild lions or buried to the neck in desert sands so buzzards could peck out their eyes. Daniel had been successful up to now in interpreting Nebuchadnezzar's strange visions, and the king had respected even the harshest of portents. But the young Judean dreaded the day the king would reject what he had to say.

"Not mine," the king said now. "But yes, I have need of your ability to construe dreams." He glanced at the soothsayer who was still standing, half bowed. "Sit, my friend." He gestured to a cushioned bench placed on one side of his gigantic throne.

Daniel settled himself, arranging the draperies of his rich gown, a hand pushing his thick black hair away from his forehead. "Whose dreams then, Great King?"

"My children. The three eldest," Nebuchadnezzar said, sighing. "Amel-Marduk, Kasšaya, and Nitocris. Each one has come to me this week and reported a confused vision of grave import, rife with portents and signs—each suggesting that their dream points to their future as imperial ruler."

Daniel's eyebrows rose. "The girls, too?"

"A natural question," Nebuchadnezzar concurred. "But they are *my* daughters. You may have heard of Queen Semiramis, who ruled Assyria some three hundred years ago. I suspect either daughter could rise to such heights if called upon. Neither claims the throne for themselves, however. Kasšaya, at least, says she will rule alongside her husband-to-come."

Daniel pursed his lips. "Still, it is unusual."

"Again, they are my daughters, Belteshazzar. Their ambitions do them credit."

Daniel subsided, waiting.

Nebuchadnezzar was silent for a moment, looking off into the distance. When he spoke, Daniel heard constraint in his voice. "I fear all three have invented these night visions in concert with their personal magicians to influence the succession."

Daniel suppressed a grin. The rivalry between Princess Kasšaya and her two younger half-siblings was well known. "Quite possible," he mused. "But I would need to hear each one from their own lips to be able to judge."

Nebuchadnezzar nodded. "I will have my chamberlain arrange it." He fixed his gaze on Daniel's face, adding, "You will not reveal to them what their dreams mean under pain of death. You will hear them all, and once you have divined their meaning, you will tell me and me alone. Is that clear?"

Daniel bit his lip before composing his face. He understood the king's reasons, but his royal master had neither understanding nor care of how difficult refusing to answer the demands of his imperious children would be. But Daniel had been in Babylon long enough to learn how to navigate the shoals of palace politics. He trusted he would find a way to do so once again.

Nebuchadnezzar looked down at the tiled floor, eyes wandering over his empire. "They cannot all rule after me. But, like wolflings, they snarl and snap at one another, each one vying for my attention. Are all children so jealous of one another, Belteshazzar?"

Daniel felt the emptiness of his lap and grimaced. "I will never be a parent, you know, Majesty. And, as an only child, I had no siblings myself. So I am not qualified to answer your question."

Nebuchadnezzar shrugged. "No matter. My chamberlain will inform you when he has arranged your audiences with my children."

The first meeting was with Nebuchadnezzar's eldest son by his newest wife, Queen Amytis of Media. Daniel had to wait nearly an hour past the appointed time before a bedraggled prince, reeking of manure, presented himself in the smallest of audience chambers. Amel-Marduk was accompanied by members of his cortege and a handful of priests of Marduk. As they crowded into the small room, the smell of sweat and horses rose off the courtiers. Hunting armor clanked, while the gowns of the priests swished across the marble floors.

"Belteshazzar," Amel-Marduk greeted him, a toothy grin showing as the Judean bowed low, "you have not been waiting long, I trust?"

Daniel swallowed his irritation. His years in Babylon had taught him much, and one of the first lessons was that each princeling was a law unto himself. Had he played the role of tutor and told Amel-Marduk that promptness was the politeness of princes, the king's son would either shrug or punish him for impudence. Daniel thanked the Most High that he had not been made a tutor to any of the royals—his own position was precarious enough.

But Daniel also knew the prince's discourtesy was not personally pointed. After all, tales of the prince's behavior—his cruelty to his slaves, his courtiers, his tutors, and his priests, his abuse of varied bedmates, even his misconduct toward his royal parents—were rife throughout the kingdom.

"Nothing is more pressing than waiting upon your pleasure," Daniel said, bowing again.

The prince strode across the room and poured himself a cup of wine from the hammered bronze decanter sitting on a marble table. He quaffed it and poured more. "We were off hunting ibex—hot on the trail of a beauty with a striped horn. Nearly brought him down too."

"It's a pity he escaped you, Highness," said one of the courtiers with a pointed glower at another. "Next time, perhaps, Zaidu will not yell out and spoil sport."

Zaidu glared in response. "Had you not nearly ripped open my mare's flank with your short sword—" he began.

Daniel watched the squabbling, amused. Amel-Marduk's courtiers were in a constant state of internecine warfare, each vying with the others for the spoiled prince's favor.

"Your bickering makes my head ache," the prince grumbled. "Shut up, would you?" He turned toward Daniel. "I've been commanded to tell you of my dream. Milik-Harbat here"—Daniel warily bowed toward the priest in his dark robe and thick turban—"has already told me that it means I will be king after my father dies. I don't understand why I must tell you as well."

Daniel nodded. "Your royal father's commands cannot, of course, be ignored," he said carefully. "But I am curious to see if my interpretation agrees with that of my esteemed colleague. If you will indulge me, Prince?"

Amel-Marduk sighed loudly. "This is a bore. Oh, well…." He paused dramatically. "My dream. It was dark, and I stood at the peak of the Ziggurat of Marduk. There was lightning and thunder, and heavy rains fell upon me. But they weren't rainwater. The drops that gilded my tongue were the most delicious wine I have ever tasted—and all Babylon knows that I know wine better than any man in the kingdom. Don't they?" He looked to his nobles, who tried to outdo one another in their murmured praises of Amel-Marduk's ability to select the finest of wines.

Daniel stifled a smile. The prince was usually brought to bed sodden with wine and heavy with rich food. The wine's quality had little to do with Amel-Marduk's gluttonous desires.

"So, I drank deep, my mouth filling. It was as if a river flowed through me, every mouthful more delicious than the last. At last I felt weary. I stretched out to sleep, when suddenly, the great seal of Babylon pressed itself upon my chest. It grew until it nearly crushed me—but I rose to my feet as lightning flashed about me. Then my servant woke me. So—that's all. Straightforward enough, yes?"

Milik-Harbat reached up and adjusted his priestly turban. When he spoke, his voice was reedy, thin, despite his square-shouldered stance. "There can be no doubt what this portends. Our prince will reign supreme after his father. And even the heavens will tremble at his reign."

Daniel smiled warily. "I can see why you believe that to be true, priest of Marduk. Thank you for relating your dream, Highness."

Amel-Marduk stared at him. "You agree, then? You will speak with my father and tell him he must declare me his successor?"

Daniel looked toward the ceiling's cedar beams. He could neither ignore Nebuchadnezzar's commands nor Amel-Marduk's question. After all, Amel-Marduk was likely to succeed his father—as little as Daniel liked the notion—and the prince's grudges were legendary. "It seems likely, but I need time to ponder, Highness. And your father has commanded me to speak with him first."

Amel-Marduk looked satisfied, even smug, and Daniel's tense shoulders relaxed. The courtiers surrounding them buzzed with excitement. Only Amel-Marduk's most favored friend, Belshazzar, a rising star among Babylonian nobles, scrutinized the Judean soothsayer with narrowed eyes.

3

Sarah and the Captain of the Guard

"YOU, YOU...OH YES AND YOU, definitely," said the guard, pointing to Sarah and licking his lips.

Sarah shuddered. "What do you want with me?" she asked. But she knew the answer.

One of the other Judean maidens tied to her shrugged. "It might be an escape from this," she said bitterly, nodding at the ropes coiled around their wrists.

They were all bound—right hand to the left hand of the person behind them, left hand to the right hand of the person before them. Ten people formed a group. Sarah tried to count the number of groups but gave up after reaching one hundred. The chain immobilized them, forcing them to shuffle in march step. Curses arose when someone stumbled, whips cut into all their backs when someone slowed.

Sarah kept careful count of the days, naming them silently as the sun peeked over the horizon and light teased her eyelids. She feared slipping into nothingness, of accepting her fate as a captive. So she named the days in the mornings, repeating them as she moved painfully forward, and released them every day at sunset. They'd been two weeks on the road. The prisoners whispered that Nebuzaradan, the Captain of the Guard, feared the Hebrew God's wrath if he allowed the Jews a moment to pray for His mercy. So until they departed Judea, the Hebrews slept only an hour at a time, standing upright against one another like horses, forced to nod off under the unblinking eye of the summer sun. Then the whips would sing out and the appalling trek begin anew.

As she was prodded onward, Father's last words bedeviled her with their sing-song persistence, every word sounding in time with her steps. *God abandoned us. Trust in the world to come. God abandoned us. Trust in the world to come.*

God certainly had abandoned her, but the world to come seemed bleak and full of despair.

This morning, they had finally crossed the border into Aram, which had once been the Kingdom of Israel. Their journey took them north rather than eastward across the dangerous reaches of the desert. Sarah knew they were looping through the conquered cities of the vanquished Assyrian host. A hundred and fifty years ago, these cities would have been bustling with their cousins, the Israelites. Sarah had heard the stories, how the Kingdoms of Israel and Judea had once been united under King David and then King Solomon. But when ten of the twelve tribes rejected King Solomon's son, Rehoboam, the kingdom split into two. Sarah's family, living on their ancestral farm near Jerusalem, belonged to one of the two tribes loyal to the Davidic line. When the Israelites were exiled from their homes by the Assyrian armies more than a century and a half earlier, many Judeans claimed that this was a judgment on the ten tribes for abandoning their God-appointed king.

After the Israelites were forced from their land, Father had explained, Canaanites rushed in to take their homes and farms. They lined up now to jeer as the endless procession limped by. Listlessly passing the mocking faces, Sarah wondered: Would pagans lay claim to the abandoned cities and villages of Judea? Would some foreign family seize the farm? Imagining some stranger living in her house and farming her father's land, a pang of bitter yearning rose within her, so intense that even the chorus of Father's last words could not subdue it.

Now that they had reached Aram, Nebuzaradan felt it safe to halt their cruel journey. Still tethered, they sat in huddled groups on the rocky ground. The guards cut away those who had died, stinking corpses whom the captives had dragged over countless miles. The soldiers piled the dead in a shallow gully, carelessly covering them with rocks and sand. The Judean priests pleaded to be allowed to pray over them. But Nebuzaradan refused. Sarah gagged as birds of prey perched on the loose rock cover, ripping dead flesh with their beaks, flying off with dripping carrion. Even the battle-hardened Chaldean soldiers covered their noses and mouths at the stench. They forced the cavalcade farther down the road to escape the smell, the prisoners moaning as the soldiers prodded them back on their blistered, bloody feet.

The Babylonians pitched camp under the shade of tall cedar trees. They set guards over their captives but allowed them to talk freely for the first time since leaving Jerusalem two weeks ago. As Sarah placed one foot after the other day after day, her father's refrain ringing in her head, other words had bubbled up, desperate to escape. Images bombarded her: her father slaying her mother, the dagger sticking out of her father's back. And then emotion flooded her: how helpless she'd felt at her near rape, and how horrified she'd felt at the callous burning of her home.

She forced herself to call upon quieter memories of her childhood. Long afternoons spent beneath the eucalyptus trees or high up on the terraces working in the fields. Working with Mother in the kitchen, watching her direct the servants, knead bread, and prepare offerings for the Temple. The soft pinkish hue of the white stone farmhouse in the early evenings as the sun set over the hills of Jerusalem. The warmth of the barn, nuzzling the young sheep and milking the goats. The excitement of market day, bringing fresh produce to the market, finding excuses to visit the well where the young men congregated, lingering there despite her father's objections. How she used to preen before the eager smiles, wondering which of the lounging youths Father might pick as her husband. Everything that was gone, forever.

But now that she was permitted to speak her sorrow, words stalled in her dry throat.

As she sat, limply leaning against the back of another captive, Sarah looked over at her cousin, roped to a different group. Reuven's eager young strength had always made her compare him to an overgrown puppy. But now, sitting slumped against his neighbor, he seemed to struggle with his own memories. Sarah motioned with her head, waving without hands. Reuven nodded in return, lower lip quivering as he tried to force a smile. Seeing his grotesque grimace, the tears Sarah had suppressed for so many miles streamed from her eyes, making sluggish furrows in the caked dirt on her face. She and Reuven stared at one another for a long moment, the only survivors of their family's house.

Her heart went out to her twice orphaned cousin. He had already known too much sorrow. His parents and three brothers had succumbed to a spring sickness that left him miraculously untouched. Coming to live with her family, he had ignored Aliza's mothering and Baruch's gruff attempts to help him feel like a member of the household. Sarah tried to comfort him with food that she moved from her plate to his own, but he just picked at it, leaving most of it untouched. It was Yoram, whose strong, broad body always reminded Sarah of their father, who finally pulled him out of his grief, teasing him mercilessly and plying him with an endless list of chores. Reuven, almost too exhausted to stand, finally protested near dusk at the end of the first week. Yoram had laughed, taking up a second shovel, singing out at the top of his lungs as they cleaned the animals' stalls together. Reuven had grown to adore his older cousin. But now Yoram was dead. They were all dead.

After two weeks of silent disbelief, forced to do nothing but place one aching foot ahead of another, Sarah succumbed to grief. She longed to fling herself onto her cousin's chest, to howl in mourning for everything they had both lost. For the God that had abandoned them. For the world to come, which seemed full of sorrow and terror.

The guard who selected her ignored her wet face. He sawed at the cords that sweat and dust had made hard as iron, freeing Sarah from the human chain. He grasped her by the forearm, yanking her to her feet.

Sarah's limbs were numb after being tied so tightly for so long. She shook her arms, massaged her prickly forearms and wrists, then stumbled after the girls the guard had selected. They picked their way through the enervated ranks of captives toward the captain's quarters.

Sarah studied the other three girls through narrowed eyes. Each of them, she realized, were selected for their burgeoning beauty, shining forth despite the filth of the trail. All were unmarried virgins with uncovered heads. All wide eyed, frightened. One girl kept whimpering, a sad, tickling sound she tried to suppress by clamping a hand to her mouth. A second girl's tears streamed down her cheeks. Sarah caught her trembling lip between her teeth and bore down, using the pain to stop from being infected by their fear. She thought of what her father would say if he saw her now and squared her shoulders. "Shut up," Sarah hissed under her breath. "Are you weaklings that you let the enemy hear your moans?"

The captain's vaulted tent was spacious—large enough for a table in one corner, draped with a dun-colored cloth and laden with food and earthen jugs of water and wine. A wide cot stood in a second corner and an area of woven rugs and plush pillows in a third. A young Judean prisoner sat stiffly on one of the cushions, strumming a battered dulcimer. He was slender and tall, with olive skin and dark chestnut hair that nearly touched his shoulders. He swallowed hard as the girls were ushered inside, his soulful black eyes reflecting their fear and pain. The young musician glanced at Sarah, his expressive eyes seeming to offer her courage. She drew a deep breath and nodded tightly at him.

Nebuzaradan stood with some officers at the table, pointing to a map and barking orders. A tall, broadly built man with graying hair, the captain wore a sleeveless tunic of metal mesh. His naked, muscular arms were scarred, and what Sarah could only imagine must be a battle wound ran from his forehead down his lean left cheek into the grizzled, salt-and-pepper beard of his projecting chin. He moodily plucked grapes from a large bunch tumbled in a woven straw bowl, making Sarah's mouth water. The captives received only bread and water in the mornings and a thin gruel at night and the sight of fresh fruit was almost too much to bear.

Nebuzaradan turned. His face lit up at the four beauties, taking in their jutting hips and budding breasts. He waved his officers out. Their eyes lingered on the women's curves. It took a sharp "Go!" from the captain before they dragged themselves away.

"I approve your choices," the captain told the guard, throwing him a gold coin, which the soldier caught deftly. "I'll take that one for tonight."

He pointed straight at Sarah. The guard led the other three girls back outside. The fear Sarah had tried to ignore nearly overwhelmed her. Her face puckered. The musician sounded a twanging chord on the dulcimer just as she was about to throw herself at the captain's feet and beg for mercy.

The captain laughed. "Do you know her, Seraf?"

"No," the prisoner said. "But surely she is too young for you, noble Nebuzaradan."

The captain grinned. "I like them young, Judean musician."

"You would ruin her, Captain. No man would take her for wife after you finish with her."

"A beauty like that? Of course they will. What if I give her to you as a gift if you please me during this journey?"

Sarah watched, feeling sick to her stomach, as the musician looked at her differently now, appraisingly, a fire in his eyes that hadn't lodged there before. Despair made her reckless. "I will sleep with no man before I have moistened my throat, which is parched from this weary journey," she declared.

The captain's eyebrows rose. "She is young, yes, but she has spirit. She pleases me. Drink, girl. Have some food too."

"But very little," the musician murmured. "Otherwise you will be sick."

Hard though it was to follow the dulcimer player's advice, Sarah knew he was right. She took a sliver of roast hen and a few grapes. Rather than drinking the heavy red wine sitting in a ceramic jug on the table, she poured herself a cup of water.

As she ate, the musician played. The tunes he chose were soft and lilting—almost as if he wanted to lull the captain into sleep. Nebuzaradan sat back against the soft pillows and yawned. And yawned once more.

His eyes drooped. Would the musician's quiet tunes succeed in preventing—or at least postponing—her rape? Sarah sat breathless, waiting. The officer's body sank into the cushions. Seraf played even more softly. In a moment, the captain would be asleep....

An officer walked in. "Sir!" he called out, clicking his heels together as he shot a hand up in salute.

Seraf gasped, exasperated. Sarah wanted to cry.

Nebuzaradan shook himself awake. "Yes?"

The officer handed him a parchment, which the captain unrolled, read, and handed back. "Take it to Kofu," he commanded. He stood, stretching.

"Out," he barked at Seraf. The musician reluctantly rose, putting his dulcimer under his arm. Panic gripped Sarah's throat. She looked around.

"Captain," she said, her voice filling the tent. "I see dice on the table. Do you gamble?"

The captain laughed. "What soldier doesn't?"

Despite her father's forbidding it, Sarah had learned the rules of dicing from Yoram, out in the barn when they were supposed to be doing their chores.

"Good," Sarah said. "I propose we play for my virginity. If I win, you will leave me be."

Nebuzaradan frowned, the scar on his face whitening. "You overstep your bounds, Judean girl."

Sarah swallowed. "Are you afraid you might lose?" she taunted him, willing her voice not to break.

The captain growled. "I fear nothing. Cast the dice."

Sarah sent a silent supplication to God. She threw. Two sixes stared up at her.

Nebuzaradan let out a gruff roar of laughter, then looked at Sarah regretfully. "I can't best that. We'll play again tomorrow. Tonight I will take another girl."

A guard led her out and seized one of the others, who wailed and kicked at him, but was thrust inside. Sarah felt wretched, watching her.

Seraf followed Sarah. "Clever," he told her.

Sarah sighed. "My luck can't hold for the entire journey."

The musician laughed, his almond-shaped eyes crinkling at the corners. Sarah saw a tinge of gold in their dark depths.

"You don't know that," he said. "What do they call you?"

"I am Sarah, daughter of Baruch. And you?"

"Seraf, once a musician at King Zedekiah's court."

"You are older than you look, then," Sarah said, surprised.

"I was very young when I played at the king's court. I apprenticed as a musician at the age of four and was performing before I was ten. I am twenty-two now."

"That explains why you are so skilled." Sarah nodded. "I saw how you tried to lull the captain to sleep with your music. Thank you for trying."

Seraf smiled. "You did not need my help. You are beautiful and brave both, like Deborah the Prophet."

Sarah smiled back at him. But her smile wavered as she noticed how his eyes rested on her lips for a long moment, then moved lower on her body.

4

Kasšaya's Dream

A WEEK ELAPSED BEFORE THE Princess Kasšaya was willing to meet with
Daniel. Daniel heard through the palace grapevine that she had argued
with Queen Amytis and left the court in a huff, saying that she would
visit her mother's people. But it could not have been a successful trip,
for Kasšaya returned to the palace after a few days, closing herself in her
rooms in a royal tantrum, and no one could prevail upon her to leave
her apartments.

Nebuchadnezzar grew impatient and went himself to her rooms.
Daniel never learned what he said to her, but a day later the chamberlain
summoned him. Daniel dreaded this meeting even more than the one
with Amel-Marduk, for Kasšaya's temper was well known, and she clearly
was already in an ill mood.

So when Daniel arrived at her reception chamber, he was astonished
by Kasšaya's serene calm. "Welcome, noble soothsayer," the girl said, as
though honey oozed from the corners of her mouth. "I am always delighted to see you."

Instantly, he grew wary. Kasšaya, unlike her heedless brother, was
adept at palace politics. Prostrating himself, he said: "Kind princess, I
am honored by your delight."

Kasšaya reclined on a cushioned divan, resting languidly against a bank of pillows, her saffron-colored gown drawn up around her knees, the bodice draped carelessly, allowing a peek of a smooth white breast. The large, airy room looked out upon a small courtyard. A fountain in its center filled the room with the gentle sound of flowing water. Curtains swayed in the slight breeze, and a slave stood over her mistress, fanning her. Kasšaya dismissed him with a wave, then gestured to her hand-maiden, who placed a platter of dates and a flagon of wine on a low table. Daniel obediently sat on the stool Kasšaya pointed to.

"I know Father already explained that I do not aspire to the throne myself—lowly female that I am—but I am proposing it for my husband." She reached for a date and popped it into her mouth, delicately removing the pit between two long fingers and dropping it onto the table.

Daniel smiled at her. Perhaps she was in a good enough mood that he might attempt some humor. "Have you celebrated your marriage recently, Princess? I had not heard. My congratulations."

She laughed lightly. "Surely you know me well enough, Belteshazzar, to recognize that my marriage ceremony will be trumpeted throughout the kingdom. And that you, the most renowned soothsayer in all of Babylon, the seer who knows all, could not possibly be in ignorance of the fact."

Daniel placed a humble hand on his chest, playing the game. "I only wish you spoke true, Highness. But perhaps you have an eye on someone? Possibly even have become betrothed and kept the fact private?"

Kasšaya lifted an eyebrow. "I understand why you ask these impertinent questions...."

"I do not mean to be impertinent," Daniel hastened to say.

"I'm certain not. But you want to know how I am so sure that my husband will be a suitable ruler, when his identity is still cloaked in the mists of time. Is that not so?"

Daniel nodded warily.

"I had the omens cast, and my fortune teller prophesizes that the man I marry will be stronger than any three men combined, a leader among men, and a heroic commander of our armies. Of course, I would be satisfied with nothing less. With me at his side, bestowing the royalty of my birth upon him, there can be no doubt that we are destined to rule Babylon. Such a powerful couple would serve the empire better than either of my two half-siblings. Amel-Marduk is a pampered weakling, and Nitocris a conniving bitch. How either of them…."

Daniel raised a hand, hoping to cut her short. "Perhaps you should tell me of your dream now, Highness."

Kassaya nodded. "Of course. Let me bring it to mind." She settled back against the piled pillows, closing her eyes. Her lashes, darkened by kohl, lay upon faintly flushed cheeks. Raising her hands behind her head, she rested them lightly on her dark curls, pinned in extravagant whorls, secured by gold pins. "I dreamt of a grasshopper flitting across the land, dancing in the sunshine, making a ceaseless racket, getting drunk from drinking dew. It fluttered about, a careless creature, joined by a band of feckless friends. They ate everything that flowered, including the crops, drinking all the water, draining the canals. The land suffered under their gluttony, reverting to arid desert."

"A dire prediction," Daniel mused.

Kassaya peered at him under half-opened eyelids. What she saw in his face seemed to satisfy her, for she closed her eyes again and continued, her voice hushed. "Then an army of ants appeared, orderly, row after row, lining up against the horizon as the sun rose over the suffering landscape. An ant king and queen stood before their ranks, tall and proud, wearing golden diadems and shining armor. The soldier ants obeyed their every command. The king and queen led the ant army and vanquished the grasshoppers, eating them whole, crunching their wings and bodies in their jaws." Kassaya sat up, pulling her feet from the divan to the floor and leaning forward. "Do you want me to tell you what my fortune teller told me this dream means?"

Once again, Daniel raised a hand. "I need to ponder it myself, Highness."

Kassaya shrugged. "I know Father commanded you to tell him the meaning first. I respect that. But afterwards, I would like you to come and share your thoughts with me. About my dream—and the others. Yes?"

There was no gainsaying the princess. Daniel rose, bowed, and hoped his nod in her direction would be enough. It wasn't.

"Belteshazzar? You'll come?"

Daniel swallowed hard. "I will do my best, Highness."

Kasšaya smiled sweetly at him. "That's all I ask." She waved him away.

As Daniel made his way down the long corridor, Kasšaya's hand-maiden stopped him. Daniel knew her name was Bara'a. She'd been kind to him once when, as a young exile fresh from Judea, he had lost his way in the winding corridors of the palace.

"She has not told you the entire dream," Bara'a whispered as she pulled him into a narrow room. "But you must promise me to not let her know I told you. She'd whip me—or worse—if she knew."

"I won't say a word," Daniel replied. "But I do need to know the dream in its entirety."

Bara'a looked at the floor, keeping her voice to a mutter. Daniel leaned close. "She woke that morning screaming from the nightmare and told me the whole while still in the vision's thrall. What she related to you was correct—the grasshopper, the ants led by their king and queen. But she deliberately left out the horror of the dream's end."

Daniel held his breath, waiting.

"The queen ant grew and grew, as if big with child. She deposited her eggs inside a richly appointed chamber. But only one broke open—and a grasshopper emerged, who ate all of the other eggs and the mother ant as well."

Daniel shivered despite the heat of the day. No wonder Kasšaya deliberately left out that pertinent detail.

"Thank you, Bara'a," he told her, patting her arm. "You've given me much to consider."

5

Nitocris's Dream

NITOCRIS, UNLIKE HER SIBLINGS, WAS eager—even impatient—to speak
with Daniel. They met in one of the palace gardens, where she sat on
a marble bench beneath a grape arbor heavy with fruit. She patted the
bench, wordlessly inviting him to sit next to her.

"Last again—as always," Nitocris complained.

"I met with you all in the order dictated by your royal father's chamberlain," Daniel replied, annoyed at the defensive tone that crept into
his voice.

Nitocris placed her long, sharp fingernails on his forearm. "I know,"
she murmured, sounding sympathetic. "We are all Father's to command
and must bend the knee to him."

Daniel resisted the urge to squirm away under her touch. He regretted the conditions of their meeting—completely secluded beneath the
arbor's lush leaves, with no one to bear witness to what the young princess
might say or do. Nitocris, despite her youth, was reputed to be difficult
to satisfy in bed, insatiable, much like the older brother she adored. Both
she and Amel-Marduk had wide and varied tastes and selected partners
accordingly. It was rumored that she liked the unwilling ones best.

Thinking of how similar her bed sports were to her brother's prompted
Daniel to ask a question that had troubled him. "I know how fond you

are of Amel-Marduk," he began, eyes raking the princess's face for any sign of stiffening. "So I was surprised when your father said that you, too, were visited in the night by a vision of yourself on the throne."

Nitocris drew back and Daniel was afraid that he had, indeed, over-stepped. "Is that what Father told you?" she hissed. "That I want to unseat my beloved brother?"

Daniel scrambled to recover the misstep. "Perhaps I misunderstood, princess."

"Perhaps *he* misunderstood," Nitocris flashed back.

A cold bead of sweat ran down Daniel's back. "Perhaps," he said, desperate to placate her.

Her eyes narrowed and she was silent for a minute, then two. Daniel felt the thudding of his heart and chided himself. It was ridiculous to be afraid of this mere child—after all, Nitocris hadn't yet left her teens behind. Like her older sister, she had blossomed into a woman early, or perhaps she used artifice to look older. As the seconds ticked by, Daniel studied the young royal. Her eyes were rimmed with kohl, her full lips painted a deep scarlet—pomegranate juice, perhaps, or a slurry of raspberries. She dabbed her body lavishly with a heady perfume more appropriate for an older woman. Her breasts, too, hefted upward under a diaphanous gown, were as heavy as a matron's, their nipples, visible through the thin cloth, stained the same red as her lips. Bleached white arms were ringed in jangling gold and silver bracelets, and her thick calves bore the imprint of the fine leather straps of her jeweled sandals.

Daniel's contemplation of the princess was interrupted by her sharp voice. "I'm sure Kassaya's dream was all about supplanting Amel-Marduk," she demanded. "Was it not?"

A trap. One Daniel knew he had to evade at all costs. "I am not at liberty...." he began.

Nitocris laughed. "What else could it be, Belteshazzar? Grasshoppers eaten by an army of ants—honestly, it doesn't take a soothsayer to in-terpret what she means. A transparent effort to convince Father, one I'm certain"—once again she leaned forward and let her sharpened nails graze Daniel's thighs through his robe—"you will expose for the fiction it is."

Daniel shifted out of her reach, squirming inwardly as her scarlet lips parted in a wolfish grin. "I am instructed to reserve my thoughts about each of your dreams...."

"Until you hear them all and tell Father your conclusions," she said, finishing the sentence for him.

Daniel reminded himself that she was just a girl. But a cold chill shook him, wondering what other tricks age would teach her. What power might she wield over her impulsive, impressionable brother? And that's when he understood.

"Your dream, Highness, isn't for you, is it? It's meant to support your brother."

Daniel watched, astonished, as Nitocris's composure faded. "I'm not sure of that," she said, painted eyelids lowering to the ground while her feet shifted in the sandy soil. "Perhaps—perhaps that is true. But as much as I'd like it to be, it doesn't seem to be...."

Daniel's heart pounded again at a second realization. While Amel-Marduk's night visions might have been as manufactured as his father suspected, Nitocris was about to relate something she had actually dreamt. "Tell me about it," he said gently.

Nitocris nodded, taking a deep breath. "The Ziggurat called to me, told me to climb the steps to the top. A boy was in my way—a boy wearing a crown much too heavy for him. He whined about its weight. I have never seen him before, not in real life, but somehow in the dream I knew that he was a puling, complaining weakling, unworthy of the crown. At the top of the Ziggurat, the supreme god Marduk's dragon, Mušḫuššu, roared, angered at this boy king. His fury filled me with strength, and I pushed the boy, toppling him off the Ziggurat, so that he plummeted to earth. Marduk was pleased, inviting me to climb to the apex of the Ziggurat where he undressed me with his own divine hands. He lay with me—it was the most exquisite sensation as he entered me—and after expelling his seed, left me panting at the peak, all of Babylon applauding us from below, the crown resting just beneath my hand."

Daniel stared at her, astonished. "Whose child was it, this boy king?"

Nitocris hunched her shoulders. "I don't know. That's what troubles me, soothsayer. He was not Amel-Marduk. Possibly one of his sons? Yet—how could I hurt anyone connected to him?"

"Perhaps the boy was not related to you at all?"

Nitocris stared at him for a moment, then shook her head emphatically. "No. This boy was too much a coward and a fool to have seized the kingdom from our family."

There were, of course, other possibilities. The boy might have been one of her younger brothers, the ones who had been born after Amel-Marduk. But Daniel knew that wasn't so. He had never shared this with the king, but his own visions about the younger princelings convinced him that not one of them would survive to claim the throne. The only remaining possibility—one Daniel refused to voice, for fear of the princess's fury—was that this must be Kasšaya's son. Which meant Kasšaya would inherit.

Daniel rose to his feet. "Was that the entire dream?" he asked.

Nitocris's head was lowered, her eyes on the soil beneath her sandals. "That was all."

Daniel bowed. "I must consider what I've been told, then."

Nitocris looked up, eyes narrowed. "It can't be my sister's spawn. I swear that I *will* kill it if it is. Marduk has entrusted me with a sacred duty; I will not fail him."

Daniel felt dread creeping up the back of his neck. He turned and strode away as quickly as dignity would allow.

6

Sarah Loses

SARAH'S LUCK WITH THE DICE ran out on the fourth night.

She stared with horrified eyes at the one and the two she had cast. The captain leered at her, a slow grin lighting up his face.

"Couldn't I try again? I threw too fast..." Sarah reached out quickly. If she just acted confident, perhaps....

But Nebuzaradan smoothly scooped up the dice. "Don't be foolish, girl. It's my turn now." The dice clicked in his hand, the pieces of bone tossed together in the little pocket of his flesh. Then he threw them onto the dun-clothed table. Two fours.

Seraf rose from his seat on a cushion, dismay written across his slender face.

"Send the others away," the captain ordered, looking at Sarah and licking his lips.

The guard hustled the other girls and Seraf out. They had to take Seraf by the arm to thrust him forth.

"Take off your clothes and lie down on the bed," the captain ordered calmly.

Sarah could tell he was used to being obeyed. She tried to think of something to prevent this from happening. *Just one more night's reprieve,* she thought. *Please. I'll do anything. Please....*

The captain looked at her as she stood stock-still in the middle of the large tent. He reached out, his hand grazing her small breast as he made his way up her chest to the nape of her neck. He gripped her, fingers rough against her skin.

"It won't hurt, not a lot," he whispered, looking directly into her eyes. "I've taken my share of virgins. I can be gentle. But you must take your clothes off. Now." He stepped back and stood watching her, eyes narrowed, as though considering if she would obey him.

Sarah's fingers felt wooden as she pushed her shift off her shoulders, letting it fall in a wrinkled circle around her ankles. She trembled in the cool evening air. Nebuzaradan's hand reached out and caressed her, moving from her neck to her white breasts to her waist. She stepped back, away from his grasp, almost tripping on her dress.

"Lie on the bed," the captain instructed. "It will be easier for you."

But Sarah couldn't move. *This is what Father's knife was supposed to save me from*, she thought. *He should have killed me first, before Mother. If he had, I'd be safe now.*

Nebuzaradan, eyes glinting, removed his armor. She looked away, trying not to see how his excitement for her grew. He stepped toward her, slid one muscled arm into the small of her back, and pushed her, face first, into his cot. She closed her eyes and waited. *This isn't happening*, she told herself. *God cannot be this cruel.*

There was no fumbling. *He has probably ravished hundreds of women*, Sarah thought, as she felt his warm, battle-roughened hands parting her thighs. A part of her was grateful that he did not grope and clutch at her. His motions were deliberate, controlled. He entered her from behind. She felt a sharp pain, a tearing deep inside her, and cried out, recognizing it as the moment she was ruined, the moment she had to surrender everything she had hoped for in her young life—a husband, a home, children to love. Slow at first, Nebuzaradan began to move faster, shoving her face deeper into the cot, making it difficult to breathe. As the captain enjoyed her body, hot helpless tears escaped her cheeks, wicking into the scratchy wool blanket beneath her.

Hours later, she stumbled out into the darkness. The camp was asleep. Her body felt bruised, thighs sticky with his fluids.

"Sarah?" came a whisper from the black shadows just outside the captain's tent. Seraf stood, looking at her uncertainly.

She turned away, shame searing her.

"It's not your fault," the musician murmured. "No one blames you."

She gestured that she wanted to be left alone. But Seraf grabbed hold of her hand and dragged her, stumbling, into his arms. Her head fell upon his shoulder as she leaned against him. Sarah wanted to sob, to let the pain escape, but something hard building inside her blocked her tears. She couldn't let go of her disgrace. She wondered if she ever would.

She stood, stone cold inside Seraf's protecting arms. He must have felt how rigidly she was holding her body. He stepped back and surveyed her, holding her at arm's length.

"You need some sleep," he finally murmured. "Let's get some sleep."

She nodded, limping away to find a corner of the prickly grass to sleep on. Seraf hovered nearby, as if unwilling to let her out of his sight. She lay on her back and looked up at the stars twinkling coldly above. Even the night sky looked unfamiliar. She heard Seraf sigh softly. Then she let her eyelids droop, collapsing into an exhausted slumber.

The next morning, Sarah awoke to bird song and lay still. Any movement rubbed the irritated core of her body. She opened her eyes. There, looming above her, was her cousin.

"Is it true?" he shouted. "Did he take you last night? Did the Chaldean captain ruin you?"

She closed her eyes again, willing him away. Her head throbbed at the temples. Reuven's red face reminded her of her father, how he would have railed at her for succumbing. *Go away*, she thought, trying to hide behind her shut eyelids. But Reuven wouldn't leave. She felt his hand on her forearm, yanking her to her feet. She opened her eyes again, seeing the compressed corners of his mouth, dotted with flecks of saliva. He shook her like the little straw doll she had dragged around as a toddler. The doll that had burned with the rest of their home.

"Did he?" Reuven asked, his teeth clenched, shaking her roughly.

"Stop," she cried, shame and fury raging within. "Let go."

"It's not her fault," came Seraf's voice from behind. "She's suffered enough."

Reuven released Sarah and whirled. "This has nothing to do with you, whoever you are. Sarah is my cousin, under my protection."

"Under your protection? Where were you last night, then?" Seraf goaded him. "When Nebuzaradan forced her to his bed?"

"Sarah, who is this?" Reuven demanded. "Why does he think he can speak for you?"

Sarah felt sick to her stomach, watching the two young men eyeing one another, like dogs vying for the same stick.

"He's a friend," she said. "He's been kind to me."

"Kind to you how?" Reuven snapped.

"Kinder than you're being, that's certain," Seraf retorted.

With a roar, Reuven launched himself upon the musician. The two dropped to the dirt, arms flailing and fists pounding. Reuven was broader, more muscular, but Seraf was older and warded off the wild blows with trained skill.

A cry of "Fight!" rang out, and a crowd of young men came running, as well as some of the guards. They roared encouragement, excited by the two men raining punches upon one another.

Sarah's shrill voice could hardly be heard above the men's shouts. "Seraf! Reuven! Stop!"

But they ignored her, raising a smoke of dirt as they tussled. She looked around wildly, trying to find something to break up the brawl. All she could see was dirt and rocks. Sarah scrabbled in the road and rose with two fistfuls of small stones. She flung them at their two wrestling bodies with all the strength she could muster.

The tiny rocks must have stung. Seraf and Reuven broke apart, indignant, clambering to their feet, looking wildly into the small crowd that surrounded them.

"Who threw that?"

"Who dares?"

Sarah stood with her fists balled at her waist, furious with them both. "What are you thinking? Why are you fighting?" she demanded of the two panting men.

They both stared at her for a moment. Reuven was the first to speak. "I don't know, I was just so angry. And then this stranger came along…."

"Angry? At whom? At me?" Seraf demanded.

"At Sarah! He slept with her! Ruined her!"

"What was she to do? What would you have had her do?"

Sarah could barely look up, ashamed that her humiliation was being proclaimed so loudly in front of the crowd gathered around them. Reuven, too, suddenly appeared aghast at his hasty words. He ducked his head and kicked at the rubble in the roadway with one foot.

"She had no choice," Seraf continued in a less heated tone. "Don't you see that?"

A long silence followed. A cry of "Breakfast!" was heard in the distance. The crowd dispersed. Sarah felt every one of their pointing fingers and condemning whispers. She thrust her head up defiantly, her face and neck crimson and hot.

Reuven glanced toward his cousin and swallowed, hard. Sarah watched his Adam's apple bob in his throat.

"Are you…are you all right?" he whispered.

She nodded, holding her lower lip in her teeth, refusing to lower her head again. With a quick stab of her hand, she dashed away the tears that flooded her blinking eyes.

"Your mouth is bleeding," Seraf said to Reuven, pointing at him.

"And that eye of yours is going to swell up," Reuven replied.

They relapsed into tense silence.

"I'll get some water, to clean you both up," Sarah muttered. "And then we'll have breakfast. Stay here."

"Sarah, I…." Reuven said, swallowing hard.

"Don't say it," Sarah replied. She was afraid of any more words, fearful that they would break her, succumbing to a shame she knew she would always carry. "What is there to say, anyway?"

7

Sarah's Dream

SARAH CLIMBED THE HILLTOP, GLADNESS *filling her heart. Above her, her family home beckoned, the long white building with its thick walls warm in the chill Jerusalem winters and cool in the heat of its summers. Mother hung laundry on a long line between trees just on the edges of the kitchen garden, a sight as natural as the brilliant blue sky and the rainclouds. Sarah knew Father, Yoram, and Reuven were in the fields, for where else would they be when the sun was directly overhead? Dina sat on the stone slab in the back of the house, shelling peas with her withered fingers, pods often missing the bowl and tumbling to the dry earth, snatched up by chickens pecking busily around her feet.*

Sarah's arms filled with sloshing water buckets. She hadn't noticed their weight until she crested the hill. Yet, heavy though they were, she floated over to the barn, where she poured water into the trough for the sheep and goats—a never-ending stream of water that made her giddy with delight. The barn reeked of sunshine and home, the smells of steaming fur and animal waste a comfort.

Then she was in the kitchen, breathing in thick fumes of bean stew and barley beer, roasting lamb turning on the spit, the fire sizzling with its slaking fat. Her mouth filled with saliva. The odors permeated the air, inviting her to eat. Her mouth was suddenly crammed with lamb, and she chewed the rich meat, juices escaping her greedy mouth and running guiltily down her chin. She wiped her mouth with singed fingers and reached out to snatch another stolen piece....

But then she was no longer in the kitchen. Instead, she was on the hilltop overlooking the farm—outbuildings, barns, fields of barley, and terraces where they grew olives and grapes arrayed beneath her. As she watched from her floating perch, the fields bubbled with red, streams flowing into the farmyard, flooding the kitchen garden, pooling on the steps. Sarah turned to see her mother's body stretched out beneath the clothesline, Dina leaning lifeless against the doorpost, Yoram with an arrow in his back, staggering up from the city, only to fall onto the earth, leaking blood from his mouth and ears....

Her father strode up from the fields, a knife the size of a hoe in his hands. "Sarah!" he bellowed, his voice echoing off the mountainside. "Sarah! You're next, daughter. You're next."

Sarah woke with a start. She lay outside the captain's tent, body aching from his ravages, face wet with tears. The sky was just beginning to lighten, stars fading as the horizon turned orange and blue. She choked back her misery, but it festered inside her, the dream haunting her. *The Chaldeans have taken everything from me. I will never again see my home, never again hug my mother or hear Yoram tease me. Or obey Father, willingly or unwillingly....*

At the thought of her father, a shudder overtook her. *How could he?* She put her hands up to touch her wet cheeks. He had always been strict, always unforgiving. But to have killed her mother? To have intended to plunge the knife into her? Into Reuven?

The Chaldeans may have stolen my home, but Father did something much, much worse, Sarah realized. He stole any peace of mind she might have summoned up in remembering it.

Seraf, lying on the ground next to her, stirred. She stretched her aching body. It would be another long day on the march toward exile—an exile Sarah carried not only on her soiled body and aching feet but buried so deep in her heart that she would never be able to cleanse herself from it.

8

Daniel and the Three Dreams

DANIEL THOUGHT LONG AND HARD about how to explain his conclusions to Nebuchadnezzar. The king, for all his power, was a simple, straight-forward man who would not like the convoluted future that the three dreams augured. Daniel waited for the inevitable summons, praying to the Most High to somehow imbue his tongue with silvered magic and deliver himself from the king's nearly certain wrath.

The thought of silver made him recall an earlier dream he had in-terpreted for the king early in his service, of a huge statue with a gold head, silver chest and arms, bronze belly and legs, and feet of mixed iron and clay. Nebuchadnezzar had accepted that he was the gold head, and that other kingdoms, lesser than he, would follow his rule. Perhaps that dream could once again be the answer, Daniel thought, tossing sleepless on his cot in the palace.

The summons came after a restless night. Daniel entered the throne room and was brought up short by seeing all three of the king's children arrayed before him.

"I thought," Nebuchadnezzar told him, the corners of his mouth lift-ing upward in amusement, "that it would be easiest for you to tell us all at the same time, Belteshazzar. I understand that my children have each demanded you report back to them, after speaking with me. We might as well all hear the same wisdom from your lips together. Yes?"

Daniel willed his shaking legs to stand upright. "You are wise, oh great king," he said, spreading his hands before him. "I am honored not only by your wisdom but also by your kindness in sparing me the task of recounting my thoughts to each of your children in turn."

Kassaya shifted in her seat, leaning forward. "Yes, yes, honored, wisdom, kindness, who cares? Tell us, whose is the true dream?"

A bead of cold sweat traveled down Daniel's back. "Not yours, princess," he said. "For you only tell half-dreams."

She straightened, gasping. "Are you calling me a liar? I'll have you thrashed and thrown to the jackals!"

Daniel shook his head. "You are not a liar. You did, indeed, have the night vision you related. But you failed to tell me the whole. Did you not?"

Nebuchadnezzar glared at his eldest daughter. "Is that true?"

Kassaya looked away. "I…. The rest of the dream made no sense. It was too clouded and confusing. I couldn't describe it clearly, to you or to myself."

Daniel willed his trembling limbs still. "I understand that, Highness," he said, nodding as if in agreement. "For the rest of the dream was not just confusing but disturbing. No wonder you tried to forget it. I would have, in your place."

Kassaya's eyes slit nearly shut. She was too intelligent, Daniel knew, not to understand that he was twisting her words. But she would say nothing in front of her father for fear of having to admit to the rest of the dream. At least for now, he was safe from her.

Amel-Marduk laughed. "So we can forget big sister's dream. What of mine, soothsayer?"

"It is clear to me, Highness, that you will succeed to your father's throne after him—with all the glory that ascension bestows upon you. But only after your father's golden reign comes to its natural close, after a long and fruitful rule." Daniel turned to Nebuchadnezzar and bowed low. "You are the golden head of the great god statue still, noble king. Long may you reign!"

Nebuchadnezzar seemed to relax, while all three children were quick to murmur their avowed loyalty to the king and wishes for his long life. Daniel was thankful no one asked if Amel-Marduk's dream was fabricated. Perhaps he would escape this incident unscathed, after all. *In truth, God is good to me*, Daniel thought, *though he scourges my people—as even now, new captives make their way to us.*

But then Nitocris, draped in a gown so sheer that it was practically invisible, looked at Daniel through thick eyelashes. "And my dream, Belteshazzar? What of that?"

"You are a loyal daughter and a loyal sister, are you not?" Daniel asked, hoping to sidestep her question. "You have always supported your brother. You will continue to do so."

"But…." she began.

But Nebuchadnezzar waved her question away. "Very well. I am satisfied. All the more, as my own wishes in the matter will be carried out. Leave us, Belteshazzar."

Daniel prostrated himself and was about to back out of the throne room when Kassaya huffed past him. Daniel walked calmly into the courtyard, finding her hovering by a bubbling fountain.

"You…." she hissed at him.

He leaned forward to mutter into her ear. "Your dream will come true," he told her. "But only after your father's death and your brother's ascension to the throne. You are looking for a shortcut, to elbow your brother out before it is time. Doing so would prove fruitless and could undo all. There is no point in telling your father that you and your husband will rid the land of the flighty grasshopper. And you and I both know who that will be."

She reared back, looking at him through narrowed eyes. "Truth?" she demanded. "And the rest of it?"

He took a deep breath, the trapped space under his armpits growing damp. "As you said," he said slowly, "the end of the dream was cloudy and unclear. And while dreams can foretell the future, there is also room for personal destiny. You, princess, have a strong will. Unlike your brother, and like your father, you can shape the future to become what you wish."

He watched her leave, looking exultant. *And yet, all of it will come true*, he told himself. *The time will come when Babylon simply exchanges one grasshopper for another.* And what, he wondered, would become of him then?

9

New Lives

ON THE THIRD DAY AFTER they reached the massive blue tiled gates of Babylon, Seraf drowsed near the captain's wagon, his thin cheek resting on Sarah's shoulder.

"You," a soldier poked him. "Musician. Get up."

They were camped outside the city walls, near the banks of the wide Euphrates River. Nearly four months had elapsed since that first dreadful day setting off from a burning Jerusalem. They had traveled north through Aram, turning south just before reaching the city of Rezeph, and then following the Euphrates River to Babylon itself. The soldiers, who claimed they could have made the trek in less than half the time unencumbered, cursed the captives' slowness as they limped forward. But even the captain recognized that they could only move as swiftly as the slowest old man or youngest child, and that all the whippings he ordered could only speed the feeble incrementally, or even slow their steps further.

The midsummer sun blazed down upon the open campsite, but a bank of palm trees provided shade and the river sent up a cool breeze morning and evening. During the past few days, soldiers had marched off with groups of Judeans. None returned. They were sent to new lives as Babylonian captives, Nebuzaradan explained to Sarah. Since their arrival, he had less time for her. When he'd disposed of his captives, the captain was commanded back to Egypt to subdue yet another rebellion. He was busy studying maps and sending dozens of couriers off with new orders. Sarah felt deep relief at his preoccupation. She'd been ordered to the captain's bed almost every night of their trek. Perhaps her initial resistance had intrigued Nebuzaradan. Or perhaps he sensed that she wasn't fully broken.

As the guard addressed Seraf, Sarah's head jerked up. She motioned frantically to her cousin, seated a short distance away under a palm tree. Reuven joined them.

"Are you Seraf the musician?" the soldier asked gruffly.

Seraf slid his cheek off Sarah's shoulder. "I am." Seraf rose slowly, the challenge ringing in his voice frightening Sarah. She and Reuven had learned how quickly the musician could take offense.

"He's with us." Sarah scrambled to her feet. "Tell him, Reuven."

"The three of us stay together," Reuven said.

"That's right." Seraf raised his chin as he draped an arm around Sarah's shoulders.

"I have orders to take you with the other court musicians," the soldier told Seraf. The Chaldean's mouth rode up, sneering at the Judean's black glare. "Come now."

"He's with us," Sarah repeated, looping her own arm around the musician's waist.

With lightning speed, a dagger appeared in the soldier's hand. "Move, girl," he growled. "I've killed Judeans before. I won't hesitate now."

Reuven grabbed Sarah's arm and pulled her away. He and Seraf stared at the guard for a moment, as if considering their options. Sarah didn't know whether to feel relieved or sad watching the defiance fade from Seraf's face.

He turned to Sarah and hugged her tightly. "I will miss you," he murmured in her hair. Seraf's eyes burned as he slid out of their quick embrace. He turned to her cousin and whispered something into Reuven's ear. Reuven put out a hand. The two friends clasped each other's forearms. Then Seraf was pushed from behind and marched off. Gone.

Two afternoons later, in the blazing heat of noontide, the soldiers walked through the remaining Judeans, calling, "Farmers. We're looking for men who can till the soil. Who knows barley here?"

Reuven and Sarah glanced quickly at one another. Sarah's father had raised barley. They knew how to farm.

Reuven waved a hand high in the air. "Here, guard. I lived on a farm—I know barley."

The guard stared at Reuven's eager grin, then shrugged dismissively, looking Reuven's emaciated body up and down. "Too young. What are you—thirteen? fourteen?"

Sarah thought fast. "He's older than he looks," she retorted. "I've seen him out in the fields working from dawn to dusk, doing a man's work."

"Can you farm a plot of land on your own? You'll pay high taxes, Judean, but what you harvest beyond your quota is yours to keep."

The cousins looked at one another, barely believing their ears. To have their own farm! It was more than they could have hoped for.

"Yes, yes. I can do it. Sarah, get ready. She comes with me," Reuven told the guard.

"Not so fast. Who are you to decide anything? Who's this—your wife?"

"My cousin," Reuven said. "I have no wife."

"He needs me," Sarah said. "I know the work."

"We're only taking the wives of married men," said the guard.

"She's my betrothed," insisted Reuven doggedly. "Among our people, being handfast is as good as being married."

Sarah gasped and poked Reuven in the side. "We're not.... I mean...."

"Our fathers intended it." Reuven grabbed Sarah's arm and drew her close.

Sarah stared at her cousin's stolid expression, the way he set his chin. Just like her father. She blinked back tears, touched by Reuven's willing- ness to provide for her. She remembered how he had pushed away the choice morsels she placed in his bowl, back when he was mourning his family. So much had changed since then, but they were still protecting one another.

The guard groped inside a satchel, pulling a clay tablet and a stylus out of his pack. He stared at Sarah, taking her in from head to toe, lip curling. Sarah could almost hear him thinking, *A shame to bury this one on a farm.* She shivered, thinking of what her future might have been without her cousin's generosity. A brothel, somewhere, or sold off as a bed slave. No other Judean would have married her now. Except perhaps Seraf—but he was gone.

"Make your mark here," the soldier said, pointing at an empty row.

Reuven leaned over and inscribed his name.

Sarah moved closer to her cousin, barely breathing as she felt their fortune turn to good. But at just that moment, Nebuzaradan emerged from his tent, saw them, and approached. Sarah held her breath.

"What have you to report?" the captain asked the guard, who straightened, saluting.

"This Judean is being assigned a farm. He wants to take the girl with him. This one," the guard motioned toward Sarah, "whom he says is his cousin and his betrothed."

Nebuzaradan laughed. "See, Sarah! I told you. You found yourself a man willing to take you despite being a virgin no longer."

Sarah's cheeks flushed. Even if Reuven accepted her to wife, she would never be completely free of her shame. If only her luck with the dice could have kept her from the captain's embraces altogether.

The memory of those nights seared her, a tattoo marking her as loathsome, reviled. As the days passed, no matter how she struggled, the captain became increasingly demanding. Sarah staggered as she was forced to march, her body aching after Nebuzaradan contorted her limbs in unnatural ways, exploring every part of her. The captain was an athlete and she his prize. He saw his conquest of her body as his right as a victor.

"I thought of taking her home with me, but my wife would just throw her into the streets when I left on my next campaign," Nebuzaradan said now. "But I can't see her wasting away on a farm."

Her nights with the captain might have been degrading, but Sarah had learned from them. She placed a tentative hand on his muscled forearm. "But if it's what I want?" she murmured, looking at him from under lowered eyelids.

The captain shook his head. "No."

Trying to ignore her cousin's astonished glare, Sarah moved the hand slowly up the captain's arm. She watched, feeling the unaccustomed power of her sensuality work upon him. She shuddered deep inside, keeping her gliding fingers light, seductive. The captain's dark frown softened at the edges.

"Well," he said, "I suppose if you want...."

"Captain!" called a voice from behind.

The party wheeled to face a beautifully dressed woman attended by a retinue of slaves and a personal guard, approaching from a few feet away. The woman floated serenely above the rocky ground. She seemed untouched by her surroundings—the dusty campsite, the menacing guards, the emaciated prisoners gawking at her.

She stopped a few yards away. "Nebuzaradan, Captain of the Guard, don't you know me?" she asked, her voice rich, assured, slightly amused.

Nebuzaradan stared at her, stunned, then fell swiftly to one knee. After a second's hesitation, the guard beside him did the same, bewildering the Judeans.

"Your Highness." Nebuzaradan's head almost touched the ground in supplication.

"Rise, Captain," said the young woman, taking the last few steps toward him, delicately placing long fingers adorned with gold rings on his right shoulder.

Sarah gaped at her. The princess wore a light dress spun from flax, dyed a soft peach color. Her right arm and shoulder were left uncovered, and her bare arm was decorated in gold bangles that jangled as she moved. Her lustrous black hair was looped into dozens of spirals and piled on top of her head, secured by heavy jeweled pins. Her dress was cinched at the waist by a girdle of beaten gold, and her feet were shod in a soft pair of goatskin sandals, their laces tied halfway up her calves. Next to the young royal, Sarah felt awkward, filthy. She tugged at her ragged dress, wishing it covered her better.

The princess moved her languid gaze from the captain toward Sarah, and a slow smile grew on her rouged face. "She's a beauty, Captain. I came to select a handmaiden to tend my perfume storeroom, a daughter of Judea lovely in face and body. The most beautiful of all the captives. I think this is the girl."

"Bow before Her Highness the Princess Kasšaya, daughter of our great King Nebuchadnezzar, Judeans," the captain commanded, noticing that neither Sarah nor Reuven had abased themselves.

If they had been in Judea, the cousins might have argued that they kneeled only before their own king and the Lord God. But this was the new life and, being captives, they were unsure of the customs of the country. Sarah reached out and grabbed Reuven's forearm, urging him to his knees as she kneeled gracefully before the princess.

"Obedient. That pleases me," said Kasšaya, picking up Sarah's chin and turning her face from side to side, smiling at the faint blush that mottled her cheeks. "White skin, lovely green eyes. Body just about to flower. You must have had her, Captain—you have a reputation for bedding the loveliest of your captives. Is she truly as exquisite as she seems beneath all that filth?"

"A young, supple, beautiful girl," said the captain, regret at losing her tingeing his voice. "One whom fortune shines upon. As it does even now by securing your favor."

Kasšaya dropped Sarah's chin. "Come then, girl. We must give you a Babylonian name, so my tongue does not trip over your guttural Hebrew syllables. What is your birth name?"

Sarah's lips tightened to prevent a cry of protest. The Chaldean invasion had killed her parents and her brother. The soldiers had burned her family's farm. Her virginity had been ripped from her. Would they take her name as well? But looking at the armed men—the captain, the princess's guard, and the soldier collecting farmers—Sarah knew better than to object. Just as Seraf had been marched away to serve as a court musician, she would tend to the princess's perfume storeroom. Perhaps Reuven would be luckier than them both, on his barley farm.

"I am Sarah, Your Highness," she murmured, casting her eyes down.

"I will call you Shamrina, a much more melodious name. Come now."

Sarah glanced toward her cousin, whose clenched jaw showed how he struggled to resign himself. She placed her fingers on his arm. He turned away, hunching his shoulders.

The guard, who had stood by, silent and amused as he watched the interlude, shook his head. "So. No wife for you, Judean, hey? But if the beauty is gone, at least you have a farm now. Come, it grows late."

Sarah, feeling more alone than she had since the soldier's dagger had pierced her father's back, walked away from her cousin, following the princess's retinue toward her new life.

10

Seraf and Daniel

THE SOUND OF HAMMERS REVERBERATED through the palace. Nebuchadnezzar had instructed his builders to add more rooms to the queen's already spacious apartments. Amytis, daughter of old King Cyaxares of Media, was described as the world's most beautiful queen: tall and stately, comporting herself with infinite grace. Seraf wondered what it would be like to perform for her.

He hugged his battered dulcimer to him. It was a miracle it had survived the terrible journey. Only Sarah had transformed the trek into something bearable. She and Reuven had helped him through the brutal days. Last night, tossing and turning on his lonely cot in the crowded slave quarters, he found his restless thoughts lingering on them. Where were his friends now? He had heard that several of the Judeans had been set up in trade or in farms, others sold into slavery. Had fortune smiled or frowned upon them?

As for him, he thanked God for the gift of music. That gift, at least, had never failed him. Stretching his back now against the cool marble walls, he mused on how he had come to arrive here, to serve as musician to the Babylonian queen. As a child, he'd apprenticed at King Zedekiah's palace, performing for the Judean royal family under his master's watchful eye. Then, eleven years ago, Judea made the fatal mistake of siding with Egypt against Babylon. Babylon had shown a measure of mercy when they captured Jerusalem the first time, only exiling the royal family and their court. The Chaldeans bestowed the territory back to the Hebrews, appointing a governor, requiring only loyalty and tribute from the bereft nation.

But still, as a boy walking through the echoing hallways of the abandoned palace in Jerusalem, Seraf felt shame for his lost king. Seraf sang David's old hymns of longing and loss and tried to find some vestige of romance in defeat, but the reality was merely painful. While the Judean governor, Gedaliah, was a fine ruler, he had neither leisure nor taste for music. Seraf spent the empty years practicing his craft and wishing something—anything—might restore Judea's pride.

And then it did—and Seraf learned to be wary of wishes fulfilled. He winced, recalling Gedaliah's slaughter by Judean rebels. Giddy with triumph, the dissenters dragged the governor's dead body through the palace hallways, smearing them with a slick red trail that left the coppery scent of treachery behind. The young insurgents camped in the throne room, arguing day and night about how to defend themselves from the inevitable Chaldean onslaught.

As if on cue, the indignant Babylonians returned in force. This time, there was no restraint and no mercy. The rebels were put to the sword, the city leveled, the Temple destroyed, and every citizen of rank was exiled to Babylon—including merchants and landed farmers like Sarah's family.

The destruction of the city spelled the end of Seraf's dreams. He had hoped someday to become one of the Temple musicians, to serve God through his music. To play during the rituals and ceremonies, fingers spelling out his devotion to the Almighty. He might have had sons and daughters with his talent, children he could teach to play and sing. But when the Temple was burned, Seraf's invisible, nameless God was defeated, vanquished by the Lord Marduk, head god of the Babylonians. And the life Seraf had wished for vanished in the bloody residue of defeat.

Now Seraf sat kicking his heels in the queen's antechambers with three other musicians. He knew them well—Tekoa the flute player, Rivai the harpist, and Oreb, who could play any instrument handed to him. They had all served together in the Judean royal palace.

Despite the heat, the antechamber was dim and dank. Seraf shifted on the hard marble bench, easing the ache in his lower back. They had waited for hours.

"It is nearly midday," said the harpist. "Perhaps she does not mean to hear us perform today."

"She is Queen of Babylon, daughter of King Cyaxares of Media and Empress of the known world," Oreb replied wryly. "The convenience of a small group of Judean musicians doesn't matter to her."

"It's just that I'm hungry," Rivai complained. "What do you think they'll feed us?"

"Whatever it is, I'll eat," said the flutist. "My stomach has been rumbling for hours."

They settled back to wait again. The thought of food troubled Seraf. His upbringing had been strict; he adhered to the laws about what one should and should not eat. Despite—or perhaps because of—their slim rations on the road, he had managed to observe the regulations thus far. But could he continue to do so in King Nebuchadnezzar's luxurious court?

Another hour passed. A beautiful young man entered the room. The court musicians straightened, for he surely must belong to the royal household. He was tall, lithe, with bright black eyes that shone out of an olive complexion. His dark hair curled back from a high forehead and fell onto broad shoulders. He wore a flowing gown of rich colors—shifting blues and greens with touches of saffron. A diadem rested on his forehead and his long fingers were bright with hammered gold rings.

The musicians rose and bowed. Seraf was thankful his master had drilled him in the graces of court life—how to nod your head when praised, bow to royalty, the manner in which you wipe your mouth when dining in the royal presence. *My manners might not be as sophisticated as a Babylonian's*, he thought ruefully, *but at least I am not an unpolished rustic.*

"Welcome, Judean musicians." The man's voice was deep, resonant. "I am Belteshazzar, the king's seer. But when we are alone, please call me Daniel, for my ears long for the sound of home."

Seraf's eyes roamed over the regal figure. "You are from Judea?"

"I was taken during the first exile as a child, together with our king and his family. I was brought to the palace with my three friends, and trained to become Chaldean, part of the king's retinue. I serve Nebuchadnezzar as soothsayer and interpreter of dreams."

"You must have been young when you were taken," said Oreb, "for you are not very old now."

Daniel threw back his head and laughed. The throaty sound was like the rich blare of a battle horn, Seraf thought, bemused by the courtier's amusement. Daniel was clearly even younger than he, though his assured smile belied his youth.

As they all stared, Daniel cut his laugh short and shrugged, still smiling. "Young? Me? On the contrary, one grows quickly in this palace. But I forget my manners. I have come to bid you to the table my friends and I keep, where we eat simply but well. Though, if you prefer, you might dine at the court table, where the fare is richer."

"You do not partake of the king's table?" Oreb asked.

"No," Daniel said. "The priests bless all meat in the name of Marduk and Ishtar, and the butchers take no care how they slaughter the beasts. The court kitchens serve food we Hebrews have been taught is impure."

"No meat is served at your table?" asked Tekoa, his face falling.

Daniel laughed again, his chest expanding in merriment. "It has been more than four years since flesh has touched my lips. But you would not think so to look at me, would you?"

Seraf's eyes widened. He studied Daniel head to toe. The beautiful youth did not seem any the worse for abstaining from meat. Some yet undefined quality in Daniel drew Seraf to the courtier. "I'll join your table," he said.

Rivai and Oreb muttered agreement. Tekoa shrugged. "I'll come with you today. I'm not certain I can forgo meat for a lifetime, however."

"You are welcome today." Daniel indicated with an elegant wave of his arm that they should follow him. He led them through the winding corridors with the natural grace of one raised to command.

They reached the room where the Hebrews ate, finding it overflowing with people. Some, with burnished skin and worn, stained clothing, Seraf recognized from the long trek. But others were well dressed, with lustrous skin and plump faces.

Daniel's rich voice carried effortlessly through the crowd. "It is like a vision come true to see so many of us gathered in one space!" he cried, heading toward his seat at the head of the table. Several men and women embraced him as he made his way through the crammed room.

"My friends," he proclaimed, arms outstretched to include them all, "our Israelite brethren, some of whom are here with us today, were forced from their homes by the Assyrians nearly one hundred and fifty years ago. Many settled here, in Babylon. When we, the first Judean exiles, were brought here by Nebuchadnezzar more than a decade ago, we found them half-wary and half-hopeful that we exiled Hebrews could become as one people. By joining together in meals and in prayer, I believe we have done so.

"Now you new exiles join us. Yours was a cruel passage to an unfamiliar home. You must fear what is in store for you. But you will learn that life in Babylon is one of plenty. And life here in the palace is particularly filled with enticements.

"You may be tempted to slip away from your Hebrew roots. Many of us struggle to remain steadfast to our faith. We are seduced by the lure of the gods of Ishtar and Marduk, Sin, Damkina, and Ea. Their temples overflow with riches and their ways are strange and compelling.

"But I urge you to remember the promise the Almighty gave Abraham in the desert not far from here: That we will be a prosperous people residing in our own land. We do not despair of a Return, a rescue from exile not unlike the one we were favored with during the days of Moses. We pray for it, and our poets compose poetry of longing and hope. We have new musicians here," Daniel nodded at Seraf and his friends, his smile encouraging, "who will learn to play these songs.

"Every man has a small basin at his place. We will now wash our hands and praise the Almighty in silence before we eat. Please join me."

Seraf found the small ritual comforting. He craned his neck to discover who the Israelites might be. His mother often told him of a great-grand aunt who had married into one of the Ten Lost Tribes. He smiled, thinking he might find family among those vanquished by the Assyrians a century before.

The fare on the table was simple: grains, vegetables, and fruit. But it had been prepared by someone with skill in spices. After so many years of feeding richly at the Judean court, Seraf wondered if he would rise famished from Daniel's table. Instead, he felt a comforting fullness without the aching stomach that so often followed a feast in the Judean royal palace.

A man attired in elegant sage robes trimmed with fawn-colored ribbon made his way around the table, greeting the newcomers. He stopped to talk to the musicians, "I am Abed-nego, named Azariah by my parents. Welcome to Babylon."

"Are you one of Daniel's friends?" asked Seraf, recognizing the same fluid grace of bearing.

Azariah smiled gently. "And he is one of mine. Daniel is a great man in Babylon. He was given remarkable talents by God, including visions and the ability to speak truth to power. He persuaded Melzar, master of eunuchs, to give us this room and fare for our pleasure."

"What had Melzar to do with it?" Oreb asked. "If Daniel is so powerful…?"

Azariah shrugged. "A powerful eunuch is still a eunuch."

"You have undergone…?" Tekoa asked, grimacing and reaching into his lap involuntarily.

Seraf, not wanting to follow his example, gripped the seat of his chair.

"Alas, most of us who live in the palace and serve the king are forced to live as men who are not men."

"Will we have to?" Seraf whispered, horrified. He thought of forever losing the beautiful Sarah, who haunted his dreams, and of any possibility of their children. Tears stood in his eyes.

"I cannot say. But you are to serve the queen, so it is likely. They cut me many years ago, but it is a pain unlike any other." Azariah stood still, face pulled tight as he recalled those ugly days. *He must have been so young*, Seraf thought.

Azariah came out of his trance with a shake of his shoulders. "But this is not a subject with which to welcome you to the palace. I apologize.

I look forward to hearing you play." He drifted off. The musicians stared at one another, aghast.

"How can they bear it?" Rivai croaked.

"How will we?" Tekoa replied, his face white.

11

Sarah and the Princess

THEY MARCHED SARAH THROUGH THE streets of Babylon, a guard making sure she trailed in the princess's wake. The streets were wider than those of Jerusalem, the roadways kept in better repair. There were signs of new construction on nearly every street corner. Palm trees and other greenery peered out of the high walls, concealing large mansions, stately houses of a reddish brick, rather than the pink stone she was used to. The streets bustled with richly garbed men and women who stared contemptuously as she was led past. The rushing River Euphrates sent up a cool breeze. In the distance, an enormous, tiered structure dominated the cityscape, smoke rising from its top level.

Upon arriving at the Summer Palace, Sarah was bathed several times, the months on the captive trail turning the heated waters brown as accumulated filth leeched from her body. Slaves washed her hair, scraped her rough skin with pumice, and anointed her body with salves and ointments. When she was clean and clothed in a simple white shift with green-banded sleeves of ribbon, flowers braided through her dark hair, and kohl painted around her green eyes, a slave brought her to the princess for inspection.

Kasšaya was sitting with her father's wife, Queen Amytis, the two laughing at the antics of a half-sized acrobat brought from Nineveh to amuse them. Sarah had eaten well since she'd arrived at the palace, but her mouth still watered when she saw the luscious repast set before the women. There were flat baked breads to be dipped into a crushed chick-pea mash or drizzled with olive oil, pickled cucumbers and small peeled white onions, roasted goat, fresh-grilled pike, pheasant's eggs baked in their shells, and date cakes sprinkled with sesame and honey.

"Ah, the handmaiden from Judea," Kassaya said, as Sarah paused by the door. "Queen Stepmother, this is my newest slave. Shamrina. The Captain of the Guard singled her out for his favors and his bed. I purchased her to tend to my fragrance storeroom."

Amytis looked up languidly, dark eyes bored and vacant. Sarah's beauty made them narrow in concentration. The queen stared at the slave coldly. She leaned forward, selecting a cake sticky with syrup and sesame seeds. "I wouldn't care to have such a girl as one of my attendants," she said. "Too great a distraction."

"My perfumers are all eunuchs," replied Kassaya. "And it is a pleasant conceit to have a beauty who delights the eye fetching a fragrance that pleases the nose."

Amytis shrugged, tossing her half-eaten cake away and snapping for a moistened cloth to wipe her fingers. "I asked Nebuchadnezzar for some slaves to tend to my garden. Did you hear how he is bringing all my favorite plants from my homeland in Media and creating a special garden for me?"

Sarah watched Kassaya stifle a yawn. "I heard."

"But the Judeans are farmers, not gardeners, it seems," Amytis said, idly putting a hand up to pat her elaborate plaits. "They do have some fine musicians, however."

Sarah's heart skipped a beat as she thought of Seraf. She knew the musician was attracted to her—in the same way that young men had buzzed around her when she visited the well in Jerusalem or made her way through the marketplace. But Seraf was different. He'd been willing to be her friend as well as her admirer. Sarah smiled thinly, remembering how the musician had watched out for her during the terrible journey.

Kassaya leaned back into her cushions. "I heard my father gave you the Judean royal musicians. Do they amuse you? It is so hard to find true talent among the captive rabble. At least the first group of Judeans brought here were nobles. But these! Father's governor to Judea, Neriglissar, told me he found them a proud and stubborn people. And the ones left behind in Judea, the shepherds and beggars, are even worse."

"Your slave girl is blushing," commented Amytis, glancing at the angry flush rising into Sarah's face. "If you bleach her cheeks, they won't redden in that vulgar fashion."

Kassaya waved Sarah into a corner. She crouched down, waiting to be dispatched back to the perfume storeroom. *So this is what it's like,* she thought indignantly, *to be a slave. They think I have no feelings. My body—my legs, my cheeks—they own them. Like the captain did.*

Sarah was raised to consider her virginity her most precious treasure, and her body something to shield from the gaze of strangers. But Nebuzaradan had swatted aside her pleas of modesty as though they were mites found on his saddle. Sarah's face flushed again, remembering the nights when he'd used her as he might his horse or his armor. *But I am free of him,* she reminded herself firmly; the captain had ridden off on new conquests. She took a deep breath to banish the sickness she felt in the pit of her stomach when recalling those curtained nights. She forced herself to think instead of the perfume storeroom. She would be left alone there, among the bottles and flasks. Sarah looked forward to living in that fragrant space in solitude.

The acrobat was waved away. Amytis motioned to a slave standing at the door, whispering something in his ear. Kassaya looked at her stepmother, one eyebrow raised.

"It is so long until nightfall," Amytis said plaintively, picking up a small cup of seed tea, "and I'm bored. The men have their wars and politics to attend to, but we women?"

"If we were poor, we'd have children to care for, a household to tend," Kassaya replied.

Amytis shuddered. "I thank Ishtar she did not make me poor. Ah!" She glanced up as the door opened. Her small retinue of Judean musicians stood there, carrying their instruments.

Sarah shrank back, tingling with shame as she noticed Seraf in their midst. She had been the freeborn daughter of a well-respected farmer when he met her. He had known her as a captive, as a ruined maiden—but not as a slave. Despite the baking heat of the late summer afternoon, she shivered inside her thin dress.

Amytis commanded, "Come in, come in. Daughter, these are my new musicians. I offer you their services for the afternoon."

The tightly tucked corners of Kasšaya's mouth showed Sarah how Amytis's presumption annoyed the princess. But the princess hid her irritation behind honeyed tones. "A good thought, Queen Stepmother. Some amusement for the long, dull afternoon."

Sarah looked around, counting the servants, the musicians, the tiny acrobat. How many people were pressed into bondage to alleviate the boredom of these two privileged women? Sarah's family had many servants, but her mother would have scoffed at the idea of sitting with idle hands. She had a farm to run, children to raise, a home to tend. And on those rare afternoons when she found a few hours of leisure, Aliza would busy herself with charitable deeds, mending clothing for the poor or carrying a basket of food to the ill and indigent.

As the musicians started to play, the familiar melodies made Sarah straighten. The rustling of her dress distracted Seraf. He glanced in her direction and his mouth dropped open. Sarah saw him struggle to preserve his concentration on the notes of his dulcimer, a sudden blaze building behind his black eyes. She flashed him a quick smile before ducking her head. A discordant note made her glance up, half amused. Seraf bit his lip, looking like a young boy caught with his lessons unlearned.

Sarah's throat tightened. During the long journey, she'd had to endure the physical strain of the march and the perpetual threat of the captain's bed. But she and Seraf had survived it, and now were captives under the same roof. Slaves together.

Had the Babylonians not disrupted her life, her parents would have found her a good husband. Now it was up to her to find someone who might protect her and give her children. Would Seraf make a good husband? She sat back and studied him. Yes, he was handsome, with his chestnut hair falling to his shoulders and deeply expressive dark eyes. She already knew how kind he could be. She glanced down, noticing how the cool linen of her dress had crumpled beneath suddenly restless fingers. She hastily smoothed the wrinkles in the fabric.

Amytis put up a hand, cutting the musicians off mid-song. "Regale us with a song of love and tenderness," she commanded. "Something joyful. Thus far, your music is too melancholy."

The harpist strummed a few bars, and the musicians sang a round, their combined voices building into a paean of joy:

> Awake, O north wind, and come,
> O south wind; blow upon my garden,
> that the spices thereof may flow out;
> let my beloved come to his garden and eat his
> sweet fruit.

Seraf kept glancing toward Sarah as he sang. She rested her back against the marble wall and let his music wash over her.

12

Sarah in the Perfumery

"GET THE ESSENCE OF BLUE lotus from Jahu, and pour it off into the blue glass bottle," Geb instructed Sarah.

Sarah eased around the tables carefully, making sure to keep her skirts tight against her legs. On her first day in the perfume manufactory, she had brushed against one of the bowls, knocking the container of blanched almonds soaking in oil to the floor. Geb stood almost nose to nose with her, screaming vile threats. Sarah, unaccustomed to being treated thus, thrust up her chin and stood her ground, but trembled inwardly in shock. The unfortunate slave who had to re-boil water, drop in handfuls of almonds, and slip them from their loose skins, made the sign of the evil eye in her direction for days afterward.

Geb, an Egyptian slave, oversaw Princess Kassaya's perfumery. Once he calmed down, he told Sarah how he'd been seized when Nabopolassar, King Nebuchadnezzar's father, fought the Egyptians during the decisive Battle of Carchemish. Geb, who'd served the Egyptian royal house of Necho, was well versed in the ancient art of perfume making.

Dozens of slaves worked under him, like bees serving in the confines of a hive. All day long they crushed iris roots, plants, and berries; soaked fragrant woods in the purest of oils; and boiled various mixtures on small fires. Sarah watched as they released the fragrance of the blue lotus, the lily, and the rose. Cedar bark was brought from the north to Babylon by camel caravan, and men whose faces were darker than night brought Geb aromatic woods from Africa. Sarah reared in alarm when she first saw their dark countenances. The group's leader grinned, reaching out to touch her glossy dark hair and peer into her green eyes.

"What is he doing?" she gasped, shying away from his long fingers, pitch black on one side with dead white palms. The overseer asked a question in a language Sarah had never heard before. The African cupped her chin with one hand and pointed at her eyes, speaking in a string of lilting syllables. His fingers were warm, insistent against her skin.

"He's never seen a girl with devil eyes before." Geb laughed. "Says you'll bring bad luck."

Sarah backed away, a chill chasing up her spine. "Tell him to leave me alone." She retreated into her storeroom sanctuary, slamming the door shut, refusing to emerge until he left.

The perfumery slaves extracted resin from the slivers of African wood. Sarah took the resulting myrrh and frankincense, bottling them in jars of alabaster and cloudy green glass.

A few days later, Geb ordered the princess's butcher to slaughter an ox. The scraped fat was brought in heavy white lumps to the perfumery. The slaves boiled it down and poured off exact portions. They used small sieves to purify the oil, then mixed it with fragrant essences.

Sarah, holding the bottled musk to her nose, was amazed at the oil's heavy, almost overwhelming aroma. "Where do these bottles belong in the storeroom?" she asked Geb.

Geb shook his head. "We send the musk to the temples of Ishtar and Damkina as an offering from our mistress," he explained. "They are her favorite goddesses. Take the musk to Melzar, the master of the eunuchs. He will arrange to deliver the oils to the temples."

Sarah gathered the vials in her apron and set off, hoping she would not lose her way in the great palace. Kasšaya's quarters were in the southeast corner of the complex. The office of the master of the eunuchs, Sarah knew, was on the opposite end, near Nebuchadnezzar's rooms.

As she wound through the long hallways, Sarah experienced an unexpected surge of well-being. *I might be a slave,* she thought, *but I'm healthy, strong, well dressed, and well fed.* Her soft white linen dress, drawn over one shoulder in the Babylonian fashion, felt light and cool against her skin. Her sandals were laced up her shapely calves; her hair fell in loose curls over her shoulders. As nobles passed her in the corridors, she made the appropriate obeisance, standing aside to let them pass. The men's gaze lingered on her curves while the women's eyes slit appraisingly. Until the captain had taken her, Sarah had always been flattered by the attention she provoked. Now that her virtue was protected as a member of Kasšaya's household, she could permit herself to enjoy the stares once more.

But as one young noble's ogling grew too penetrating, she remembered how her parents had harped on the need to remain modest. She pulled at the cloth that barely skirted one shoulder, wishing she could cover her bare arm. Her father would have whipped her naked flesh if he'd seen her.

But he was dead, she remembered. They were all dead: father, mother, and brother. A pang of grief smote her, remembering her old life, the life stolen from her. Why was she alive when they were dead? Why had she not perished as well? But she denied the wave of shame that threatened to overwhelm her, squaring her shoulders. It was not her fault that the Chaldean soldier took her father's life before he could kill her. *Had he lived, I would be as dead as they are*, she told herself. Despite her guilt at surviving, she couldn't deny the simple fact: She was alive. Sarah threw up her head, feeling blood race through her, right down to her fingertips, her toes. She stood proud and joyous at the end of a long stretch of corridor, every nerve tuned to the preciousness of life. Her father, mother, brother, all might be dead, her home lost, but she would survive. Despite everything that had happened to her, she would survive.

And after all, she reasoned, smiling, she lived here in the palace. So did Seraf. She knew he wanted her. They could make a life together: marry, have children. It wouldn't be the life Sarah thought she would have—but it could be a good life, nonetheless.

She turned a corner. Melzar's quarters were straight ahead. She eased by a small line of slaves waiting there. She knew from their averted glances and the way they pulled in their breath as she swept by them that they were no longer men.

Sarah sickened at the thought of a gelded man. She'd been taught that castration was a sin. A man who was cut could no longer have children. Procreation, Sarah's culture decreed, was the primary goal of man and woman. The laws of Moses were clear and direct: Be fruitful and multiply. But since coming to Babylon, she'd learned this nation held chastity in higher esteem than fertility. The men and women who served their pagan gods submitted to a lifetime of celibacy. The royalty of the Empire considered themselves kin to the gods, so they forced their servants to be chaste, just like the priests of the altar. Melzar oversaw the cutting of most males who served in the palace, particularly if they served the royal family.

Sarah stepped gingerly through the ranks of the eunuchs. She had a childlike prejudice against touching them. Melzar's door was slightly ajar. Sarah pushed it open.

And froze. There, standing naked, eyes averted and body flushed by shame, stood Seraf. A royal physician knelt at his feet, measuring his manhood with a pair of calipers. "I can cut this one three days from now," he told Melzar, who used a clay tablet and stylus to make a mark. "He is well endowed. We'll remove his penis as well as his ball sack."

The sacred oils rolled out of Sarah's apron and crashed onto the marble floor. The entire chamber was suffused with a heady odor. Sarah strangled the scream that rose in her throat, but a whimper nonetheless escaped.

Seraf's head jerked up and his agonized stare burned her face. Sarah turned and fled.

But she could not resist one glance backward as she went. Seraf stood watching her run, his unclad body leaning toward her in yearning, dark eyes awash in despair.

13

One Night

THE NEXT NIGHT, SARAH TOSSED and turned on her thin sleeping pallet, the soles of her feet throbbing from the whipping she'd received for dropping the musks. The trapped fragrances of the tiny storeroom were cloying, the air thick with malevolent spirits. Sarah could not banish the image of Seraf, naked and despondent, from her thoughts.

Outside her pitch-dark room, dozens of slaves slept on the floor of the perfume manufactory. One of them moaned under his breath, softly murmuring in a foreign tongue. So many wasted lives, Sarah thought, all stoppered up like the fragrances they bottled.

She couldn't sleep. She rose from her bed and limped to the single window in the storeroom, a slit in the wall overlooking the garden. She stood, trying to breathe enough fresh air to help her relax. Her breath felt strangled in her chest.

She couldn't stand it. She needed to find her way outside, even at the risk of another beating. She slowly opened the door to the storeroom. A dozen snores assailed her ears. Creeping like one of the cats the Egyptian Geb kept as sacred pets, she twisted and turned past the prone bodies of her fellow slaves. She felt her way to the door, opening it just enough to slip through and find herself in the garden.

Above her, a thousand stars sparkled, vivid and glittering in the moonless sky. Sarah walked through the rose bushes into the lily garden. The palace architect had placed a tiny artificial pond exactly in the middle of the plantings for the floating water lilies. Sarah knelt beside it, scooped some cool water in her cupped hand, and splashed her face.

"Sarah!" someone murmured in her ear. A strong arm reached around her waist and pulled her close. "Hush."

Heart beating wildly in her chest, she knew instantly who it was. Seraf.

"What are you doing here?" she whispered, leaning back against his slender frame.

"I came looking for you." His voice was edged with—what? Regret? Pent-up desire? "I didn't think I would find you, but I had to try."

"What are they going to do to you?" she asked, turning to put her arms around his neck. "When I saw you, I…."

"Shh," he murmured. "Let's not speak of it."

In a daze, she took him by the hand and led him out of the lily garden to a small, secluded grape arbor. One of the palace landscapers had placed a bench beneath the glossy leaves. Thick clusters of globed fruit dangled above them. They sat.

"I don't know how to say this," he told her. "Sarah, they're going to…."

"Let's not speak of it, you said," she begged. "I can't bear it."

"It's all I can think of," he said, bitterly. "That—and you."

"I'm here," she said simply. She put her hand out, taking his. "I'll always be here for you, Seraf—no matter what."

He reached for her chin, cupping it in one warm hand. He raised her face, lowering his head so his lips touched hers. Seraf's kiss, hesitating and delicate, was nothing like the captain's firm, possessive salutes. Seraf's lips trembled against hers. Her mouth felt soft, yielding. Then he pulled back, breaking off the embrace.

She reached for him, twining her arms around his neck, finding his lips again. Their second kiss grew deeper. She pulled one hand away from his shoulder, running it down his arm, moving soft fingertips across his chest. He pulled her closer, hands roving over her body. Her pulse danced as her legs turned limp. She pushed the cloth of her shift off her shoulder, releasing small, rosy-tipped breasts to the night air. He stooped and kissed them, lingering on her curves. Sarah gasped and moaned.

The sound of a cricket made them draw apart, startled. Seraf took hold of her shift, covering her body with a trembling hand.

"We cannot do this," he murmured. "If you became pregnant…they would destroy you."

"I don't care." Sarah leaned close so he could smell the subtle perfume that always lingered now in the folds of her gown.

Seraf shifted out of reach. "Listen to me," he muttered, turning his face aside. "In two days, I will be gelded. When I threatened to escape, I was warned that runaways from the palace are flayed alive, bodies dumped in the desert, still beating hearts left for the vultures to tear to bits. I cannot face such a death. So I will stay and endure…my disgrace." He stopped for a moment, swallowing hard. "Since the evening I first saw you, I was entranced by your beauty, your bravery, your quick wit. But my desire doesn't excuse my putting you in danger, even though.…"

"Even though…?" Sarah whispered.

"Even though I want you. I will always want you."

"What if we were to pledge our troth to one another?" Sarah asked softly. "Could you not tell them we are to be married? Wouldn't that stop them from cutting you?"

"No." Seraf shook his head. "We are all gelded. Even the great Daniel and his friends."

Sarah felt as though cold water was sluiced over her. She shivered. "Do you not want a wife? Children? We could flee the palace together," she begged him.

Seraf's lips tightened. "What do you think? Of course I want you. I want to fill you with our children, raise a family together. I've wanted it since we met in the captain's tent. But we're slaves for life, you and me. We can't do what we want, not now, not ever. And how could I put you in harm's way? What would they do if you became pregnant?" He paused. Then, in a more hopeful tone, he said, "Though, perhaps, they would think it was the captain's baby and not punish you."

Sarah shook her head. "My red flows have come upon me since arriving at the palace. Kassaya's slaves know—they gave me cloths to protect my gown. Any child I bore would be yours."

Seraf folded his arms and edged back farther. "We must not, then," he said.

Sarah stared at the musician. He looked so forlorn. She wanted to help him, ease his pain, even briefly. Give him a memory that he could cherish. After all, would he even survive the operation? And if he did…. She reached up and felt his cheeks, the stubble rough beneath her fingers. The feel of him clouded her reason.

He felt it too. The misery melted from his face, his body relaxing. He put his arms back around her. His hands moved lower on her body, sliding along her linen shift, finding the spot where a clasp secured the garment. He slipped past it to the warm flesh of her hips. His fingers brushed her small, taut stomach, then dipped to her thighs. Sarah's legs grew weak. Her body began to move against his roving hand, almost against her will.

Let it happen, she told the cold, rational part of herself that warned her to stop. *It's only one night. Give him this one night.*

Then she stopped thinking altogether. His fingers reached deep inside her, making her arch against him, moaning as he played upon her as though she were his dulcimer. His delicate musician's fingers found her nub and teased it, her gasp floating out into the night air.

He tilted her backwards, stretching her on the bench. With one hand, he pulled his manhood from his robe. She reached for it, brushing against the hot, humid tip, making him groan. Her knees fell apart and he moved between them. This felt nothing like the captain's enthusiastic plundering of her body. This was something altogether different.

She felt him make his way inside her, mouths merging in a breathless kiss. The night swirled around them, the stars touching the horizon. The light fragrance of the garden wafted over them. He was moving within her now, and she was moaning to his motion.

"Sarah," he gasped. "Oh, my darling Sarah."

She opened even more to him. Something was happening to her, something that made her forget everything but the two of them and the sensations of their bodies. She was rising, somehow, her body climbing a peak and she was gasping to reach the other side. *Almost there*, she thought crazily, *I am almost…*.

Her body flooded with his seed at the same moment she felt herself reach the peak she'd been straining for. They clutched one another, letting the glorious waves dance over them.

And then, it was over.

Sarah sat up, suddenly aghast at what she had permitted. She pulled against his restraining arms. "I must go," she gasped.

"Just one minute more," he begged her.

She knew he wanted to hold her tight against him and try to forget. But if they found them together, they would both be whipped. She struggled against his hands and worked herself free. In an instant, she was gone.

14

The Making of a Eunuch

Seraf awoke in a pool of blood.

He cried out, waves of pain engulfing him. Ibi-Sin, the physician's apprentice, slithered over on soundless feet, clapping for slaves to bring towels. Ibi-Sin took one look at Seraf's white face and poured a drink from a clay ewer, dropping powder from a vial in it and stirring the mixture with an olive wood stirrer.

The apprentice's left arm curved around Seraf's shoulders, lifting him to a sitting position. "Drink," the soft voice urged. "You'll feel better soon."

The liquid, thick with undissolved opiates, made Seraf gag. Suddenly, he broke out in a sweat, retching and vomiting up the contents of his stomach. The room filled with the sharp, foul smell and the other patients groaned and complained.

Seraf lapsed back into a semi-conscious state. He felt hands moving around him, but it didn't matter any longer. The thought of all he had lost assailed him. He was impure, could never again approach the holy sites. Even if, by some miracle, he was restored to Judea and the Temple rebuilt in his lifetime, his dream of performing his music there was now a withered vine, blasted by his maimed body.

And then there was Sarah. She had given him a single night's memory, but could that sustain him for a lifetime? His future stretched before him, bleak and unrelenting: a life in thrall to the Chaldeans, never to have his own home, his own household, his own family.

Let me die, was his last waking thought, as he let go, falling into a black pit of unconsciousness.

It was impossible to know how long he lay there. When he next woke, it was dark.

Ibi-Sin, who did not seem to need sleep, looked down at him. "So you decided to live after all," he murmured, feeling Seraf's forehead and wrists with cool hands. "We thought we had lost you."

Tremendous pressure pushed against Seraf's lower stomach. "I want to piss," he muttered weakly. His urgent need chased every other thought away.

Ibi-Sin straightened, lips pursed. "Bring a basin and two other orderlies," he said to a slave who hovered nearby. In a moment, a basin of tightly woven river weeds, lined with tar, was thrust into Ibi-Sin's hands.

"All right, Judean," the apprentice said. "We're going to help you sit. You'll feel weak and dizzy, but we'll hold you. Pretend nothing has changed and just let yourself make your water. Do you know what I mean?"

Seraf, still woozy, wasn't sure. Strong arms helped him sit and swing his legs to one side of the cot. One slave held the basin, while another reached down and pulled…something.

Seraf cried out, pain rushing over him like sea waves. What had they put inside him?

"It's a pissing tube," Ibi-Sin said, large black eyes searching Seraf's face. "Go on, piss."

But Seraf had lost the urge. Despite the pressure in his lower gut, which grew more acute as he sat upright, he couldn't make himself go.

Ibi-Sin shook his head. "I was afraid of this. There's always one or two in a group. I'd hoped we'd be luckier, this time."

"What…?" Seraf started to ask. But then, pain assailing him again, he subsided.

"Lay him back down," was all the physician's assistant said.

A half hour later, with the lightening colors of pre-dawn seeping into the room, Seraf couldn't stand it. "I need to piss!" he yelled, his frantic desire overtaking every other sensation.

In an instant, Ibi-Sin was by his side. "Are you really going to do it now?" he asked. "Don't waste our time if you're not."

"If I don't relieve myself, I'll die," Seraf shrieked, making a few of his fellow inmates stir and cry out for quiet.

"Quite possibly," Ibi-Sin replied, his heavily kohled eyes raking Seraf's face.

Slaves pulled him up again, arms around his back. "Help him stand," Ibi-Sin instructed them. "Sometimes that helps."

Seraf felt his knees buckle and sway, but one of the slaves draped an arm under his armpits and held on. "How do I do this?" Seraf muttered, feeling the strange object rubbing and chafing inside him.

"Just let go," Ibi-Sin told him. "Don't think about it."

Seraf tried to clear his mind, but the tube inside him blocked the impulse. "I can't...." he cried out.

"Bring water," Ibi-Sin said to one of the orderlies. "A cup and a pitcher."

"Let me lie down," Seraf begged.

But Ibi-Sin shook his head. "You're going to drown inside yourself if you don't let out the urine that's built up," he said. "We may have already left it too late. Here, give him a drink."

"A drink?" Seraf moaned.

A full cup of water was tipped down Seraf's throat, then another. The pressure inside him was like a dam after a rainstorm, threatening to burst open. He cried out.

"More?" the orderly asked.

"Let's try the waterfall trick," Ibi-Sin suggested.

The slave stood behind him, taking a cupful of water and letting it pour back into the pitcher, over and over. The sound of rushing water concentrated Seraf's need to relieve himself. It was all he could think about. But still it did no good. He groaned.

"Think about something else," Ibi-Sin murmured.

Gritting his teeth, Seraf made himself recall something else. Sarah…
her softness, the way she had opened to him, the taste and smell of her.
But the deadness in his midsection when he remembered Sarah horrified
him. Shaking his head to clear it, Seraf conjured up his favorite childhood
memory. A festival day when he had been an apprentice. He had spent
it with a friend on the banks of the River Jordan, trying to catch a fish.
They hadn't succeeded, but the day remained precious in his memory,
the two of them sitting by the rushing waters in the shade, boys content
to be quiet together and simply enjoy the warm summer day.

There was the sound of water in the basin beneath him. Gasping in
relief, Seraf realized that a stream of urine flowed from his body. Slowly,
the immense pressure in his stomach eased. He pissed until there was
nothing more inside him and he sagged back into the orderly's arms.

"Put him to bed," Ibi-Sin told the slaves. He bent down and sniffed
at the urine, then stuck a finger in it and tasted. "Seems like you'll live
after all, Judean," he said, raising his head.

For a moment, triumph swept over Seraf. He was going to live. But
once he had been resettled in bed, a slave washing away the drops of urine
that stung his legs, draping cool sheets over him, thoughts of what he had
lost struck him like an earthquake. Mutilated. No longer a man. How
could he face the world this way? Face Sarah? Shutting his eyes, Seraf lay
still for many hours, numb as stone.

15

The Human Scarecrow

THE DAYS BEGAN TO MELD together. Sarah heard that Seraf was healed, but he refused to see her. She told herself that he needed time; that she understood his deep shame.

As she waited, she spent her days in the tight quarters of the perfume storeroom, carefully placing bottles on the shelves, waiting for the princess to summon her to replenish the supplies of scent she kept in her quarters. The overwhelming fragrance of the storeroom was too much for Sarah most mornings, and she woke feeling queasy.

As soon as she could escape her storeroom duties, she crept outside, finding a shady spot where the heat did not beat down on her uncovered head. She sat under the grape arbor, reliving her one night of passion with Seraf.

The Judeans who dined at Daniel's table heard that many of their fellow captives were starving, especially those tending the land. The new exiles had arrived at the peak of high summer. The farmers had no crop to sell and nothing to trade.

"We should feed them," Daniel declared one day at the midday meal. "We who are well fed have a responsibility."

Sarah wondered about her cousin. How was Reuven faring? Where was he living? She set aside a portion of every meal to feed her fellow

Judeans. That was easier to do some days than others, for certain dishes she had enjoyed before repulsed her now. On other days, it took all her strength not to bolt down her entire meal and beg for more.

Daniel set up a booth to distribute food to the starving exiles. When she could slip away from her duties, Sarah joined the other Judean slaves and handed out bread, olives, and yogurt. She scrutinized every face, asked everyone for news of her cousin. No one knew anything.

The long, sun-struck days slipped into cool, short nights. Sarah began to check her bedding for her red flows. Every morning she pulled the thin blanket off completely, running her hand over her cot. There was no sign of her womanly cycle. She told herself not to panic. There could be any number of reasons why her courses might have stopped temporarily. She began to make marks in the dirt floor every morning. The tracks grew deeper as she clutched the stick tighter and tighter.

One afternoon, as she left the palace courtyard, Sarah recognized Seraf's dulcimer. She peered over a low wall and saw him sitting on the ground, playing, his eyes shut. A small knot of Judeans had gathered, listening closely. Sarah's breath caught in her throat, seeing her cousin seated among them. Reuven was sunburnt, his face drawn. His frame seemed too broad for the flesh that stretched across it. But his arms were thick with sinewy muscle.

Sarah shut her eyes and thanked God that Reuven was alive. She drew closer. Before she could raise a hand to greet her cousin, Seraf began to sing:

> Show me mercy, O God, show mercy,
> in you my soul takes refuge.
> I will hide under the shadow of your wings
> until tragedy passes.

Many women wiped away tears and the men shuffled their feet in the dirt, as if afraid to reveal their emotions. As she listened, Sarah felt the catastrophe anew:

> I am among the lions;
> I lie among ravenous beasts—

men whose teeth are spears and arrows,
whose tongues are sharp swords.

The psalm's end was meant to evoke joy and faith in the Almighty. But the cloud overshadowing Seraf's face grew ever darker:

Great is your love, reaching to the heavens;
your faithfulness reaches to the skies.
Be exalted, O God, above the heavens;
let your glory be over all the earth.

Seraf put down his instrument. "Is that the song you wanted?" he asked Daniel, who sat on a cushion on a garden bench, shaded by the fronds of a palm tree.

"It was," Daniel replied, rising with a fluid motion. A slave hurried to collect his cushion. "Thank you, Seraf."

Seraf inclined his head, but the pain in his eyes was still palpable. "I am glad my music brings you comfort."

Daniel placed a hand on Seraf's shoulder. "It will do the same for you in time."

Another slave came running from the palace. "Belteshazzar, the king waits upon your counsel," he said.

Daniel nodded and walked gracefully away, rich robes trailing behind.

The crowd around the musician thinned, and Seraf shut his eyes wearily. Reuven stood up, looking uncertain.

"Reuven!" cried Sarah. "I'm so happy to see you!"

Sarah ran into Reuven's extended arms, and the cousins hugged one another. Sarah was glad to feel the tensile strength of Reuven's grasp, despite his worn appearance. Seraf sat apart, watching them, his face still dark with grief.

Sarah broke from Reuven's embrace. "I hoped you'd come. Where do you live now?"

"On a barley farm near Tel Abib, a town located some leagues from Babylon, near the Chebar Canal," he told her. "A two-hour donkey ride. Are you allowed to leave the palace grounds? You could come visit my little hut of brick, my tiny portion of land." Reuven turned to the musician. "You might bring her, Seraf."

Seraf smiled thinly. "I don't know if they will permit it, but I will ask. Melzar will know."

"Melzar?"

"He is—my master now."

Reuven looked confused. "I thought you served the queen."

"I am one of the queen's musicians, but Melzar is master of her servants." Seraf changed the subject, looking at Reuven's small woven basket holding a handful of olives, half a loaf of bread, and some dates. "Don't you need more food than that? It doesn't seem like enough."

Reuven turned beet red. "I don't want to take more than is right. Many are starving in Tel Abib. It is hard to start a life from nothing."

Seraf nodded, lips pressed tight. "You remind me how lucky Sarah and I are. We are well fed, well cared for."

Reuven looked from one to the other. "But are you happy?"

An image of the marks on her floor flashed before Sarah. She shaded her eyes, trying to hide her mounting panic.

Seraf quickly changed the subject. "How are *you* managing? Have you found someone to help you?"

Reuven grinned. "A neighbor of mine comes when I most need him. I never call him—it's as if he knows. A wild-eyed fellow who talks in a lisp and faints dead away in the heat of the sun."

"He doesn't sound like he could be much help," Sarah mused.

"No, but he always appears when I need him."

"That must be a relief." Seraf waved his hand toward a nearby bench.

Reuven and Sarah sat close together.

"Let me tell you about the first time I met him," Reuven said, uncharacteristically eager to talk.

He must be lonely, Sarah thought, living in that brick hut all alone.

"I was sowing my crop of bitter vetch—tiny beans that can grow in the heat of the summer. My master, Chori, knowing barley seeds would scorch in the field, gave me a sack of vetch instead of the barley I'm supposed to plant to pay my taxes."

"Taxes?" Seraf asked.

"Every landowner who gives a captive farmer land owes the king nearly a third of his crop in taxes. Chori said bitter vetch would ready the soil for next year, and he'd use all I raised to feed his livestock. But first I had to agree that he could take twice as much of his share of my barley quota next year, if he paid my taxes this year."

"Twice again would make it..." Seraf pondered.

"Difficult for me to live, but not impossible." Reuven nodded. "But for a while I wondered if I would even get the bitter vetch into the ground. For I was all alone. As Sarah will tell you, when you try and plant seeds on your own...."

"The birds," Sarah said wonderingly. "How did you keep them off?"

"At first I didn't. I would prepare a row with my hoe, strew the seeds—but before I could return to the top of the row to cover them, the birds had already carried the beans away."

"You can't be in two places at once," Sarah explained to Seraf. "It was often my job to chase the birds. Or my father hired a boy if my mother needed me elsewhere."

"It was a miserable day," Reuven continued. "Horribly hot. Every time I yelled to scatter the birds, they'd fly off for a bit. But as soon as I picked up the hoe, back they flew."

Sarah held her breath. She knew from harsh experience that birds could decimate a crop. And if they did, what would Reuven's landlord master do to him?

"But then," Reuven continued, "The birds no longer landed on the field. A man stood in the middle of my rows, arms stretched wide. He had wild sandy hair, a beard that grew straight out of his chin, and a tunic of loose rags."

"A human scarecrow!" Sarah said.

"Yes. And he said to me, in this low, ringing voice"—here Reuven deepened his own voice, mimicking the stranger—"'I will keep the birds away. You must continue to plant in this strange field. All of Judea must raise their crops far from home now.'"

Sarah shivered at the weird pronouncement. She glanced at Seraf. His face had cleared of grief. Instead, it was rapt, fingers moving soundlessly over his dulcimer as though he were composing a tune to this strange tale.

"I asked him who he was. He looked toward the sky and answered, 'God's friend. And yours. I was heading to Tel Abib when I saw your struggles. So I turned off my road and will stand here while you complete your work.'

"I thanked him, and he asked if I were new come from Judea and what had happened to the rest of my family. I tried to speak of it, but the words stuck in my throat.

"He said, 'I am sorry. New injuries are always the hardest to bear. You keep working. Work and time will heal your wounds. I will watch that the birds do not eat your crop.'"

"He must have impressed you—you remember what he said so clearly," Sarah said.

Reuven nodded, continuing, "For hours, I plowed and planted the fields. It was so hot, sweat dripped into my eyes and I grew dizzy from the sun. The stranger hummed under his breath, something about God and wheels of fire and angels sitting inside the wheels. I wondered if he were insane."

"Wheels of fire and angels?" Seraf shook his head. "He sounds crazy."

"Finally, I finished planting and gathered my tools. The stranger began to tremble. I thought he was exhausted, so I invited him to rest, to eat something. Not that I had much to offer.

"But he put up both hands, as if to hold me off. 'Wait,' he said, voice shaking. His face went purple, and, to my shock, he collapsed on the ground, kicking and choking."

Reuven paused dramatically. Sarah could not drag her eyes from his face. After a moment of silence, Seraf ground out, "So?"

"I once saw a child have a fit in the market in Jerusalem. Someone reached into his mouth and held his tongue. They said, afterwards, it was so the child didn't swallow it during the fit. I had no choice and opened the man's mouth. His tongue was thick and throbbed with strange veins. I grabbed hold and held on.

"The man jerked with a massive shake and lay still. I released his tongue and put my head to his chest, trying to hear his heartbeat. Then he spoke, startling me.

"'I am sorry if I frightened you,' he said. 'God's grace is hard to bear sometimes.'

"I ran for the bucket I'd used to dampen the newly planted seed. It still contained an inch of water. I spilled some over my hands and wiped the man's face, then made him drink from my cupped palms.

"I asked if he had friends or family I could summon. But he shook his head. Then he said another odd thing.

"'It is fitting you have plowed your fields with bitter vetch. You will water it with tears for three generations.' I wanted him to stay still, but he shook me off and rose. He was walking away when I called out to him again, to ask his name.

"He just kept walking. But then he threw his name over his shoulder. It came back to me, echoing in my ears. 'I am Ezekiel,' he cried, 'son of Buzi and long captive of this evil land.'"

Reuven subsided. Sarah and Seraf stared at him.

"A strange experience," Seraf mused. "And he has been back to help you, you say?"

"Several times," Reuven said. "I could not have managed without him."

"Sarah," cried one of the perfumery slaves. "You are wanted inside."

"I must go," Sarah said reluctantly. "Come back and see us soon, Reuven."

Reuven rose and gave Sarah a hug. "You're getting plump," he whispered in her ear. "At least I don't have to worry about you, do I?"

"No," said Sarah, swallowing hard, placing a hand on her rounded stomach, "you don't have to worry about me at all."

16

Sarah Discovered

Summer was over. If they were back in Jerusalem, this would have been a season of rejoicing. Newly bathed, clothed in their best garments, carrying their sacrifice to the Lord, Sarah's family would enter the vast courtyard before the Temple, Father bringing their harvest offering to be blessed by the priests. The family would join other pilgrims in singing as musicians played joyful hymns. Mother would slip Sarah a coin to buy a ribbon for her hair, while her stern father watched over the two boys, keeping them from the clusters of young men who used the holiday as an excuse to tip the wine flask a few times too often.

But now there was no rejoicing. The exiled High Priest of the Judeans decreed that there should be no Sukkot festival. They could not celebrate this joyous holiday of the land when they were so cruelly separated from it.

Sarah could no longer pretend that she was not ripe with a harvest of her own. Her stomach bulged and, in panic, she begged for a new dress. But despite its width, it was still too flimsy. Dismayed how the jutting of her womb showed whenever she moved, she knotted a light linen shawl over her midsection, concealing her body as best she could.

The baby began to move within her. She didn't know what to do.

Seraf must still be miserable, Sarah told herself, which was why he continued to avoid her. She longed to share her secret with someone but flinched from afflicting him with still more wretchedness.

At the morning meal, the Judeans talked of gathering to mark the festival of Sukkot despite the High Priest's proclamation. Daniel was in favor.

"We must discover new ways to worship the Most High, even though our Temple lies in ruins and our homeland is destroyed," he told the Hebrews assembled at his table. "I will request permission for us to go."

Sarah thought it best to refuse, to hide from suspicious glances. But the enthusiasm of the other Judean slaves was infectious. Just as the last of the three carts carrying the slaves to Tel Abib was about to depart, she clambered onboard. Seraf, his expression grim, hunched next to Daniel in the lead cart. *Daniel must have made him come*, Sarah thought.

Daniel stood, looking regal in a rust-colored cloak rich with green and yellow beaded trim, his black curls pulled back in a hammered bronze clasp. Balancing by placing his hands on the shoulders of those sitting next to him, he called for a song. Seraf and the other musicians straightened and began to play. The palace slaves, gladdened by this rare holiday, joined in. And so, after two hours of singing and laughing, they rode into Tel Abib.

Looking about her, Sarah saw the desolation of this small town on Babylon's outskirts. Called "the mound of the deluge" because it so often flooded when the Euphrates rose into the Chebar Canal, it swarmed with pestilent mites. The brick huts the Judeans lived in were made from silt and river clay, set out in square molds to bake in the desert sun. They looked cramped and cheerless, shaded only by dwarf palm trees.

Riding through narrow streets crowded with hawkers and small, dark-eyed boys, Sarah was relieved she'd not been sent to tend one of the small booths crammed in the marketplace. After months of tranquility in the palace, the noise and smell of humanity made her head ache.

The carts dislodged the slaves at the town well, situated in a small square. Friends and family rushed up to greet them. Sarah felt bewildered, craning her neck to find her cousin, lost amid more people than she'd expected. The exiles milled about, not quite sure what to do. Some gathered in small groups to pray. Others sang about the land they had lost. Sarah, trying to push through the crowds, was stopped by a cry from the steps of one of the largest of houses.

"People of Judea!" came the call. Sarah recognized Daniel's rich, stentorian tones. "I have a letter to read to you all. From Jeremiah! Jeremiah in Egypt!"

The name of the prophet who had predicted their exile into Babylon sent a wave of excitement through the crowd.

Daniel put up a hand for silence. "Jeremiah is in Egypt now, but he bids us in this missive to live according to the will of the Lord." His deep voice rose above the hubbub. "Listen!"

Women hushed their babies. Young men stopped carousing in the corner of the town square. The crowd leaned forward as one.

"He writes: 'Build houses and live in them; plant gardens and eat their produce. Take wives and have sons and daughters, take wives for your sons, and give your daughters in marriage, that they may bear sons and daughters; multiply there, and do not decrease. Seek the welfare of the city where I have sent you into exile, and pray to the Lord on its behalf, for in its welfare you will find your welfare.'" Daniel tucked the sheet of papyrus inside his gown.

Jeremiah's words were repeated throughout the crowd, men and women interpreting it to one another. Clearly the first part of the message meant they must remain strong, remain a people, continue their lives. But the second part—seeking Babylon's welfare? That was more difficult to comprehend. How could they seek the welfare of an enemy? How would Babylon's success mean their own?

Daniel raised a hand and again the crowd hushed. "I hear your questions. I understand your confusion. But I beg you, look at me. Look"—he waved a hand at the three richly dressed young men standing close behind him—"at my companions. We were torn from our homeland as children. Brought here as captives. But we found peace and prosperity. By helping Babylon, we helped ourselves. And doing so, we found ways to remain true to the One True Lord even on foreign soil."

"You mean you've become a traitor to your people by serving a tyrant," a voice called out. "You sought wealth and comfort, but at what cost to us?"

Daniel's face darkened. "Who says so? He who speaks should step forward."

No one moved. Sarah held her breath.

"Only a coward calls out accusations from the safety of a crowd!" Azariah said, stepping forward to clap Daniel on the shoulder.

Daniel reached back, patting his friend's hand. "Would you call Azariah here a traitor? He braved fire to remain true to God. As did my friends and fellow captives, Hananiah and Mishael.

"Listen to my story, which occurred before you arrived. Heed me, you new exiles who are so quick to condemn. Jealous of our success in serving King Nebuchadnezzar, the king's advisors encouraged him to erect a great statue of gold and silver on the plain of Dura, requiring all to bow in worship. The king's heralds brought his royal servants to the idol, proclaiming that anyone who refused to worship it would be cast inside a fiery furnace. I was far from court, contemplating the dreams the Lord had sent me, and so was ignorant of our danger. But when my three friends were summoned, they refused to bow to the statue.

"Furious, King Nebuchadnezzar demanded that the three Judeans be brought before him. He asked why they would not abase themselves before his idol. What did you reply, Azariah, friend of my heart?"

Abed-Nego smiled. "What did I say? That I would not bow down before an idol, no matter who threatened me. And that my God would rescue me from the hottest of furnaces."

"And did He?" Daniel prompted. "Hananiah, you tell what happened next."

A third man stepped forward. Unlike his two dark-complexioned friends, he had red hair and fair skin, reminding Sarah that according to legend, King David had been a redhead.

"The king demanded that the furnace be made so hot it would kill a man to stand three paces before it," Hananiah continued. "The soldiers who bound us and pushed us into the heart of the furnace suffered greatly from its heat. But we did not feel it, for God sent an angel to protect us."

"Mishael," Daniel said, dragging the last of the companions forward, "tell us what you felt inside that furnace."

Mishael was shorter than his three friends and his plump, kindly face blushed as he faced the crowd. He shrugged. "We cannot tell you more, for while God shielded us from harm, he also robbed us of our memories. I can only tell you what the king said when we were finally brought forth—that we walked freely in the furnace, talking with the Lord's angel."

Daniel turned to the crowd. "There! Are these the words of men who betrayed their people and their God? My friends were willing to die for our faith, to perish rather than bow before idols. How can you question our loyalty?"

"How do we know that actually happened?" a voice cried out. "What if it is just a tale you invented to beguile us?"

Daniel's face turned nearly purple with suppressed rage, hands clenching together. But before he could respond, a wild-haired man climbed onto a pile of bricks, hovering over the crowd. He was dressed in dirty rags, his face peeling with sunburn.

"I, Ezekiel, son of Buzi, have been moved to speak to you all," he cried.

Sarah started, recognizing the name as the strange man her cousin had spoken of.

"The Lord castigated the People of Israel who would not believe, who worshipped graven images in their own land," he shouted.

All eyes turned toward him.

Ezekiel's limbs trembled, but his voice remained strong. "You who were justly punished by the Lord God do not have the right to question Daniel or his friends. They are true to the Lord even in this evil land. They live in luxury but do not turn from the Most High. They withstand temptation and act humbly before *Adonai*. Would that their accusers would do the same."

Despite some muttering, Ezekiel's proclamation ended the squabble. The populace drifted away.

Sarah pushed through the crowd, looking for Reuven. Her shawl, carefully wrapped around her midsection, caught on the sharp edge of a bronze bangle and was half dragged off her. Sarah clucked in annoyance, pulling to free the cloth.

"Whore!" came a cry from behind her. "Harlot!"

Sarah whirled, the shawl dropping from her hands. A thick-bottomed Judean matron, heavily clothed in mud-colored garb, pointed at her.

"Look at her, the shameless wretch!" the woman cried in a penetrating voice. "I remember her. The Captain of the Guard took her to his bed. And now she has the nerve to walk among us, her slut's dress barely hiding her guilty womb!"

The woman, whose bronze wristlet had caught Sarah's shawl, ripped the snarled end away and threw it at her feet. "You are right, Zilpah! See how she seeks to conceal her shame with rich rags! How plump and well-fed she looks, while we starve. She must entertain men nightly on her couch in the king's palace!"

"What should we do to her?" Zilpah asked. "What does she deserve?"

"Stone her!" some young boys, attracted by the uproar, cried.

The women took up the shout. "Stone her!"

Dizzy with fear, furious at their false accusations, Sarah snatched her shawl from the dusty ground and wrapped it around her. But eager hands grabbed it back. Two farmers, set on by their wives, gripped Sarah by her forearms and forced her through the crowd. Boys pulled her hair as she moved past them, unraveling the intricate braids woven for the festival. A clod of mud struck her. As it slid off her cheek, a second smacked her mouth.

"Put her up there, where we can stone her," someone shouted.

Sarah was forced onto a low mound of sun-hardened clay. Heart pounding, limbs weak, her memories flashed back to the soldiers who'd tried to rape her in her father's home. But these were her own people!

She tried to speak, but her mouth was so dry that all that emerged was a wheeze. She forced saliva into her mouth and tried again. "Stop!" she called, willing her voice to rise over their taunts. "Listen!"

Another clump of dirt hit her, followed by a pelting of river stones.

"Stop!" came the shout. Reuven stood before her, shielding her with his body. "What is this? What are you doing?"

"Move away," hissed the heavy-set matron. "We are teaching this harlot not to walk the streets where the sight of her offends law-abiding people."

The wild-eyed man in tattered clothing pushed his way through. "Move away from the whore, friend, lest you be hurt when the stones are hurled," he told Reuven.

Reuven did not budge. "Sarah? A whore? Be careful, Ezekiel, of speaking untruths in the marketplace."

"Stand back, I said," Ezekiel bellowed, eyes blazing under unruly strands of hair.

But Reuven was not cowed. "I said untruths and I mean untruths. How can you accuse her without proof?"

"The proof is in her belly," Zilpah sneered. "Ask her if she is not with child."

Sarah's head dropped to her chest. Had she suffered the agonies of the trek to Babylon only to die at the hands of her own people? "It's true," she muttered. "I'm pregnant."

"She was forced," Reuven cried. "I was there. The Captain of the Guard took her. Would you call her harlot when she was enslaved and raped?"

"Has Judean justice gone begging in the streets of Babylon?" came a voice behind them. Daniel approached; eyes alight with anger. "What is this?"

Seraf stood behind him, clutching his dulcimer.

Sarah wanted to fling herself at Daniel's feet, but hands clasped her elbows, raising bruises as they squeezed her flesh. "Oh, prince of Judea, help me!" she cried.

Reuven turned to the hostile crowd, eyes bulging in fury. "What should she have done, captive as she was?" he hissed.

"She could have killed herself," Zilpah said. "Like a decent Judean girl."

Someone in the crowd sniggered. "Lucky the captain didn't choose you, woman. You'd have killed him when he'd turned over in bed and seen your face in the dawn."

"Quiet!" Daniel cried, as the matron flushed beet red. "This is not a moment for levity."

"Ask if the baby is truly the captain's," cried a girl with a yellowed pocked face that likely scared off potential husbands.

Sarah trembled, hardly able to stand. She was tempted to lie, to save herself and her yet unborn babe. But as she opened her mouth, her father's face flashed before her. He had wanted to kill her to prevent her from shaming the family. She would not dishonor his memory by telling a falsehood. "It is not," she whispered.

"What did she say, Reuven?" Ezekiel asked.

"I didn't…. I couldn't hear…." Reuven stammered.

Sarah's head rose. "The baby is *not* the captain's," she screamed, casting aside her shame for a moment. But her courage waned as a flight of stones stung her legs and arms.

Some of them hit Reuven as well. "Move away," Ezekiel yelled. "You have your own patch of bitter vetch to sow. This is none of your concern."

"She is my cousin," Reuven cried out. "That makes it my concern."

"Who fathered the child, then? You?" the pock-marked girl mocked. "Her *cousin*?"

"I'm the father," Seraf said, putting his instrument down on the ground and joining Reuven. "If anyone is to be killed for the sin of fornication, it should be me."

"You?" laughed one of the boys in the crowd. "How did you do it, gelding? With your pissing tube?"

Sarah tried to will Seraf away, to protect him. "Do you think we chose these abuses? This life?" she shouted.

Reuven looked at Seraf, confused. The musician's eyes glittered dangerously, his mouth set in a straight line.

"Seraf," Reuven whispered, "what do they mean?"

"I was cut when I entered the queen's service," Seraf muttered in response.

Reuven was still mystified. "I don't…."

"He's a eunuch, Reuven," Sarah hissed.

"A…." Reuven could not keep the disgust from his face.

Seraf ignored it, turning to the crowd. "I lay with her two nights before the royal surgeon cut me. I begged her to bed with me, to give me the chance of fathering at least one child. If anyone is punished, it should be me."

"The Law says they both should die by the stones," Ezekiel called out. "Judeans! This is your chance to prove that the Law applies even in this evil land."

"Judeans!" Daniel cried, his deep voice carrying through the crowd. "This is your chance to prove that the Law also means mercy. For does not the Law say to be fruitful and multiply? Can you not see why this man and woman acted as they did, alone and without recourse in the great palace of Nebuchadnezzar?"

"The Law is clear on the sin of fornication," Ezekiel yelled back. "The whore and her lover must be punished. He cannot wed her and put this right.

"I would be willing," Seraf shouted. "I am still willing. But I am no longer a man any girl should marry."

Some of the mob stooped for stones. Seraf pushed Reuven away. "Stand back," he said, reaching for Sarah's hand, his dead white face oddly composed.

Sarah clung tight, wishing she could change their destiny. Even as slaves, they might have been happy together. Now, only death awaited them. Death and pain.

Hands reached up; arms pulled back. In a moment, Sarah knew, the stones would come whizzing, enough to batter and kill them both

"*I* am willing," Reuven cried, stepping before Sarah and Seraf, shielding them.

Those about to hurl their rocks paused.

Daniel moved beside him. "Stop! Listen!"

"*I* will marry Sarah," Reuven cried. "I will give her a home and raise the child as my own. And I warn you—let any man—or woman—call my wife a whore, and I will come to their home with whips and punish them!"

Sarah stared, seeing a look of her father in her cousin's set face. His courage, his loyalty, moved her. As for her—this was not the life she'd wanted. But it was life.

Sarah still clutched Seraf's hand. A glance passed between the two men. Seraf helped her down from the clay mound. He picked up her hand, kissed the palm, and handed it to his friend. He turned, retrieving his dulcimer and standing aside as the two cousins walked away.

17

Seraf's Promise

SOMEONE HAD TO TELL KASŠAYA. Because Sarah was still recovering from the shock of the stones, Seraf volunteered to seek an audience with the princess. It had to be soon. Geb would report her absence to Melzar before too long.

The day after the holiday, Seraf approached Daniel following their midday repast, and asked, "What do you think the princess will say?"

Daniel pursed his lips. "It depends on Kasšaya's mood. Sarah is her property. The princess could demand her return—or her death. You must make Kasšaya sympathize with Sarah's plight. But make no mistake— eventually someone will have to pay for the loss of a slave."

"But Sarah could not stay and have my child here, could she?"

"You doomed her the moment you slept with her. Why do you suppose you've been cut, Seraf? So this would not happen."

Seraf flinched at the disapproval in Daniel's eyes. "I was desperate. Have you never known what that feels like?"

The strangest look flitted across the man's face. "Someday I'll tell you what it felt like to prophesy to the king the first time. But today you must appease Kasšaya. Perhaps flattery. She is a woman, after all. And approach her before nightfall, before news of a runaway slave reaches the king."

Seraf sat for a few minutes, strumming his dulcimer. Deciding his plan would not improve by waiting, he set off.

Outside Kasšaya's quarters, a handmaiden wept over the red weal of a whiplash on her palm. The princess was in a foul mood, she whispered. Too many fermented figs the night before had soured her stomach. Then the handmaiden had pulled on a clump of Kasšaya's snarled hair as she dragged the horn comb through the tangles. The little whip Kasšaya kept on her dressing table was swift and painful.

Seraf bit his lip. Foul mood or not, he couldn't wait. He took his instrument out from under his arm and started strumming.

The door to the princess's rooms was propped open, perhaps in hopes of a cool breeze. Seraf caught a glimpse of Kasšaya as another handmaiden soothed her temples with scented oil. He hoped music might calm her. One of the marvels of music was how it soothed away anger, illness, anxiety. As he sang, her eyes slipped shut and she seemed to doze off:

> I am feeble and sore broken:
> I have roared because of my heart's disquiet.
> Lord, all my desire is before thee;
> I groan so you will hear me,

"Who is singing?" she murmured, as her handmaiden pushed her gown aside to massage her shoulders. "Bring him here."

Fetched inside, Seraf bowed so low he glimpsed only the gold-painted toes in the princess's open sandals.

"Sit in that corner and finish your song," she commanded.

Picking up his dulcimer, he continued:

> My heart pants, my strength fails:
> the light of mine eyes is gone.
> My lovers and my friends stand aloof from my sore;
> my kinsmen stand afar off.

"Why do you sing so?" the princess murmured, nearly swooning under her servant's hands as she skillfully kneaded the royal neck. "Are you in trouble?"

"Yes, Your Highness," Seraf said. "In terrible trouble." He continued to sing:

> I am ready to halt, my sorrow is always before me.
> I will declare my error; I will atone for my sin.

> Forsake me not, O Lord: O my God, be not far
> from me.
> Hurry to help me, O Lord my salvation.

Seraf put down his instrument and abased himself again. The princess looked at him under drooping eyelids. "Your music is lovely. Whatever the trouble, I will help. If it is within my power, consider your problem vanished as in the evening mists."

Seraf put a hand over his chest to still his pounding heart. He had not expected to sway the princess so quickly. Could he trust her? Would Sarah's loss make her forget her promise?

"Your Highness, you may wish to punish me for my trouble. You mustn't feel bound to help."

Kassaya drew herself up. "What do you mean?" she asked indignantly, waving the servant off. "Royals of the House Nebuchadnezzar never go back on their word. I have sworn to help, and I will."

Seraf prostrated himself before the princess, lying prone on the ground at her feet. "I fear for the life of my unborn child," he said. "I fear for the life of his mother. I ask that you take my life for theirs."

Kassaya signaled that he should rise. "Are you not a eunuch? How did you get someone with child?"

Slowly, Seraf stood. "Before I was cut, I lay with one of your handmaidens. My doing, not hers. It was as though a fever came upon me."

"Send for the girl and we'll find a place for her child," Kassaya sighed.

"She is not in the palace, your Highness. She will marry a Judean. He will give her a home and my child a second father."

"A runaway?" Kassaya hissed, her heavily kohled eyes narrowing.

Seraf prostrated himself again, forehead touching the floor, peering upward through half-shuttered eyes.

Kasšaya glared, face creased in annoyance. "Get to your feet," she snapped.

He half rose.

"Stand," she roared. "Tell me the name of this handmaiden who's fled my service."

"Sarah, your Highness. The one you named Shamrina."

Kasšaya's face mottled in anger. "That one? Amytis was right after all. Too beautiful. But I liked seeing her lovely face when she brought me my perfumes."

Kasšaya tapped her long-tapered fingernails ominously on a marble table. Seraf cowered, crouching submissively, holding his breath.

"My father has taught me that a princess cannot go back on her word, once given," the princess said. "Shamrina is free to wed this Judean. But there must be a price paid."

Seraf bent his head. Daniel, prescient as always, was right.

"If the child is a daughter, she must enter my service at four years of age," Kasšaya decreed. "I am soon to wed the warrior, Neriglissar, and will start a family. Her daughter must tend my son."

"And if it is a boy, Your Highness?" Seraf asked, barely able to utter the words. *What have I done?* he thought, shattered. *I have enslaved my own child.*

Kasšaya considered. "I am not interested in a boy. If it is a boy, you must pay me the price of a slave, one I will select from the newest of captives. If it takes your lifetime, I will be paid."

18

Daniel at Prayer

SERAF COULD FIND NO PEACE as the months passed. He healed completely—the enforced march having strengthened his body. But he could not stop from dwelling on his shame. He was gelded, no longer a man. He was enslaved in a country far from his own, his God vanquished by the idols of Babylon. He feared having to take a daughter from Sarah and could not bring himself to tell her of the threat. And he longed for her despite not being able to lie with her. When he visited the newly married woman, she shrank from him, clearly despising what he had become. But at first the sick longing he felt in her presence was better than blank despair.

He was there one day when the baby kicked. He saw a slight ripple move across the tiny mound in her stomach and her instant inward look.

"Oh," she cried, grabbing his hand. "Feel the child!"

It was as if balm had been poured on his wounded manhood. Life flowed under his fingers and then quieted. He let his hand curve around her small belly, the flesh beneath her rough gown warm and inviting. He watched her wake from her private dream to look down at his fingers, remember what he was, and shudder slightly.

"It's still now," she said.

He thought she controlled an instinct to throw off his hand and removed it, asking, "Are you feeling well?"

She looked worn and tired. Her rough dress—so different from the breezy, diaphanous gowns she had worn in the palace—was stained and wrinkled.

She sighed. "I'm keeping food down finally. But I'm so tired. And I must go help Reuven in the fields."

Any excuse to leave him. He felt she wished him elsewhere. He began to visit less.

While the thought that Sarah was repulsed by him hurt, while he dreaded the child's birth in case it was a girl, her revulsion and his dread were only part of what troubled him. Seraf was no more religious than most men, but there was an aching void in his life. As court musician, he'd attended all Temple sacrifices, supplying music for the rejoicing afterward. No such occasions existed now. There was no day of rest, no Sabbath, because the Babylonians celebrated none. Every day was like the next. It wearied him. God had abandoned him together with the rest of the people who'd considered themselves His Chosen. Seraf could not bow down in worship to the things of clay and stone that littered the queen's chambers. And God surely could not exist here in Babylon, in this unclean land.

One afternoon Queen Amytis lay down on her bed to rest before a ceremony planned in her honor down the River Euphrates. Seraf considered visiting Sarah, but his soul shriveled at her likely unwelcome. Instead, he wandered aimlessly through the enormous palace, finding corridors he'd never seen before. Miles of marble echoed beneath his feet as he walked. Had he been a woman, it would be a relief to find a corner and weep. But he was yet too much a man.

On this quiet mid-winter afternoon, the king was out hunting. Most left in the palace followed the queen's example and napped. Seraf felt utterly alone, lost among the winding hallways of the palace, carrying his burden of deep, unremitting shame.

But then, rounding one more corner, he caught the sound of... something familiar.

Baruch Ata Adonai, Elohainu Melech Ha'Olam, Seraf heard murmured in a sing-song voice.

He crept closer. A chamber door was ajar and a shape indistinguishable in the low light was speaking to the Most High Lord in the words of a Temple priest, but in a manner wholly different—personal and restrained. Seraf's soul opened like a flower touched by rain after long drought. He swallowed hard and thrust the door wide.

Daniel knelt by his open window, hands on the sill, eyes resting on the vast reaches of desert that separated him and the lost city of Jerusalem. A slight breeze bathed his face in its damp coolness. Seraf, staring, recognized a peace residing within the exiled seer that Seraf had deemed lost forever.

Daniel stiffened. Without turning, the king's advisor motioned to a servant. The servant, a thin stick of a man, moved between Seraf and his view of Daniel at prayer. "This is a private moment," he said firmly, pushing Seraf back and shutting the door in his face.

Seraf swallowed unbidden tears and walked through the cold marble corridors. That night, his fingers felt stiff against the strings of the dulcimer. He was not the only one in a foul mood. The queen found fault with her meal, the entertainment, and the small gnats that had no respect for royalty. The ride upriver in the barge was cut short, and a cart called to convey the queen back to the palace. The musicians had to tramp several miles home. As they rounded a bend in the road, the city spreading before them, they encountered a knot of young nobles walking by the river.

"Musicians!" one of them called. "Give us a song, will you?"

Rivai winked at his fellow musicians. "If it's a song you want, gentlemen, we must see the silver glint of your money first."

"Money, is it? You'll be paid," swaggered the largest of the young men. "Where are you from?"

Oreb shrugged. "Judea. Brought to play for the queen from among the captives."

"Judeans! Sing us one of the songs of your own land!"

The musicians looked at one another. "Perhaps one of the Psalms of David," Oreb sighed.

"I will not defile David's songs by singing them under the poplars of Babylon!" Tekoa growled. "We should have hung up our harps long ago and refused to sing."

The thought of life without music distressed Seraf. He had lost his land, his God, his love, and probably his child and was finding these all hard. But life without music? The idea was unbearable.

"I will sing a song of Judea, young nobles," he said, gritting his teeth, "if you solemnly swear to your gods to let us depart in peace afterward."

The men looked at one another and, amused, agreed.

Seraf brought the dulcimer up and strummed on it. The other musicians stared at him, waiting to recognize the tune. When they did, Oreb shook his head but put his flute to his lips. Seraf sang:

> O God, why did you cast us off forever?
> Why does your anger smoke against your
> grazing sheep?
> Your adversaries roared inside your Temple; marking
> their place with ensigns.
> They were like men who lifted up axes in a
> thicket of trees.
> They broke all the carved work down with hatchet
> and hammers.
>
> How long, O God, will our enemies reproach us?
> How long shall they blaspheme Your name forever?
> Why do you draw back Your hand, Your right hand?
> Take it forth from Your bosom and consume them!

As he sang, the nobles sniggered, nudging one another, but at this point, one of them broke into the song. "Consume them? You would call upon your gods to harm us? Shame!"

Seraf removed his hand from the dulcimer. "Pay us and we will take ourselves off."

Grumbling, the young men sprinkled silver coins, each one impressed with Nebuchadnezzar's profile, at their feet. Rivai and Oreb stooped to collect them. Tekoa had already started downriver. Seraf stared straight into the eyes of the noble who'd reproached him.

"I have always heard that Judeans are a stubborn people," mused the young man, his dark kohl-rimmed eyes blazing into Seraf's stormy black ones.

Rivai and Oreb abandoned the last few stray coins and took Seraf by the elbows, forcing him to bow as they backed away.

"You want us to land in a worse position than we're in now?" Oreb hissed in his ear.

A sudden twinge of pain in his groin made Seraf's face crumple. "Worse than this? Unmanned and godless?"

"Begging and beaten would be worse," Rivai reminded him.

Seraf's gloom sat upon him like a heavy stone all the way back to the palace.

Two days later, he waited in the queen's corridors, tuning his dulcimer. She had several times offered him a new one, but he clung to his battered instrument. A little way distant, Tekoa and Oreb diced in a corner, while Rivai slept on a bench, snoring gently. A shadow fell over Seraf, and he raised his head.

Daniel stood before him. Once again, Seraf admired the man's beauty—his broad shoulders and curly black hair waving back from a high forehead, caught in a small bronze clasp that pushed the tendrils from his face.

"I have been dreaming of you," Daniel said without greeting.

"Dreaming? Of me?"

"A flood of dreams. You are troubled in spirit, Seraf?"

Seraf let his fingers roam over his instrument softly, so he would not disturb the others. He found a discordant string and bent to tighten it.

"Seraf?" Daniel stooped to look directly into his face. "I dream of fires burning and your tortured face is there. I dream of empty deserts and watch you walking across them. You wander marble corridors in the middle of the day and find no peace. I toss and turn and my head aches over these dreams. They must stop."

Seraf kept his eyes upon his instrument. He tried the string, but it still sounded flat. He turned the screw to tighten it and found his fingers were tightening too much. He tried to stop, but his fingers refused to obey. Finally, the string snapped, twanging in the echoing corridor.

"You are distressed," Daniel told him. "You are empty of life."

Seraf glanced at his vacant lap.

Daniel shook his head. "Not that."

"What else is there?" Seraf said, bitterly.

"You must find a way to fill the barren spaces inside of you. You disturbed me at prayer this week. I did wrong in sending you away."

Seraf shrugged. "Even so powerful a man as you, Daniel, should be allowed some privacy. I apologize for bursting into your quarters."

"I invite you to return with me now. We will serve the Lord together."

"How can we serve the Lord without an altar and priests?"

Daniel smiled wryly and held out a hand. "Come and see."

Seraf glanced toward the queen's quarters. Daniel gestured toward the closed door. "I'm told she is with her hairdresser and her seamstress. It will be at least an hour before she calls for music. Come now while there is time."

Seraf rose and followed the soothsayer.

Daniel led him into his room. He shut the door behind them. "When I first came here, I thought like you. But many of us have devised a way to pray to the Lord without a Temple, priests, or sacrifice. We beseech Him to remember us and promise to wait for His deliverance."

"But God was vanquished by the Chaldeans! Bested by Marduk! Why pray to a conquered God?"

Daniel's eyes twinkled. Seraf was clearly not the first man to blurt out every exile's shame.

"Listen. There is only one God, the God we worshipped in Judea. He is here, in Babylon, with us. He was displeased with us and let the Babylonians be His strong right hand to punish us. But there is still only the one Supreme Being in this world. Who would you have me bow down to and worship, if not He? He is a father whose children have gone astray. In Judea, we worshipped at strange altars and forgot to obey His commandments. But like a father, He will forgive us and restore us if we live the lives He wishes."

Seraf hunched a shoulder. More than words were needed to convince him that his God still existed. Daniel saw the shrug and paced the room for a few minutes. He returned, placing himself directly before Seraf, arms raised, making a show of all his battered gold and heavy, draped linen. "Look at me. I am richer now than I could ever have hoped to be in Judea, and more powerful. I dress in woven cloth and have the ear of the king. I am convinced this has occurred because I remember the Lord.

"But I am still a man of the people. Today I sent barley cakes to the beggars outside the gates of the city. Tomorrow is a fast day, and I will sit in sackcloth and ashes and cry unto the Most High, bewailing how I miss His land and His favor. I am grateful that my Lord has seen fit to show me how to worship Him in exile."

Daniel's soft words echoed in his spacious chambers. Seraf raised black eyes to the seer's earnest face. He wondered if Daniel could be right. The rage burning within him lessened.

Daniel put a hand on Seraf's shoulder. "Would prayer and charity comfort you, do you think? You were cut not long ago. You must still be in considerable pain. And bodily pain is only part of what ails you."

The hot tears held back for months rushed out at Daniel's gentle words, pouring forth as Seraf's head fell against Daniel's shoulder. Daniel let him cry unimpeded for several minutes. Then he brought him to the window and bade him kneel.

"Listen to what I say and repeat my words. I kneel to bless the Lord God three times a day and never rise, but I feel less bereft. I cannot tell if you will feel the same. But perhaps...."

Seraf knelt and prayed, and he felt less troubled in spirit for the time spent with Daniel, praising the Lord and beseeching Him to redeem His covenant with the people. The two rose and Daniel embraced Seraf once more.

"I must leave you to attend the king," he said. "Are you feeling better?"

"You know I will be blessed with child soon," Seraf told him. "God willing, I will have a son whom I can teach to pray like this."

"He will be among the first born to the exiles in this land," said Daniel. "It will be difficult for him. If the temptations were great in Israel and Judea, how much greater are they here?

"Come again, Seraf. I will take you tomorrow to a house of prayer, where some of us gather several times a week to serve the Lord. You will bring the boy there when he is old enough."

19

A New Generation

THE MIDWIFE WIPED SARAH'S CLAMMY forehead. "It won't be long now," she assured Sarah, who moaned as contractions shook her.

Sarah's new home was a tiny, one-room brick hut midway between Babylon and Tel Abib, which they shared with their landlord's ox. The young couple had no furniture. Reuven spread hay for their beds. In one corner, Sarah built a small hearth from sunbaked bricks of river clay, where she made watery soups from whatever scraps of food they could scrounge.

Slow hours passed, punctuated by Sarah's moans. It grew dark, daggers of late winter rain pelting down. Reuven led the ox out in the field as the animal bellowed in complaint. He sat as far away as he could from the two women, in the wet part of the hut.

Between the rolling pains that absorbed all thought, Sarah longed for her mother. The midwife was kind enough, but she was a stranger. Most of Sarah's neighbors knew of her disgrace and kept their distance. Sarah did not want to admit it, but she was lonely on this tiny patch of farm.

As the rainclouds drifted aside and moonlight peeked through the chinks in the brick, someone pounded on the door. Seraf entered, bringing a slender young Egyptian with him. "This is Ibi-Sin," he said, "the royal physician's apprentice. He can help with the birth."

Ibi-Sin looked about him with distaste. "The girl gave up the palace for this?"

The midwife stood between the apprentice and Sarah, who bit her lips to control her wailing. "It's not fitting that a man should see her nakedness," the woman protested.

Ibi-Sin laughed. "Think of me as another woman if it helps. I am surely not a man." He pushed the midwife aside and approached Sarah, taking her wrist and feeling her pulse. "Hmmm," was all he said. He bent to hear her heart through her chest, then moved between her legs and felt her womb. "She's nearly open enough," he said. "Baby should be here soon."

Reuven glared at him, then turned his outraged face on Seraf.

"He's delivered every royal baby in the palace," Seraf responded to the unspoken protest. "I trust him."

Hours passed. The midwife's daughter came to tell her that a woman in Tel Abib had started her labor. "She wants you to come at once."

"Go, go," Ibi-Sin waved her away. "More room in this cramped hut."

"Will you be all right with all these men?" the midwife whispered to Sarah.

"Trust me, I have delivered more healthy children than you could dream of," Ibi-Sin said, overhearing. "She's in good hands."

"I will visit tomorrow," sniffed the midwife, taking her daughter by the shoulders and pushing her toward the door.

"Come," Reuven said to Seraf, rising from the corner where they had crouched for hours. "We'll go outside."

"I should be here when the baby's born," Seraf protested, voice breaking with anxiety.

"I've seen one or two childbirths before, Judean. This one won't be complicated," Ibi-Sin said. "Go now, shoo."

"You'll come..."

"And tell you if it's a girl or boy instantly, yes of course."

Reuven's forehead wrinkled. "Why does that matter?" he asked, as they left the hut.

Sarah didn't hear the answer. She was panting, trying to ride through the waves of pain. They came, faster and faster, racking her young body.

"Mother," she moaned, tossing her head restlessly. "Oh, Momma. Make it stop."

The baby was born in the small hours of the morning. Ibi-Sin, handing the swaddled infant to its mother, slipped outside. Sarah held her firstborn, looking at the small bundle in wonder.

Seraf bounded through the door, face alight. "It's a boy, then?" he cried.

"Your son," Sarah told him, handing the baby over.

She watched, heart aching, as the radiant musician cradled the boy close in his arms. "My son," he murmured, kissing the top of his head.

Ibi-Sin returned, packing away his few instruments in an olivewood box. Reuven walked straight up to the doctor's apprentice. "Sarah is all right?"

"Mother and child are both doing well," the Egyptian said.

Seraf gave the baby one last kiss and handed him to Reuven. "You will care for my son?"

"As though he were my own firstborn," Reuven promised, looking into the wrinkled little face, a smile creasing his own.

Sarah sighed, looking at them both, heads bent together over the infant. They were far from everything familiar and, her stomach sinking, she realized they always would be. But for the first time, Babylon began to feel like home.

PART TWO

The Exiles

574 BCE–Year 12 of the Captivity

20

Amittai and the
Sacrifice—Jerusalem

AMITTAI'S UNCLE WARNED HIM NOT to go. But Amittai knew that all the
shepherds would talk about the next day was the sacrifice. He wanted to
see it, just once.

"It's an abomination in the sight of the Lord," Uncle Enosh said.
"Jeremiah was right when he preached against the altars of Moloch."

"Much good the Lord did us against Chaldean chariots," Amittai
muttered under his breath, looking from the hilltop to the desolate,
half-ruined city of Jerusalem spread beneath him. The Babylonians had
destroyed the city twelve long years ago, and it felt like it would never
recover. "Much good Jeremiah did us, fleeing to Egypt."

If Amittai's uncle heard him grumble, he would feel the whip lash,
just as Enosh had beat his own son, Eker. Several weeks back Eker decided he had enough and left, heading east, limping out of the family's
hut with nothing more than stained clothing, a goatskin rug, and an extra
pair of sandals. Amittai considered following his cousin and fleeing his
uncle's tyranny. But something held him fast. Fear of leaving the only
home he'd ever known, perhaps? Of leaving what remained of his family?
So he kept his complaints to a mumble.

The shepherds ate dinner together, crouching close to the ground, fingers tearing bread and dipping it in mutton stew. It felt strange to be sitting among them. Had Eker still been there, his cousin would have shuffled him off to the side, where Amittai couldn't hear the broad jokes about servant girls at the well or the solace a lonely shepherd could find within his flock. When Amittai sat down in their midst, pushing lank hair out of his eyes, the men shook their heads but didn't stop him from joining them. Amittai arranged his lanky arms and legs so he wouldn't bump the man next to him when he dipped his bread into the stew. He kept his mouth shut, listening with head ducked low, pretending to be interested only in filling the hole in his belly.

After dinner, the shepherds rose, laughing and chattering. Amittai followed in their wake, past the stone wall that marked the edge of his uncle's small property. The cold of the Jerusalem night descended swiftly as the sun dipped past the horizon. Amittai pulled his thin lamb's wool cloak close at his neck. Used to the shocking cold of the desert during nights spent out with the flock, Amittai found the chill Jerusalem nights bearable. But he was still grateful when the men quickened their pace.

They walked swiftly to a corner of the city, departing through the remains of the Potsherd Gate. Amittai had never known anything but ruined streets, the rubble of the buildings. But his uncle and some of the older shepherds complained that their city still wore the scars inflicted by the Babylonians, harkening back to a time when Jerusalem stood tall on its mountain perch.

The Potsherd Gate was a gate in name only, walls surrounding the city reduced to loose rock and open gaps. Ammonites and Samaritans had ample room to squeeze through, squatting in abandoned Judean homes, taking up residence with their families and goats. Edomites elbowed their way in as well, trading slaves and spices in the city square.

The valley of ben Hinnom was littered with broken pottery shards and decaying animal flesh. The remaining Judeans—poor and dispossessed, abandoned as not worth carrying into exile—piled trash in the shallow ditches outside the southeast walls. Gulls wheeled overhead, mouths filled with carrion.

"Watch your step, young Amittai," said Jabin, the eldest of the shep-herds, tossing a kindly warning over one shoulder. "Otherwise you'll find yourself ankle-deep in muck."

The shepherds rounded a corner and there it stood—the altar of Moloch. Dozens of people gathered for the sacrifice. Plumes of smoke rose from the fire kindled beneath the flat stone. Amittai gaped at the idol's enormous bronze bull head, glowing red from the scorching flames.

The cold night air encouraged Amittai to move closer to the sacrifi-cial fires. Jabin grabbed him by the back of his shirt, pulling him away. "Careful, boy. The Ammonites might mistake you for one of their own children and push you into the flames."

"Do they really kill their own children?" Amittai whispered, sud-denly fearful of what he was about to see.

Jabin shrugged. "They say a strong god requires a sacrifice of tears and blood. They say if we had given our young to Moloch, Jerusalem would never have fallen. Who knows? We were certainly not spared the Babylonian spears. Which of us," Jabin swept an expressive arm, "has not suffered at the Chaldean conquest?"

Amittai shivered. He had been so young, just three years old, when Babylonian forces sacked the city. One moment stayed with him, though—the moment he was torn from his mother's arms, when, shriek-ing in fear, he was flung into a corner to watch men in clanking armor force the women on their backs. The grunts and screams had terrified him, and he'd hidden under a pile of rugs. Shrieks and moans and cries for mercy kept him trembling there. Then the stomp of retreating foot-steps and an echoing silence. Amittai crept from under his suffocating cave of rugs to discover the women laying still, limbs twisted in strange contortions and flesh pierced, running with blood. He ran from one to the other, touching their still warm skin, trying to shake them into wake-fulness. When he could not, he crouched beside his mother and wept. It would be a day and a night before his uncle found him.

A chime sounded. A drum had pounded a steady beat as the shep-herds approached, but now it picked up tempo, causing Amittai's heart to thump even more quickly. Out from beyond the smoke, close to the red-hot open arms of the idol, an Ammonite priest appeared as though the ground itself offered him up.

He wore a tall-peaked hat on his head decorated with blue glowing moonstones and lamb's wool. His flowing robes were the colors of saffron and blood, embroidered with yellow thread animal figures. His pudgy fingers, with their long, tapering, painted nails, sparkled with topaz and bronze rings.

Another chime quieted the crowd. Amittai shrunk back, wishing he had listened to Uncle Enosh and stayed away. An acolyte stepped forward and spilled a powder on the fire. Sparks flew into the night air. The sweet smell of incense wafted forth. A second acolyte handed a cup to the priest.

The priest drank and then his voice rang out, echoing through the valley. "I drink this blood red wine for you, Moloch, O Great God of the Ammonites, you who are called Baal elsewhere, or Adrammelech, or Kronos. I drink at your mighty altar in Tophet, beseeching you to protect those who worship you and sacrifice to you. In fire, blood, and tears do we give you our best flesh—unlike the meek, vanquished Hebrews who polluted your land by sacrificing to a nameless deity!"

Amittai swallowed hard. Was it true? Had his people's mistake not been in their wavering faith in Elohim but in refusing to accept the true gods of the land? His uncle often spoke of hearing the prophet Jeremiah preach before the Exile. Jeremiah claimed the Hebrews were being punished for not heeding the word of God. But what if Jeremiah were wrong? How could Amittai worship a God who had allowed his mother to be raped and slain, a God who turned His face from His people and allowed so many of them to be cast forth from the land He had once promised would be theirs for posterity?

Both acolytes stepped forward, flaming torches in their hands. A line of children in pristine white gowns—two- and three-year-olds, whose lifeless eyes looked drugged—were forced forward. The priest moved among them, letting each one sip wine from his cup. They gulped it convulsively, eyes fixed ahead. One whimpered. The priest set his long, pointed fingernails on that boy's neck and forced him to drink several more draughts of wine.

Two lines of straw were laid down, leading to the altar. A third acolyte threw dung on the fire, making it smoke. The odor that rose into the air was foul. Torches touched the straw, which burst into rows of flame. The trail of fire leading to Moloch was spellbinding. Amittai found it difficult to swallow. Part of him wanted to turn and run, but something deep within him—some elemental, superstitious compulsion—forced him to watch what transpired.

The children were urged forward through the two lines of flame. The smoke made them cough but not one cried out. The bull-headed idol seemed to grow, rising from the ground. Each of the children stepped into the metallic bull's open arms, searing their flesh. The heat woke them, and they screamed for their mothers. But the acolytes snatched red hot blades from a side fire, falling upon the children and plunging the knives into their hearts. The drum beat a frenzied tattoo as bits of charred flesh flew about, the air rent with the children's dying moans.

The mothers were held back by priests throughout the sacrifice. They shrieked and tore their hair, crying with outstretched arms for their tortured children. The priest let them wail for a few minutes, then raised his hand. Whips subdued the mothers into a whimpering silence.

"In fire, blood, and tears, we have satisfied your enormous hunger, oh Great Moloch," he intoned, a smug smile creasing his flabby face.

Frantic dancing followed. Several of the shepherds paired off with Ammonite women. Jabin stopped kissing the shoulders of a pretty, plump girl swathed in a diaphanous gown just long enough to point Amittai home.

Amittai turned away, feeling his gorge rise, swallowing it back with an effort that left his forehead slick with sweat. But the thought that haunted him all the way back to his uncle's dark, cheerless hut and for many nights following, was that perhaps the priest was right. If Amittai's short life had shown him anything, it was not to spurn any means that might keep him safe from the harm inflicted by armies and men.

Yes, he decided. He would return to ben Hinnom for the next sacrifice to Moloch.

21

Babylonian Children

SARAH WOKE TO THE SOUND of crying. Someone was always crying in the tiny house—one of her children frightened by a nightmare, someone too cold, too wet, too thirsty.

Sarah glanced at her husband's still form. Reuven would wake before the sun rose. He would tramp out to the barn they had built last spring, feeding the two oxen and the three sheep they now owned. By the time he returned, he expected breakfast on the table. Then it would be time to go out into the fields.

Just once, Sarah thought wearily, *I would like to sleep an entire night through.*

But she rose, staggering into the room where the children were bedded down on straw pallets. There, crying in the corner, was her youngest child, seven-year-old Nachum. *He's too old to be crying like a baby.* The annoyed thought buzzed about her like a honeybee. But when she stooped and looked at his sweet, puckered face, her tiredness and resentment washed away.

"You should be asleep, little man," she whispered, feeling for dampness on his night dress.

"I was dreaming of the statue with the gold head and silver body," he gasped between sobs. "It was chasing Daniel."

"Shh." Sarah pulled his warm body to her. Her heart melted, as it always did, when he reached up and entwined his arms about her neck. She glanced at the other corner of the room, where her two daughters slept. They didn't even stir as she carried Nachum past. On his solitary pallet nearest the door, Sarah's first born, Uri, muttered in his sleep. Uri, twelve now, was apprenticed to Judean scribes. Seraf had arranged it with Daniel.

"You can't all live off this tiny farm," Seraf had explained to a red-faced Reuven. "You have four children now. If they and their families all lived here when grown, they would starve."

"I don't need your high court favors for Uri," Reuven had retorted, nostrils flaring.

Seraf shrugged his shoulders. Sarah watched, admiring, as the court-trained musician placated the boy's stepfather. "You've done a wonderful job raising my son, Reuven. But he isn't like you. Or like me or his mother, either. He is shy, speechless unless you put a stylus or a pot of ink in his hands. Uri comes alive on the clay or the goat's skin."

Reuven's broad forehead furrowed. "It's true that he's less than useless on the farm."

"See? So why not give him this chance? It's not as though I were bringing him to court with me."

Moving quietly past Uri now, Sarah brought Nachum into the star-drenched courtyard. The cool air made her shiver, but she knew it felt good to the flushed child, who picked up his head and looked around him.

"Things look different in the dark, don't they, Momma?"

She kissed his forehead. "They do. Now, what's this about the statue? Didn't Uncle Seraf tell you that the Lord God whispered the secret of the statue in Daniel's ear, so he could tell the great King Nebuchadnezzar not to fear for his kingdom in his lifetime?"

"Someday the stone will crush the statute, though, won't it, Momma?" Nachum whispered, his relish for the scary story returning now that he was fully awake, his mother close at hand. "And when it does, the Babylonians will be destroyed!"

Sarah couldn't help laughing. "You know it's a story though, little one? Uncle Seraf tells it as if it really happened. But it's just a story."

Nachum looked at her wide eyed. "No, momma," he insisted. "Uncle Seraf's stories are real."

Sarah smiled. Every time Seraf visited—bearing some treat from the palace—the children clung to his skirts and begged for songs and stories. They loved hearing about life under the royal roof, a life Sarah could barely remember now. More than anything, they adored his Daniel stories. Uri, who always sat next to his father when he arrived, would listen silently and then sneak off, retelling the tales by scratching the pictures they formed in his head into the dirt. Watching him one day was what prompted Seraf to find him a position with the Judean scribes.

Reuven, who had grown bitter as years of scant harvests and hungry children made his life a burden, didn't relish Seraf's visits. He would throw his arm, thickened by years of hard farming, about his wife and draw her to him, or command her to fetch refreshments. Seraf's eyes would follow Sarah as she schooled her features, an obedient wife. But when Seraf looked at her, she remembered that she had once been beautiful. Whatever loveliness she had once possessed had faded under the pitiless glare of the sun and the unremitting labor of a farmer's wife. But Seraf's dark gaze made her feel desirable once again. And Reuven knew it.

Sarah sighed, cradling her son to her. She was forever grateful to Reuven, but he treated her more like a servant than a wife. Was she wrong to recall her one night with Seraf—to imagine what life might have been like had they been allowed to marry?

But then she frowned at her own disloyalty. Reuven had saved her from stoning. He married her when no one else would. What did it matter if he were dour and rough? He was just an echo of her life on this farm. The same tasks, the same duties, day after day.

Had her parents ever felt this way? Exhausted, wanting nothing more than to collapse in the hay rick, oblivious to the day's cares? Her heart went out, hundreds of miles to the west, to her real home. Her parents had not just survived. They found meaning tilling the soil. Because it was their homeland, blessed by the Almighty. Something she would never know.

Our farm, Sarah thought, weary once more, hoisting her son up onto her hip and carrying him back to bed, the strange night sky glittering coldly above. *Whatever became of our farm?*

22

Amittai and the Farm

571 BCE–Year 15 of the Exile

UNCLE ENOSH WAS DRINKING IN the yard with a grizzled old man when eighteen-year-old Amittai brought the sheep up the hill. A glorious sunset peeked over the stony ridge of the distant mountains, spreading golden light over Jerusalem's ruins. Amittai was annoyed when his uncle waved him over. The sound of the sheep bells in his ears, his mind was on dinner and a tryst with one of the Ammonite serving women after the sacrifice that night. He was in no mood to be polite to some old man.

"Here's the boy." Uncle Enosh clasped his elbow. "My brother Dotan's son."

The old man looked him up and down and spit on the ground. "Is he a hard worker?"

Amittai yanked his arm away. "I am," he said, throwing out his young chest proudly. "Are you?"

Uncle Enosh swatted him on the forearm. "Watch your manners, boy," he said. "This is your new master."

Amittai took two steps back. "My new master…? But…?" Something heavy moved in his chest. Life with Uncle Enosh was not easy, but he was family. With Eker gone, Enosh was the only family Amittai had left.

In the three years since Amittai had adopted the Ammonite rites, he had grown from a boy to a strapping young man. He stood taller than most of the other shepherds, his shoulders broad and his lean body muscled by the miles he walked daily. He knew a man's pleasures now too, lying with the women who served Moloch, loving the touch and feel of their smooth skin, their warm centers spreading to his eagerness. Nor were the Ammonites the only ones who desired him. Despite the eyes cast down in modesty, he could feel the hot, surreptitious glances of Judean maidens when he passed the city well. Scandalized they might be, but they still wanted him.

"They tell me he attends the sacrifices," the old man said, "I won't have that."

Enosh shrugged. "I never cared enough, but you can beat the habit out of him."

Amittai felt like one of his uncle's sheep when they were penned at market. Any protests would sound as plaintive and pitiful as the bleats of those poor beasts. Amittai was dirty from the day spent walking up and down rocky hillsides. He wanted time to wash before dinner, to eat copiously from the common bowl, and then to lie with a girl. He didn't want to stand there while two old men treated him like a simple animal with no sense and no tongue.

"I'm off now." Amittai shrugged at them both, turning away.

Enosh reached out with a thick arm and grabbed him. "Stand still, fool!" he cried. "Show some respect. Hod wants you for his only daughter. He has a new farm, one of the abandoned ones. He needs a strong son-in-law to work it. Mind your manners, and you'll have a much better future than I could provide."

That stopped Amittai. He could just picture himself living on a farm of his own. But there was one important thing to consider.

"What's she look like?" he asked. "Does she squint? Is she fat? Pock-marked?"

Hod shook his head. "What does that matter?" He spat onto the ground again. Amittai could see one of Hod's teeth was loose, and it bothered the old man. "You're not asking the right questions."

"The right questions?"

"How big is the farm? What do you grow? What's the land like?"

"I'm not a farmer," Amittai admitted. "Do you keep sheep? I know sheep."

The old man rose and brushed out his lap. He was taller and stood straighter than Amittai expected. "I don't keep sheep. I grow barley and olives. Figs and pomegranates. I have a small vineyard with grapes that make a fair wine. I work the land for three seasons every year and then I rest with my storehouse full and my feet toasting near the fire. While you're out on the hillsides in all weathers, huddling under your cloak as wind and rain pelt you."

"I can learn to farm," Amittai growled. "But the girl…she must be ugly if you won't say."

"She's not," Hod said, his mouth turning up at one corner. "But I won't wed her to anyone who takes part in the abominations at ben Hinnom."

"I can forgo them after I'm married."

"You'll forgo them from this point forward, or I'll find another husband for my girl! It's only because of my fondness for your father that I'm here at all, shepherd boy."

Amittai thought of the nights he had lain sleepless after the sacrifice. Despite sating the urge in his loins that almost always followed the bloodletting and heady wine, the nights at ben Hinnom often left him sick and despairing. Truth be told, he welcomed a reason to let idolatry go.

"I'll do it," he said, spitting onto the ground to show his uncle and his prospective father-in-law that he was old enough to make his own match. "When's the wedding?"

23

Uri and the Idols

URI WAS BROUGHT TO A room lined with heavy stone benches where Babylonian scribes mastered their craft. The youngest children, sitting in a circle on the floor, were handed a piece of round, wet clay dotted with their master's inscriptions down one side. They copied the words, using water to wet the drying clay and rework their mistakes until their version was a perfect match. Bending young backs over tablets for hours at a time was hard. The boys squirmed and fidgeted, and their long-legged, long-armed, thick-bearded master—whom they called Baba to his face and Hairy Spider behind his back—would bring out his leather lash and send the thongs of his little whip stinging on their bare thighs or their necks.

The older boys grabbed a bit of the wet clay mounded up next to them, shaping it quickly into a small tablet. The oldest apprentice rapidly recited a tale of the gods, or a tax report, or a manual about how best to irrigate the fields. Their styli dotted the clay swiftly, making small triangular wedges that their master checked. He crumbled the drying clay of a mistake between his long fingers, smearing the residue on the boy's face, making him wear it untouched the rest of the day, drying and itching.

It was here, Uri's Judean master thought, that young Uri could most easily master the art of the scribe. He paid Kur, the Babylonian master, a hefty sum for the year. Unlike the Babylonian boys, Uri lived at home.

He would arrive daily just as they were lined up before the row of clay figures, praying to the gods before starting the day's work.

"Why doesn't Uri bow?" young Agga asked Kur, seeing how the Judean lad stood at the back of the room until they rose.

"He has his own devotions that he performs at home," Kur replied, casting a darkling look toward Uri, who squirmed under his glare. Did the master wonder if his refusal to bow to the idols would bring bad luck to the classroom?

That evening, eating a hot summer's dinner of goat cheese mashed with olives with his mother, stepfather, half-sisters, and half-brother, Uri asked, "Why don't I join the other boys when they dedicate their day to Marduk and Sin?"

Reuven looked at the fifteen-year-old boy, then leaned over the table to pick up another chunk of barley bread. He put it in his mouth and chewed as he stared, making Uri flinch before his dark frown. "I told you no good could come of this," Reuven said, the words garbled in his stuffed mouth. "What was Seraf thinking?"

"He thought Uri would be suited as a scribe," Mother replied. She reached out and smoothed a brown curl back from Uri's forehead. As always, the touch of his mother's fingers helped him bear his stepfather's quick temper.

"But why not?" Uri persisted. "I'm the only boy who doesn't."

"It's not fitting," his mother said. "Your father can explain when he visits next time."

"I'm his father," Reuven growled, glaring at his wife. "I'll explain after we eat."

"Only if you know what to tell him," Mother retorted.

Having two fathers who loved you wasn't always easy. At least Mother was there to calm the household's often stormy waters.

Reuven finished his meal, drank some of the family's homemade barley beer, and rose. "Come on, then," he said, "We'll walk to the far fence and make sure it's still holding after last week's winds."

As they walked in the blue twilight, Reuven put a heavy arm around Uri's shoulder. Uri wanted to shrug it off, but knew he'd offend his stepfather. The weight of Reuven's arm seemed to intensify as they walked, like a yoke around his neck.

"We Judeans don't bow down to idols," Reuven said. "Why would you even want to?"

Uri regretted raising the subject at Reuven's table. He should have talked to Mother privately. Or better yet, spoken with his father when Seraf visited next. But it was hard to know when Seraf would be able to get away. He hadn't been feeling well lately. Uri had overheard him telling Mother that he had a bad infection in the place where his manhood used to be.

Uri had wanted to die the day he learned his father had been cut. He'd been nine years old—just a little younger than his half-brother Nachum was now. Seraf had taken Uri to the palace to buy his son's freedom. It had taken him nine years, Seraf told his son proudly, but he had finally earned enough to pay off the debt to Princess Kasšaya. The princess was married now to a Chaldean courtier, a mighty warrior. Uri often heard the story of how she might have claimed him as a slave, had he been a girl rather than a boy. He thought about that as his father led him through the thick palace gates, secured by the king's heavily armed guards.

Seraf brought Uri to the royal exchequer, where a scribe took the coins and made a note on a piece of clay. Seraf kissed his son and handed him the tablet.

"Keep this safe, son," he said. "It means your future is your own."

In a holiday mood, Seraf brought the boy to meet Daniel, who nodded kindly at him and gave him a sesame cake. Seraf's friends, the musicians, played a special song for Uri that brought tears to his father's eyes, a song of longing for Judea. They ate lunch at Daniel's table and Seraf walked his son proudly through the palace corridors, introducing him to the other palace slaves.

As the long afternoon waned, Uri grew tired. He tugged on his father's sleeve, pulling Seraf down to his level.

"I need to pee," Uri whispered, ashamed to have to admit it.

Seraf laughed. "Come on then."

They walked out to the privy behind the slave's quarters. Uri, half turned from his father, felt better after relieving himself. But as he tucked his penis back into his short tunic, he turned to see his father making his own stream on the ground. And there, instead of a rod of flesh, was a hollow tube.

"What's that?" Uri pointed, wide-eyed and frightened.

Seraf turned away, cursing under his breath. He tucked the contraption under his robe and turned back to his son. In a few clipped sentences, he explained.

The shock on Uri's face seemed to cloud his father's joy. He brought him back to the farm. Inexplicably sad, Uri ran to his mother and hid his face in her skirts.

"He's your son, all right," Seraf snapped at her. "Hates the idea of my being gelded. You should be pleased—he's as ashamed of me as you are."

Sarah's hand stroked Uri's short brown curls. "I never...."

"But who cares about the feelings of a eunuch, right, Sarah?"

Sarah grew rigid. Uri picked his head up out of her skirts. Tears fell down her beautiful pink cheeks. Uri looked at his father as Seraf turned away.

Uri flung himself from Sarah's clasp and grabbed the back of Seraf's robe. "Why are you so angry at Momma?" he sobbed. "It's my fault. She never said anything bad about you. I'm sorry. I love you. Please don't be mad at Momma."

Seraf turned, gripping Uri's arms. "Shh, shh," he said. "It's all right, son. Don't cry. You're too old to cry."

Uri put his arms around his father's waist and clung to him. "Don't be angry at Momma," he wailed. "Don't be angry at me."

Seraf knelt to gather the boy into his arms. "I am not angry at anyone," he said. "Not you and not your momma." He reached out an arm. "Sarah. I'm sorry," he told her.

She shook her head, stepping back. "You're right, though," she said. "I have never been able to let go of the shame. Yours—or mine."

"That's nonsense," Seraf said. "Come here and give your son a hug—and me too."

Sarah moved into the circle of his arms, kissing her son on the head. The three of them stood there for a few minutes, rocking together. It was the most complete Uri had ever felt.

But it had been a fleeting moment, soon interrupted. Flinching now as Reuven's strong arm on his shoulders ushered him off the path to look at the fence, Uri realized he had felt out of place his entire life. Maybe it had something to do with his mother's shame. Or the fact that his father was not truly a man. Maybe the other children knew this. Maybe that was why he was teased and pushed during their brief morning and afternoon recesses.

Reuven let him go as they approached the fence, but Uri could still feel a phantom heft of his thick arm across his back.

"They are things of dirt and stone, not real," Reuven said now about the idols, peering at the fence, pulling it to test its strength. "Our Father Abraham destroyed all the clay gods in his father's shop at Ur and was left unscathed. You could go to the front of your classroom and smash them all…."

"Smash them all?" Uri gasped, aghast.

"I'm not saying do it, I'm saying you could. And nothing would happen if you did."

Uri thought of Kur's little whip. He thought of the glares the other boys always gave him when he sidled past their bowing bodies to get to his seat.

Uri shook his head. "Something *would* happen."

"Are you contradicting me?" Reuven bellowed.

"Something would happen," Uri repeated. "They would hurt me."

"There are no gods inside! They can't hurt you! Are you stupid?"

Uri looked at his stepfather, whose face was red with exertion and anger. His fingers curved around the fence posts, his grip rustling the strong muscles on his forearms. With a sudden pang, Uri realized he knew something Reuven could never quite grasp.

The gods inside don't have to hurt me, Uri thought. The fact his classmates believed the gods existed within the figures was enough.

He sighed. Belief came so easily to some people, he thought. He wished he had his stepfather's simple faith in the invisible God. He wished he could bow before Marduk and Sin every morning and be like everyone else. He wished....

On the way back to the house, he felt his stepfather's anger fading. His face, which had creased red with bluster, looked uncertain now, as if he wanted to apologize to Uri, to make it right between them. But Uri knew Reuven's pride wouldn't let him. So the boy put a hand around his stepfather's massive waist. Reuven hugged him tightly and then set him back down with a kiss planted wetly on his forehead.

"You're a good boy, Uri," he told him. "A good boy."

Uri smiled, gratified. If his straightforward, honest stepfather told him so, it must be true.

24

Jerusalem Wedding

AMITTAI'S BRIDE, KEREN, STOOD BY his side as he repeated the words that made them one flesh. Despite a year's betrothal, he had never seen her face and couldn't penetrate the heavy veil she wore. He recalled a story his uncle had once told him—that of the forefather Jacob being hoodwinked into marrying the wrong woman. As the ceremony progressed, Amittai grew convinced he was marrying the ugliest woman in Jerusalem.

I'll leave the city if that's the case, he told himself. *I'll go someplace where I can buy a flock of sheep and stay out in the wilderness beyond Jerusalem. I won't be made a fool.*

The moment came when the young couple was to drink from the same wine cup. Amittai drank, then handed the goblet to Keren. He scrutinized the brown hand that extended from a wide sleeve and clutched the stem of the cup. It was a strong, calloused hand, a hand that knew hard work, not the soft, white fingers of the serving girls of Moloch. Keren lifted her veil just an inch, enough for Amittai to see a wide, smiling mouth with a freckle decorating one side of it. Keren had a good set of teeth, unstained and unchipped. Then the veil dropped again.

These small glimpses of his bride set Amittai's blood afire. *I'll have her whether I stay or not,* he thought, shifting his stance so the wedding guests wouldn't be scandalized by his untimely bulge. *She's mine now, to do with as I will.* The thought made him breathe heavier. He waited for the moment when he could remove the veil and reveal his prize. It finally came. He took the headdress between fingers that suddenly trembled. The veil—just a flimsy piece of cloth after all—flipped upward. And there, beneath it, was Keren's face.

Something moved inside him at the sight of her, an emotion he didn't recognize. She was neither beautiful nor ugly. Her face was wide and friendly, her eyes blue and smiling. A sprinkle of sun freckles spread across her flushed cheeks. Her hair was brown and curly, and she stood eye level to him, calmly studying him just as he studied her. He was shocked at how easy it was to find the woman of his heart. What had he been doing with Moloch's handmaidens? He flushed, ashamed. Why had he been playing with other women's bodies when Keren had kept herself chaste, waiting for this day?

But he shook the unsought tenderness away. He was a man, after all, and she nothing more than a woman. His woman. The lust that had ripped through his body earlier returned as he led his bride to a small room where they would sit secluded for too short a time, symbolic of the night that was to follow. He wanted to take her then and there. But something in her trusting look made him stop. He exhaled heavily through an open mouth, forcing himself to think of something else. He did not want to frighten her, he told himself. She was his now. He owned her. He could wait.

The wedding feast separated them again. She was surrounded by the women of her family—cousins, sisters and aunts. Her mother, like his own, had perished at the hands of the Babylonians. He was ushered over to the menfolk, seated in the place of honor. Enosh drank a cup of wine to him and to the farm.

"She's not a bad piece." His uncouth uncle laughed.

Amittai wanted to smash his head in, but restrained, grinning senselessly. The shepherds sat on the ground in a circle of their own at the edge of the crowd, belching and laughing, fingers shiny with grease, making Amittai shudder to look at them. *They are crude,* he thought. He couldn't wait for them to be gone so he could convince his father-in-law that he was not like them. He would show Hod that he deserved this unexpected life—Keren and the farm.

He had finally seen the farm last week. It was a beautiful plot of land overlooking the city. The terraces—which Hod had repaired at no small expense—held olive trees, dates, and barley fields. A barn—still half ruined—could be expanded to hold grazing animals. Enosh had already given Amittai a contract with one of his shepherds as a wedding gift—two years of services and a small herd. Awkward but sincere, Amittai had hugged his uncle to seal the unexpectedly generous bargain.

While they walked the land, Hod spoke of the family that had owned it last. "The father was stabbed in the back by a Babylonian dagger, the mother killed by her husband's hand, so the Chaldeans would not ravish her. The son was hacked to pieces in the city. Their old maidservant, Dina, told me of it. The other two children—a daughter and nephew—were carried off."

Talking of the previous owners made Amittai uncomfortable. Who cared, after all? The land was his now, waiting for him to rise in the mornings and tend to it. It was like Keren, his bride, unawakened and unaware of the delights of the marriage bed. Both waited for his hand.

Amittai could not eat. He walked around the wedding party, grinning at the guests. Keren's family eyed him warily. "Why a shepherd boy?" Amittai overheard someone asking Hod, who answered, "King David was a shepherd boy. Amittai was my friend Dotan's son, the son I have selected in my old age. Insult him and you insult me."

Amittai's eyes were on his bride as she stood laughing among her family. *She's mine*, he told himself, *the land's mine, and she's mine.* And the thrill of possession, a headier sensation even than lust, swept through him.

25

Uri and Ezra

URI WAS SEVENTEEN WHEN HE finally left Kur, the Babylonian scribe, and began to work with his Judean master, Baruch ben Neriah. The room Baruch ushered him into was small, dust motes dancing in the strong sunlight. Through an open door in the back of the room, Uri could see where Baruch lived—a cramped room filled by a rumpled sleeping pallet and several clay pots bubbling on a narrow hearth. Baruch followed Uri's gaze and took two steps past him, pushing the door to his living quarters shut.

Baruch pointed Uri to a table, mounded some clay beside him, and told him to wait.

"What am I waiting for?" Uri asked.

But Baruch ben Neriah was already at the entrance to the small hut, looking out onto the busy streets of Tel Abib.

Uri was nervous. He knew how to write in three languages now. He could read several more. His swiftness in writing earned him praise from Kur, a man not given to lauding apprentices. But Baruch ben Neriah's temper was unknown. What would he be like to work with? What would it be like writing down the stories of his own people, rather than the odd, mystic miracles of the Babylonians?

"Where have you been?" Uri heard Baruch demand, as a slight young man, maybe a year or two older than Uri, slipped through the door. His hair was unusually light, his skin fair. And his eyes! Uri had seen blue eyes before, but none so bright and intense.

"I am sorry, Baruch. Father asked me to write down some of the Temple proceedings, so the old customs could be restored when we return."

"Your father still dreams of a Return?"

Uri looked up, noting Baruch's derisive tone.

"Of course." A rising inflection in the young man's voice made Uri turn to stare at him.

Baruch ben Neriah pursed his lips. "Come meet Uri," was all he said. "He's just come from Kur and will work on the Writings with us."

Uri stood, unsure whether to extend his hand. The other scribe looked him up and down.

"Is Uri pure?" The young man sneered. "Or has his time with Kur seduced him? Does he worship at other shrines?"

"Answer," Baruch said to Uri. "He has the right to ask."

"I answer no man when I do not know his name," Uri shot back, annoyed.

"You don't know Ezra ben Seraiah, son of the High Priest of the Temple and a direct descendent of Aaron?" Baruch shook his head. "I keep forgetting you are not of priestly lineage."

"Not of priestly lineage and yet training to be a scribe?" Ezra looked like he had just bitten a lemon. "Surely not."

Uri flushed. "I can write as quickly as any scribe from Judea," he said. "And I have never bowed my head to Marduk or Sin, so I am ritually pure."

"Did you bathe at the mikveh before coming here?" Ezra persisted. "You cannot write the Holy Name without doing so."

"I didn't know."

"I can see that you didn't." Ezra looked pointedly at the dried clay on his arms and fingers. "Baruch ben Neriah, why did you not send this poor boy instructions? Or a minder?"

"I may not be of priestly lineage, but at least I am polite to strangers," Uri retorted. "Master, if you want me to go to the mikveh now...."

"You don't even know that the mikveh opens at dawn for the men and closes by morning prayers?" Ezra asked with scorn. "If you go now, you'll find yourself among women cleansing themselves from their monthly courses. Fool." The young scribe turned away.

Uri's hands balled into fists. He itched to hit the condescending priest's son. But Baruch shooed them both to their tables.

"It will be many days before he must write the Name," Baruch explained to Ezra. Uri did not like how he appeased the arrogant scribe. "I want you to take him to the mikveh a week from today and show him what he must know."

"You want *me* to do it?" Ezra snapped. Then he sighed. "Fine."

It was a bad week for Uri. He was cuffed several times by his new master when he could not write quickly enough. "Soon," Baruch explained, "You'll be sent among the wise men to write down every word they say. And they speak quickly when they become excited by the tales they remember of the Lord's glories. You will not be allowed to interrupt them, and if you cannot keep up…."

"It will be like sending a donkey to write it all down," Ezra muttered in Uri's ear, softly, so Baruch would not hear. "How can you record miracles you cannot understand?"

Before the week was up, Uri nearly came to blows with Ezra a dozen times. He pulled back, however, recalling that he was to be entrusted with sacred duties. His behavior must be as spotless as his body or his soul. Uri wondered what Baruch would do to him if he gave in to temptation and pummeled Ezra one day. He fell asleep at night dreaming of Ezra's bloodied face, unable to suppress a wide grin, even while he reprimanded himself for such unholy thoughts.

Finally the morning came when Ezra was to take him to the mikveh. Uri woke before dawn, rising silently so he would not wake Nachum or the girls.

"You're not thinking impure thoughts, are you?" was the first thing Ezra said as they stood on the mikveh steps. "You can pollute the water for the rest of us by impure thoughts."

"You think a lot about purity, don't you?" Uri challenged him. "Does that mean your own thoughts are impure?"

Ezra pulled himself up. "Do you know who I am?" he demanded. "Do you know who my father is?"

Uri shrugged. "Once that might have meant something. But now? My father works as a musician in the palace. He plays for the queen. He's played for her husband, King Nebuchadnezzar. He is good friends with Daniel, the king's advisor. Your father was High Priest of a destroyed Temple. Who is to say whose lineage is more important?"

"Your father is a musician?" Ezra prodded him. "What did he do in Judea?"

"He played for the king there before Nebuchadnezzar exiled him. He's always played for royalty."

"I thought your father was a farmer."

"That's my stepfather."

Ezra shrugged. "Perhaps there is more to you than I thought. Come on. Let's get this immersion of yours over with."

Uri was standing in the middle of the spring-fed pool, enjoying the blood-warm water—neither too hot nor too cold—when Ezra's eyes suddenly opened, as if in shock. "Your father serves in the palace?" he asked.

When Uri nodded languidly, Ezra hissed, "Get out of the water this instant."

The sting of command in his voice was such that Uri reacted instantly, clambering up the wet steps to stand, shivering, naked, before the boy with the flashing blue eyes.

"Don't cover your privates," Ezra instructed.

"Why? What's the matter?" Uri stammered.

Ezra looked over Uri's shaking body minutely. "Your father would be cut to serve the queen. A castrated man cannot enter the mikveh. I must make sure you were not gelded as well."

Uri flushed, remembering his shame at learning of his father's deformity. Had his reaction been this cruel?

"You're intact," Ezra said, sounding almost disappointed. "Get in."

Uri plunged back into the water, feeling the warmth embrace his shivering limbs. He relaxed into it.

"I can't believe," Ezra sneered, "you had the nerve to compare my father to a gelding."

All the fury Uri had been holding back came bubbling up. He slipped under the water, moving quickly to reach for Ezra's ankle. With one, swift pull, he yanked the other boy underneath and held him there for several long seconds. When he let him up finally, Ezra was sputtering and gasping for breath.

"You needed to learn a little kindness since you've mastered purity," Uri said, walking to the edge of the pool.

Ezra's mouth thinned. "I won't forget this, farm boy," he gasped.

Uri looked back at him, at Ezra's white, narrow chest and spindly arms. "I'm happy to remind you any time you like," he retorted. "Just let me know when you need another lesson."

26

Seraf's Death

IBI-SIN BROUGHT THE NEWS TO Sarah. "He's near death. The infection has spread throughout his body, into his armpits and neck. He's stopped urinating. He asked for you and Uri to come say goodbye."

"Oh, poor Seraf," Sarah said, wiping her hands on a piece of cloth and piling the dough for the barley loaves she was kneading into a wicker basket, turning to her eldest daughter. "Rahil, you'll finish the bread baking for me."

"Can't Mara do it, Mother?" Rahil whined, slouching in the corner of the room. At eighteen, all Rahil cared about was painting her fingernails and toenails and finding different ways to dress her hair. She constantly bullied seventeen-year-old Mara into doing both of their chores. Mara—sweet, easy-going Mara—would perform Rahil's tasks cheerfully, feeling amply rewarded when Rahil didn't elbow her out of her small corner of the bed they shared.

Sarah worried about Rahil and tried to convince Reuven it was past time to find the girl a husband. But Reuven, strict with Uri and Nachum, turned a blind eye when it came to his daughters.

"Next year," he'd say. "I cannot afford her dowry this year—not for the type of husband she deserves."

"And what type of husband would that be?" Sarah replied. "Surely not the wealthy husband she says she wants."

"And why not? Is she not the very picture of you, when you were younger?"

Frankly, Sarah saw more beauty in her youngest daughter. Mara's sweet smile was easier to gaze upon. Rahil was apt to jut a hip and flash her black eyes, flaunting her dark loveliness.

Sarah chastised the girl whenever she left the house with her heavy Judean garb pulled off one shoulder, provoking endless arguments that ended with Rahil flouncing off. And Sarah, hands on her hips, watched that Rahil did her chores and didn't just foist them onto her sister.

Sarah's blood boiled now at the thought of leaving gentle Mara behind to acquiesce to her sister's selfish whims. "Mara will come to comfort Uri," she declared.

"She goes to the palace, and I bake the bread? How is that fair?" Rahil complained.

"She visits a dying man to console her brother," Sarah snapped. "How can you think of that as a treat?"

Mara stood looking at them both. Behind her quiet eyes, Sarah thought, was a flash of bright strength that made Sarah recall her youth. If only the girl would speak up and not let Rahil bully her! "Go," Sarah said to Mara now, "change into your best dress. The tawny-colored one. And use Rahil's combs to put up your hair."

"To visit a dying man?" Rahil sneered.

"To visit the palace." Sarah's palms itched to slap her, but she refrained. She dispatched Nachum to fetch Uri from Baruch ben Neriah and went to change her own clothing.

The three of them walked through the palace gates in late afternoon. Ibi-Sin had left word with the guards to allow them to enter without escort. Uri, a constant visitor, knew his way through the winding corridors. After years of service to the queen, Seraf was housed in the towered section of the palace where privileged slaves enjoyed tiny private chambers. As they clattered over the marble floors in their loose sandals, Sarah noticed how Mara pulled the eye of most of the men and many of the women.

She is lovely, Sarah thought, nearly as beautiful as Sarah herself used to be at fifteen. But Mara had a calmness about her that allowed men, after a long, satisfying glance, to turn away. Her beauty was worn quietly, like a gauze veil floating over her features. Sarah's own attractiveness had been too overt, just like Rahil's. At least she, unlike Rahil, had never used tricks to make men stare and click their tongues.

The stench in Seraf's room was overwhelming. His body was puffy and distended, his gaze dark slits sitting in fleshy hammocks of skin. He was covered by a light drape, and, as they entered, was complaining to Ibi-Sin that it chafed him.

Sarah clung tightly to her son's hand as they crossed the threshold. Even Uri, who had witnessed his father grow increasingly frailer during his many visits, was appalled to see signs of the end so clearly. Seraf's dark hair lay lank and thin upon his pillow. His skin resembled old parchment, worn and scaly. But he smiled to see them enter, waving away Ibi-Sin and his basin of foul-smelling medicine, grasping Sarah and Uri to him with thickened fingers.

Mara stood at the back of the small room, giving Seraf a moment with his family. Sarah questioned Ibi-Sin closely about the medicine in the basin and asked how often the bedclothes—which seemed crusty and soiled—were changed. She made such a fuss over the state of the bed that Ibi-Sin, his black outlined eyes snapping, stalked off to fetch a house slave to change the linen. Mara simply stood, waiting for a moment when she might help her mother.

The moment came. Seraf began coughing uncontrollably. Sarah, impatient, was already pulling at the sheets at the bottom of his bed. Uri looked around for some water. Mara—used to Rahil's bossy shouts—was quickest, bringing a cup of tepid lemon water to the man she called Uncle. She leaned over him, supporting his back as she helped him sip from the cup.

"My dear Seraf," came a rich, imperious voice from the door. A woman, decked in gold and silver jewels, her gown a rich burgundy red embroidered with emerald and turquoise chips, stood in the entrance-way. Sarah dropped the handful of linen she was holding. She and Uri prostrated themselves before the queen. Only Mara ignored her, watching

Seraf as he grasped her wrist, tipping more of the soothing drink into his parched mouth.

"Rise, rise," ordered Queen Amytis, gesturing distractedly at the Judeans. "Seraf, my poor Seraf. You gave me so many beautiful hours of music. I came myself to bid you farewell."

Mara moved away gracefully, ducking a small curtsey as she moved off. The queen's eyes followed her.

"What a lovely child!" she said. "She reminds me of someone, Seraf. Who is it?"

Barely able to speak, Seraf motioned toward Sarah. Sarah bowed again. "She is my daughter, Your Majesty. You may recall I served your stepdaughter, the Princess Kaššaya, for a short time before becoming pregnant with my son. Uri here is Seraf's son."

The queen barely glanced at the young scribe. She studied Sarah's face. "Ah, yes. You were Kaššaya's pretty pet in the perfumery. She was annoyed that the two of you could not control yourselves. I remember," the queen smiled maliciously, "how she broke some vases in her rage. Wasn't there a price to be paid, Seraf, for taking her slave?"

"Yes, Your Majesty," Seraf croaked, putting out a hand for Sarah's. "She demanded the price of a slave, which I paid after many years of additional labor."

"And so your son is a free man. Well done. But it wasn't just a matter of paying the price, was it? I remember something else, yes?"

"Perhaps you mean that the Princess Kaššaya demanded their daughter, if Sarah had one, to serve her. But Sarah had me—a boy," Uri stammered.

"But—I'm confused. Surely this is your daughter, Sarah?"

A jangle of alarm rode up Sarah's back. Looking at her son and daughter, she read the sudden fear in their faces as well. Seraf's eyes closed, and he breathed more quickly, as though even he, despite his near-stupor, caught a whiff of the danger they stood in so unexpectedly.

Mara stepped forward, swallowed hard, and spoke in such composed tones that Sarah stared at her daughter in admiration.

"I am Sarah's daughter, but to Reuven, her husband. Uri is the only child she and Seraf had."

"I see," said the queen. She thought for a long moment. "But surely that doesn't matter. You *are* Sarah's daughter, are you not?"

"I am," Mara replied, her voice shaking a little.

"Your Majesty," whispered Seraf. "I paid the price for the slave. Forgive the bluntness of a sick and dying man. But you can have no claims on this child."

From the sudden slanting of Amytis' eyes, Sarah realized that Seraf's hasty assertion was a mistake. She stepped forward. "The child in question was—is—this young man. Uri works now as a scribe, Your Majesty, serving our community. Uri, tell Her Majesty how grateful you are that her stepdaughter allowed your father to purchase your freedom."

"Extremely grateful, Your Majesty," Uri faltered. "I...I'm a man who writes the words of others all day, so I have few of my own. Excuse me if I don't speak well. But I am eternally grateful to the Princess Kasšaya for giving me my freedom."

Amytis pursed her lips and turned toward her musician. She put a linen handkerchief to her nose to block the stench rising from his putrid body.

"Did you know that Kasšaya is about to give birth to another child?" the queen asked Seraf. "Years ago, I suggested to Nebuchadnezzar that he wed her to a Medean prince, but he chose instead to reward his courtier, Neriglissar, with her hand. She has had three children thus far, but they have all been useless girls."

Sarah could see that Seraf was finding it difficult to concentrate. She was angry that the queen was squandering their last hours with him. Controlling her rising temper with difficulty, a sudden memory rose unbidden: crouching in a corner in the Princess's rooms, wondering what it was like to have so much power that you could disregard everyone else's feelings and needs.

Amytis continued, "I want to give my stepdaughter a present if she finally manages to produce a son. I think this girl would be a perfect gift."

Mara turned to her mother, clinging to her hand. Sarah wrapped both arms about her. She gasped, "Press me into service, Your Majesty, but let my daughter go free."

Amytis looked Sarah over, shaking her head. "You are too old. What beauty you had once—and you were exquisite, I remember—has been marred by years of farming. No, your daughter is fresh and young. It is right she serves a prince of the blood. She will make an excellent hand-maiden to my stepdaughter."

Seraf opened his mouth, struggled to speak, and shut it again. He closed his eyes. Sarah saw the enormous strain he was under, summoning forth the little strength left to him. Finally, he managed to wheeze out, "Kaššaya gave me her word. Daniel always told me the word of a royal was sacrosanct. You cannot do this."

Amytis shrugged. "Her word, not mine. I made no such promise. Come, come, surely we are making too much of a very slight matter. The girl will live in luxury as she tends to a prince of the blood. If she serves well, she will eat richly every day, dress in the finest linen, and the kind eye of Ishtar will shine upon her. What future do you Judeans offer her? A life of drudgery in a brick hut as the first or second wife of a farmer or tradesman? I am doing the girl a favor. We will talk no more of this. My servants will fetch her when the time comes—if Kaššaya delivers a boy."

Seraf shifted his body with an effort, wincing in pain. "I will not survive to know if the child is girl or boy. I will not last past the time when the first stars dot the sky tonight. If my music meant anything to you, Your Majesty, grant me a deathbed wish. Do not take the girl."

Amytis sighed. "It is true you gave me much pleasure, Seraf. Come, rest peaceably. I will leave you with your family now."

Seraf was correct when he told the queen he would not live to see more than a few stars in the sky. When the first of them shone forth, seen through the narrow slit in the wall of his room, he breathed his last.

Sarah clung to her children, thinking of those days, long ago, when the Captain of the Guard had singled her out for his favors. "Seraf was so kind to me when I lost everything," she told them. "He helped me survive the greatest humiliation of my life."

"A good man," said Daniel, who had joined them for the last hour, summoned by Ibi-Sin.

The Egyptian was there too. "Brave in the face of pain."

"And a good father," Sarah said, smiling at Uri through her tears.

Uri could not speak. He reached for his half-sister's hand and wept on her shoulder. Outside the window, the stars appeared one by one, twinkling coldly above them.

27

Keren's Light

THE FIRST YEARS OF MARRIAGE were the happiest of Amittai's life. His wife, freckled, strong, with a broad smile and wide hips, brought him untold joy in the marriage bed. And the string of children she delivered—a boy, two girls, another boy—filled his heart with pride.

Amittai rose with the dawn and lay down in the early dark. The ruined old farmhouse, restored to sprawling comfort after several excellent harvests, suited him, and he would often walk from room to room, trailing a hand over the whitish pink stone walls. While he embraced the hard, relentless work of farming, once or twice a year he would take his flock of sheep and enjoy a day hiking the beautiful stony foothills surrounding Jerusalem, his oldest boy with him. Ophir would tag along happily, pleased with a day's leisure from farm chores.

On one such occasion, a beautiful sunny day when the crops were sown and the only thing to do was to water and wait, Amittai met Jabin, the shepherd. After many years of service, Jabin had parted ways with Enosh to build his own flock. Amittai flinched to recall that it was Jabin who'd taught him the lure of Moloch's handmaidens. With that memory uppermost, Amittai turned away after a brief exchange of pleasantries.

"Too good for us, now, are you?" Jabin crudely spat on the ground.

Amittai saw young Ophir's eyes widen as he watched the thick wad of saliva drip down the side of a rock. "No, no," Amittai protested. "It's just—there isn't enough grass for both flocks to graze."

"It's not that, is it? I'm too rough for your little boy. I remember when you were his age—running to catch the sheep and round them up. You were a handy soul to have around. Bet your boy can't do it."

Ophir flushed. At six years, he was already sensitive to taunts.

"He's handy at the chores I ask of him. That's good enough for me," Amittai retorted, draping an arm around his son.

"What, mucking out the barn and planting seed? Any idiot can do that. It takes skill to keep a flock, though. Outthinking the sheep—that's hard work."

"No harder than outthinking nature's whims. I know. I've done both. They both take skill. Patience. Farming takes more strength and endurance, sheep herding more cunning. That's the difference." Amittai grinned inwardly, as Jabin shrugged and waved them off. How had such a statement come from his own mouth? His son was staring at him in—was that admiration? It was years of living with Keren, Amittai thought. His wife could talk when the mood took her—when the moon rose, or the first wildflowers filled the valley. He would grunt and let her talk and enjoy the flow of her thoughts.

What would she think of this landscape right now? Amittai wondered. The purple, green, and brown hills rolling in the distance, the brilliant cloudless blue sky stretching like a promise that went on forever. And the solid, glittering, white hot disk of the sun, now sinking toward the horizon. *God's country.* Overseen by Chaldeans it might be, but it was still the Most High's homeland. His Promised Land.

Amittai and Ophir spent the rest of the afternoon in the next valley. Ophir listened carefully to his father's instructions about how to round up a stray sheep and blundered through the task. Amittai praised him, anyway, remembering all those years when he himself had received only stray blows and the occasional cuff on the ear.

They returned home as the sun tipped its last rays over the hillocks. Ophir said his legs ached, but Amittai was proud that he pushed on, stolidly ignoring the tearing pain in his calves and thighs. He scooped his son up after they deposited the sheep into the barn, bringing him the last few yards to the house on his shoulders.

"It takes strong legs to make a shepherd," he told him, swinging him around, holding his small, smooth face against his soft beard, treasuring the sweet warmth of his young breath on his cheek. Ophir put both arms about his father's neck, clinging. It was a long second of bliss for them both.

"Supper's on the table," Keren said, a bright light in her eyes. She smiled, watching father and son embrace. She reached for the boy, who went eagerly from father to mother. "Did you have a good day out walking, Ophir?"

"Mmmm," said the sleepy boy, nestling in her neck. "What's for supper, Momma?"

Keren carried him off, naming the dishes. Amittai went outside again to wash the stink of the day from his body. He stripped to the waist and doused himself in cold water from the well. *I am still a strong man*, he thought, patting his muscular chest. He wondered if Jabin would go to the sacrifices that night. *It's no wonder the Most High abandoned us*, he thought, remembering the nights of fire and burning flesh with a shudder.

Seated at the table with his family, Amittai ate heavily. Keren swallowed a few bites between tending their noisy children's needs. There was a knock on the door, and Keren brought her father to the table. The children greeted him with hugs and kisses, and he laughed with them, finally seating himself beside Amittai and taking the basin of soup that Keren ladled for him. The men ate in contented silence, punctuated only by murmurs of appreciation for Keren's cooking.

"What news from the city?" Amittai asked as the children slid away from the table and Keren poured both men another cup of barley beer.

"There's talk of rebuilding the altar on the Temple Mount," Hod said. "But both the Ammonites and Edomites are trying to stop it through protests to the governor, the Rab-mag."

"Can they stop us?" Keren asked, putting slices of honey cake down by her father's elbow. "Other exiled peoples have been allowed to have altars to their gods."

"The Rab-mag is considering it," Hod said. "It boils my blood that these people are elbowing in on our affairs."

"I see more and more of them in the marketplace," Keren agreed.

Amittai was silent. He didn't want his picture of God's country—that exquisite moment of viewing the fertile hills and valleys spread out before him—to be spoiled. He took a long swig of his beer, then wiped his mouth with the back of his hand. "Spent the day with the sheep today," he told his father-in-law. "It never used to weary me like this."

Hod shrugged. "A long day doing nothing. Of course, you're tired. Tomorrow you're back in the fields?"

Amittai rose, annoyed at Hod's disparagement of sheep herding. "Yes. Naturally. Keren, bid your father good night."

Keren shot him an irritated glance but rose obediently. Hod drank down what was left in his cup and pulled himself to his feet.

"Sleep well, children," he grunted, leaving by the kitchen door.

Before Keren could chastise his rudeness, Amittai pulled her to him. "I couldn't wait another moment to be alone with you," he spoke into her soft ear.

"I have to clear up, the children...Amittai!" she giggled, as he kissed the nape of her neck and patted her ample hip.

"Work quickly, then wife," he said, releasing her. "Quickly."

28

Mara the Handmaiden

MARA HEARD THE BABY STIR and she stopped crying. Her pillow—so much softer than the pillows at home and yet so much harder to sleep on—was drenched with her tears. Sometimes it seemed it would never dry.

The baby stirred again. In a moment, he would pierce the air with his thin newborn wail. Mara sat up, covering her shoulders with the gauzy scarf that was all she was allowed as a handmaiden. She perched on the end of her sleeping pallet, groping in the dark for her sandals.

The baby's mouth opened, and he let out a screech. Mara staggered over, exhausted from lack of sleep. Where was the wet nurse? *Probably asleep in bed*. Rahil would have called Silili a stupid cow. Mara giggled at her sister's likely comment. *Stupid cow*. An apt nickname for the fat, placid, milk-rich slave who ate all day and waddled rather than walked from place to place. But then Mara sobered. It wasn't the woman's fault. Silili was trapped. A slave. Just like Mara.

"Shh, shh, shh, little Labaši-Marduk." Mara half sang the baby's full name before reverting to her nickname for the tiny boy. "Hush, Bashi. Ba-Ba-Bashi," she crooned.

The baby screamed even louder. He was drenched and soiled. Mara held the struggling, bawling child at arm's length, laying him down on the tall cedar chest that was spread with a soft rug. She reached inside the ornate chest and pulled out a cotton diaper from the pile inside it. Mara was still amazed at the softness of the cotton that she used to swathe the infant's bottom. These diapers were made of cloth spun in far-off Egypt, brought to Babylon by trade caravan. Silili the wet nurse had explained that once the guards at the Ishtar Gate felt how soft they were, the traders were escorted directly to the palace to pay tribute to the mightiest of grandfathers. Nebuchadnezzar himself bestowed these diapers upon his beloved daughter as a birth gift.

Of course, another birth gift had been presented—Mara herself. Removing the gold, jewel-encrusted pin that secured the wet diaper carefully, inserting the point in the rug so that the baby could not pass his tiny fingers over it, Mara remembered again the day she'd been brought to the palace.

She'd been working in the garden with Rahil. Her mother sat on the shallow steps of the brick hut, peeling small new onions outside so the pungent fumes wouldn't permeate the small farmhouse. Sarah steeped the delicate onions in spiced oil and vinegar, marinating them, sealing the jars for the family to eat during the rainy season. It was one of Mara's favorite winter indulgences. Mara's father and her brother, Nachum, were out in the fields.

Standing to stretch at the midpoint of her second row, Rahil suddenly straightened and put a hand over her eyes to shield them. "There's a chariot coming."

Mara and Sarah looked in the direction of Rahil's pointed finger. The lands surrounding their farm were flat and one could see for miles in all directions. The swiftly moving chariot was coming from the capital city.

"Probably not heading here," Sarah said, gazing at the chariot. "They'll veer off toward Tel Abib."

But Rahil had found a distraction and kept interrupting her work to look toward the chariot as it drew closer. "Momma," she finally said, "the chariot isn't going to Tel Abib. It would have turned by now."

Sarah wiped her oniony hands on her apron. In a motion much like her daughter's, she placed a hand above her eyes to screen them from the glittering mid-afternoon sun.

"Run and fetch your father and brother," Sarah told Rahil.

"Can't Mara go?" Rahil whined. "I have a water blister on my foot."

"I'll go," Mara said, glad for the excuse to stretch her back.

Sarah pursed her lips. "Good. That will give Rahil time to catch up with you. You've weeded four rows to her two."

"Oh!" Rahil looked about her for inspiration. "But shouldn't we have a fresh drink ready in case they are coming here?"

"I'll take care of that," Sarah said.

Rahil flounced back down in the dirt.

Mara approached her father and brother, pointing out the chariot. Mara recalled how Reuven put his warm, heavy arm around her shoulders as they walked to the farmhouse together.

The thought of her poor father made her want to weep again. Instead, she picked up the baby, fresh and fragrant with the perfumed oil she used to clean his little bottom and carried him into the wet nurse's room. As they entered, Silili rose sleepily up from the cushions and put her arms out for the infant.

Labaši-Marduk fastened his lips greedily to the wet nurse's ample left breast. Mara sank down on the marble floor, shivering in her thin dress. She shuddered to think how furious her father would be to see her dressed this way, the cloth of her dress sheer enough to see through, her left shoulder and arm completely exposed. Good Judean maidens did not dress that way, Mother had repeated over and over again when Rahil pined for light clothing and beautiful ribbons and jewelry. Her sister would be jealous of Mara's transparent cream shift, embroidered with a row of small lotus petals around the hem and neckline. As a royal slave, Mara wore her hair up now too, secured by combs decorated with seed pearls and tiny gem chips. Mara, trembling with cold as she huddled on the floor, her knees drawn up to her still-thin chest and her arms wrapped about them, smiled sadly as she thought how Rahil would connive to steal her combs. Oh, but her sister was welcome to them—welcome to everything she wore—if she could only go home again!

By the time Mara, her father, and Nachum had come from the fields, the chariot had drawn up before their door. Sarah was pouring the chariot driver a cold, sweet drink of herbs and honey steeped in barley water. The chariot driver was a young palace guard, breastplate gleaming in the sunlight, short linen skirt riding high over his bronzed, muscular legs. Rahil was twitching her left sleeve, trying to expose more shoulder, smiling at the guard to make him look her way. But it was not Rahil he was interested in. When the group from the fields walked up, the guard said, "Ah!" took the proffered cup from Sarah and downed it in a single gulp.

"I am Reuven, who leases this land and pays my master tribute," Mara's father said. "This is Nachum, my son." Reuven didn't introduce the women. It would be unseemly.

"Welcome to our home," Nachum said, trying to sound more dignified than his uncertain twelve-year old voice would permit. "How may we serve?"

"I come with a commission from Her Majesty, Queen Amytis," the guard said, "Which of these women is Mara, daughter of Sarah?"

Reuven cut his eyes at his wife, his glare hard and bitter. Reuven had blamed Sarah when they had all returned from the palace after Seraf's death. He'd been furious that she'd attended the sickbed, fearful it would remind their neighbors of the old scandal. And he was horrified at their encounter with the queen.

No one else spoke and the guard repeated, "Who is Mara? It is you, is it not?"

Mara remembered how he had pointed at her. How her eyes filled with tears.

"That's answer enough," the guard said. "Can any of you read?"

"My stepson, Uri, can," Reuven said. "But he is not here. He comes only in the evenings, after he finishes his day's work as a scribe to the elders of Judea."

"Well, he can read this to you then," said the guard, handing Reuven a clay tablet. "But I can't wait. I'll tell you what it says, word for word."

Drawing himself up, controlling his horse with a strong hand on the reins, the guard proclaimed, "I, Amytis, Queen of Babylon, chief wife of Nebuchadnezzar, King of Kings, daughter of Cyaxares, king of the Medes, mother of Amel-Marduk, he who will be King in the days to come, hereby decree that Mara, daughter of Shamrina, now known as Sarah, and of Reuven of Judea, subject of Babylon following the Exile of her people, is to be brought to the palace to serve as a handmaiden to the Princess Kaššaya, wife of Neriglissar, upon the blessed birth of their son, Labaši-Marduk. This in accordance with the promise made by Seraf, late musician of Queen Amytis, that Shamrina's daughter would serve the princess. Mara, daughter of Shamrina, is to be brought to the palace at once. Signed, this sixteenth day in Nisannu, a day of glory trumpeted by the gods for the birth of Labaši-Marduk of the royal bloodline."

As the guard reached the end of the decree, Mara and Rahil were weeping.

"But Daniel—Belteshazzar—told me on Seraf's deathbed that he would appeal to Queen Amytis. That he would remind her that the price for a slave had been paid," Sarah pleaded, wringing her hands. "He told me not to worry."

Reuven, his eyes darting sparks of fury, stood hunched, his hands balled into massive fists. "And you believed him? Why did you take her in the first place?"

The guard, who had kept one eye on Reuven throughout the reading, now reached for his dagger and pulled it from its sheath.

"I would advise you not to fight this proclamation," he said. "I am a veteran of many wars, including the one in your homeland. I will not hesitate to carry out my Queen's ruling—even at the cost of all your lives."

The horse, perhaps sensing the tension, whinnied, and reared forward and back. The guard brought it under control with a quick tug at the reins. Feeling as though a heavy stone perched on her chest, Mara realized there was no recourse from the queen's proclamation. But her father's quick anger could cause the family untold disaster. She stepped forward.

"I am ready," she told the guard. "Let me fetch my belongings, and I will come at once."

The guard nodded, a look of understanding lurking in his dark eyes. "Good girl! You won't need your belongings—they would only be burnt at the palace. Hop up."

Reuven's jaw hardened. Something inside him seemed to snap. He took three steps over to Sarah and, his heavy fist rearing back, punched her full in the face. "Whore!" he snarled at her. "Slut! I should never have saved you from the stones. I should have let them kill you—you and Seraf's bastard with you. You have brought me nothing but heartache, whore."

Sarah fell backward onto the ground, moaning at the sudden blow. Holding her jaw, she cried, "Nothing but heartache? How can you say that, looking at these children? I gave you everything...."

"You never loved me. Not the same way you loved that gelding."

Sarah's shoulders slumped. "There are different kinds of love."

Mara stooped to comfort her mother, but the guard pulled her into the chariot. "No," Mara cried. "Let me at least say goodbye."

But the guard turned the horse and started out of the yard. Rahil crouched over Sarah, but Nachum ran after the chariot long enough for Mara to shriek at him, "Tell Momma I love her! Tell her to come see me! Papa too! Nachum, tell them!"

"I will," he promised, finally stopping. Mara saw him growing smaller through tear-filled eyes—saw her sister kneeling in the dirt over her mother, her father stalking away. And then the dust of the road obscured them from view.

Silili took a practiced finger and broke the baby's hold on her nipple. She swung the infant onto her shoulder and burped him. A thick, pottage-looking mixture came from his tiny mouth. Mara rose, found the cleaning cloth, and wiped the spit-up from Silili's broad shoulder.

"He's thriving, sweet little man," the wet nurse murmured.

Mara yawned. She took the cleaning cloth, now covered in thick spittle, and brought it out to the hall where another slave—the one responsible for cleaning the baby's excretions—was lying on a pallet of straw. *At least that's not my life*, Mara thought, prodding the sleeping girl with one foot. This was a slave from Cilicia, a child recently captured from Kassaya's husband's victorious land and sea campaign. Mara pitied her. The girl was younger than Sarah had been when her mother was exiled, and she had clearly been mistreated and probably ravaged by Babylonian soldiers. Silili—who seemed to know all the gossip in the palace—whispered that the girl's tongue had been cut out when she had screamed too loudly for her mother. Mara, who hated not knowing the child's name, called her Cilci after her homeland.

"There are some soiled diapers in the baby's bed chamber as well, Cilci," she told the child now, "and there will be more soon."

The child took the cloth from her and stumbled off. Mara returned to the room, waiting for the baby to finish eating. She carried him back to his bedroom. It would be foolish to put him down yet—he was grunting and straining and would simply fuss if he were laid down to sleep. So she held him against her and swayed back and forth, willing him to finish pushing, so she could change him and return to her sleeping pallet.

Mara had often heard how her mother had been brought to the palace and cleaned in a bath of many waters before being anointed with oils, her hair dressed and body arrayed in new clothing. She'd never pictured such a thing happening to her. But that was exactly what did happen. The bath servants cut away her Judean garb, tut-tutting over its roughness. They laved her with soap made from fat and wood shavings, scented with lilac blossoms. And they gave her this thin dress, a dress that she blushed to wear.

Queen Amytis's eyes lit up when Mara was brought into her ante-chamber. Mara prostrated herself before the queen.

"Ah! My birth gift to Kassaya!" Amytis said.

Only desperation could have prompted Mara to cry out as she did, using phrases she had practiced in the bath, "Oh, mighty Queen! You promised my Uncle Seraf not to take me when he begged a deathbed boon! Do the promises of Babylon's royalty mean nothing?"

But the queen simply glowered at the girl and said, "I promised him nothing, merely told him to rest easy. Has no one told you not to speak unless you are bid?"

Silenced, Mara couldn't control the tears that came streaming from her eyes. Amytis ignored them. Her pain obviously made no difference to the queen.

Amytis commanded Mara to follow her into the throne room. Pointing to the pile of soft diapers in one corner of the room, the queen told to the girl to wait. Nebuchadnezzar entered, a trail of courtiers following him. Mara stared at the King of Kings, seeing how grizzled and worn he looked, how tired. Kassaya arrived on her husband's supporting arm, followed by the wet nurse who proudly bore the infant. The baby was asleep but woke with a start when Neriglissar took the bundle and laid it on the ground before the throne.

"Your newest subject, Your Majesties," he told Nebuchadnezzar and Amytis.

Amytis motioned to Silili to pick up the mewling infant and bring him closer. The royal grandfather peered into the blanket and chucked the small thing under his chin. The startled baby wailed, piercing cries echoing in the large throne room.

"Good strong lungs," Nebuchadnezzar commented, waving to Silili to remove the infant.

The wet nurse cuddled the baby to her as she began to bow herself out. But Amytis motioned her to wait. "We have birth gifts for the babe," she said, clapping her hands for Mara.

Mara approached, carrying the bundle of Egyptian cotton. The new parents felt the softness of the diapers and smiled their thanks.

Amytis smiled. "And the girl, Kassaya. Does she not remind you of someone?"

Kassaya peered into Mara's tear-swollen face. "Perhaps...."

"Think back, oh, nearly twenty years ago, when the second group of Judean exiles were brought to Babylon. You picked a girl to serve in your perfumery, did you not? A beauty?"

"I seem to remember...." Kassaya murmured.

"This is her daughter, brought to serve you and the babe."

"Oh!" Kassaya said. "A sweet gift, stepmother. Thank you." She turned away, fingering the diapers once more. "But these, Papa dearest—these diapers are truly wondrous. We are so grateful."

Is my life to be ruined for someone who cares so little for my services? Mara remembered thinking, watching Amytis's face fall.

So it seemed. Amytis, pouting over Kassaya's lack of enthusiasm, waved the girl away. The wet nurse, only too glad to hand the baby over, thrust the wailing child into her arms. And Mara had been carrying and caring for the baby ever since.

The baby finally managed to push out the stool that was bothering him. Mara changed him once more, then sang softly, settling him in the royal crib, beautifully fashioned from cedar and ivory inlay. Covered by blankets of the softest wool, the infant fell asleep instantly. Mara picked up the stinking bundle, brought it out to Cilci, and crept back into bed. With any luck, she would have a full two hours of rest before the baby woke again.

Lying still and exhausted, she told herself not to think of home. But the tears refused to heed her, and she wept once more before absolute fatigue overtook her.

29

Zakiti and Uri

ZAKITI WOULD MEET URI BY the Ishtar Gate, waiting by the mosaic relief of dragons and lions. She carried a jug or basket, so the soldiers on guard wouldn't think she was one of the loose women who sauntered by the city gates plying their bodies to any willing passerby. Tucking the jug against her hips, large lips pursed in impatience, Zakiti waited for Uri.

He was always late, always showed up on the run, parchment scrolls and clay tablets falling from the large cloth bag that he wore on a strap around his neck. He would stoop to pick them up, but more would tumble out. The soldiers laughed. Zakiti took her lower lip between her teeth so she wouldn't giggle, dark eyes glittering with amusement. With a crowd of Babylonian and Medean merchants clamoring to marry her, how had she fallen for such an odd figure of a man?

They walked together through the massive gates into the city, careful to keep distance from one another so no one would suspect. Today Uri led them through Nebuchadnezzar's famed processional avenue to a hidden alley oasis, with a low bench and tiny fountain. Once they were seated close on the bench, Uri's sweet breath tickling her cheeks as he whispered awkward endearments in her ear, Zakiti remembered why she loved this preposterous Judean. Heart pounding, she trembled in his arms.

Her father would never let them marry, never. It wasn't that Uri was Judean. Nutesh had his finger in every trade in the city of Babylon and beyond, loading his vast ships with barley, dates, mustard, cardamom, sesame, and wool to convey them to distant lands. He respected the Judean merchants who'd been forced to dwell in his city, exiles arriving the year he'd married Zakiti's mother. Their idol-less worship bewildered Nutesh, but they were good honest men who understood how to spit into the wind, clasp a hand on a shoulder, and shake on a deal.

She'd first met Uri in a merchant's shop. Zakiti had been sent by her father's third wife to purchase some ostrich feathers, for burning them daily during the last months of pregnancy ensured a safe labor. Uri had come to the shop for a new set of styli. The shop owner had been busy and Zakiti, mistaking Uri for a shop assistant, asked him to fetch the ostrich feathers. Uri, who knew the shop well, took one look at Zakiti's liquid black eyes and obeyed.

But Uri was not a shop clerk. Zakiti was shocked to learn that he sat all day with a group of crabbed old men who, to recall their days of glory, wasted daylight telling one another stories of all they had lost. Uri would sit over parchment or clay and scribble their tales, their aged eyes watering in longing for this homeland he'd never seen. Uri, who could reduce her limbs to jelly, was stained by ink he made from the crushed bodies of beetles and powered thistle root, his arms scaled with clay, which Zakiti would rub away as a prelude to seduction.

Zakiti knew there was only one way to marry Uri. She used her lips, the arms she bleached by the light of the moon, the ample curve of her hips, to goad him past his defenses. He told her it was wrong, protested that what they both wanted was an abomination in the sight of this invisible, nameless Lord of his—and laid with her nonetheless.

At night, Zakiti prayed to Damkina, the Earth Mother, to help Uri's seed reach her womb. She delicately placed an open pomegranate on the altar of the goddess, ripe with wet, red beads. She lit the incense burner, bent her head, and beseeched Damkina to give her life.

30

Uri's Shame

URI HURRIED INTO BARUCH BEN Neriah's house in Tel Abib. He constantly had to rush these days, running from Ezekiel's home, where the prophet would gasp out another strange prediction, to the homes of various elders, then back to Baruch's brick hut to transcribe his hasty notes into something more presentable.

The stories he heard! It was hard to make sense of them all. One elder told him how the world was made in seven days by dividing light and darkness, water and land. Another said the world was a vast desert, which the Most High watered with the same rivers that surrounded the many lands around them now—the Pison and the Gilion, the Hiddekel and the mighty Euphrates. Writing out the different accounts made his head ache.

"Just write them down," Baruch told him crossly. "It's not your job to understand."

But Uri wanted sense in the universe. So he worked on the creation story for days, trying to resolve the inconsistencies.

"They want you at Zachariya's house tomorrow, to transcribe the Law's dietary considerations," Baruch told him, watching the young scribe lean over the tall table where he stood and wrote. "You can't spend all your time on stories."

But Uri thought the stories were the most important part of his duties. He spent days reconciling the two tales of the world's beginnings. He was not completely happy with the result, but when he read out his two stories of Creation to the old men, they wept and praised him. While Ezra reveled in the Law, Uri found himself immersed in the accounts of the beginning of the world. In time, Baruch ben Neriah knew which scribe to dispatch for which task.

"They want someone to relate the story of the apple to," Baruch said one morning.

Ezra groaned, but Uri's eyes lit up.

"That means more about Adam and Eve—they who were placed in the Garden of Eden naked and knew no shame," Uri mulled.

"Praise the Most High that He taught us the difference between nakedness and clothes," Ezra shuddered. "Imagine walking the streets of Babylon naked! It would be worse than the way the Babylonians dress."

Uri turned so that Ezra would not notice the sudden flush coloring his face and marking his guilt. Zakiti.... For him, she was the perfect Eve. Her transparent and loose clothing, her warm breath on his face, her sweet pliant body offered without artifice or coyness. He could imagine how God created Eve from Adam's body because Zakiti fit so perfectly to him. Uri could easily conceive of her as his missing part, that rib removed to form her.

"You know," Baruch whispered to Uri, fired by Uri's enthusiasm despite himself. "There is another story about Adam, one the elders only whisper. I'll find someone to relate it to you. About a woman who was equal to Adam."

A woman equal to Adam! Uri's head pounded as he thought of it. If he had learned anything, it was that the Most High's world depended on man overseeing the foolish whims of women. He came home nowadays to the sound of his mother and stepfather endlessly arguing. Rahil would bring him a cold drink where he sat in the yard to escape their yelling.

"They miss Mara," she told him. "He blames her."

"Ezra would say that Mother's being punished for her sin," Uri said. "Lying with a man who was not her husband. That's how God works."

"Is it?" Rahil's voice grew shrewish. "And why should God worry about our poor parents? Doesn't He have more important things to worry about? Is the Most High that petty?"

Uri wrote the story of the apple. Eve was tempted and ate, and shame grew upon her. The idea of the serpent made Uri uncomfortable. Evil—how did it manifest itself in the universe? Was it something from outside of Eve or something within that made her disobey God?

And what if God wanted her to disobey?

After days of agitated reflection, Uri decided to break with Zakiti. She was Eve to him, and Eve was weak, tempted by the evil within the serpent. Fallen by her own sinful act. He waited for Zakiti at the place of their usual tryst, the Ishtar Gate. The dragons on the mosaic relief made Uri think of the serpent in the story of Creation. *God made the rules*, Uri thought. *It was not for man to understand, just to obey.*

But despite waiting until the sun set to the west, Zakiti never appeared. Happy for a day's reprieve from the inevitable flood of tears and the pang of parting forever, Uri returned home.

"Tell us what you wrote today," Nachum begged him that night, as he so often did. The boy was becoming strong and brown from his days out in the sun. Uri was almost ashamed when he stood next to him, his own skin so pale and the only muscles he could boast of in his wrists and fingers. Rahil, plaiting a ribbon in her thick, dark hair, pretended to sniff. But as he told the story of Eve and the apple, her stool crept closer. And then closer.

Sarah wandered in, and he made room for her next to him in the small circle. She wordlessly reached out and grabbed hold of his hand. It was the only time of day, Uri thought, that anything resembling peace fell upon his mother's face.

But then, Reuven called for Sarah.

"I wonder," she said, dropping a kiss on Uri's forehead, "if Eve felt trapped. Women have so few choices—how could she have known this was a bad one?" She went outside to her husband. The three children waited for the inevitable yelling to start. Uri spoke louder to drown it out. But some of it filtered through, nonetheless.

"I told you we should hide her. Send her off to some other family. But no, you said, the queen will forget. But the queen didn't forget, did she?" Reuven roared.

"She promised Seraf. I heard her. Daniel said he'd intercede. So I thought...."

"You thought! You watched them carry her off—and did nothing. What kind of a mother are you?"

"What kind of husband strikes a woman and blames her afterwards?" Sarah shouted back, then lowered her voice. "Besides, she's not dead. She'll be treated well. Have plenty to eat. More than you could ever give her. She might even be happy there."

"Happy. As if anyone can expect happiness in this life."

"*You* should be happy. You wanted to marry me, and you did. You wanted a farm, and you have one. You wanted children...."

"I wanted my children to live here, on my land!"

"It's not your land. Your land is far to the west of us. Our farm. Back home. This—is just temporary."

"Sarah of Jerusalem, tough as a mountain cat, pretending to believe in the Return?" Reuven sneered. "Don't make me laugh, wife. You never listened to that foolishness before."

"You call me foolish? And is the way you are treating your wife not foolish? Cruel? None of what happened is my fault."

"It is!" Reuven called. "It is God's punishment for your fornication with Seraf!"

Uri felt a small, wet splash on his hand. Nachum was crying, though he tried to hide it. Uri leaned forward and spoke even more loudly, almost shouting the story. Sarah must have heard him, for she led Reuven farther from the house.

The next day, Baruch sent Uri to Olmert, a man so old he could barely speak. "He will tell you the story of Lilith, whom some say was the first woman," Baruch said.

"But that's nonsense," Ezra said. "Mere superstition. Why are you wasting Uri's time?"

Olmert lay in the hot sun on a thin rug in a Tel Abib alleyway. Uri leaned close, letting the old man's musty breath wash over him as he related, in faltering syllables, the story of Lilith.

"God created her equal to Adam," Olmert whispered, "and Lilith refused to sleep beneath him. A sin. A woman should submit."

Uri scribbled rapidly. It was hard to hear the old man. Bending over him as he lay flat on the woven rug made Uri's back ache. But the story made him catch his breath with excitement.

"She said the ineffable Name of the Almighty and flew off, having grown wings," Olmert continued.

"She actually said the Name and was not struck dead?" Uri wondered aloud.

Olmert told how Lilith became an avenging demon, only stopped from killing all newborns by God's angels. How she caused men to dream of her and waste their seed on their bedsheets. The old man looked around fearfully as he told this part of the story.

"I should not let you write this down," he finally said. "You will give Lilith too much power if you write this story down."

"I just write," Uri said. "It's not up to me what is included and what not. The priests from the Temple and the older scribes decide that. I'll tell Baruch ben Neriah of your reluctance."

The old man fussed with the thin blanket that covered his withered limbs. "Lilith has been the bane of my existence," he whispered, looking toward the house where his daughter-in-law bustled about, making his evening meal of barley gruel. "Women...you cannot trust them. They suck your soul to get what they want. If you ask me, they're all just like Lilith."

Uri went straight from the old man to the Ishtar Gate, determined to find Zakiti. Once again, she did not show up. He was bewildered, almost hurt. *Had she decided to end it herself, pretend it never happened?*

Instead of heading straight home, he stood for a while, looking up at the massive blue gate with its crenellated bastions, its glittering blue tiles adorned with white and ochre bulls and dragons. He'd been told that the gate's walls were thick enough to allow a four-horse chariot to turn with ease high above the city. Passing the heavily armed guards, he entered the processional avenue, taking one guilty glance into the secluded niche where he and Zakiti had spent so many intimate hours.

He walked past the massive palace where his mother and father had served as slaves, where his half-sister was immured inside its marble walls. He should visit her, he knew, but he felt guilty at the thought. Wasn't it his fault that she had been claimed as a slave?

Before him towered the Ziggurat, with its eight stepped stories, a long straight staircase leading as if into the heavens. He himself had never mounted those stairs, of course, but Zakiti had told him that midway up were benches allowing those who wished to reach the tower floor to rest from the long climb.

Turning from the Ziggurat, he entered the market district with its bustling stalls. Uri never entered the market without realizing anew that Babylon was the center of the world, that all roads led to its rivers, that conquered kings paid tribute to its might, and that the illustrious city contained every richness imaginable. The scent of spices and roasting meat pervaded the market's narrow alleyways, and the wind rustled vibrantly colored skeins of woven cloth from as far away as the lands of Asia. The clamor of tradesmen bartering with slaves and housewives echoed off the thick brick walls. Booths were piled high with exotic items brought to Babylon from subject lands. The market was where he'd first met Zakiti, in a small shop he frequented for scribal supplies. He couldn't help but smile, recalling her mistaking him for a shop clerk.

Zakiti. Why did everything in this majestic city of Babylon remind him of her?

He passed through the Market Gate into the residential part of the city, with row after row of red-brick houses that glowed golden as the sun sunk lower in the horizon. The richer quarter boasted large homes surrounding gardens and courtyards constructed of fire-baked bricks. Houses on the narrower streets pressed up against one another, sunbaked walls crumbling whenever infrequent rain pelted the city. Zakiti had once described her father's home—a mansion of immense size, filled with spacious rooms surrounded by greenery, tended to by a retinue of slaves, including the nursemaid who had cared for her since birth. How was it that a girl so well favored by fortune cared for him—a poor scribe living on a barley farm midway between Babylon and Tel Abib, an exile of a despised people? He didn't wonder that she had decided not to meet him.

Turning, he left the city for the long walk home, pondering what to do about her. Did he have the right to seek her out, to demand an explanation? She was just a woman. What gave her the right to end it?

He arrived home to find his stepfather in the yard, sitting with a small, portly Babylonian who wore a rich trader's garb of woven cloth, a heavy sash thrown over one shoulder, secured at the opposite hip with a heavy brooch of figured silver.

"Is this he?" the trader asked Reuven, who was pouring them both more wine.

"This is Uri, my stepson," said Reuven, turning a baleful glare on him.

The trader rose. "I am Nutesh, father of Zakiti, who will bear your child when the winter rains begin."

Uri felt the ground threaten to come up to meet him. He touched the table to steady himself. Reuven, watching his stepson's face, must have seen the guilt written there. He picked up his cup of wine and threw it in Uri's face.

"Just like your mother. You'll get out of my house, now, tonight," he told Uri, who coughed and spluttered as the liquid hit his eyes and nose.

Sarah burst from the house. She had been listening, probably standing behind the door. She ran toward her son. But Reuven grabbed hold of her forearm and pulled her back.

"Now you'll learn," he snarled at her, "what it's like to lose the child of your heart. This one, I don't care about."

"You do care," Sarah cried back, yanking her arm away and clasping her son to her. She looked at her husband with wild eyes. "You can't fool me, Reuven. You love Uri as much as any of our children. Remember holding him in your arms? Remember swearing to Seraf to be a father to him? I understand you, husband. It's because you care so much that you treat us so."

Reuven stared at her, astonished. Uri gently peeled her clinging arms away.

Nutesh, who'd hastily drawn his stool back to avoid being splashed by the wine, now turned to Uri, his voice stern as he asked, "You'll marry my girl? You won't leave her in shame?"

Uri closed his eyes. Adam and Eve learned to wear clothing when they discovered their nakedness. Zakiti had tempted him, and, like Adam, he had fallen. He would cover her shame and his own with the garb of marriage.

For a moment, Ezra's smug, sanctimonious face swam before Uri. What would Ezra say when he learned Uri had wed a Babylonian? Would he still be permitted to serve as a scribe?

But Adam had taken Eve's hand as they walked out of the Garden. Uri could do nothing less.

31

Amittai and the Amorite Raiders

"A MITTAI!" HE HEARD KEREN SCREAM. "The west field's on fire!"

Amittai dropped his hoe. He ran, panting, to the field. The crop was nearly ready to harvest, and for several evenings Amittai had lingered there, savoring the sight of the long grasses waving in the breeze. But now the barley sheaves he had cultivated so carefully were ablaze, sparks flying from one seed head to the next, the wind whipping the flames.

"Keren!" Amittai cried. "Send the children!"

The children came running, dragging buckets of water. Quick-thinking Keren organized them into a chain, passing water from the house well hand-to-hand. But the flames were spreading too quickly.

"Yael," Amittai called to his oldest daughter, "Go to Jerusalem to your grandfather and fetch help!"

His daughter ran, her sandals a blur of speed. The rest of them passed the buckets of water as quickly as they could. But the wind kept blowing and just as they dowsed the fire in one part of the field, another broke out.

Amittai's young children struggled under the buckets. Keren, her freckled face smudged with smoke and dust, urged them on. It would take at least another half hour for Yael to return with help—if Hod were home. Could they stave off the fire that long or would it take the field?

"Amittai son of Dotan!" a voice called out. Above them, from the hills where the grapes and olives grew on terraces, stood Hanun the Amorite, a knot of grinning men behind him. "We have missed you at the fires of Moloch!"

"Have you done this?" Amittai yelled to him. "Is this fire your doing?"

Hanun's wolfish grin on his thin, pointed face made Amittai shudder. "Would a friend do this to a friend? Of course not. Would you like our help?"

Amittai looked at his wife. Keren shook her head ever so slightly. Hanun laughed uproariously, throwing his head back.

"I had heard Judeans were cowed by their women, but I've never actually seen it before. Are you going to let her tell you what you can and cannot do? Or are you going to act like the man of the household?"

Amittai ignored him, plucking another bucket from Ophir's outstretched hands, and extinguishing more of the flames. But the fire was growing out of control.

"If you help us," he called to Hanun after a moment, "what do you want in return?"

Hanun's eyes narrowed. "You offend me. Mine is a simple act of friendship and brotherhood. From one neighbor to the next."

"You are not my neighbor." Amittai stomped on a small burst of flame near his foot. "You are an Amorite. You do not belong in Judea."

Hanun turned. "Farewell, then. But I would not sleep too lightly these next few nights if I were you, Judean. Who knows when the fires will return?"

Amittai sent an anguished look at Keren. She hung her head, unable to meet his gaze.

"Wait, Hanun!" Amittai called. "Come help—as a friend."

Hanun turned back and grinned. He motioned to the men behind him, who swarmed over the field with buckets of dirt. The flames were quickly extinguished.

"Lucky we happened by," Hanun said. "And with buckets of soil at the ready, no less."

"Lucky," Amittai muttered warily, his eyes scrutinizing Hanun's foxlike face.

Hanun kept looking around him, his constantly moving eyes roving over the house, the barn, and the fields. "We're thirsty," he said, putting an arm around Amittai's shoulders. "Tell your women to fetch us some beer or wine. We'll drink together, eh?"

"Keren." The name sounded flat as it emerged from Amittai's mouth. There was a plea in his noncommittal tones—and shame.

His wife seemed to understand. Keeping her head bent, ushering the children into the house, she prepared a tray with cups and pitchers of beer and wine, adding flat bread and goat's cheese to the platter. Through the open door, Amittai saw her moving about the storeroom, her movements wooden. She brought out the first of the trays, setting it down before the men, then backed away, her eyes never looking up, as they grabbed for cups and poured.

"Ah!" Hanun swallowed the barley beer in large, thirsty gulps. "Let's have another!"

Amittai reached forward, grasping the handle of the beer pitcher to pour his unwelcome guest another drink. Hanun looked at him, feral eyes narrowed.

"But you don't drink yourself, Amittai! What sort of friendship is this? A friend does not let a friend drink alone."

Amittai picked up the one remaining cup and poured a half measure of wine into it, downing it in one gulp.

"Good man, good man!" Hanun smacked him soundly between the shoulder blades. Then he stretched out his long legs, leaning back in the chair. "It's going to be a lovely evening. Come with us to the sacrifice, hey? It's been a long time since you've been cupped between the ample thighs of a server to the great god Moloch. Don't you miss the fire and the willing flesh, sitting here lonely and chaste on your acres, nothing to amuse you but counting sheep and children?"

"I'm content at home," Amittai said. "What do you want from me, Hanun?"

Hanun shook his head. "You Judeans. Ever suspicious of a simple reaching out in friendship. Why should you suppose I want anything?"

Amittai put his cup down with a thud and rose. "I thank you then, as a friend. My family is tired from fighting the fire and would like to rest. Ask your men to finish drinking and go."

Hanun brought his pointed tongue between his teeth and tsked. "Where's your oldest boy, hey? He's old enough not to be hiding behind a woman's skirts. He should be out here, drinking like a man."

Amittai looked at his feet. "Ophir is well enough where he is."

"Nonsense! Send for the lad. I would like to see him—" Hanun leaned forward, his eyes fixed on Amittai's face. "—as an act of friendship."

Amittai turned and yelled, "Ophir!"

The boy—not yet ten years old—came out of the stone house. "Yes, Father?"

"Our guests wish you to join the men. Sit and I'll pour you some wine."

Amittai saw his son swallow hard before he hastened to obey, crouching on the ground near him. Hanun looked the boy over as if he were indeed a fox, thinking about making a small jackrabbit his supper. Amittai poured Ophir a half cup of wine into his own cup and handed it to the boy. Ophir drank thirstily.

"A good-looking boy," Hanun commented. "Is he strong?"

"He is," said Amittai slowly, wondering what the Amorite wanted with his son.

"What is going on?" came a voice from behind them. Hod, panting as though he had run a long way, stood there. Little Yael could be seen farther down the road. "Yael told me the field was on fire and I should fetch help. I have men coming in wagons behind us."

"Thank you, Father." Amittai's eyes tried to convey a soundless message to his father-in-law. "But Hanun and his men...just happened to be passing by. They helped us extinguish the blaze." Amittai looked at his son. This was a chance to extricate him from Hanun's reach. "Ophir. Run down the road and tell the men coming to help us we no longer need them. Mind you thank them politely for me, boy."

Ophir rose and ran off.

"Sit down, Father," Amittai said, relieved that his strong-willed father-in-law was there to support him. Together they would discover Hanun's real purpose. "Have some wine."

Judging from his frown and hunched shoulders, clearly Hod didn't want to drink with the Amorites. Perhaps the plea in his son-in-law's eyes made him sit.

"This is a nice piece of land you've given Amittai," Hanun commented, unabashed by Hod's arrival. "How did you get hold of it?"

Hod drew himself up and stared directly in Hanun's face, their eyes locking. "What do you care how I bought the land?"

"I heard it wasn't so much a purchase as a bribe to a Chaldean official." Hanun looked casually away into the west field with its ruined and charred stalks of barley. The sheer audacity of the careless gesture stole Amittai's breath. His father-in-law turned purple at Hanun's insinuating tones. "It used to be Baruch's land, did it not?"

Hod, his bottom lip caught between his teeth, ignored the question, and looked at his son-in-law. "You say Hanun and his men just happened to be here when the fire broke out?"

Amittai nodded.

"There has been a rash of fires in the farmlands surrounding Jerusalem," Hod said. "I wonder how they're being started?"

Hanun turned back and laughed. "Amittai asked me more directly than that, Hod. Could it be your son-in-law has more courage than you?"

"And what did you tell him?"

The steel in the two men's eyes was a mutual challenge. A long, tense moment followed.

Hanun broke the staring contest and laughed, shrugging. "I said setting fires was not an act of friendship. Amittai agreed that we were friends." He sat back in his seat, looking very much at ease. "And you, Hod? Can Hanun and his men count Hod among their friends?"

"Hod would ask if there is a price for this friendship," Amittai's father-in-law snapped.

Hanun shook his head ruefully. "Not as large a price as the bribe I know you paid for this piece of land—but perhaps with a similar result," he said.

"What does that mean?" Amittai asked. Would Hanun finally reveal his purpose?

"You have two boys, do you not? I have seven daughters. Seven! It's hard for a man to provide for so many girls." Hanun leaned forward, took up the pitcher of barley beer, and poured a third cup, draining it to the last drop. "The last of the beer. Oh, well," he said, drinking greedily.

Hod frowned as the Amorite put the cup back on the table. "Are you proposing to match Amittai's son and one of your seven daughters?"

Hanun grinned, his pointed tongue flicking out to catch a beer drop lodged in his beard. "How pleased I am to have you both as friends!" he cried. "What an excellent idea!"

Amittai rose. "Enough nonsense," he growled. "My son will not wed an Amorite."

Hod got to his feet as well, his hand resting lightly on the dagger in his belt. "We will bid you good night, Hanun," he said, spitting the words through gritted teeth. "And you are lucky that we are both in forgiving moods."

Hanun shook his head. "You do not understand, I'm afraid," he said, standing and glancing toward the men behind them, whose eyes were riveted on Hod's dagger hand. They rose, forming a tight half-circle around Hanun and the two Judeans. "I'm looking to provide for my third daughter, Tobija. This farm—when it's not charred to the ground—strikes me as a good place for her to live and raise a family. She'll be close to her sisters, whom I'm settling in farms throughout the countryside.

"Tobija is a good girl—a trifle skinny, perhaps, but lots of men like their women that way. She's handy at the hearth and in the garden. Ophir will enjoy bedding her, when the two of them are old enough." Hanun glanced back at the men who stood behind him, their eyes hooded and alert, like hawks before they swoop down on their prey.

"I say the betrothal ceremony should take place in two days' time, here at the farm. A good opportunity to seal our friendship. The children can wed when the girl is old enough. Probably in three, four years.

"What say you, Amittai? It's a good match for your boy, and it means that no one will dare set a fire on your land again. They'd have to answer to me if they did."

Hod reached for his weapon, but one of Hanun's men swiftly slashed at his hand with a blade hidden in his fist. Cursing, Hod dropped his dagger and nursed his hand.

"Can we talk this over and let you know our decision tomorrow?" Amittai asked.

But Hanun pursed his lips and shook his head. "Not the act of a friend, I'm afraid. I wouldn't be able to protect you from another fire. Tonight, for example. Or from someone taking one of your pretty girls and, well, mistreating them."

Amittai turned to Hod, who shook his head and looked away. Amittai glanced over his shoulder and saw his wife standing in the door, clutching the two girls to her, her face puckered with fear.

If there were only someone to appeal to! But their Chaldean overseers didn't care who owned the land, so long as someone paid the taxes. Judean, Amorite, Edomite, Samaritan—in Chaldean eyes, there was no difference. And any fellow Judean who came to Amittai's aid was bound to find his own farm or shop under fire, his own women threatened.

"Two days, then," Amittai said, sending an anguished look over the fields he had grown to love. "We will prepare a suitable feast."

32

Royal Hide and Seek

MARA AND THE SEVEN-YEAR-OLD PRINCE, Labaši-Marduk, were playing hide and seek throughout the palace.

The palace was a wonderful place for the game. There were so many corridors to turn down, so many rooms to explore. Labaši-Marduk's grandfather, Nebuchadnezzar, had stopped his expansive construction throughout the city of late, but until he had done so, mighty temples had risen under his command, and the palace of the royals had become a virtual city of marble and fragrant cedar beams.

Mara knew not to stray too far from her young charge when she hid. She peeked through her fingers when it was Bashi's turn, deliberately watching what direction he took. She had lost him in the bowels of the palace just once. She had roamed for hours, calling his name frantically, fetching Cilci to hunt with her. She finally found the boy chatting with some supplicants as they waited in an antechamber for an audience with the mighty king. The next day Kassaya, learning of his adventure, screamed at Mara for nearly an hour before dispatching her for punishment. Mara had not needed old Melzar's stinging lash on the soles of her feet to realize she couldn't let that happen again.

Bashi was now nearing his grandfather's quarters. Mara followed him surreptitiously, her heart pounding a little as Bashi turned the corridor into Nebuchadnezzar's court room. Everyone in the palace knew that Nebuchadnezzar was afflicted by some strange disease. Mara wished she had forbidden Bashi from roaming in this part of the palace. But he was a royal child—strong-willed, spoiled, and self-centered. He rarely heeded his nursemaid.

Luckily, the throne room was empty. Bashi stood, gazing on the chiseled scenes decorating the walls. The gray-stone mural revealed his grandfather standing proudly in a chariot led by a rampant pair of steeds, his bow arm extended back over his armies. A lion followed the chariot, tended by a man who brandished an enormous shield. Thousands of armed men marched behind. Before him, the vanquished Egyptian pharaoh, Necho II, recognizable in his conical hat and strange square beard, cowered like a cornered animal. Elsewhere in the room, the artist had captured the Battle of Carchemish: Babylonian troops crossing the Great Nile, reeds waving as they waded across, swords held aloft. Other sections of the wall showed other victories—over the Phoenicians, the Syrians, the Cimmerians, and the Judeans. Mara gazed, blinking hard, at the scene depicting the burning of her people's Temple and the battering of Jerusalem's walls. A line of chained people was led down a hill, and she touched the figure of a young woman, head lowered, weeping. It might easily have been her mother.

Beneath Bashi's feet was a mosaic map of the world. He skipped from tile to tile, naming the lands his grandfather had brought to heel, careful to avoid walking on the great dragons and water eels that floated at the ends of the earth. He slipped into the massive gold throne, etched with geometrical lines of flowering trees and circular patterns and flanked by enormous statues of Marduk and his goddess bride. He sat, laughing, feet swinging beneath him.

"Mara," he called. "Come see me. I'm King of Kings!"

Mara came running. "Bashi, get down right now," she gasped.

But Bashi shook his head. "You," he commanded, laughing, pointing at her, "must bow before me. On your knees, slave!"

"That isn't funny," Mara hissed. "You'll be punished if you're found there!"

Bashi stood on the high throne, jumping up and down. "Punished? I'm a prince of the blood! No one would dare. They'll punish you instead. That's what you're afraid of."

Mara stared, eyes round. That was indeed what she was afraid of. At age seven, Bashi already understood too much. Such keen understanding might save his life one day, Mara knew. But it did not make for an innocent childhood.

A movement outside the room frightened her into action. She gathered up the young prince.

He struggled in her arms. "Let me down!" Bashi kicked her shins and set his teeth in her arms. One particularly nasty bite forced her to drop him. He pulled her hair viciously and ran, choosing one of the doors at the back of the throne room, which slammed shut with a reverberating echo.

As Mara started after him, she saw two men standing at the threshold. Panicked, she looked about frantically for a place to hide, burying herself in the folds of a long curtain hanging behind the throne.

"I don't know what to tell you," the man Mara recognized as Daniel said, walking slowly into the room, his olive-complexioned face drawn with exhaustion. "It's as if one of the demons they talk about in this land has taken possession of him. He crawls on the floor on all fours like an animal, eating grass and snarling rather than talking. I don't know how long we can conceal his illness from the kingdom."

"Ezekiel says it is the Almighty's doing, as punishment for destroying the Temple," Abed-nego replied. "Do you think he's right, Daniel?"

"I really don't know," Daniel replied. "Ezekiel's prophesies are too impenetrable for me to unravel. Besides, it's politics that worry me. Amel-Marduk wants to be named regent, which would be a disaster. The prince is heedless, spoiled—and worst of all, irrational. The priests love the idea, of course. They think they'll finally get the power Nebuchadnezzar has always denied them, even while they pretend to adore him. Of course, it is only a matter of time before we see the prince crowned in earnest."

"But why don't the priests love the king?" Abed-nego pondered. "He's built the most beautiful city in the world here in Babylon. I won't enter them, of course, but I hear the temples Nebuchadnezzar constructed to their false gods are even more magnificent than the palace and the garden."

"That garden." Daniel sighed. "If I told you how much money was wasted on that garden...."

Mara knew they were speaking of the Hanging Gardens, a green paradise created to remind Queen Amytis of her home country.

"It's a beautiful spot," Abed-nego murmured.

"Oh, doubtless. But the expense! All his victories have made Nebuchadnezzar complacent. And this strange ailment comes at a bad time. I hear talk of this new king to the east, this King of Anshan. What's his name again?"

"Cyrus of Anshan and Persia. But he rules tiny kingdoms, part of Medea. Nothing to worry about."

"The Assyrians once thought Nabopolassar was nothing to worry about. But our king's father laid low the once mighty city of Nineveh and defeated the Egyptians. It is the hungry kings that complacent and prosperous rulers need to fear. And this Cyrus is both—and ambitious besides."

Once, Mara would not have been able to keep the names straight. But nearly eight years of palace life had taught her that the royals lived a life of often shifting factions. Just yesterday, when Mara had bathed Bashi in his mother's marble pools, Kasšaya had sat in the courtyard just within earshot, grumbling to her husband Neriglissar that her half-brother would never be capable of governing the kingdom properly. She'd also complained of her stepmother—this, Mara knew, was nothing new—saying that Amytis was secretly receiving missives from Media supporting young Cyrus's ambitions. The Medeans saw the upstart Persian, Kasšaya said, as a way to contain Babylonian ambition. Kasšaya's spies had intercepted clay tablets Amytis had been expecting and brought them to their mistress.

"It is treason for her to receive such messages," Kasšaya said to her husband, as the two of them huddled over the clay shards. "But Father doesn't heed my warnings now any more than he did when we were all younger."

Neriglissar, his armored chest plate clanking whenever he moved, shrugged gracefully. "And your Father has been suffering these strange episodes lately. Nitocris is the only one allowed to tend to him. Perhaps you should ask your sister the true state of his health. All sorts of stories are circulating around the palace. You and I—we should know the truth."

"Nitocris!" Kassaya snapped. "She would tell me nothing. She's as much Amel-Marduk's creature as if we were Egyptians and the priests allowed brothers and sisters to marry!"

Mara laved fragrant soap on her young charge and doused him in warm water, bringing him into the courtyard wrapped in a warm swath of Egyptian cotton. The talk veered from royal intrigue to Bashi's training in weapons and reading. Both parents questioned their son, their faces showing concern that the young prince wasn't learning quickly enough. Mara's heart sank as she realized she would be summoned that evening to Melzar's chambers for another foot thrashing—and so she was.

The thought of Melzar's favorite punishment woke Mara from her remembrances to a sense of her surroundings. She could not dally any longer. Feeling the wall behind her with splayed fingers, she realized there was a door in the wall. Pushing it open, she found herself in a corridor heading away from the immense court room. Limping slightly, Mara made her way back to Bashi's chambers, hoping to find him there and that she could coax the young prince once again to apply himself to his studies.

33

The Story of Samson

Uri stood over his table transcribing the story of Samson the Nazarite. As he wrote, he glared at Ezra, who had suggested that Baruch ben Neriah dispatch Uri for this assignment. Uri had seen a slight smile flit over Ezra's sanctimonious face as Baruch laughed and agreed.

Uri wrote:

> And Samson went down to Timnath and saw a woman in Timnath of the daughters of the Philistines. And he came up and said to his father and mother, I have seen a woman in Timnath of the daughters of the Philistines whom I want to marry. His father and mother said, Why not a woman from among the daughters of thy tribe or among all the people instead of a wife from the uncircumcised Philistines? And Samson said to his father, Get her for me, for she pleases me well.

Ezra put down his stylus and stretched. "I've heard there is disorder in the palace," he said, in an unusually friendly tone. "Amel-Marduk is not the leader his father was. What have you heard? Have you spoken with Daniel or your half-sister lately?"

Uri peered at him, eyes slanting. "Do the affairs of Chaldean royalty interest you? I'm surprised."

Ezra smirked. "Jeremiah urges us in his letters to make the affairs of Babylon our own. I'm just trying to do what the prophet commands."

Uri shrugged. "I haven't heard much. But I'll tell you what I know later. I want to finish this section before midday."

Turning his back on Ezra, he bent over his work. He wrote of Samson's violence against the woman he married, of her infidelity, how Samson handed her to his friend after she betrayed him. A bitter taste congealed in Uri's mouth, writing of Samson's anger against the Philistines, his uncontrolled rages and large-scale slaughter. Uri wished he'd been assigned a different task. But—as Baruch had said so many times before—a scribe writes what he is bid without question.

In the years since Uri had become a scribe, he had written many strange things. The history of the Israelites and the Judeans was full of stories of terror and lust, of God's rage against the people who did not heed Him, of the unremitting violence needed to protect the land God had ceded to His people. Some of the tales were wonderful and beautiful, but many sent Uri home to Zakiti and their young daughters, wondering if life were not better in Babylon than fighting over a small piece of arid, rocky land far to the west.

But no land was ultimately safe. Uri, visiting Daniel in the palace, was welcomed as Seraf's son as well as in his capacity as a scribe. A middle-aged Daniel needed someone to write his own life story. Since Nebuchadnezzar's death, Daniel's status in the court had waned. The once powerful king's advisor was forced to give way to a new generation, whose rash counsel plunged the empire into mistake after mistake. But Daniel remained in his spacious quarters in the palace and was still privy, through a network of friendships built up over the years, to what transpired in the inner circle close to Amel-Marduk, the new King of Kings.

And Mara, whom Uri visited whenever he went to the palace, overheard court gossip from the young princeling and his mother. Kassaya was bitter about her half-brother's accession to the throne, for he excluded her from all court affairs and even moved her family into less-comfortable rooms to make way for an increasing number of nubile concubines.

"My sister whispers that Princess Kasšaya's husband would make a better king than Amel-Marduk," Uri told Ezra and Baruch during the midday break, taking bread and cheese from a small woven basket and pouring out barley beer to drink. They sat around a small table in the corner of the room, where the midday sun shone through an open window, illuminating the thick dust clinging to every surface.

"I heard that Amel-Marduk spends his money on drunken parties and on women." Ezra looked around cautiously. There was no telling who might suddenly enter the scribes's sunbaked brick building.

"But he freed Jehoiachim, our long-suffering Judean King, from his prison cell," Baruch reminded them gently, fingers trembling as he raised a piece of flat bread to his mouth. "Jehoiachim eats at the king's table now."

"Where he is witness to drunkenness and licentiousness." Ezra's mouth twisted in sour disapproval. "My father visited Jehoiachim this week in his new quarters in the palace. He tells me they sat together for hours, crying for the Judea we have all lost." Ezra looked into the distance, disapproval fading as sorrow crossed his face. "They've grown old and tired here."

"All the while young Cyrus of Persia goes from victory to victory," Baruch mused.

"Cyrus will be stopped before he reaches the gates of Babylon," Uri asserted. "Even if Neriglissar and Kasšaya don't agree with the new king's rule, Neriglissar is a good general. He will defend the country to the death."

"We need to do more than just halt Cyrus's march," Ezra said. "If the country stops receiving tribute from lands once under Babylonian rule, Amel-Marduk won't have funds to waste on wine and women."

"Which won't be good for us subject people," Baruch agreed. "But what can we do about it, after all? Best to live our own lives and trust to God Almighty to protect us."

As he did in Israel against the Assyrians or in Judea against the Babylonians? Uri wondered. But he did not say so aloud. Moodily, he poured himself another drink and unwrapped the figs Zakiti's servants had packed for his dessert.

Baruch was called away by some of the younger scribes, leaving Uri and Ezra to finish their meal together. "How are you getting on with Samson's story?" Ezra asked.

Uri glared, suspecting Ezra of sarcasm. "He was a strange man."

"I've heard those stories since I was a child. My grandfather was fond of telling my brothers and me about how Samson regained his strength. You agree, don't you, that all of Samson's troubles came from consorting with Israel's enemies? Marrying into their families, going to their parties? God gave him the strength to resist and what did he do? Allowed a woman's smiles and soft body and constant pleading to defraud him of his secret, then let her shear his hair and steal his strength."

Uri shrugged. "Are you trying to teach me something, Ezra? Ezra the pious. Always finding some way to tell me that my marriage is a sin."

Ezra brushed crumbs from his thin lips. "You could put her aside even now, you know," he said. "Samson's Philistine wife was given over to his friend."

"Samson was a newlywed," Uri retorted. "There were no children involved. Even if I wanted to leave Zakiti—and I do not—I would have to leave my girls as well."

Ezra shrugged. "Girls don't matter. If you had sons, now…but even they would not truly be Judeans. Better to marry a second wife, a Judean girl this time, and raise a family who believes in the One True God."

"It must be nice to have no feelings," Uri retorted. "No heart. You have no heart, Ezra."

He was surprised to see a hurt expression cross Ezra's face. The two of them had worked together for so long that they couldn't help growing attached to one another, despite approaching life in exile differently. Ezra wanted to maintain his Judean heritage and cordon the Hebrew people off from the Babylonians, fearing contamination. Uri, with his Babylonian wife and family, with the new-found wealth of his wife's dowry, had been introduced into the Babylonian *awilu* class. They lived in a spacious house not far from his married half-sister, Rahil, and numbered Babylonian and Judean merchants among their friends. Uri's work as a scribe was highly regarded. The respect Zakiti's friends showed him helped reconcile his new wife to the fact that he continued to work.

"Papa provides us with enough money, you know," she had told him early in their marriage, as he rested his head lightly on her protruding belly and whispered quietly to the growing child inside her. "You don't need to work."

He kissed her stomach and sat up. "You would have me live on your father's generosity? That is not the Judean way."

"My brother does not work, and my father is proud that he does not need to. I don't see why you cover yourself in clay or ink every day." She pouted prettily.

Uri laughed and kissed her puffed-out lips. "You would grow bored if I did not have stories to tell you," he said. "I seduced you with my stories, you know."

"Hah!" Zakiti laughed. "I seduced you, not the other way around."

At the time, Uri had laughed and tickled her, and they ended up making love for the rest of the afternoon. But now, many years later, Uri realized that it was true. His wife had been the seducer. Look at the snares both Samson's Philistine wife and the woman, Delilah, had set for poor, simple Samson. Were not all women deceitful and alluring?

Yet he knew he was a happy man. Who would not be happy with all he had in life? A loving family, a luxurious home, a position of respect in both his community and hers. Who needed more?

Ezra finished his meal and rose. "My grandfather told us where Samson's true weakness lay," he said. "It wasn't just that he couldn't say no to women. It was that he wasn't smart enough to see that he was being ensnared. He drank with the Philistines, bedded their women, and forgot his own people, his own God. Are we any different?"

Uri shrugged. "We all live such brief lives. Why not embrace the good things in it?"

Ezra's face darkened. "I despair of you sometimes, Uri," was all he said before turning away to his own work.

That evening, Uri watched as Zakiti sang their youngest daughter, little Atara, to sleep. Bent over the cradle, her face soft in the twilight, Zakiti was the very picture of motherhood. But then he harkened to the words of her song, "Little one who dwelt in darkness, why do you cry? You will rouse the gods of the household, shush, now, pretty one."

The toddler's eyelids fluttered against her round cheeks, then stilled as her chest moved in restful slumber. Uri drew Zakiti into the courtyard where the other children were playing in the twilight. Zakiti still hummed the lullaby under her breath.

"Can't you sing the child something else?" Uri asked. "Something without gods in it?"

Zakiti smiled, showing her pretty teeth. "And what did Ezra say to make you uneasy with your Babylonian family today?" she teased him.

He didn't answer. Instead, he sat down in the courtyard and drew his two older daughters on his knee. "I have a new story for you," he told them as they cuddled close in his arms. "Once, in Israel long ago, in the days before David the King, there was a man named Samson. And Samson was very, very strong...."

34

The Coronation

560 BCE–Year 26 of the Exile

"Hurry, Mara, hurry," Labaši-Marduk said, almost jumping from excitement. "You're too slow!"

Mara sighed, putting up one hand to still his bouncing knee, awkwardly using the other to finish lacing. "There. Your sandal is tied, Your Highness."

The prince grinned. "After mother and father are crowned today, I am heir to the kingdom, Mara. Have you thought of that? Have you?"

Mara looked up at the young boy. A stripling of eleven, he was thin and consumptive looking. Bashi was a fussy eater, a frantic and excitable boy who would not do more than watch as his instructors tried to teach him the science of warfare. If Neriglissar had been at home more often.... But he was too busy conducting battles against the Kingdom of Anatolia. Bashi suffered from headaches if he were pressed to exert himself, and Kasšaya always took the boy's part.

"You upset him. Again," she would say, kissing Bashi's white forehead. "He needs patience and kindness, not discipline and rough treatment. He is a prince of the greatest empire the world has ever seen, and battle is in his blood. Wait long enough, the boy's strength will astound you all." She would send him off with Mara into a darkened room where Mara would press cloths infused with lavender against his aching temples.

Years of obeying the willful and selfish dictates of her mistress and young master had inured Mara to Kassaya's illogic. Mara survived her days minute by minute, turning her skilled fingers and inventive mind to the task of placating the young prince when he fussed and fumed.

She stood now, reaching past him for the apron of hammered gold he would wear at the ceremony. Made of the thinnest of metals, decorated with intricately engraved lines of winged lions, it pulled at the rest of the garment.

He squirmed as its weight was draped across his shoulders. "I don't like this apron after all," he complained.

"You must wear it, Your Highness," Mara said. "Your mother specifically instructed me to dress you in it."

"I don't like it," he whined, moving his shoulders irritably. "Fix it so it isn't heavy."

What do you want from me, boy? Mara thought. *The apron is fashioned from gold.* But seeing the baleful expression on his face, she reached down to spread the cloth out, distributing its weight more evenly across his narrow frame.

"It's heavy," he whined again.

Mara held the boy close to her for a moment, smelling the odor of lilies that rose from his fair hair. "You will make the kingdom proud of what a strong prince they have," she encouraged him. "You will stand straight and tall as your parents are crowned King and Queen of the world's greatest empire and everyone will point at you and admire you."

"Yes!" Bashi crowed. "But you must hurry, Mara! It's late!"

Kassaya's handmaiden, Uttu, came in. "The prince and heir to the throne is called for," she said, winking at Mara.

"See, Mara! Foolish cow! You need to be quicker," the boy said, pushing her away. He started out but turned at the door. "I look like a prince of the blood, don't I, Mara?"

His eyes looked anxious. Mara smiled at him. "You look every inch a prince of the blood, my darling Bashi," she told him. "Your parents will be proud."

Bashi ran off, following Uttu. Mara attended to the messy room, tidying the cosmetics and discarded clothing and the jewels Bashi had peevishly decided he wouldn't wear. In many ways, Mara thought, he's more like a girl than a boy. Not wanting to miss the coronation ceremony, she thrust her musings aside to hurry through her work.

Hurry, Mara, hurry. As she ran down the nearly deserted palace corridor on her way to the immense temple where Neriglissar and his wife were to be crowned, the words echoed in her brain. *Hurry, Mara.*

She stopped, feeling cold sweat dot her forehead. Dizzy and sick, she leaned against the cold marble of a pillar that supported the arched roof of the corridor. *Hurry, Mara.*

"Hurry, Mara," Kasšaya had hissed at her on that dreadful night. Was it only two weeks ago? "Go watch and then come back and tell me what happened."

Mara shook her head. "I want no part of this," she whispered. After years of bending her will to the whims of the royal family, even this murmur was an act of defiance.

And the princess knew it. "I will beat you if you do not obey!" Kasšaya screamed at her. "I will beat the very flesh from your bones!"

Mara remembered how her mouth grew arid as she protested, "It is a sin to murder or to be a part of a murder." She barely believed she possessed the courage to defy the princess. "I cannot do what you ask me."

Kasšaya brought out her whip. "Murder? You call it murder?" she hissed. "You're a fool, Mara—you and your invisible god. We vanquished your god long ago. We of Babylon vanquished all the gods. We are supreme, and my husband is Marduk's tool to protect our empire and keep us supreme. Go and tell me what you see!" The lash of Kasšaya's whip caught Mara's wrist. She snatched her hand away.

"Why me, mistress?" Mara moaned. "You have dozens of handmaidens of your own, body servants and eunuchs. Why send me?"

Kasšaya came close. "Because," she hissed, "you are chief handmaiden to my son, who will reign after Neriglissar. One day, I may need you to tell him what his parents did on his behalf. Do you understand?

Now—hurry, Mara!" She pushed Mara out into the hallway where the handmaiden stood, trembling, undecided.

Just as she stood now, feeling sick and unsure. A blue mantle swept by her, then stopped and turned. "Mara?" came Daniel's voice. "What is the matter, child?"

Mara smiled wanly at the man. Daniel was aging. His long, flowing hair was threaded through with silver, but his broad shoulders still supported a strong body. And there was nothing old about the snap in his deep, dark eyes.

"Mara?" Daniel asked again. "You are not at the coronation?"

"I am on my way," Mara replied. "I was delayed..."

Daniel smiled. "We'll walk over together. I am curious to compare this coronation with the one we had just two years back, when Amel-Marduk took his father's crown."

Amel-Marduk... at the sound of his name, Mara shivered again.

"You are cold, child?" Daniel scrutinized her face carefully.

"A little," Mara said, taking his still muscular arm. "But it will pass."

The two Judeans hesitated at the entrance of the temple. "Ezekiel would have harangued me for entering, saying it was sinful, a place of abomination," Daniel commented wryly. "In many ways, I miss him, now that he's passed on."

"Uri's friend Ezra would agree with him," Mara said. "We Judeans do not lack for people who tell us how to behave."

Daniel shrugged gracefully. "It's hard to be both Judean and part of the royal circle. Politics and religion have never been comfortable partners."

Mara stepped into the wide temple antechamber. "Except for today, when the priests joyfully crown and anoint the new king and queen."

"Yes. Come, let's hurry."

Because Daniel was recognized by the guards, they were ushered to a place close enough to hear most, but not all, of the priest's words, standing among the representatives of the lesser countries. Closer to the thrones of hammered gold were the royals of the more important nations—Egypt,

Assyria, Chaldea. Fewer had come than were summoned. Mara had over-heard Kasšaya's complaints that Cyrus of Persia was making too many inroads into the Empire, but that at least her strong husband would now be in a position to stop him.

Chief among the celebrants was the Babylonian royal family—Labaši-Marduk, who, despite Mara's care, had wriggled out of his apron of gold, leaving it lying carelessly on the chair behind him, his sisters, arrayed in transparent gowns of white and silver, their foreheads encircled with gem-studded circlets, and his aunt Nitocris, who, daringly, wore a gown of purple as though she were the one being crowned. The Dowager Queen Amytis was still magnificent, wrapped in black silk with a tower-ing headdress of gold leaf. She stood three steps removed from the royal party, her dark attire an unspoken reproach. Neriglissar's accession to the throne meant the end of her influence over the crown.

"She speaks of returning to Media," Daniel whispered to Mara, as the handmaiden's eyes rested on the old queen—queen mother no longer.

"Kasšaya would welcome her departure."

"She mourns Amel-Marduk's death, that is certain," Daniel mur-mured, then turned his head to watch as the priest approached Neriglissar.

Snippets of the coronation ceremony filtered through over the cough-ing, rustling, and whispers of the crowd.

"Marduk in the assembly of gods gave rule and power to Neriglissar," cried one of the priests, passing a crown of gold encrusted with jewels over his head. Someone handed the new king the standard of the armies.

Neriglissar proclaimed, his deep voice reaching every corner of the vast room, "With this standard, I will conquer the enemies of Marduk."

The chair bearers took Neriglissar by the arm and led him to the throne. Standing beside him was Kasšaya, looking beautiful and glowing in a dress of deep purple, her dark hair dressed high on her head, studded with jewels.

Staff bearers ran up, bearing the great seal, which they draped over Neriglissar's shoulders, securing it over his neck with a chain of heavy gold links. It glinted on his broad chest.

"Once, Amel-Marduk pretended to dream of the seal pressing heavily against his chest. I remember thinking how his fabrication actually came to pass the day he was crowned," Daniel commented. "The seal looked overlarge against Amel-Marduk's thin frame, especially after his father bore it so gracefully. It suits Neriglissar better."

The smell of incense wafted through the temple. The priest approached Neriglissar, who was now firmly seated on the throne, his wife beside him.

"O Lord, O King, may you live forever! May you conquer the lands of your enemies! May the king of gods, Marduk, rejoice in you! May Nabu, the scribe of Esagil, make your days long! May Erra…your sword… may you avenge Akkad…"

The priest began mumbling a long litany of the gods and how they needed to be served by the new king. Mara felt her attention wander. She didn't want to look at Bashi, who was slouching in his chair. His sisters poked and prodded him to sit up, and he kicked and hissed at them. Nitocris sat placidly, ignoring the children. Amytis's eyes were fixed on Kasšaya. Mara could see the hate in them.

A stronger smell now, of burning oil and spilled wine, made Mara recall that terrible night, when she had crept into King Amel-Marduk's antechamber. The room was in disarray, half-naked girls lounging on couches, food, oil lamps, and wine cups strewn about.

Amel-Marduk sat in the middle of the confusion, body half slumped into his seat. While he was only Bashi's half-uncle, Mara saw in him what her young charge might become—lazy, dissolute, uncaring, spoiled. Amel-Marduk was not the man his father had been. She'd heard countless stories of how he spent his days drinking, dicing, and fornicating—with women, with boys, and with beasts. He was wont to keep his counselors waiting for hours, kicking their heels in his antechamber, while he dallied in bed or rode out to hunt. Or drank. Of course, if the rumors were true, he tended to drink during the sessions with his advisors as well, keeping a servant with a never-ending flagon of wine constantly by his side.

"Mara," came a voice next to her as she stood, trembling, on the threshold of the king's rooms. "Did you bring it?"

Mara reached with a shaking hand into the bodice of her gown and pulled out the pouch that Kasšaya had draped around her neck on a ribbon. "Here, master," she said. "It's here."

"Good," Neriglissar murmured. "Pour its contents into Amel-Marduk's wine cup. Make sure you are undetected."

"Not me," Mara backed away. "I won't do it, master. It's a sin."

Neriglissar's strong sword arm shot out and grabbed Mara in a painful grip. "A sin? What do you care about that—that—insect over there? He is harming Babylon. He is harming the kingdom. We must restore order and harmony. Do you not see?"

What Mara saw, in Neriglissar's dark eyes, was a glint of madness mixed with iron resolve. "You do it, then," Mara cried. "You're the soldier, the hero. I'm just a lowly slave girl."

Neriglissar pulled her closer to him. "You're the perfect one," he hissed. Mara felt fumes of wine wash over her as he spoke. "No one would suspect you."

"They will kill me if they discover me," Mara moaned.

"I promise they will not. Now"—Neriglissar shoved her—"hurry up. Hurry, Mara."

She inched forward. The king leaned in to throw his dice. His drunken courtiers roared and cheered. The king won the toss.

"What is my prize?" Amel-Marduk shouted, beaming at his small victory. "What did I win?"

"Would you like a girl, a virgin?" Neriglissar cried, pulling Mara up with him. Mara felt her knees buckling under her.

But Amel-Marduk looked at her and sneered. "A handmaiden. She can pour my wine, but I want something more lively in my bed. Here, Antos, run and get me one of those Nubian boys that were just brought in. A young one. And you, girl, pour me more wine."

Mara, her entire body shaking, stepped up to his flagon and poured a brimming cup of wine. Half hiding the cup by turning her body to the wall, she took the pouch from inside her gown and dispensed its contents into the cup with trembling fingers. She closed her eyes and prayed to the Lord God to forgive her. *He is an unworthy ruler, Lord*, she prayed. *Just as Judith gave Holofernes drink and beheaded him to save us from the*

Assyrian general, let my pouring this potion into Amel-Marduk's wine bring Your people a better future.

She put the wine cup down and backed away. The courtiers had all turned to ogle the procession of gleaming Black boys brought forward for the king's pleasure. As he leered at them, quaffing the wine, Amel-Marduk suddenly choked. Neriglissar, watching him with eagle eyes, stepped forward and quickly tipped the cup so that the rest of the contents streamed down Amel-Marduk's throat.

Amel-Marduk sputtered and coughed. Quick as thought, Neriglissar took the cup, with its thick paste of poison and wine lying at its bottom and thrust it into Mara's hands. Mara hid the cup in her gown as Neriglissar placed his own cup down before the king.

"I don't feel well," the king muttered.

"Go now, Mara," Neriglissar prompted her in a harsh whisper. "Dispose of the cup where no one will find it and return to my wife. Hurry, now!" Neriglissar turned to the king. "Your Majesty? Perhaps you have had too much wine? Or not enough?"

"Not enough," Amel-Marduk muttered, his hand at his forehead. "Give me more."

As Mara left the room, the king was drinking from Neriglissar's cup, looking more and more unwell every second. As she reached the end of the corridor, she heard Nitocris' sudden wail, the shouting of the courtiers. Mara dropped the cup into a bronze urn and ran.

A sudden shout of the crowd startled Mara out of her reverie. The newly crowned king was standing before them, arms outstretched, greeting his subjects. She shuddered slightly, then felt Daniel's eyes on her face.

"Are you all right, Mara?" he asked her.

"Of course," she said, evading his searching glance. "I should head back to the palace. They are preparing the feast, and I will need to help the young prince dress. Be well, Daniel. I must hurry now."

PART THREE

Liberation

555 BCE–Year 31 of the Exile

35

Mara and the New King

"What do you see, Mara?" the High King hissed.

"I don't see anything, Your Majesty." Mara looked at the hallway through a crack in the door. "All seems quiet out there."

"This is ridiculous!" Labaši-Marduk exclaimed. "I'm King! I should be ruling from the throne, not hiding in a closet!"

Mara sighed. She knew better than anyone that the newly made boy-king was still only a twelve-year-old child—spoiled, thoughtless, and completely unfit to rule. And she was not the only one who thought so.

The boy's father had died near dawn yesterday morning after suffering for weeks from a putrid infection of the throat. The royal physician recognized the rattle of death when he heard it in the king's clogged chest and called the queen and the court to attend the deathbed. Mara accompanied the young prince.

The room was dark, shaded against the morning light. The king tossed and moaned, struggling on the high mattress, irritably tossing aside his heavy covers. It took only a few hours before Neriglissar took his last breath. Kassaya took his crown from the low marble table where it lay next to the king's side and placed it reverently on Bashi's narrow skull. For a moment, the boy straightened, trying to rise to the occasion. But the moment passed.

"It's heavy," he whined. "Do I have to wear it?"

"We'll make you a lighter one later, darling," his mother soothed. "But bear it for now."

"It's cutting into my forehead," he complained. "And slipping down."

"Mara!" Kassaya called. "Bring something soft that Bashi can wear between the crown and his head."

Mara nodded and slipped away. The mid-morning sunshine streaming through the windows made her blink as she hurried down the marble-tiled hallway. In Bashi's quarters, she entered a back room where his old diapers were stored, along with other remnants of the prince's childhood. As she pulled out a diaper, Mara shook her head ruefully. Little had Nebuchadnezzar thought that the baby whose bottom these soft cloths had swaddled would someday succeed to his throne. He would be horrified, Mara realized, if he knew how heedless and spoiled the boy was.

Mara returned to the hushed deathbed, adjusting the diaper under the crown.

"Is that better, my love?" Kassaya asked.

"It's still heavy," Bashi whined. "What do we do now?"

A small coterie of nobles and priests, including the High Priest of the Ziggurat of Marduk, stood shifting from foot to foot in the back of the king's bedchamber. The High Priest now turned to Kassaya and Bashi and bowed low. "Your Majesties might step into another room while we prepare the body for internment," he suggested.

Belshazzar, chief among Babylonian nobles, powerful for his influence over the military and once Amel-Marduk's most favored courtier, abased himself before the queen mother and her son. "Wise advice," he agreed. "We'll announce the king's death to the populace. Why don't you withdraw to reflect on your loss?"

Kassaya shook her head. "The king, my much beloved husband, may be dead, Belshazzar, and I may wish to weep tears of gall and bitterness. But the king, my much beloved son, must announce his father's passing. The people waiting outside will acclaim him King of Kings. I warn you, do not overreach your position."

Belshazzar shrugged. Mara knew the noble had not wanted Neriglissar to rule as king. Despite Neriglissar's marriage to a princess royal, Belshazzar had disparaged the warrior's common blood. His whispers that Neriglissar was unfit to sit upon Nebuchadnezzar's golden throne had circulated like hissing asps through the court. And the noble clearly had the same reservations about Labaši-Marduk, Neriglissar's son.

Bashi, bored, had removed the crown to play a game with the diaper, wadding it into a ball and throwing it in the air. A sneer flitted across Belshazzar's face before he twisted it into the sickly-sweet smile of the courtier.

"Of course, Your Majesty." He prostrated himself before Kasšaya. "Present the boy to the multitude. It would be my honor to oversee the preparations for the funeral and coronation. I will return before nightfall when the priests bring the body to the temple."

He bowed himself out. Just as he left the room, Bashi griped in a penetrating voice, "Oh, let's get this over with. I'm hungry!"

All that seemed like a lifetime ago. Had it only been yesterday? The rest of the day passed in a blur of ceremony. Bashi's whining grated on everyone's nerves. Kasšaya had to coax him to stand before the shouting, waving subjects who crowded the courtyard for a glimpse of their new ruler. Bashi fidgeted through the long, drawn-out ritual, complete with the incense and prayers required to remove his father's body from the palace and install it in the Great Ziggurat. The climb up the steep steps, lined with wailing professional mourners, seemed to take forever. Before they were a third of the way up the ascent, Bashi called for Mara's arm to support him, and she had to half carry him the rest of the way.

Kasšaya grew increasingly worried when Belshazzar did not return as promised. Bashi sullenly told her he didn't care where Belshazzar was, just so long as he stayed away. Exasperated, Kasšaya sent Bashi off to bed. It was dawn when she came to rouse Mara, the alarm on her face making Mara shiver as she quickly dressed the half-awake young king. As Mara hunted frantically under the bed for the sandals he'd kicked off the night before, the queen mother pulled him aside and whispered urgent instructions in his ear.

Mara let the door of the small chamber slide shut. "Your Majesty, are you certain that your mother intended us to hide here?"

"That's what she said," Bashi muttered. "Go hide, Bashi, and take Mara and some soldiers with you. They'll protect you."

"She's certain Belshazzar intends to dethrone you?" Mara persisted.

"I told you and told you." Bashi shook his head, rolling his eyes toward the low ceiling of the cramped closet. "Stop acting like a dolt. When Belshazzar left, Mother sent a spy to follow him. He went straight to the army barracks and talked to some generals. They all want some noble—I forget his name—to take the throne. They don't want me. Mother says maybe they'll try to kill me. But they won't, not with you here, isn't that so, Mara?"

He's a foolish child, Mara thought, heart beating a frightened tattoo. *All those tutors, all that training, and this is what we raised. What my poisoning Amel-Marduk has brought us to.*

"Isn't that so, Mara?" A look of fear crossed Bashi's face when the handmaiden didn't immediately reassure him.

"Of course," Mara calmed him. "Hush, Bashi. Your mother will take care of everything."

"And then I'll cut off their heads." The boy laughed, making a chopping motion with one gleeful hand. "That will teach them!"

They waited in the small chamber for more than an hour. Bashi grew restive. Mara's head drooped and she nearly drifted off. But then she heard them.

The sound of soldiers' boots marching on the marble floors.

Mara grabbed Bashi's hand. The three soldiers who were there to protect them hesitated, then pulled swords from ornate scabbards. *Palace guards*, Mara thought. Not battle trained. Second-born sons whose noble fathers purchased a place where they could dress up and eat in the mess tent every day.

Not the type of soldiers you'd want to defend you against trained troops.

The footsteps drew nearer. Bashi, frightened now, cowered against Mara's chest. She wrapped her arms around him, praying silently to the Most High to be delivered from death.

"Where are they hiding, you bitch?" snarled a woman's deep, distinctive voice.

"It's Aunt Nitocris!" Bashi hissed.

Nitocris...Amel-Marduk's sister, Nebuchadnezzar's and Amytis's daughter, widow of the courtier, Nergal-sharezer. Half-sister to Kassaya. There was no love lost between the two. Nitocris had never forgiven Kassaya for Amel-Marduk's death, accusing the royal couple of foul play in whispers that echoed maliciously through the court's marble corridors. Neriglissar had ignored Belshazzar's insidious taunts, realizing the courtier was too powerful to confront. But he was not the man to put up with dangerous gossip from a mere woman. So he banished Nitocris to Haran, a city far to the north. When had she returned to Babylon? And what had she to do with the plot to dethrone young Labaši-Marduk?

"Let go of my arm," cried Kassaya. "You will all pay for this... this...!"

"Where are they? Don't think I won't kill you, Kassaya. I'm itching to plunge my dagger into your heart," Nitocris growled. "It's no more than you did for my brother, eh?"

"What is she talking about?" Bashi murmured, frightened eyes raking Mara's face.

Mara shook her head, a cold shudder moving up her spine. After all her years of service to the royal family, she was going to be killed for a brat of a boy king. Her thoughts flew to her family. Her poor father, mercifully dead now. Her mother, growing older on the farm. Mother would weep for her. No one else, though. *What a waste my life has been*, Mara thought, cradling the frightened boy close to her heart because it was all she could do. *What a waste*.

"Stop!" Kassaya cried, pain radiating through her frightened tones. "Let me go!"

Bashi straightened, gently moving out of the shelter of Mara's arms. Mara saw the resolve in the boy's eyes, saw the man he might have become, had he not been pampered his entire life. *That too*, she thought sadly, *had all been a waste*.

Bashi reached past Mara and turned the handle of the door.

"Bashi!" hissed Mara, aghast. "Don't!"

"They'll kill her if I don't," he said, and pushed the door open.

After so long in the dank closet, Mara's eyes were blinded by the flaming torches the lead soldiers held. She blinked, and the scene before her flew into focus. Too many soldiers to count stood in straight rows behind the two women. Kassaya's black robes of mourning had been torn from her shoulders and several of the gems sewn to the gown dangled precariously. Tear stains smudged her heavy cosmetics, looking as if rivers of black ran down her cheeks.

In sharp contrast, Nitocris stood tall and proud in a gown of purple and green, a diadem twinkling on her forehead, face flawless, mouth drawn into a pitiless sneer of disdain. Mara realized there was not an ounce of pity anywhere in her bearing or her face. And her eyes! Mara shuddered as she stared into the depths of hatred simmering in Nitocris's eyes.

They all froze as the young boy-king emerged from the closet, Mara creeping out behind him.

"Who calls for Labaši-Marduk?" he cried, shoulders straight and head held high. "Unhand the queen mother and bow in obedience to me, your High King, or I'll have you killed like the dogs you are."

There was a moment, just one, when Mara thought the boy's unexpected dignity might prevail. But then Nitocris threw back her head and laughed, breaking the spell.

"Stand your ground," she ordered the soldiers, men bronzed and muscular. Battled-trained troops. Very different from the palace guards who cowered in the back of the closet.

Nitocris continued, "My new husband, Nabonidus, is High King, acclaimed by the nobles of the court and the priests of the Ziggurat. They have judged this pathetic boy unfit to rule."

For a moment, the only sound was of strained and heavy breathing. Labaši-Marduk and Kassaya slumped, growing small at Nitocris's contemptuous stare.

Then Nitocris commanded the unthinkable. "Kill them both."

In an instant, swords flashed out. The first two soldiers moved swiftly forward.

"No!" Kassaya cried out.

"Mara!" Bashi yelled, reaching out his arms for her.

Mara was rooted to the ground. In horror, she watched as the two royals were skewered on razor-sharp blades. A rasping gasp was torn from Kassaya's throat, a heart-wrenching groan from Bashi. The metal glinted blindingly as it drove into their bodies. Mara screamed. The tip of a blade pushed through Bashi's back. His eyes rolled up into his head. The guards, grunting, withdrew their swords. The two bodies wilted against the wall and collapsed to the floor with a heavy thud, fresh blood leaving a viscous trail on the marble walls.

Mara shrieked again, then clapped a hand to her mouth. She waited, heart pounding painfully. A second passed, then two. A sharp command, and the soldiers turned briskly and marched off, leaving one guard behind to accompany the new queen.

Mara crouched, sadly touching the rapidly cooling bodies of the dead queen and her son. Tears leaked from her painted eyes, rolling down her cheeks. She was free, she suddenly realized, nearly prostrate from conflicting emotions. Devastated at the death of her heedless young charge, for—despite everything—she had loved him. But joy flooded her mourning heart as she realized that, after all these years, she could return home. Too late for a husband or children, she could be maiden aunt to her nieces and nephews, help her aging mother, weed the vegetable garden once more. Free.

She rose, trying to keep the giddy expression of release from her face, feeling the thoughtful eyes of the new queen upon her.

"Mara…." Nitocris said slowly, looking her up and down, the bangles on her arms jangling imperiously. "You've been with my sister since her son was born, have you not?"

Mara bowed her head in trembling assent.

"A favorite of Kassaya's. It will please me to have you serve me. Come."

"Your Majesty," Mara whispered, her voice breaking as the clang of prison gates swung shut in her heart once more. "Could I not just…go home?"

Nitocris ignored her, strolling leisurely down the long marble corridor, gown trailing majestically on the marble tiles. After a long moment, Mara lifted one foot and then the other, following in the wake of her new mistress.

36

Chava and the Ziggurat

552 BCE–Year 34 of the Exile

When Chava was young, she and Grandmother Sarah sometimes drove the donkey cart into that most magical of cities, Babylon. Then her grandmother would take her by the hand and walk with her to the Great Ziggurat.

"There, darling," Grandmother would say, pointing with a wrinkled hand to the tremendous triangular edifice, its enormous steps swarming with priests and worshippers come to sacrifice to Marduk, "that is where the Babylonians tried to build a tower to the heavens and challenge God."

Grandmother Sarah brought lunch with them, for she refused to eat food sold by street hawkers. Chava longed to sample the spicy minced lamb patties or pastries drenched in pistachio shavings and honey, sold from small booths. But the comfort of Grandmother's familiar flat bread and dried fish, dates, and sweet soft cheese, helped her walk resolutely past. They'd find a bench by the river and sit to eat, enjoying the cool breeze that flowed up from the rushing green water.

In all the great city of Babylon, Chava would think, only Grandmother and I have time to sit and do nothing in the middle of the day.

Chava knew such leisure would not last long. She was nearly five now, the youngest in a family rich in children and poor in land. Her mother, Mirav, already wanted to hire her brothers out. Her father, Nachum, refused to allow it. If Mirav had her way, all but her older brother, Joshua, would be apprenticed during Zag-mu, the Festival of the New Year. Chava would hear her father and mother arguing about it at night, long after she was curled into the warm cot she shared with Grandmother.

"We cannot feed all these mouths on the barley you harvest," Mother complained. "I have tightened the cord about my waist so often, the two sides meet around my middle."

"A man should have his sons and daughters grow up around him," retorted Father.

"A man should have flocks of sheep and goats, a milk cow, and long acres of fields sown with wheat and fruit trees, not just a few hectares growing barley," Mother snapped back.

"When my father received this land, he was instructed to grow barley," Father said. "If we grew something else, the master would take the land from us. How would we eat then?"

Chava pictured her mother throwing her hands wide open to heaven, her sharp outthrust chin making her father wince. "You know there are other ways for the children to earn their living." Sarcasm dripped from her like fat from a spit.

Father would turn away. "I am still master of this house," he'd declare, walking out into the balmy night.

"A poor one," Mirav would yell at his back.

The little girl wasn't upset by their shouting. All her life, Mother had wanted more than she was given. Chava's brothers were happy enough to put their spoons down half-fed, as long as they could gather around Uncle Uri when he visited, to hear the stories he had inscribed that day. But sometimes, when the nightly argument went on too long, chilling the warmth of the room, Grandmother would reach out a quavering hand and caress Chava's soft brown hair in the moonlight.

"It's nothing, darling," she would murmur. "Just your parents' way."

Chava knew that, but she would sigh and sigh again, so Grandmother's comforting hand continued to rub her head, lulling her to sleep. Often after such a disturbed night, Grandmother would take her to the Ziggurat, or to old Queen Amytis's gardens, a series of terraces creating an artificial mountain of beautiful flowerbeds, fountains of spilling water, and towering trees. Grandmother would tell her how Uncle Uri's father, a musician who'd lived at the time of Queen Amytis and King Nebuchadnezzar, would play in the gardens, flanked by the lush plantings.

"What happened to him?" Chava asked once.

Her grandmother's eyes clouded over in memory. "He died, darling. A sad death." Sarah shook herself, patting her granddaughter's head. "But he was a kind man, a good man. He and your grandfather and I all walked many miles together, in the wake of the captain's wagons, all the way from Judea to Babylon."

Chava would snuggle against her grandmother, content. It was a game she played with herself: How long before Grandmother mentioned the magic word? Judea....

"What was Judea like?" she then allowed herself to ask. "What was our home like?"

Sarah would gaze at the azure depths of the flowing Euphrates River and sigh. "You can't possibly want to hear this again child," she'd protest.

But the half smile on her face was all the permission Chava needed. "Oh, yes, Grandmama. Tell me about the farm and the city of Jerusalem and the Temple and everything."

So in the shadow of the Great Ziggurat of Babylon or shaded by the green terraces of the Hanging Gardens, seated by the mighty river that cut the city into two, Sarah would keep the memories alive for her granddaughter. It was Chava's favorite childhood tale—better than the tower that men built to touch the face of God, better even than Uncle Uri's stories of the Creation and the Flood, the brutal enslavement of the Hebrews by the Egyptians, or the tales of the Judges and the great and conquering kings. There by the banks of the river, Sarah would tell Chava the story of a home the little girl thought she would never see.

37

The Queen of Heaven Cakes

548 BCE–Year 38 of the Exile

ZAKITI PUSHED THE STRANDS OF hair that had escaped her gold pins off her damp forehead. "I don't understand why we couldn't have done this at my house," she complained. "It would have been so much cooler."

Her sister-in-law, Mirav, blew on the fire, crouching over it as if to protect it from the whip of the hot desert wind that blew through every crack and crevice of the little farmhouse. "Because we're teaching my daughter this time, not yours," she said. "She doesn't have the luxury of a house with a courtyard and servants to stoke the fire. She'll have to do it here."

Zakiti shrugged. "I don't see what difference that makes."

Mirav ignored her, turning to the little girl who hovered nearby. "Chava," she said, raising her head and dabbing at the line of sand that had settled in the corners of her mouth. "Go fetch more sticks."

Zakiti stood at the open doorway and watched as Chava ran off, clearly only too glad to escape the scorch of the baking stones. They had heated for several hours now, glowing red in the hazy, hot summer heat. But then Zakiti turned back to the kitchen, evading the swirling wind that moved like a malevolent being, reaching into mouth, ears, and nostrils and choking them with thick desert dust. The heat was bad enough, but it was preferable to the wind and dust.

Chava returned, having wrapped branches from the fig tree in her skirts to avoid touching the milky bark that would make her skin itch. She let them drop, rubbing her eyes. "It's too windy out there, and the wasps are bad today," she said. "I thought they were going to sting me."

"Fig sticks don't burn well," Zakiti said, sighing. But she stuck them into the fire anyway.

The baking stones made the little brick house radiate with heat. Chava, a trickle of sweat dripping down her neck, asked if she could go back outside. But the stones were ready and so was the batter.

"Watch me pour them out in a crescent shape," Zakiti instructed Chava, picking up the bowl containing a thin mixture of honey, crushed barley flour, water, and eggs. "There's no milk to spare, Mirav?"

Mirav shrugged, mopping her wet brow with a cloth. "Not in this heat."

Yet another reason why Zakiti's house would have been the better choice that morning. But she bit back the comment. "Well, the Queen of Heaven must accept our poor portion," she said, pouring the batter directly onto the flat rock. The batter spit and simmered.

"How do you do that?" the little girl wondered, her eyes wide.

Zakiti smiled. She was proud of her skill in creating the mystical crescent shape. As soon as the cake began to bake, she took a peeled stick and carved the lush image of a woman into the thickening batter.

"She certainly looks fertile enough," Mirav commented, nodding approvingly.

"When will I look like that?" Chava pointed to her flat chest. "Like my cousins?"

The women laughed. "When you're a little older than seven," Mirav told her daughter. "I promise, in a few years from now the Goddess will give you a woman's curves. When you're ready to have children of your own."

Zakiti invoked part of the prayer as she completed the drawing. "Let the favor of thine eyes be upon me, oh Ishtar. With thy bright features, look faithfully upon me. Drive away the evil spells of my body and let me see thy bright light." She flipped the cake over to bake on the other side.

"You said Ishtar," Chava said, watching as the cake puffed around the shape etched into it. "Is Ishtar the Goddess of Heaven?"

"She has many names. We Judeans call her Asherah," Mirav explained. "It's your aunt who calls her Ishtar because that's what they call her here in Babylon. But she's a secret for women only. Don't tell your father."

The little girl nodded and Zakiti handed her the bowl of batter. "Your turn now."

Chava moved toward the hearth, tipping some batter onto the stone in the space Zakiti had left her. As she poured, Uri and Nachum burst into the room, agitated and grim-faced, startling them. Chava splattered the batter onto the floor.

"What have I told you, Mirav?" Nachum bellowed. "How dare you disobey me?"

Uri pushed past him. With a quick sweep of his hand, he brushed Zakiti's nearly baked Queen of Heaven cake onto the dirt floor, grinding it into the ground with his sandaled foot until nothing was left but crumbs.

"How dare you!" Mirav screeched. "It took us all morning to get the stones hot enough."

"And what did I tell you last time about these cakes?" Nachum yelled just as loudly. "Zakiti has an excuse, perhaps—the customs of her youth mislead her. But you, Mirav, daughter of Judea—you should know better. You disgrace us by baking in sacrifice to your false Goddess!"

Zakiti glared at him. False goddess, indeed!

Mirav put her hands on her hips. "My mother back in Judea made Goddess cakes! My father always laughed at her, but he ate more of them than anyone. And we live in Babylon now, not Judea. Why shouldn't I sacrifice to the Goddess?"

Nachum opened his mouth, but fury seemed to rob him of words. Zakiti saw the pulse dancing in his jaw and stepped back, out of reach. The air crackled with more than desert dust. Then Uri stepped between the couple.

As always, her husband barely spoke above a whisper and as always, everyone leaned forward to hear his every word. "Yes, the women of Judea worshipped the Goddess. Only this morning at the Academy of Sages, we spoke about the prophet Jeremiah, may his memory be blessed. Jeremiah said such practices angered God. It is why God broke his covenant with us. Let us pray that, like Noah's journey on the ark, God's anger lasts only a short time. But if we wish for a Return to our homeland, we must vigilantly avoid practices such as Goddess sacrifice."

Zakiti, face already hot from the blaze of the fire, felt herself flush with indignant fury. "You speak of Noah, but you mean Atrahasis, husband. Atrahasis, who dismantled his house to build an ark and survived the rain that flooded the world. I told you the story long before you ever wrote about this Noah. You jumbled the facts, making your own tale from them. You say your invisible God wanted to punish man's sins by the deluge. But it was just Enlil and Enki, gods of sky, wind, and water, who commanded the rains, flooding the world because it was overcrowded!"

Uri shook his head. Keeping his voice low and calm, he replied, "You told me about Atrahasis, yes, but that's just a fable, told to amuse ignorant men at the campfire after they sacrifice to their pagan gods. God told Moses our history at Mount Sinai, a history I am privileged to write, despite any sins," here Uri looked up and down Zakiti's body, making her cross her arms across her chest, "I have committed. When I forbid you to sacrifice to false gods in our home, that did not mean you should pollute my brother's house with impious acts."

Zakiti ducked her head to conceal her intense anger. How dare these Judeans—defeated and exiled—call her gods false and her acts impious! But she knew better than to say so.

Uri took her gently by the elbow. "We will leave now."

Mirav stepped in his path. She, like Uri, spoke quietly, but her voice carried a frisson of menace. Zakiti knew her sister-in-law was most dangerous when she doled out her words one by one. "Your wife came here by my invitation, brother-in-law. I wanted my daughter to learn from her, just as I learned to make Queen of Heaven cakes from my mother and grandmother. We need our own power in the heavens to care about the things that matter to us—raising our children and keeping them from harm, protecting the land from war, famine, and pestilence."

Uri's head tilted to one side, considering Mirav's arguments. "Jeremiah himself could not sway the minds of the people and could not persuade them not to bake their cakes. Like you, sister, they protested that they would always sacrifice to the Queen of Heaven. They pledged themselves to continue to pour drinks to the goddess and burn incense to her—all because their mothers and grandmothers had taught them to do so.

"But heed my words, little Chava," here Uri turned toward the girl, who furrowed her brow as if trying to make sense of all the confusing, grown-up arguments, "anyone who tells you to sacrifice to a false god is wrong. They are things of stick and stone, made in a potter's kiln—not alive, not divine. They cannot change the wind or rain, make the crops grow tall or heal the sick. Only the one true God can do these things. Do you understand?"

Obedient girl that she was, Chava nodded.

Zakiti seethed inside, watching.

"Good girl." Uri nodded at the heavy mud pottery bowl the child still clutched to her chest. "Throw that batter out. No one will eat food prepared for a false goddess in this house." He took Zakiti's elbow again. "Come, wife. We'll head home now."

Zakiti loved Uri, but sometimes he was insufferable. She yanked her arm away and stalked out of the house.

38

Amittai and the Clash
of Cooking Hearths

AMITTAI SAT AT THE KITCHEN table with a heavy heart. The day was ending, the sky etched in orange and pink clouds. Ophir washed at the well just outside the open back door, preparing himself for the sacrifice. Ophir's Amorite wife, Tobija, face excited and flushed, bustled about the hearth, preparing food for her two toddlers. Ophir came in, hair still damp and broad chest exposed through his tunic's open lacing.

"It upsets your mother when you go to the altars of Moloch." Amittai's voice held the weary quality of someone who'd spoken the same words many times before.

"Mother knew you attended the sacrifice," Ophir replied quietly. "She still married you. She will not cease to love me because I honor my wife's rites."

"I carry my shame with me—shame I witnessed the death of those innocent children, shame I partook of the temple whores." Amittai lowered his voice so the children playing in the corner would not hear him. "I would prevent you from bearing such a burden."

"Hanun wants me there tonight," Ophir said. "He told me so."

At the sound of Hanun's name, a look of disgust flitted across Amittai's face. "Your mother says they spit at her in the marketplace whenever your father-in-law returns from his raids. They accuse us of hiding the coins he bullies out of the poor families of Judea. It is sinful that you heed that man."

"I didn't ask to be married into his family," Ophir shot back. "That was your doing, not mine."

Amittai's shoulders slumped. "I had no choice. You might find that hard to believe...."

Tobija, pretending she was not listening, timidly sidled over to her husband and father-in-law. "The children's dinner is almost ready, Ophir. Will you let your mother know I will be done with the cooking hearth soon?"

After months of trying to master the complexities of a ritually pure Judean kitchen, Tobija asked Keren if she could use part of the larder and a corner of the hearth as her own. There, she prepared the food of her childhood—lamb boiled in its mother's milk, a mixture of pig lard, flesh, and gruel laid out in sizzling pancakes before the excited children, and, on rare occasions when Hanun's travels took him to the shore, sea creatures such as snails and shrimp.

Ophir, who could not stomach his wife's cooking, still ate at his mother's table. Several times Keren suggested she could cook for the entire family, but Tobija refused.

"I want my children to eat the food of my childhood, and my father to be served the meals he loves when he comes to visit," she insisted.

Keren, her usually smiling face shadowed by frustration, merely stipulated that the smells of forbidden cooking be dissipated before she prepared meals for her husband and son. So Tobija cooked with the door propped wide, summer and winter.

Hanun had not visited Jerusalem for months. Amittai heard he was busy raiding the countryside. Battles between the upstart Persians and their enemies preoccupied the Babylonian overlords. Any order the Chaldeans might have once imposed on the captive country had long ago eroded. Now neighbor fought with neighbor, and the Judeans were beleaguered as Edomite, Amorite, and Philistine marauders insisted on taking their land, crops, or some other form of tribute.

But Amittai and his family were safe. Hanun was respected among the foreign marauders, and the family's property remained intact while

Amittai's neighbors were robbed, their lands torched. Keren wept that the women in the marketplace turned their faces from her. Amittai was forced to sell his crop to the Chaldeans, as Judean traders found excuse after excuse to avoid dealing with him.

Amittai rose, not wanting to watch his grandchildren gleefully spooning down meat shards prepared in a milk sauce. He found his wife sitting outside by the well.

"Father says that Cyrus is fighting Croesus, King of Lydia, in Sardinia," Keren said. "Is Lydia close to Babylon, husband?"

"I believe so." Amittai put an arm around his wife. "But why should you care?"

Keren snuggled into his shoulder. "Cyrus released the captives of Ecbatana when he conquered the Median capital," she mused. "I wonder if he will free the Judean exiles if he conquers Babylon."

"Cyrus may have succeeded thus far," Amittai admitted, "but do you really think anyone's going to vanquish Babylon?"

Keren shrugged. "Where are the mighty Assyrians today, husband? My great-grandfather once talked of them as we talk of the Babylonians—as if they were invincible. But they weren't."

Amittai looked over his fields. A stubborn wafer of sun, lingering just at the horizon, spread a golden haze in the rich, blue twilight. "You dream of a Return, wife?" He pulled her closer into the crook of his arm. "What would become of us if the original owners of this farm were to come home?"

Keren shrugged. "They were forced out two generations ago. Whoever used to live here is probably dead. And why would they reclaim this land? We are Judeans—we have rights, too."

"It's a right your father stole," Amittai reminded her.

Keren pulled away. "Don't say that. Father bought this land for us fairly and honestly!"

Amittai was careful not to let amusement appear on his face. If Keren had a fault, it was her unswerving loyalty to her father. Well, it wasn't a bad trait. He wished Ophir had it.

One of Ophir's little ones, a smudge of milk on his left cheek, ran up to them. "Grammy, Grammy, you can go eat now, Momma says," he crowed, crawling into his grandfather's lap.

Keren rose. "I'll go make our dinner."

Amittai sat with the bouncing toddler on his lap for a long while, singing a shepherd's song to him. The little one's eyes began to sag. Amittai carried him into his mother, whom he found in the interior courtyard. Tobija took the child and held him close, murmuring a wordless lullaby as she kissed the top of his head. *She is a good mother,* Amittai thought. *If only she were a Judean woman....*

"Your father is back in Jerusalem?" Amittai asked, keeping his voice low.

Tobija cradled her son closer. "He returned last week. I hope he will come soon to visit the children. Ophir and I will see him tonight at the sacrifice."

"Your father is always welcome," Amittai said, not caring that irony frosted his words. "As he knows."

Tobija hunched over her son. *She is a sensitive girl,* Amittai reflected, *easily bruised.* Usually he tried not to upset her. But tonight, Keren's question had made him curious.

"Our neighbors say that your father was recently in the north. Perhaps he has word about the battles Cyrus of Persia is waging."

Tobija just stared. She was not like Keren. If she had only felt accepted, Tobija would have been happy in the sheltered cocoon of the farm, her husband and children her only concerns. Battles waged outside her gates did not interest her.

"I will go put the boy down and we will go." She left the courtyard.

Ophir entered a few seconds later. He was dressed in a soft, white tunic, slashed with blue trimmings. It was new and, at a glance, Amittai recognized it must be a gift from Hanun. His eyes slanted and he turned from his son.

The smell wafting from the hearth made Amittai's stomach growl. He would prefer to eat as soon as he came in from the fields. But the children had to be fed first. Tobija might well have fed them before sunset. But they always clamored to play with their father when he came home. Ophir and Tobija loved those few minutes when the little ones would clamber about their father's knees. He carried them around the yard, bumping and jostling them, throwing them high into the air as they giggled.

Amittai looked at his wife. Keren's eyes were glittering, her mouth screwed tight. "One of the children dumped their food on the floor tonight, and Tobija missed a spot on the table leg when she cleaned it up." Keren spoke through a clenched jaw. "I had to boil water to purify everything again."

"She probably didn't see it," Amittai soothed her. "She tries so hard to leave everything spotless."

"You may be right," Keren snapped, "but accident or not, it fouls my table."

Ophir walked in. "Is dinner ready, Mother? We need to hurry."

Keren stood still, closed her eyes, and breathed heavily in and out. She opened her eyes, and her face was distorted by a wide, false smile. "Just a moment," she said.

"Your mother had to clean..." Amittai started.

But Keren whirled on him. "No matter!"

Moving swiftly, she loaded the wood platters with a stew of lamb, small potatoes, and carrots, laying thick slices of barley bread on top. They sat, mouthed the prayers of thanksgiving for the meal, and ate.

"We have to work on the back fields tomorrow, Father," Ophir said, breaking the silence as he dipped his bread into the drippings of savory stew. "I'm worried about the coming storm."

"Yes," Amittai agreed. "If the seers in Jerusalem are right, the rainy season will start early and be long and wet. We need to get the crop in as soon as we can."

"If we need to hire extra farmhands..." Ophir let the sentence trail off.

Amittai shook his head. "Hanun's men are busy elsewhere. This year, I'll hire some of the farmers whose crop was ruined by raiders."

"But Father..." Ophir, seeing his father frown, ducked his head and hastily sopped up the rest of the juices with his last remaining crust of barley bread. "A good meal, Mother, thank you." He dropped a kiss on the top of her forehead, leaving the kitchen.

"Won't Hanun want you to hire his men this year?" Keren carried the empty bowls away.

"He'll be disappointed for once. He won't hurt his daughter's crop. I think we'll be safe enough if we help our neighbors." Amittai sat back, feeling satisfied both by the meal and his decision.

A clatter of falling dishes startled him. Amittai turned his head. Keren was staring at a spot on the section of the hearth where she prepared the meals. Her eyes focused on a small puddle of hardened milk sauce.

"We're leaving now!" came Ophir's voice. They heard the front gate open and close. The voices of the young couple drifted up through the open door and then faded.

Amittai rose but the sound of his wife's tears stopped him. "He commits sin every time he watches that abomination," she sobbed. "And someday they'll take the children, and the entire family will be lost to us. Lost to God."

Amittai approached her, wanting to fold her in his arms, but Keren pushed him away. "And you! You did even worse. You not only watched them kill innocent children, you partook of their whores! Drank their wine! Oh, I wish I had never married you! Like father, like son!"

She ran, weeping, from the kitchen. Amittai looked helplessly at the mess of wooden plates on the dirt floor at his feet. He knew better than to touch them. But it seemed like he should be able to do something to restore order and harmony to his home.

He walked outside, into the deepening night. By the light of the rising moon, he circled the farmhouse. There, on the south side, where the fields lay fallow this year, might be a spot. He took a long stick and dragged it behind him in the dirt. If he opened a door in the back side of the house, and made a small, second room with a cooking hearth....

Hanun and his men would supply him with the wood and stone he would need. He would close his eyes to where the supplies came from. They would build the room while he hired Judeans to work with him in the fields. And in this way, perhaps—for the shortest of times—he might earn a moment's respite.

39

Chava at the Academy

CHAVA LIKED NOTHING BETTER THAN bringing Uncle Uri his lunch at the Academy of Sages.

Chava's three cousins, Asnat, Irit, and Atara, once loved to visit their father too. But it was considered immodest for a girl older than twelve to appear at the academy, where wise men contemplated the wisdom of the ages. Over the years, the academy had transformed itself from a modest brick building into a beautiful, widespread complex of buildings clustered around a tall marble fountain, set among green bushes and statuesque date palms. Spacious columned rooms housed debates and lively lessons. In smaller chambers, men and boys quietly contemplated the Torah and the Writings. In these buildings, Israel and Judea's displaced priests and scholars met as Moses of Egypt had commanded, in a High Court of the Hebrew people. A vast amphitheater nestled like an upturned giant hand behind the buildings. On calm, starry nights, sages gathered on stepped seats to hear lectures by one of their number.

Chava loved walking down the wide corridors to the room where the scribes worked. As she passed, a straw basket swinging on her arm, she would peek at the boys whose heads bowed over clay tablets and scrolls. Teachers coached the younger boys through their lessons. In other rooms, elders would argue over what should be included in the Writings—were the words the work of God or man? Did they belong collected with the sacred texts?

Uncle Uri always put down his stylus when she arrived, grabbing her by the elbows and swinging her around the room. "This is my exquisite niece, Chava," he said, introducing her every single time. "Isn't she just a little rose of Judea?"

Then he dipped into the basket and brought out the sweet Aunt Zakiti packed for dessert. "I have a toothache again today, child," he confided in a loud, carrying whisper. "You'll have to eat my cake as well as your own."

After they ate the rich food, Uncle Uri took Chava by the hand and led her to the garden. There, seated on a smooth stone bench next to a side fountain, he stretched and yawned, sometimes even pretending to fall asleep.

"You can't sleep here!" Chava told him, half-giggling, half-horrified at the thought.

"But I'm so sleepy after all that food," he teased her. "I worked hard on a special story today. Do you want to hear it?"

Chava wiggled ecstatically in her seat, nodding that yes, she wanted to hear it. Uri launched into his tale. Like magic, an audience of boys settled around them. Generally it was just a class or two, but some days the entire lower school gathered to hear the scribe Uri tell them a lunch-time story.

This day, Uri told them about King Solomon and the bee. Chava noticed Uncle Uri's fellow scribe, Ezra, leaning against a date palm, watching. The courtyard was crowded with young boys. They fidgeted, jabbed one other with their elbows, threw pebbles, and shouted.

Uncle Uri said to Chava, "I can't hear myself think, never mind tell you a story. We'll have to wait."

"Oh, no," Chava replied, stopping her giggles with an effort. "Just whisper in my ear."

"But then we couldn't hear it," complained one boy, who sat so close to them that his knees touched Chava's dangling feet.

"It's too noisy to tell a story." Uri shook his head. "I'll come to the farm and tell it to you tonight, Chava."

But a chorus of hisses was followed by the boys settling their bottoms more firmly into the ground and sitting upright, quiet and expectant.

"See," said the eager boy, "we're ready."

Uri told them how the Queen of Sheba, to fool the great and wise King Solomon, challenged him to find a real flower among manufactured ones. A bee who owed the great king a favor after stinging his nose, buzzed into each one, discovering the real flower by its sweet nectar.

The boys filed back to their classrooms, talking excitedly about King Solomon the Wise.

"I must return to my labors as well, little Chava." Uncle Uri handed her the empty basket. They walked past the date palm where Ezra stood. Uncle Uri stopped short, one eyebrow raised in wonder. "I didn't think you'd listen to the entire children's tale," he commented.

"They settled down to listen, didn't they? Even though they were ill behaved to begin with," Ezra mused. "I wonder if that also would work on their parents?"

"A good story, I find, holds most people's attention for as long as you tell it and for just as long again," Uri said. "Wouldn't you agree, little Chava?"

Chava nodded. Years later Chava would remember this conversation in the serene gardens of the academy. But right now, she thought Ezra was just being his usual prickly self.

"An idea worth remembering." Ezra turned away.

Uncle Uri kissed Chava on the forehead and followed his fellow scribe.

All the way home, Chava looked for bees hunting out the nectar of the flowers. Solomon, she thought, had made a particularly wise choice of friend.

40

The Price of Freedom

547 BCE–Year 39 of the Exile

"THERE SHOULD BE ENOUGH HERE," Uri told Mara as he handed her a heavy leather pouch filled with coins.

They sat in Queen Nitocris's water garden—a green space of man-made waterfalls, limpid pools, and gravel-bottomed rivers. A canopy of lush trees shaded them from the noonday sun. The half brother and sister, grown past the age of easy affection, shared little more than the claim of blood. Uri wore the modest dress of a Judean scribe, ritual fringes dangling outside his coarsely made gown. Mara was arrayed in a thin dress of pale-yellow layers, her still-narrow waist encircled by a leaf-green girdle, her still luxuriant hair dressed high on her head with brass combs. Uri noticed how the artifice of cosmetics softened her aging face. Kohl shadowed Mara's eyes, and a bright green powder was pressed into her eyelids.

Mara took the leather satchel, hefting it to feel its weight. She let it drop. "You couldn't afford this alone."

Uri looked at her, curious at the note of constraint in her voice. But then he laughed, shrugging. "Not on a scribe's salary, you mean? Of course not. But Zakiti's father is generous. My portion came from a gift he gave us during the Lubuštu holiday."

"And the rest?" Mara asked, poking a finger into the sack, nudging the coins so they clanked against one another.

"Rahil was happy to pay her part."

"She's never come to visit," Mara said. "During all these years, not once."

"You know Rahil," Uri shrugged. "Lucky for us she married well. She would not have made a good wife for a poor man. Our sister prospers as the wife of a rich Babylonian merchant, the first among his three wives. He told me last night he's opening a new shop in Haran, close by the Temple of Sin."

"Yes," Mara said, head bent as she rummaged through the coins. "Nabonidus wants to move back there to serve the god Sin. Nitocris is still deciding if she will go with him or stay here to help her adopted stepson, the young Belshazzar, rule as regent in his stead."

"It's hard to believe Nabonidus would leave Babylon just as Cyrus threatens the kingdom," Uri mused. "None of us in the Academy of Sages know what to make of him."

"He's no Nebuchadnezzar or Neriglissar." Mara nodded. "He longs for the simpler life he led before he became king. Most of his days are spent with the priests and astrologers of the Temple of Sin. He says his work on the life force of the world—the mystic combination of Sin, the goddess Ishtar, and his son, Shamash—is more important than defending the gates of Babylon."

"It pains me to hear how unbelievers waste their energies and lives pursuing false paths toward enlightenment," Uri mused.

Mara looked up, her expression sour. "You sound like a wise old man," she said. "All pompous self-assurance, all-knowing about God's intentions."

"Mara?" Uri was startled by the bitter edge to his half-sister's voice. "Have you lost your belief in the Most High?"

Mara's chuckle was thin and humorless. "I have witnessed murder and helped to murder. I have been partner to waste and selfishness my entire life." She paused, her gaze glancing off her bare shoulder. "I may appear immodest, but nothing but a withered stranger stares back at me when I look into my glass."

She thrust the pouch at Uri. "Take your money, save it for your children's futures. Nitocris will never permit me to purchase my freedom."

"She mistreats you?" Uri looked down at the coins but didn't reach for them. Mara left his question unanswered for a moment. He did not want to press her.

Mara tossed the bag into Uri's lap. He caught it so the coins would not scatter, placing it firmly on the marble bench between them.

"No more than most and less than some." Mara shrugged, finally answering. "I have learned to placate her. And I am used to whippings."

Uri pushed the bag at her. "Please, Mara. I will go see the chamberlain if you won't. It is our dearest wish—Mother's, Rahil's, Nachum's, and mine—that you be freed."

"Nachum?" Mara sounded surprised. "Nachum couldn't afford to contribute...."

"But he did!" Uri protested. "It wasn't much, but he put in what he could."

"Mother is well?" Mara asked. "She hasn't been to visit in many weeks. I worry about her."

A shadow passed Uri's face. "She finds it hard to walk long distances now," he admitted. "But she is still healthy and strong of heart, God be praised."

"It's hard to believe she's all that's left."

"It's God's way. Our parents pass on, and we must strive to become what they were."

"I don't think anyone could become another Sarah," Mara said. "She was—is—special."

"There is only one Sarah," Uri agreed.

An awkward silence lengthened between the siblings. Mara ended it by rising. "Give my love to the family. If Nitocris decides to travel to Haran, I may not see any of you again."

"Mara." Uri rose, thrusting the pouch at her. "Take the money. Buy your freedom."

Mara's hands moved behind her back. "No, brother. You asked me if I had lost my belief in the Most High. The answer is far worse."

Uri stared. Her face suddenly appeared ravaged, as though the shadow of every sleepless night and furrowed tear could be traced upon it.

"I believe in Him—and I hate Him," Mara whispered. "He has given me nothing but pain and suffering. He robbed me of all I might have held dear. He is nothing but a taunting bully."

Uri laid a hand on her shoulders. "Mara, no one is saying your life has not been hard…."

Mara stepped back, out of his reach. "My life? If it were only my life, brother…. But I see what life has become for all of us, how different from the world Father and Mother and Uncle Seraf grew up in. Why did the Lord forsake us? Why did He break his promise to us?" Mara forced a laugh out of a throat that sounded parched and sore. "All my life I've waited for a sign that God loves His people—and instead, I was sold into slavery, into a world of baseless desires and heartless ambitions. He rewarded my mother by allowing a soldier to rape her and took her lover's—your father's—manhood. He gave my father a dry portion of land and a wife who was grateful to him but could never love him."

Mara turned away. "And you and Nachum? You married out of the faith and Nachum struggles to keep his brood fed on a tiny farm that will never belong to him. Only Rahil—selfish, grasping Rahil—did your Almighty see fit to reward." Her shoulders sagged. "No, I won't buy my freedom, Uri. I hoped for honey cake and your Lord God gave me a thimbleful of stale crumbs. I will stay where He has placed me and dine on them."

"The Persian King Cyrus is coming to destroy your queen," Uri said. "What will happen to you then?"

Mara's shoulders hunched. "I have discovered that one mistress is very much like another," she said. "I will be someone's slave always, brother." She took a step away and then swiveled around, her hands outstretched. "Give my love to everyone, especially Mother. Tell her I hope she finds the strength to walk all the way back home when Cyrus lets us go free."

"Mara…." Uri said, his heart twisting with pity.

But Mara turned again, walking over the stone cobbles into the palace, never once looking back.

41

Sarah and the Idols

RAHIL PLACED THE LITTLE SILVER-EDGED basket of candied citrus peel before her mother. "I asked Ninsun to buy these from the market for you, Momma," she said, her tone that of a parent giving a child a treat. "Aren't they nice?"

Sarah glanced at the intricately worked basket. The price it would fetch in the marketplace might feed Nachum's children for a week. "Thank you, child," she said, picking up a peel and nibbling a small corner.

Rahil rose, restless. "I don't know where the boys are. I told them to come home early today."

"Do they like their studies at the academy?" Sarah forced a bright note into her question.

Rahil sighed, casting her eyes dramatically heavenward. "No, Momma. Remember? They're apprenticed to their father and work in his shop in town."

Sarah chewed more of the candied fruit peel. "Of course," she murmured after a pause. She wished she could keep her grandchildren's names straight and remember what they were all doing. But since losing Reuven to illness two years ago, having lost that last connection to her home in Judea, her world felt like it was covered with gauze. She could peer through it, but the details were lost.

"Momma, let's talk again about your coming to live here." Rahil sat and took her mother's wrinkled hand. "I have more room than Nachum, and they're practically starving, Mirav says."

"Mirav exaggerates," Sarah replied, gently moving her hand away. "It's my farm. My home. I can't leave it, child. It's all I have left."

"Argh!" Rahil made a disgusted sound deep in her throat, half-swerving in her chair.

Sarah knew her answer made the child unhappy. But when was Rahil ever anything but dissatisfied? How could she explain to the woman that she shuddered at the thought of living with her? *My own daughter*, Sarah thought. *I should not feel that way.*

"Rahil," Sarah patted her arm, "you know how much I love you and the children."

"You would be much more comfortable here," Rahil whined, indicating the richly appointed room with a wave of her hand.

Sarah looked around obediently. Rahil's home was beautifully decorated, with finely worked carpets on the walls and the marble floors. The huge antechamber where they sat was supported by wide pillars, the room open and airy. *You could fit half of our little brick house in this room*, Sarah thought, glancing about her. Low couches were covered with embroidered cloth coverings and cushions. Niches in the walls held silver boxes and goblets and exquisite pottery vases painted in vibrant colors.

"When we first came from Judea…." Sarah started to explain.

But Rahil's face puckered into a pout. "Oh! Not that again! Don't you know how tired everyone is of hearing you?" She looked callously into her mother's astonished face. "When we first came from Judea…." she mimicked in a sing-song voice, "I was sold into slavery…. Your father had to fight off the crows…." Rahil stood up. "No one cares, Momma. Those days are long gone. Let them go!"

"Let them go?" Sarah's voice quavered. She felt as though her daughter had struck her.

"Let them go," Rahil repeated, her eyes narrowing as she scrutinized her mother's appalled face. "Really, Momma. Just let them go."

Sarah put her hands down by her sides, pushing her tired body upright. She didn't want to remain in Rahil's house another moment. How dare the child disregard her memories? The long days on the road, her humiliation as the captain's bedmate, the trouble she and Reuven and Seraf had shared? *The young are so unkind*, she thought. But before she could make her way to the door, her three grandsons ran in.

"Grandmama," they cried, colliding their young bodies against her.

She put a shaky arm around them. "Let me look at you," she started to say, but they had already run off.

"It's time for prayers," the second wife, Ninsun, said from the doorway.

The children, who could not eat dinner until they prayed, trooped noisily to the line of idols kept in a small chamber adjacent to the garden courtyard. Sarah had seen the idols during earlier visits, ugly winking objects of clay and wood. How was it possible that her own grandchildren—her own daughter—bowed before these things?

But unless she completely closed her ears, she couldn't help but hear their prayers:

> It is you, Marduk, who are most honored among the
> great gods
> Your destiny is unrivaled, your utterance in Anu,
> O Marduk, you are the most honored among the
> great gods
> From this day onward unchangeable will be thy
> pronouncement

Their small voices stumbled over the hard words. Sarah thought of how her children had had difficulties with their prayers to the One True God. But they had learned them! How could Rahil have surrendered her religion so easily? She leaned back into a cushioned seat, sighing a little. All her daughter had ever wanted was a rich husband, a comfortable home, and the warm bath of belonging. But while Rahil might be married to a Babylonian, they were still not her gods, not her people.

Through the open doorway, she saw the children bowing to the long row of gods, offering obeisance to each as they chanted the idol's name:

> Niura is Marduk of the hoe
> Negal is Marduk of the attack

Zababa is Marduk of the hand-to-hand fight
Enlil is Marduk of lordship and counsel
Nabu is Marduk of accounting
Sin is Marduk the illuminator of the night

Sarah heard Rahil's loud tones. Her daughter always prayed to these strange gods with fervor, as though she wished to convince everyone of her piety.

Shamash is Marduk of justice
Adad is Marduk of rains

Sarah thought of returning to Nachum's house—her house. But if she left before they finished their prayers, Rahil would complain that she had disrespected her husband's beliefs.

The children finally finished and came running back in.

"Look, citrus peel," the youngest, Mered, cried. The three boys converged on the little table and gobbled up most of the treat.

"Don't ruin your dinner," their nursemaid chided from the doorway. "There's spiced lamb skewers tonight."

The thought of meat—which she had not eaten for more than a month—made Sarah's mouth water. After all, Mirav would not thank her for coming home unfed. Sarah felt her way to a chair. She watched the children squabble and Rahil screech that they should stop fighting. The second wife—Sarah could only remember that her name was Ninsun with effort—scurried over to distract them with promises of sesame cakes after dinner. Sarah sat back, shut her eyes, and wondered when the meal would be served.

42

Packing to Leave

MARA PICKED HER WAY THROUGH the bundles and heavy chests that littered the cobblestones of the palace courtyard. Just inside the arched doorway, she heard her mistress, Queen Nitocris, berating her husband, the King of Kings.

"Our marriage legitimized you! You are forsaking everything I worked so hard to attain! How dare you decide your worship of Sin is more important than the defense of your kingdom…."

Mara wished she did not have to go back inside the palace. In this mood, Nitocris was apt to fling vases and vent her spleen on the closest slave's back. The last time Nitocris and Nabonidus fought, she'd grabbed Mara by the neck and thrown her down the stairs, abusing her for bringing tepid lemon water. Mara rubbed her still-bruised hip.

"So he goes?" came a voice from the shade of the Cyprus trees. Daniel sat watching the slaves rush back and forth, piling more bundles in the yard. Servants were loading the chests high in several horse-drawn wagons, securing them with tight knots of heavy rope.

Mara sat beside Daniel. "He goes."

The aging royal advisor was growing frail. But he still kneeled beside his open window three times a day to pray to God, and still maintained his own dining hall in the palace. Mara often sat at his elbow, prompting him to recall how Uncle Seraf would sit beside him. "He was a good man, your uncle."

Mara guessed that Uri had gone to see Daniel soon after she refused his coins. Daniel had sought Mara out, inviting her to pray with him, telling her stories of how God's mercy had lightened the load of many Babylonian exiles.

"My friend Azariah still works among the poor Judeans," he said. "He brings them the charity God commands we extend to one another. Join us when he next comes to visit and hear his stories."

Mara smiled and agreed to come. But nothing, she told herself, could alter her rage against God. Daniel's stories only illuminated God's injustice. It was man who was compassionate and merciful, cruel and vengeful. God had little to do with how men treated one another.

"Nabonidus will find more peace in Haran than he would here in Nitocris' arms," Daniel said now, laughing.

Mara smiled. "They do make an incongruous couple," she said. Nabonidus was a dumpy, short man, wont to wear coarse woolen tunics and slippers rather than the robes of a king. A mole sprouted on the side of his nose and several hairs grew from it. Nitocris, on the other hand, was every inch a Babylonian royal. A tall, shapely woman, she colored her hair to preserve its rich, black hue and painted her face so that—from a distance—she retained the look of a younger woman. Cosmetics hid brown spots on her smooth white hands, and Mara spent hours pumicing her back and shoulders so she could wear diaphanous gowns, her body rising from them like a cold, marble statue.

Just yesterday, in fact, Nitocris called upon her body to sway the gods into changing Nabonidus's mind. Deciding she must not have properly honored Marduk, she arrayed herself in a loose robe and was carried in a palanquin to the Ziggurat, where, sitting atop the highest step, she let her gown drop and sat naked before the multitudes.

"It is said every woman in Babylon should perform this rite once in her lifetime," she explained, almost giddy with excitement as passers-by stared at her. "I am not so old that the sight of my body is disgusting to mighty Marduk—or to the men who serve him."

The thought of Nitocris and Nabonidus in bed together made the court chuckle. But the truth, everyone knew, was theirs was purely a marriage of convenience. They shared a couch just once, Nitocris's body servant whispered—on the night of their marriage. Nabonidus took no joy from Nitocris's grasping thighs and pointed nails. So he retreated to his library, filled with esoteric scrolls and clay tablets. Nitocris visited the marketplace of Haran the following day, purchasing several slaves for her bed pleasures. Mara was often dispatched to fetch one of them—everything from a Nubian with polished muscles to a tall, scraggly blonde boy from lands far to the northeast. None of them, Mara sourly noted, seemed enthusiastic about the honor of sharing the queen's couch.

"Prince Belshazzar will protect us from Cyrus better than Nabonidus ever could," Daniel said. "Not that it matters. My visions may have clouded with the years, but sometimes I still see clearly. Cyrus will break through the walls, and we'll be free to return home."

Mara felt her back crawl as though stung by water eels. Men always thought of war as if it could not touch them. Mara, remembering Mother's stories, knew better. But Daniel merely sat, calm as ever, watching the chaos in the courtyard with a thin, placid smile.

"My half-brother Uri believes in the Return. His friend Ezra never ceases to speak of it," Mara said. "But I thought you'd be more practical, Daniel."

Daniel leaned forward and patted her hand. "I am practical, Mara. The day is almost upon us when our long exile will end. I've been blessed with the ability to see—a little—of God's purpose. Most of the time our vision is blurred, and we think God has let our fates drop from His hands. But I tell you, child, He has plans for us yet.

"Don't give up on God, Mara." Daniel rose to leave. "He hasn't given up on you."

Mara sat on the bench after the seer left, knowing the longer she sat the more severe her punishment would be. But she felt unable to face Nitocris's fury. Did God indeed have a purpose in making her life so miserable? She wondered for a moment—but then shook her head, rising to drag herself into the palace yet again.

43

Uri and the Priest of Marduk

ON THIS BEAUTIFUL, WARM SPRING day, Uri gloried in the blue, cloudless sky, the sprouting of green along the banks of the river. Smiling, he strolled home, his day's work behind him. He wished his still-beautiful wife walked beside him, so they could enjoy the day's loveliness together. *We first met in the spring,* he remembered, and a surge of tenderness rose inside him.

Having visited the marketplace, his route took him past the Great Ziggurat. A few officials lingered on the massive steps. With the High King absent from Babylon, it was eerily quiet. The smoke of sacrifice did not plume forth as it usually did from the stepped building. Marduk was going hungry while Sin, in faraway Haran, was replete. *Surely it makes sense there is only one God,* Uri thought idly. *Anything else reduces divinity to the level of squabbling siblings.*

Deep in thought, he didn't see the priest rushing toward him, nearly colliding with the man in his dark black and red cloak and painted face. "Forgive me, Holy One," Uri murmured, moving aside.

"Uri?" the priest asked. "Is it Uri the Judean?"

Uri studied the priest's face, peering past the thick mask of swirled cosmetics. "Agga?"

"Yes, it's me," the priest said. "Marduk be praised, you look well, Judean."

"And you," Uri said, looking up and down his old classmate's figure. An image of Agga asking why Uri didn't worship the gods with the rest of the class surfaced from the recesses of memory. "But why are you dressed as a priest?"

"That's right—when we parted I was still training to become a scribe," Agga recalled. "That was before the dreams."

"The dreams?"

"I began to dream at night of events that would occur the following day. Kur took me to a diviner, who had me cast the holy stones and said I was blessed by Marduk. I have been in the Ziggurat ever since, first as acolyte and now as priest."

"A diviner! And does Marduk truly speak to you?"

Agga's face darkened. "Watch yourself, Judean. Do not doubt Marduk's awesome power. It is because of you nonbelievers that we face this crisis."

"Crisis? Do you mean Cyrus?"

Agga leaned in, whispering in Uri's ear. "Cyrus would give Marduk his due and reopen the Ziggurat for worship. The King of Kings is too long absent from Babylon and refuses to humble himself before the greatest of the gods."

"He rules us from Haran," Uri said. "Does it matter from what part of the far-flung Babylonian Empire the king rules?"

Agga's eyebrows lifted. "You think not, Judean?"

Uri shrugged. "I was born on a farm outside of Tel Abib, priest. Does that not make me as Babylonian as you?"

Agga pulled himself upright. "Only those who worship at the altar of Marduk can truly be considered Babylonian."

Uri grimaced. The Babylonians might have stolen the Judeans from their homeland, but they still refused to accept them. "If you priests believe Cyrus would restore the fires of Marduk, why not open the city gates to him?"

Agga's face whitened under his paint. "Who told you?" he hissed, grabbing Uri by the arm.

Uri pulled away, struggling to keep calm. "No one. It just makes sense, doesn't it? Nabonidus's allegiance is to Sin. It's been many years since a king has kneeled before Marduk, to be slapped and humiliated by you priests. You can't like that."

Agga's eyebrows rose. "You know a lot about our ceremonies for a nonbeliever," he said. "Who told you about the humbling of the king?"

"I married a Babylonian woman. Her father shared some of the details of your rituals, how you make the king abase himself before the idol once a year, then bring the other gods before Marduk in parade to swear their loyalty to the god of gods."

Agga's frown deepened. "The details of our rites are not suitable for a nonbeliever's ears," he sputtered. He straightened his backbone, his voice vibrating with authority: "You will forget you ever heard them."

Uri set his teeth in a tight smile. He'd been foolish. Despite their waning influence, the priests of Marduk still held considerable power. He wouldn't be the first exile to disappear after speaking unwisely. "Consider them forgotten. I am happy to see you again, Agga."

"And I, you, Uri the Judean," Agga said, his voice reverting to normal. "I hope you prosper?"

Uri spread arms wide. He wore a new gown, a gift from Zakiti, rich blue, embroidered with silver thread. "I married a wealthy wife."

That, too, was an error of judgment, Uri thought, as a flash of greed flickered in Agga's hooded eyes. He could see the priest trying to calculate how best to dip his fingers into Uri's pocket.

Agga put a heavy hand on Uri's arm. "You might give yourself over to the true gods, Uri. Abase yourself at the altar of Marduk. For a small fee, I would be happy to prepare the way for you. We could do it now."

Uri's skin crawled under the touch of the man's soft hand, with its long fingernails and many rings. "Another day," he said. "I'm on my way home. My wife worries when I am late."

"Ask for me at the Ziggurat any time," Agga said. "I hope to see you soon."

"Farewell," Uri replied, not promising. "Be well, Agga."

The day was as bright as it had been before, but as Uri hurried home, his face damp, the sun hid behind a thick and threatening storm cloud.

44

The Ground Shakes

539 BCE–Year 47 of the Exile

THE MORNING OF CHAVA'S FIFTEENTH birthday started like any other. She woke next to Grandmother Sarah, who was already sitting up. Grandmother found it difficult to stay asleep in the hours before dawn, although she often dozed off in her chair in the mid-morning sun and sometimes after the heavy afternoon meal as well.

"Good morning, darling," Grandmother said. "You're exactly my age when I left Judea."

Chava stretched, her feet reaching into the pockets of warmth under the blankets. It was still dark outside. A farmer's child, she'd never known the luxury of sleeping past sunrise.

"Exactly the same age," Grandmother repeated. "It's hard to believe."

Chava kissed her grandmother and rose, slipping her shift over her head and her sandals onto her feet. Sleepily, she shuffled outside, to milk their one cow—a new luxury her mother was proud of. She brought the bucket of froth-topped milk into the kitchen, where Mother portioned out large cups of it for her father and her oldest brother, Joshua, and slightly smaller cups for Chava and herself. She poured a tiny portion for

Grandmother Sarah, which Chava would later heat on the baking stones, adding honey and herbs as a morning treat.

Mother had finally prevailed last year, and Aaron and Gal, the brothers closest to Chava in age, were now apprenticed elsewhere. Aaron worked on a fellow Judean's farm an hour's brisk walk away, so they saw him every week on the Shabbat. But Gal was apprenticed to an iron smithy in Babylon, making weapons for the king's soldiers. The workers slept on straw pallets on the dirt floor, he told Chava, allowed to sleep only two hours at a time. The forge sizzled and fires boomed all night long. What sleep he snatched was punctuated by the heavy clang of iron on iron, as workers battered out the thousands of swords Prince Belshazzar would need to defend the kingdom against Cyrus.

Cyrus, Chava thought, as she drank her milk and munched a piece of bread. *Cyrus is all anyone can think about these days.*

The Persian warrior had gone from victory to victory. During one of her rare visits to Grandmother Sarah, Aunt Mara confided that the queen was worried. Cyrus had conquered Ecbatana, the capital of Media, provoking the Babylonians to ally themselves with Lydia, Egypt, and Sparta. But the pact hadn't prevented Cyrus from defeating Croesus, king of Lydia.

"A man of immense wealth, Croesus," Mara told them at dinner. "His palace was made entirely of gold. Cyrus melted it down to make armor for himself and his most trusted advisors."

"I'm confused." Chava's brother Joshua reached for another slice of fig cake. He crammed it into his mouth, talking around the crumbs. "Aren't we glad Cyrus won in Ecbatana?"

Chava saw Father and Grandmother exchange glances. Joshua might be strong, his arms and legs rich with muscle, but his brain was addled. Point Joshua in the right direction and he gave you a good day's work. But "I'm confused," was the phrase he spoke most often.

"You are thinking about the time the priests of Marduk celebrated Cyrus' victory, which Marduk supposedly prophesized three years ago," Mother answered patiently. She always protected her favorite child with calm explanations, chastising anyone who mocked his slowness.

"Nabonidus not only rejoiced when Cyrus defeated Media, he also used the opportunity to seize part of the Medean Empire for Babylon." Mara nodded. "But that was long ago, Joshua. Now Cyrus threatens *our* kingdom."

"Prince Belshazzar will defeat him," Joshua said serenely, reaching for the yogurt. "Gal says they have made more than a thousand swords already."

"He did, didn't he?" Mother replied fondly, as though he had said something wise, pushing another slice of cake toward him.

After a pause, Mara continued her tale. The priests had sent a delegation to Nitocris to beg that she open the Temple of Marduk despite the king's absence. "The priests say we face this calamity because the altars are cold."

"They can burn all the sacrificial fires they want to their false gods," Father muttered, a sour expression crossing his face, "it will do them no good against Cyrus." Chava's father was the strictest man she knew, stricter even than Uncle Uri in his observance of the one true God. The women saw the warning signs in his furrowed brow and subsided.

Putting thoughts of Cyrus aside, Chava went out to the garden to gather vegetables for lunch. She worked steadily, humming a song Grandmother had first sung a few nights ago.

"Your Great Uncle Seraf used to sing this," Sarah told the young girl. "I remembered it after all that talk of Cyrus and battles and sacrificing to false gods."

Chava had a clear, soft voice, and she sang out,

> If I forget thee, O Jerusalem,
> Let my right hand forget her cunning.
> Let my tongue cleave to the roof of my mouth,
> If I remember thee not;
> If I set not Jerusalem
> Above my chiefest joy.

Jerusalem, Chava thought. The way Grandmama talked of it, with its streets paved in gold and its silver buildings sparkling in the sun. *It's hard to believe that Grandmama was my age when she was forced from*

Jerusalem and brought to this farm in chains. Chava pulled up a carrot and contemplated it, shaking off the excess dirt. *What was it like to be born in your own country and not raised to consider yourself a* bat gola, *a daughter of the Exile?*

Chava sighed and put the carrot in her basket. She was brushing the dirt off her knees, crouching in the soft ground, when she felt it.

The earth trembled under her feet.

She picked up her head and listened. Where before birdsong and the slight summer breeze had filled her ears, now the world seemed to be holding its breath.

Then she heard it—the thud, thud, thud of an army's marching feet, followed by the sharp herald call of a trumpet.

"You are exactly the same age I was," Grandmother had said this morning. Chava left the basket tumbled at her feet and ran into the fields, where Joshua and Father were working. They dropped their hoes when they saw her excited, frightened face.

"The soldiers are coming!" she shrieked.

45

Preparing for Battle

BABYLON WAS IN AN UPROAR.

Word of soldiers at the Ishtar Gate scurried from house to house. Families who had lived for generations under the secure wing of Babylon's might panicked. Those with the most to lose—including Uri's father-in-law, Nutesh, and his half-sister, Rahil—buried gold coins in their gardens, covering the loose earth with new plantings. But even those who had little—like Nachum's family on their meager plot of land—tried to hide their small store.

"Chava," Mirav called, "put the barley flour sacks in the fig grove, tied high, where the soldiers won't look for them."

Uri watched his niece—who was growing tall and gangly—climb the slight incline to the fig trees. Wasps buzzed about, as they had since the beginning of time. She evaded them as she tied the sacks near one of their nests. At least the barley flour was safe; the soldiers wouldn't bother fighting the wasps for the half-filled sacks.

"Why are you here and not home with Zakiti?" Mirav asked, arms filled with her few treasures—some clay pots and a single shell-bead necklace that trickled through her fingers.

Uri shrugged, not wanting Mirav to scold him for leaving his wife. He went to the back of the house, where Sarah sat calmly outside, hands full of green beans.

"The last time soldiers came, they took everything," Sarah mused, rapidly topping and tailing the beans. "They destroyed everything else. Sometimes I think I can still smell our farmhouse burning."

Fear crawled up Uri's backbone. "I should go home," he said. He'd felt detached all day, moving restlessly from place to place, pretending to be amused by the pointless preparations. But his mother had a look in her still vivid green eyes that alarmed him. The stillness of total despair, Uri thought, as he kissed her withered cheek. "I will see you…afterward," he promised.

She reached up and patted his cheek. "As God wills, my son. You were always a good boy. Take care of your family."

His throat closed. Blinking hastily, he turned away.

He walked along the canals toward home. The water level had dropped overnight, panicking the Babylonians. Rumors were circulating that Marduk had dried up the River Euphrates to punish the city. Others said that Cyrus's troops had diverted the river to drain the city's flood defenses. The little water that was left—perhaps as high as a man's thigh—moved sluggishly in the man-made streams.

At home, Uri found Zakiti crying. She'd piled all her treasures onto a table and couldn't decide what to do with them. Seeing her husband in the doorway, she let out a gasp of relief and hugged him tightly. Her curving, yielding body clung to his. He put an arm around her.

"Shh, now," Uri said. "What's the problem here?"

It was just the two of them again. Their three daughters were all married, one to a Babylonian merchant whom Nutesh had named his heir, the other two to Judean boys. Uri had visited each of their homes before going out to the farm. Each daughter had wept on his shoulder and wondered if the soldiers would leave their houses intact and their possessions untouched. He'd given each girl the same piece of counsel, which he now repeated.

"These are only dead things." Uri pointed at the glinting gold and silver on the table. "I care more about the living, more about you, my darling, than all the possessions in the world."

Zakiti wept afresh, her tears dampening Uri's tunic. He held her in his arms, thoughts traveling beyond his immediate cares. He might be indifferent to the household items that his wife had assembled. But what of the academy's clay tablets and precious scrolls of parchment? Would they survive the soldiers? *My life's work*, he thought, as he cradled his wife to him, *is in those buildings. The history of my people. Somehow, I must protect them.*

Uri slid his hands to Zakiti's forearms and moved her gently aside. "I must go to the academy," he told her. "Will you come with me?"

Zakiti's eyes widened. Their young daughters had often visited him, but his wife—unbeliever that she was—had never stepped foot on the premises. When she asked, Uri always found an excuse. The last thing he wanted was for Ezra to turn his wife away. And Ezra would.

But now? Everything had changed now. He had to stand guard over his life's work, and she was his wife. He could not leave her behind.

They took Zakiti's treasures and buried them in the backyard, prizing up bricks from the courtyard. The soft, wet soil was heavy and thick, but Uri's spade moved faster than the clay, outrunning the collapse of the small pit he created. Zakiti put everything into a goatskin sack and tied it tightly. Piling heavy earth on top of the pouch, they replaced the bricks of the courtyard, careful to sweep aside any evidence they had been moved. They hid two of the most valuable necklaces in the folds of their clothing. If the Persians took everything else, these jewels would buy them food for a few weeks.

Dressed in their simplest garments, carrying enough food for three days, they made their way through the city streets, crowded with people fleeing the city. Soldiers drew ever nearer to a constant rumble of sound. Halloo'ed commands and the tramp of thousands of army boots shook the earth. Each reverberation threw the city into fresh panic. Uri's eyes widened as he saw a door forced open. The poor of the city were already looting abandoned homes, making off with bread, wine, and coin.

"Will they do the same to us?" Zakiti muttered.

"We'll consider it our tithe to the poor for the year if they do," Uri responded.

She smiled thinly, and he knew the housewife in her was mentally counting the flasks of wine and loaves of bread in her pantry.

The solid brick buildings of the academy looked serene, rising out of the Cyprus grove, unmoved by the city's alarm. Uri brought Zakiti into the cool corridors of the library where most of his work was stored. His shoulders loosened as the tranquility of the space restored his own sense of calm.

"We'll stay here," Uri said.

"How were the girls?" Zakiti asked, forehead wrinkled as she stared at the rows upon rows of scrolls and piles of clay tablets.

"All well, God be praised. I should pray that we all survive the next few days." Uri half-closed his eyes and murmured a prayer under his breath. His Babylonian wife watched him. She cast her eyes upward through shuttered eyelids. But he forebear to reprove her.

Hours passed. Neither of them had slept well the night before, and Zakiti's eyelids shut, falling into a heavy doze. Uri decided to fill the anxious hours with work. He stood at his tall table, transcribing a prayer that he had heard recently voiced at Daniel's table.

"*Baruch ata Adonai, Elohim Melech Ha'Olam, Yotser Or uvoreh Chosech*," he wrote. "Blessed are You, Adonai our God. Ruler of the world, Who forms light and creates darkness."

He put down his stylus as he finished writing the word darkness, remembering the slight young man who'd impressed them all with his glittering eyes and intense manner. Mara had stood next to her half-brother, watching the stranger with a fervent glance. She whispered that the strange new prophet, a second Isaiah, visited Daniel's table sporadically over the last few months, speaking with the assurance of a clairvoyant that God intended Cyrus to deliver Israel.

"Surely the nations are a drop in a bucket, regarded as dust on the scales," the young man said, "*Adonai* brings princes to naught and reduces the rulers of this world to nothing."

"Someone should tell that to Nitocris," Mara muttered, painfully shifting her shoulder where the queen's lash had last struck her.

Then the young prophet spoke of suffering. Uri saw Mara straighten, fixing her eyes on his face. "He gives power to the faint; and to him that has no might He increases strength," he proclaimed, "they that wait for the Lord shall renew their strength; they shall mount up with wings as eagles; they shall run, and not be weary; they shall walk, and not faint."

An immense burden lifted from Uri's shoulders, watching the transfixed look on his half-sister's face. This young Isaiah had made inroads in Mara's soul where he and Daniel had persistently failed.

Uri stopped to greet Daniel as he left, hunching a shoulder in Mara's direction. "She's finally found some semblance of peace," he said, bending low to speak into Daniel's good ear.

"He does us all good," Daniel murmured. "You should have heard him yesterday, Uri, telling us how our time of service and servitude was nearly at an end."

Uri smiled now at the memory of Mara's rapt face, then bent back to his writing. The short prayer ended, "In Your great mercy have mercy on us Lord, acting as our strength. Rock, acting as our protector. Defender, acting as our salvation. Protector, acting on our behalf."

With the city outside in a state of upheaval, Uri prayed that the young prophet's words would come to pass, and God would protect His people through this latest crisis of their history.

46

The Writing on the Wall

"Bring the prince more wine!" the royal cupbearer cried, and a dozen slaves tripped over one another to fetch it.

While chaos reigned outside the palace, inside no one dared speak of defeat. Courtiers walked tight-lipped about the corridors and any hint of the overwhelming force massing outside the city's gates was immediately squelched. To rally the morale of his courtiers, Prince Regent Belshazzar, Nitocris's adopted son, decreed his nobles must attend a banquet. During her service to both queens, Mara had seen hundreds of royal celebrations. But nothing compared with the feast laid out this evening. Dish after highly spiced dish was served on immense gold platters. Wine flowed from silver pitchers into jewel-studded goblets. So many tables were crammed in the banquet hall that the servers had to thread their way through.

Mara arrayed Nitocris in a gown of plush red, embroidered in gold thread. The queen wore a diadem on her forehead, and her bare arms glittered with heavy gold bracelets encrusted with jewels. Mara dressed the queen's thinning hair high on her head, thickening her braids with ribbons and flowers. She painted her gaunt features with cosmetics to hide aging flaws, obscuring crow's feet with kohl. She stamped her palms with red and laced up her silver sandals, tying them high on her bony calves.

"You look beautiful, Your Majesty," Mara said as the queen peered discontentedly into the huge bronze mirror taken as tribute from an Egyptian king.

"I look like a hag," Nitocris hissed. "A whore about to be taken by an enemy army. But tonight, I must still entertain this one."

Mara followed three paces behind the queen, who bestowed her painted smile upon the court nobles. *If Nitocris had been a man*, Mara mused, *Babylon would be safe today.* She, more than Amel-Marduk or Kasšaya, deserved to be her father's heir, a woman as ruthless and pragmatic as Nebuchadnezzar himself.

"More wine!" the cupbearer cried again. Belshazzar had been drinking steadily all evening, despite his stepmother's protests that he would need a clear head in the morning.

"To face down Cyrus?" he mocked. "Nonsense! We'll dispatch that upstart before cock crow."

A slave, his elbow jostled, spilled a stream of red wine from Belshazzar's cup onto the table. "Blood," giggled one of the drunken courtiers. "Look, blood."

The word "blood" was hissed from table to table. A sudden hush radiated through the banquet hall, like ripples in a stream disturbed by a flung stone. The courtier flinched at Nitocris's poisoned glare. Belshazzar, his face flushed by wine, narrowed his eyes.

"I want a different cup!" he cried, throwing his goblet against the wall. "A new cup!"

The serving men looked at one other, confused. Nitocris motioned to the royal cupbearer, who bent down before her, his nose nearly scraping the mosaic floor. "Your Prince has requested a new drinking cup. Hurry and bring one," the queen commanded.

"But, Your Majesty, every chalice we possess is already being used," the man quavered. "I suppose I could take one from one of your guests...."

Nitocris pulled out the small whip she always kept by her and let the throngs fly, flailing the back of the man's neck. He cried out and Mara flinched in sympathy, hunching her shoulders. Her movement drew the queen's glance. A thoughtful expression passed over Nitocris's face.

"Belshazzar!" she cried, voice penetrating every corner of the room. "I shall dispatch my handmaiden to bring us the vessels of her people, the ones removed from the Temple in Jerusalem, once used in sacrifice to their vanquished God. Let us drink from them. It will be fitting to remind Sin and Marduk of past victories, so they deliver glory to us in the morning once more. Will you permit?"

Belshazzar's eyes gleamed. "A noble gesture, oh mighty Queen of Babylon," he decreed, voice booming and confident. "I command it be so."

Nitocris pulled Mara to one side. "The cups are locked in a cupboard in the court treasury. Melzar has the key. Go on, hurry."

Mara felt sick to her stomach. "I won't."

Nitocris gave her a shove between her shoulder blades. "You will or you'll die," she hissed. "I'll push you out the gates of Babylon myself and into the arms of Cyrus's army. How long do you think you'd live? What do you think they'd do to you?"

Mara shivered. "Send someone else. Please!"

The queen's jaw hardened, and her hand groped for her whip. "Go."

Shaking, Mara left the room. She collapsed into the darkened curve of the corridor, uncertain what to do. How could she bring the sacred Judean vessels for the prince and his drunken company to imbibe from?

"Mara," whispered a voice above her. "Do not be afraid."

Mara looked up. Daniel stood with his friend Abed-nego. Daniel was dressed in a simple white gown, but Abed-nego was nearly invisible, swathed in a heavy black cloak.

"God spoke to me in a dream last night." Daniel put a comforting hand on her shoulder. "Fetch the sacred vessels. This is all part of His purpose."

"This is of God's making?" Mara asked, unbelieving.

"Listen." Daniel crouched at her level. "After they drink from the vessels, something will happen. They won't be able to decipher its meaning. At the right time, you must remind the queen that I was a loyal soothsayer to her father. Can you do that?"

Mara looked up at him. His face was calm, untroubled. She had spent her entire life trusting Daniel, even while doubting the God he pledged allegiance to. Would this night reveal God's purpose for her? She straightened, reading approval in Daniel's dark eyes.

"Good girl," he whispered. "Be quick."

As Mara ran down the hallway, she recalled what the young prophet Isaiah had said just the other day. Mara repeated his words: "Behold, I will do a new thing; now shall it spring forth; shall ye not know it? I will even make a way in the wilderness and rivers in the desert."

Melzar sat over a flagon of wine in his chambers, a guttering oil lamp by his side. Mara read fear in his cragged features and felt a glow of satisfaction at his discomfort. After all, he'd beaten her many times at the queen's command. She instructed the master of eunuchs to open the cupboard that held the Temple's precious vessels. Mara knelt before the open doors, head bowed, praying for a brief moment. Then she filled her arms with the glowing goblets, inlaid with jewels or etched in beautiful patterns, standing proud on their footed bases. There were too many chalices for her to carry alone, so Melzar summoned two ebony-hued slaves to help her.

Just as Mara reentered the hall, the prince pulled a scantily clad courtesan onto his lap. Mara flinched at the thought of bringing the largest, most ornate cup—probably held aloft by the High Priest on the holiest of holy days—to the reclining prince. But one look at her mistress made her scurry over and kneel before him, proffering the richly chased cup.

"Marduk be praised!" he cried. "Let me drink from the cup of this vanquished people."

The prince took a heady draft, then made the giggling girl in his lap sip from the cup. "We praise you, mighty Marduk!" he cried. "You will protect us, and we will vanquish your enemies."

The beautiful vessels passed from hand to hand through the hall, the Babylonians drinking heartily from them. Nitocris called for toasts to the prince regent, and the courtiers shouted praise to their pagan gods. Mara closed her eyes, appalled at the sight of the drunken rabble defiling the Temple's treasures. Despair weighed heavily on her, and she wondered if, despite Daniel's assurances, she had sinned.

But as she crouched in the corner, trembling and dizzy, a cry of horror rose from the head table. Shouts burst from all corners of the room.

Mara forced her eyes open to see a hand—it looked like a hand without a body—scratching a message upon the marble tiles of a wall lit by a branch of candles.

"*Mene Mene Tekel Upharsin*," the letters spelled.

"What does it mean?" The cry went up around the room.

"Is it a sign from the gods?"

"Who has done this?"

The hand disappeared. It was possible, Mara thought, peering over the heads of the nobles who'd risen from their seats with a clatter of cups, that she might have seen the folds of a black cloak moving slowly in the dark shadows. But all that remained were the white letters against the black-veined marble wall.

Mara looked at Belshazzar, whose forehead was speckled with dots of sweat, looking pallid under his bronzed cheeks. He pushed the concubine from his lap and tied the ends of his robe together, all thoughts of licentiousness frightened away. Mara turned toward Nitocris. The queen's face remained serene—she would not allow herself the luxury of fear—but her eyes narrowed as she scanned the panicked room.

"Fetch a soothsayer," one of the nobles cried.

"Yes," another exclaimed. "Someone to tell us what this portent means."

At a nod from Belshazzar, a slave slipped from the room. Mara heard his footsteps running down the hallway. As they waited, Belshazzar tried to take another sip from the Temple cup. Mara exulted inwardly seeing that the prince's hands shook too much to raise the cup to his lips. He put the cup down and stared deep into its depths.

"Any man who reads this writing and tells me what it means shall wear purple and have a golden chain strung about his neck by my own hand. He will rule over a third of my kingdom," Belshazzar cried, striving to conceal the quaver in his voice.

The servant returned, ushering in several Chaldean soothsayers, astrologers, and magicians, men with tattooed faces and paint dabs decorating their bodies. Each one examined the letters, asking how the words came to appear. They shook their heads at the story of a disembodied hand writing on the wall, but several nobles insisted the hand had moved of its own accord. They brought torches closer, touching the words with sharply manicured fingernails. One soothsayer pulled a live rat from a stick-and-dab cage, twisting its neck, flinging it to the ground to read the patterns of its blood. Another cast stones to divine their meaning. Yet a third opened a door to the inner courtyard to peer into the starlit night. As the door swung open, screams from the panicked city penetrated the hall. At Nitocris's swift command, a slave slammed the door shut.

"Can no man read this writing? Even for the rewards I offer?" Belshazzar asked, panic lacing his shrill voice.

But one after the other, the magicians and astrologers admitted defeat. With a start, Mara recalled Daniel's request. She turned to whisper in the queen's ear. "Perhaps you might wish to summon Daniel, whose Babylonian name is Belteshazzar, he who served your father so wisely and interpreted dreams for him."

Nitocris's lips tightened. "What do you know of this?" she asked, fingernails digging into the flesh of Mara's arm.

"I have heard how, in your father's time, Daniel interpreted visions and unraveled riddles that perplexed your Chaldean wise men," Mara said. "If he lives still, he might help now."

Nitocris released Mara's arms and turned toward Belshazzar. "Oh, Prince of Babylon!" she cried, "These so-called wise men are less than useless. Dismiss them and fetch in their stead a man who served my father the king.

"During my father's rule this man demonstrated such understanding and wisdom that King Nebuchadnezzar appointed him prince of the necromancers. He gave him the Chaldean name of Belteshazzar and found he had an uncanny ability to interpret dreams. He was also blessed with visions. If you would learn the truth behind this mystery, summon him!"

"Fetch Belteshazzar," the prince cried. "Bring him here at once."

In a few moments, Daniel stood humbly before the prince, bowing low.

"I am told you are wise in the realm of dreams and visions," Belshazzar said. "Is that true, Judean?"

Daniel nodded. "I have been fortunate in my prophesies," he said. "I served King Nebuchadnezzar for many years."

"Tell us—what do you make of that?" Nitocris asked, pointing to the writing on the wall.

Daniel walked over to it, examined it, touched it. He bent low, as if making obeisance to a mightier power. Then he rose and turned back to the regent.

"You have been honored. This is the doing of the Most High, Prince," he told Belshazzar.

"Yes, well, what does it mean?" the prince demanded.

"When I served King Nebuchadnezzar, there came a time when God laid a heavy hand on him, when his head muddled, and he became like a beast. Instead of meat, he ate grass. Instead of ruling wisely, he warbled tunes and snarled like a wolfling. All because he refused to heed me and deliver the Judeans back to their homeland, as was the will of the Lord God.

"And you, Belshazzar, you defile the throne by your lust—lust for women and lust for power. You take the vessels that have served the Most High and drink from them, giving them to your whores. You think you can vanquish Cyrus, he who has been foretold as God's instrument to once again free the Hebrew people from servitude and oppression."

"But what has this to do with the writing?" Belshazzar blazed, his face beet red.

"The Lord God has put out his hand to tell you the end of your days are upon you. I can dispel the mystery of the writing. But you must listen and accept what I have to say with an open heart," Daniel said.

Mara could not take her eyes from the old man's face. His long white hair sprung back in wave upon wave, flowing freely upon his once-broad shoulders. Dressed as he was in simple white linen, he stood out from the bejeweled and richly gowned mass of courtiers. Unadorned by cosmetics, his magnetic personality and deeply entrenched faith were all that he had to draw the eye. Yet he held the entire banquet hall in thrall.

He pointed to the words written on the marble wall, his hand firm and unwavering.

"God saw you drinking from His vessels. He found you wanting. He dispatched a divine hand to write these words.

"It is written: *Mene Mene Tekel Upharsin*. Listen closely, and I will decipher these words for you.

"*Mene*. God has counted your kingdom and has brought it to an end.

"*Tekel*. You were weighed on the scales and found wanting.

"*Upharsin*. Your kingdom has been broken up and given to Media and Persia."

Daniel lowered his hand and bowed. Belshazzar glared at the old man. "This is what your Lord God has to say to me?"

"It is what He has to say to us all, Prince. I am sorry my words do not please you. The words of the Lord God are often not what we wish to hear."

"I should have you killed," Belshazzar snarled.

But Nitocris saw what Belshazzar was ignoring: the effect of Daniel's words on the courtiers in the banquet hall. A few men dared to slink away, fleeing the condemned prince's presence. The rest muttered to one another, scheming how best to present themselves to the country's new ruler—a ruler whom they now accepted as inevitable.

Nitocris's eyes slit nearly shut. Her hands shaped themselves into claws. "Bring him the purple robe and the gold chain you promised," she snapped at the prince. "Take charge, or you will lose the kingdom because you are too cowardly to face a man's words."

Belshazzar, shaken by her tone, looked around and saw that she was right. Mara watched as the prince, a man used to facing the armed might of the enemy, pulled himself together. "Bring this man a purple robe and a gold chain—you will find both in my quarters!" he cried. "I give him a third of my kingdom as I swore I would. Thus should speaking truth to royalty always be rewarded."

"Keep your gifts, oh prince," Daniel said. "I speak here for the Almighty, not for you."

Mara watched, wide eyed, as Daniel turned on his heel and left. The words on the wall glowed in the light of the candelabrum. Belshazzar shakily rose from his seat. "It is time to prepare for battle," he cried out. "Who is with me?"

A thick silence followed the king's cry. With more courage than Mara thought she could have mustered, the prince began to walk from the room, his head held high. He strolled into the midst of his courtiers, smiling and nodding at them, as though nothing had upset him.

Then there was a shattering scream of pain.

Belshazzar fell to his knees. A dagger, plunged in the small of his back, blossomed from his spine. Blood trickled from it sluggishly at first, then flowed more rapidly. He groped around for the hilt, but his fingers could not quite reach it. The crowd around them parted and Nitocris rushed forward.

"*Mene...Mene...*" Belshazzar gasped in tortured grunts. "*Tekel....*" His eyes closed and he slumped forward, lifeless.

"*Upharsin,*" Nebuchadnezzar's daughter moaned, wild eyes fixed upon the marble wall.

47

Opening the Gates

As NIGHT FELL, ZAKITI GREW agitated and wanted to return home. Nothing Uri could say would persuade her otherwise.

"Why should we stay here?" she asked querulously. "I'm not comfortable—it's dusty and the echoes in the shadows scare me. I want to sleep in my own bed. The Persians aren't going to attack us tonight. No one fights in the dark."

That, Uri thought, was probably true, but how had his wife come to know it?

"We'd need to return at dawn," he insisted. "I must make sure the Writings remain untouched."

"Fine, fine." Zakiti shrugged. "Let's just go now."

They groped their way through the murky corridors, nearly reaching the exit when Uri felt another presence in the hallway. "Shush!" he hissed, clapping a hand over Zakiti's mouth. They stood in the darkness, Uri straining to see who was at the other end of the hall.

"Who's there?" called a familiar voice.

"Ezra!" Uri greeted him. "It's Uri."

"Who is with you?"

Uri noticed the strain in his voice. Ezra was as much on edge as anyone in Babylon.

"No one," Uri called, grown careless after the long day and his relief that the soldiers had not yet attacked. "Just my wife."

"You brought an unbeliever here?" Ezra gasped.

Dismay exploded in the pit of Uri's stomach. *Fool!* He knew what Ezra thought of his marriage. He had spent years separating his Hebrew life as a scribe from his Babylonian life at home. How had he come so completely to forget everything that shaped his world?

"She's my wife." The words formed imprudently in Uri's mouth. "She stays with me."

"Has she touched the Writings?" Ezra questioned, approaching to hover over them, an accusing figure even in the dark. "You know the prohibition...."

"She touched nothing," Uri hastened to assure him.

Zakiti stiffened.

"You'll return tomorrow? I wanted to come earlier, but my father delayed me."

"How is your father?" Uri asked. Seraiah, once High Priest of the Holy Temple in Jerusalem, had been ill for several months.

"Dying," Ezra said. "I doubt he will live past morning."

"But you are here now?" Zakiti asked in disbelief.

Ezra ignored her. Uri, curious, repeated her question, "Then why are you here?"

Ezra's shoulders hunched. "He's fallen into a stupor. My being there will mean nothing to him. But my being here...means everything." He peered into Uri's face. "He himself would urge me to come here. But do not think it is easy for me."

Reluctantly admiring the man so obviously torn between two colliding duties, Uri put a hand onto his fellow scribe's shoulder. "I never thought you took the easy path, Ezra," he told him. "Peace be upon you. I will return in the morning."

"Will you bring her?" Ezra blurted, slanting his eyes toward Zakiti.

A feeble grimace crossed Uri's face. Having spent a lifetime by Ezra's side, Uri knew his friend would always worry about the threat of contamination.

"Yes, of course I will. Do not worry, Ezra. She knows our rules and will not lay so much as a finger upon any of the Writings."

Zakiti kept quiet as she and Uri left the building. He shivered as they stepped into the sharply cool night. Thousands of fires from outside the gates of the city dimmed the night stars. The air was full of ash and smoke, an acrid smell that tickled the back of the throat. They walked in silence, turning from the broad boulevard into the narrower streets that led to their home.

"Am I such a foul thing that I cannot touch your Writings?" Zakiti burst out.

Uri glanced at her heated face, his stomach flip-flopping in consternation. He had never told her about the prevailing attitude in the academy, that pagans should not touch the clay tablets or the parchments that contained the Name, lest they defile the Writings. He'd always thought she understood his reluctance to let her enter the buildings. But perhaps he had just hoped she understood. It was a cruel thing, he thought, to tell her that the mere press of her flesh on the pages of his work would invalidate it.

"It's not of my making…." he started.

"But you accept it," she argued, cheeks turning red. "You think you are better than me, even though your people came here as captives and live among us as exiles. If I were banished by force of arms to another country, I would think of my captors with greater respect."

Uri bit his lip. Nothing he might say would mollify her. So he said the unthinkable: "Perhaps you *will* know what it feels like—tomorrow."

Zakiti's eyes welled with tears. She ran from him. He watched as she darted past their street toward her father's home. He didn't know whether to follow or not. He walked through the gate and into his own house, pushing open the door and walking through the rooms and back out into the garden. He sat in the dark, peering at the smoke-filled sky.

What would become of them tomorrow? He knew the Judeans hoped Cyrus would set them free, that he would allow them to reestablish their Temple and sacrifice in their own land to the Most High. He had liberated other peoples from the various lands he'd conquered. But would

Cyrus destroy Babylon as a symbol of his might? Would Uri even survive the next few hours? Would his wife? His family?

And if they did—and if the Judeans were given the choice to go home—what would become of his marriage? What would his strong-willed passionate wife choose? Would she leave the riches of her own land and follow him—to what?

Uri rubbed his eyes, red rimmed from the smoldering air. He needed to sleep but had to find Zakiti first. Making his way back out to the street, he discovered his wife fumbling at the gates to their forecourt. He put his arms about her, lifted her, and carried her into their bed, stripping her to the waist. The soot filtered down onto their bodies as they embraced in a paroxysm of desire and fear. They made love long into the night, sleeping only fitfully, wrapped tightly against each other.

When dawn came, Uri looked at his wife's sleeping body and chose not to wake her. She had finally fallen into a deep sleep, her breathing thick and measured. So that she would not worry, Uri woke the kitchen servant and instructed the girl to tell his wife that he would return mid-morning for her. Then he let himself out into the sleeping street.

The campfires outside the gate had been extinguished and the smoke that had lingered like a thick pall over the city during the night was dissipating. Uri breathed in the cold, fresh air, his sandaled feet soft on the pavement. As he walked the deserted streets, he thought contentedly of last night's caresses. Then he bade himself put carnal thoughts aside. If Ezra knew....

Uri shook his head as he thought of poor Ezra, torn between honoring his father's last moments and protecting their life's work. *I will send him home*, Uri thought, rounding the corner to pass by the entrance of the thickly protected Ishtar Gate, secured more than a month ago, closed to outside traffic.

The moment the blue mosaic gate with its animal tiles sprang into view, Uri caught his breath. A delegation of priests, dressed ornately in black and red gowns, stood arguing with a squadron of guards.

"Marduk and Ishtar bid you open the gates. Cyrus has sent word that he will honor our gods and our city, that no one will be hurt," one of the priests commanded.

"I have thrown the bones this past night and seen the gods' wishes," another declaimed. Uri glanced toward his face. Agga. Uri slunk back, hoping to evade the priest's eyes. But it was too late. Uri saw the moment Agga recognized him.

"Open the gates now, while Shamash still rises from his bed, kissing the sky," a third priest demanded. With his ornate headpiece and elaborate dress, whorled tattoos on his arms and face, and the dozens of gold chains decorating his chest, Uri felt certain he was the High Priest.

"It would be our heads if the captain saw us," the officer in charge of the squadron protested.

"Besides being treachery of the worst sort," his sergeant muttered. "Whoever thought our own priests would betray us?"

"Do not consider this an act of treason," the High Priest proclaimed. "It is the will of the gods. Obey us. If you do not, Shamash will cast you into the fiery orb of his justice."

The guards drew their swords. "We won't do it," the sergeant shouted. "Move off. We'll spit you like pigs."

Agga's eyes moved past the soldiers and looked straight at Uri, a baleful, menacing glare. Uri's heart pounded in his chest. If they opened the gates and the Persian soldiers poured in, nothing would prevent them from pillaging and looting. Uri wanted to back away, but Agga's stare fixed him in his spot. His thoughts spun wildly—what should he do? Go forward and protect the Writings? Return home for Zakiti?

"Obey!" The High Priest's voice blasted through the square before the massive gates. He pulled himself up to his full height, using the glamour of his divine office to loom over the frightened soldiers. "Marduk commands you!"

The High Priest waved toward the third divine, who carried an enormous, closed basket of straw. As he opened the lid and tipped the basket, dozens of snakes poured out, slithering about the guards's legs. The soldiers looked almost comical in their panic, trying to keep their eyes on the snakes, the priests, and the gate, all at the same time.

"Marduk will order these creatures to set their fangs in your flesh unless you do as I bid and do it immediately," the High Priest declared, eyes glinting at the soldiers's discomfort. "These are poison snakes, brought from nests found on the scorching desert sands. They are trained to attack at Shadrac's command. Shall he give it?"

"No," moaned one of the guards, who turned deathly white as a snake glided between his legs, rubbing against his boots. "I'll do what the gods wish." He slid his sword in his scabbard and stepped toward the barricade.

"Hold, Namtar!" The officer brandished his sword. But another snake darted forward and hissed at him, making him stop in his tracks.

"Shall Shadrac give the command?" The High Priest's forceful tone shattered what was left of their resolve.

"This is all your doing, priest," the officer cried, dropping his sword at his side. "You will tell my captain you forced us to do this!"

"Your captain, my lad, will lose his authority before the hour is out," the High Priest sneered. "Agga, cast the dice! Is it time?"

Uri watched as his long-ago classmate stepped forward, daintily ignoring the snake that glided sinuously about his feet. Agga threw the bones of some small animal onto the brickwork. They clattered, gleaming and polished in the dawning day.

Agga looked up. "Now!"

Uri watched, unable to move, as three of the guards strained to pull back the massive bar securing the gate. They heaved the heavy doors inward. Shadrac somehow summoned the snakes to slither back into their basket, covering them once again.

On the other side of the gate stood a man whose insignia shone upon his broad shoulders. His dark eyes gleamed as he took in the tableau before him. Behind him stood a column of armed troops, their spears pointed at the ready.

"Welcome, oh Lord General, to Babylon," the High Priest intoned, bowing low. "We welcome you to our sacred city in the name of Marduk."

"Marduk has bid my lord and king, the mighty Cyrus, to rescue your people from the treacheries of your monarch," Cyrus's general proclaimed. His voice, deep and commanding, echoed through the solid stone blocks of the opened gate. "In his name, I free you and promise that the wonders of Babylon's great city will remain unscathed. As was agreed upon by my lord and king, my soldiers will not pillage this city so long as its denizens surrender to us. Go forth and announce my capture of their beloved city."

The High Priest bowed, turning to Agga, Shadrac, and the other priests in his entourage. "Do as the general commands."

The priests melted in all directions. Agga grabbed Uri by the arm and led him a few steps away. "You should not have witnessed that, but no matter. Tell your people to surrender willingly, and they will remain untouched."

"I will," Uri said, fighting to keep his face neutral. He realized the priests were motivated by greed and a deep-rooted desire for power. By opening the gates of the city, they regained their authority, an influence lost when Nabonidus removed the seat of the monarchy from Babylon to Haran, forcing them to minister to an empty altar and forgo the annual festivals that brought sacrificial bounty to their tables.

Agga's shaky laugh admitted Uri's suspicions. "The gods' commands are not always in tune with how a moral man would act," he shrugged. "I see you think this an act of treachery."

"It doesn't matter what I think, Agga," Uri said, recalling stories he had written in which God's will passed all understanding. "I will do what you ask. The Judeans will not resist Cyrus."

"Truth be known, you all have been praying for his victory," Agga retorted, his mouth marred by a self-deprecating sneer. "We avoid bloodshed this way, all of us."

Uri nodded, moving away. "Farewell, Agga."

Uri waited until he had turned a corner before he allowed his trembling knees to collapse. He wiped the heavy dew of sweat from his brow. "Blessed be Thee, Oh Lord our God, Who has given us life, kept us, and sustained us to reach this time," he murmured. He forced himself to rise. He would go directly to the academy, he thought, and from there send word to the Judean community. Then he would hurry home and wake Zakiti with a kiss of reassurance. After that, he promised himself, he would go to the farm. He wanted to be the one to tell his mother that, this time, Sarah did not need to fear the siege.

48

Amittai's Table

THE FARMERS FROM THE NEIGHBORING hills gathered around Amittai's table: Abijah, the son of Malachai; Ladan, the cooper's son; and Kemuel and Kenan, the bastard twin sons of Eytan the landowner, whose legitimate family had been carried into exile.

Keren brought them beer and small rounds of crusty bread topped with a spread of thick honey and crushed nutmeats. She hovered, listening while she cleaned an already immaculate part of the hearth.

"They say no one stopped the Persian soldiers from marching into Babylon," Ladan said. "They drained the Euphrates River and waded in the muck."

"Rumors." Ophir reached for another round of bread. "Think of the Chaldean soldiers' reputation for fierceness. How could they not defend their capital?"

Amittai shut his eyes, thinking back to that brutal day when warriors had left his home a smoldering ruin and killed his mother and sisters. *The Chaldeans deserve defeat*, he thought with bitter satisfaction. *May their bones wither!*

"Cyrus is not a ruler like we Hebrews have known—neither Assyrian nor Chaldean," Kemuel said. "He's released other captives to their homelands. Will he do the same with our people?"

"Not one of us is farming land that truly belongs to us," said Abijah, tapping the table with his forefinger, voicing the dread everyone felt. "What happens to us if they return?"

Keren whirled, forgetting it was unseemly for her to speak to a group of men. "My father bought this land as part of my dowry," she said. "This is *our* farm."

The men looked at Amittai. "Keren," he said, voice heavy with annoyance, "go tend the grandchildren."

Keren's eyes flashed, promising Amittai an unhappy night. But she flounced from the room, dripping cloth smacking the air behind her.

"Women." Kemuel shook his head.

The other men nodded sympathetically. Ophir shifted in his chair. "But she's not wrong, is she, Father?" he asked, almost unwillingly.

Amittai shrugged. "The farm was her dowry. You don't ask where a woman's dowry comes from, not if you don't want to listen to days of complaints of how you insulted your in-laws. Your father-in-law, Tobija's father, often hints that Hod came by the land less than honestly. If anyone knows dishonest dealings, it would be Hanun."

"So what do we do?" Ophir looked his father straight in his face.

The men around the table looked away, trying to ignore the tension between father and son.

"At least you two live on your father's land," Ladan finally said to Kemuel and Kenan. "No one can say you're not entitled."

"Baroch or his children can," said Kenan, raising clenched fists from his lap to rest on the table. "If they live, that is."

"But seriously, who will return?" Kemuel asked. "The camel traders say the Judeans are comfortable in Babylon. They have homes, children, grandchildren. Many died. Many made fortunes they could only dream about acquiring here. I wouldn't give all that up. Would you?"

Abijah leaned forward and scooped up the last of the bread and honey. "I've heard the prophets are busy in Babylon," he said. "They keep the faith alive and tell those who still worship in the old way to expect a Return to rival the Return from Egypt."

"How many still worship in the old way?" Ophir scoffed. "A handful of zealots?"

"I know you don't." Amittai scowled at his son. "You need not remind us."

"You left the faith yourself, Father," Ophir said. "If Grandfather hadn't made you give up attending the sacrifice...."

"And partaking of the sacrificial maidens, hey, Amittai?" laughed Kenan, elbowing his brother. They snickered. It was well known—though rarely said aloud—that the twins often left their wives alone on the farm for days to carouse with the whores of the sacrifice. They would select two or more women and bring them to the same bed, trading as whim took them, often making their long, lustful afternoons an orgiastic chain as they sampled boys, animals and—perhaps most shocking of all—each other.

Amittai's lips curled in distaste. "Mine were the excesses of an orphan who had no one to stop him," he said disdainfully. "With Hod's help, I saw the error of my ways. And even Ophir—fool though he is for going to the sacrifices with Tobija—controls his urges, unlike some."

Kemuel shrugged, unfazed.

Ladan stared at the twins in distaste. "If the priests return, don't think your lewd behavior will go unnoticed."

Kenan flushed. "And what will you do, Ladan, when the sons or grandsons of Noach reclaim their land? When they appeal to the new Persian overlords and tell the priests you uprooted their Cyprus saplings to grow dates, and mixed fields of flax in with their barley?"

"I've been a good farmer," Ladan protested. "I did what was best for the land."

"Or for your pocket," came another familiar voice. The men skewed about in their seats. Hanun the Amorite slouched in the entryway, his cloak drawn over his face, partially concealing a smirk.

The four guests looked at Amittai and Ophir. Ophir half rose from his seat. "Good evening, Hanun," he greeted his father-in-law. "Tobija and the children are in the garden. May I take you to them?"

"I'd rather sit with the men," the small, swarthy pagan said, his still-muscular arms rippling as he dragged a stool to the table.

"Have some wine." Amittai pushed a cup and the wine pitcher toward him.

The men watched Hanun warily. He dropped his cloak onto the ground and poured himself a full cup, quaffing half of it in a series of quick gulps, then refilling the cup. "Ah," he purred, sitting back in his chair. "So, you're all terrified you'll lose your farms?"

No one said anything.

"I can help you." The Amorite leaned forward, grinning. "Amittai and Ophir have no worries—they know I'll defend their claim to this farm. Peleg, who married my Naamah just over the hillside, has no reason to worry, either. Or any of my other Judean sons-in-law. But the rest of you? Well, you're friends of Amittai and Ophir. I can draw up terms that won't beggar you."

"You want us to pay for your protection, for protection by your henchmen." Abijah looked with level eyes into Hanun's mocking expression.

"I always knew the rumors Abijah's father dropped him on his head when he was an infant were foolish talk," Hanun said, his smile twisted into a sneer. "You're much quicker than people give you credit for."

"How much?" Ladan asked.

"Half the harvest, and my men do the reaping," Hanun replied.

"Not for us," Kenan said. "Those terms would beggar us."

"Really?" Hanun replied. "You'd rather have nothing than half a farm?"

"We own the land by right," Kemuel said. "Eytan sired us both."

"He never admitted it," argued Ladan. "Your mother never got him to admit it."

Kemuel's eyes narrowed. "Look at us. Can any man look us in the face and doubt it? Mother always said we were the spitting image of the randy old goat."

"His grandsons won't be so quick to see the resemblance," Hanun said. "And while I hear they thrive in Babylon, there are a goodly number of them. Some of them will probably return to claim the farm."

"And if the case goes up to the priests for deliberation," Amittai added, "you know what they'll decide. Leave the land in your sin-stained hands or return them to the legitimate heirs? It'll be the work of minutes."

"So there's nothing to be done," persisted Kenan. "We'd pay Hanun for nothing."

Hanun grinned even more widely, showing sharp yellow teeth. "There's always something to be done," he said. "Though it will be better if you don't ask me what it is."

The men glanced away to stare into the corners of the room. Not one would meet the other in the eye as they weighed their alternatives. Then there was a thud on the table, followed by another, and then a third, as small leather pouches were dropped before Hanun. Amittai sighed as the wily old bandit scooped up the earnest money and left without another word.

49

Sarah's Table

ALL OF THE FAMILY SAT around a long board that had been carried outside and propped up on bricks, for the farmhouse was too small to hold
them all. It was a warm winter afternoon, and Sarah, who sat at the head
of the board in full sunlight, only needed a light wrap to keep her aging
bones warm.

She looked about her. They were almost all there, and she felt a flash
of pride at what she and Reuven had salvaged from the ruins of their ancestral home. Nachum was there, with Mirav sitting next to him. Their
children—the simple but able farmer Joshua; his brothers Aaron and Gal,
both hired out to work elsewhere; and Chava, the grandchild of her heart,
sat farther down the table. Rahil and her wealthy merchant husband,
Enki, perched uncomfortably on their seats, Rahil swatting disdainfully
at the small midges that should have died off with the year's first rains.
Her three sons—Tekoa, Ruel, and Mered, all of whom were growing as
rich as their merchant father—sat with their cousins.

Mara was there, swathed in a shawl Sarah draped over her thin, bony
arms. After Belshazzar's death, after Cyrus arrested Nabonidus, Nitocris
had gone mad, raging through the palace corridors. Mara told Sarah
how Daniel compared the madwoman to her father, who had succumbed
to just such fits of insanity. Mara tried to be patient with the woman's

screams and hair tearing, but when she began to foam at the mouth and bite the furniture, Mara thought only of escape. She had other reasons for wanting to leave, reasons she told her mother she could feel within her left breast when she probed it. Daniel, in favor once again as Cyrus's advisor, secured her release. Mara turned up unannounced at Sarah's door, and Sarah cried over her once beautiful daughter's gaunt frame and the dark shadows under her eyes, glad to have her back home, yet full of shame for the years that had claimed her beauty and scarred her soul.

Of course, Uri was there, seated opposite Sarah, with Zakiti at his side and the girls—Asnat, Irit, and Atara—giggling with Chava or whispering to their husbands. Asnat and Atara might have been twins, so alike they looked with their gleaming black hair and lithe figures. Irit had a look of her grandfather about her—long fingers that could embroider beautifully just as his could dance over the strings of his instrument. Sarah thought for a moment of Seraf, now long dead—and of Reuven. Had either of them ever dreamed that this day would come?

Food and pitchers of warm beer were passed from hand to hand. Had they ever gathered so many of the family in one spot before, Sarah wondered? Someone was always missing, even at weddings or funerals. She remembered her pain when Rahil barely managed to stand at Reuven's graveside for more than a few minutes before making an excuse and leaving.

But this was not just a simple family gathering, Sarah recalled, and tapped shaking hands on the table. Instantly there was silence. "Uri," she quavered, her voice nearly inaudible from age and emotion, "read it aloud to us all, please."

Uri reached into his robe, pulled out a scroll, and stood up to read:

> Thus says Cyrus, king of Persia: All the kingdoms of
> the Earth the Lord, the God of heaven, has given to
> me, and He has also charged me to build Him a house
> in Jerusalem, which is in Judea. Whoever, therefore,
> among you belongs to any part of His people, let him
> go up, and may His God be with him! Let everyone
> who has survived, in whatever place he may have
> dwelt, be assisted by the people of that place with

silver, gold, and goods, together with free will offerings
for the house of God in Jerusalem.

"So," Sarah beamed, smiling about the table. "The miracle the Most
High promised us has come to pass. I would like to pray for a moment,
to thank Him for redeeming his Word to us. Uri?" She shut her eyes.

Uri murmured the same prayer he had uttered when Cyrus entered
the city without bloodshed. "Blessed be Thee, Oh Lord our God, Who
has given us life, kept us, and sustained us to reach this time."

"Amen," they all chorused.

Sarah opened her eyes. "So. Who goes?"

There was a strained silence. Sarah could not believe it.

"Who goes?" she repeated, after a moment's pause.

"Not me." Rahil tossed her head, grimacing at her mother's glare.
"Why should I leave everything I have—for what? An uncertain share
in a small farm on the outskirts of nowhere?"

Sarah slapped the table. "The sacred city of Jerusalem is not the
outskirts of nowhere."

"It is not Babylon, though, is it, Mother? How often did you tell us
how awestruck you were first walking the city streets? Clearly what you
left was nothing like it." Rahil sat back, twisting her forearms so the gold
and silver bracelets up and down her arms jangled. "I am a rich woman,
first wife to a good husband with a spacious home, servants, and com-
forts. I remain."

"Fine," Sarah retorted, lips pursed. "Truth to tell, I expected nothing
better. But you, Nachum? Surely you and Mirav will go and reclaim our
farm? You are the farmers."

Nachum flushed. "We talked about it last night, Mother," he said
slowly. "I am still not certain we're making the right choice...."

"We stay," Mirav interrupted him. "It's not much, but it's certain.
The children stay too."

"All of them?" Sarah asked, her face falling.

"The boys are settled nicely. As for Chava, we're starting to think of
marriage. We'll find her a good husband among the Judeans who remain.
From what I hear, most will."

"Surely not," Uri said, his eyes slanting toward his half-brother's wife. "A proclamation from the academy and the remaining royal family members beseeches all to ascend to the Holy City. Of course, most Judeans will heed their call."

"So you will go?" Nachum asked his brother.

Uri looked at Zakiti. "We are still discussing it," he said slowly. "My choice is not as easy as yours, Nachum. My family has ties here."

Sarah felt sorrow etching its way into her wrinkled face. She sighed and turned from him. "And you, Mara?"

Mara wrapped the shawl around her more tightly. "I'd go if I'd be any use," she said. "But after all my years of serving in the palace, I am— brittle. The journey would break me."

"No one goes?" Young Chava rose indignantly from her place, looking not only at the grownups but at her brothers and cousins. "We finally can return home, and no one will go?"

"Sit, Chava," Mirav snapped. "You are the youngest here and a girl. You know better than to speak."

Sarah, however, reached out her arms. The young girl ran into them. "She is the age I was when I was taken from my home," she said, kissing the girl's hair. "I am heart-glad she shows so much feeling about this matter." Sarah looked up and down the table, the satisfaction she'd felt earlier dissolving in disappointment. Where before the bounty spread before them signified that she had survived life in Babylon, now it reminded her that this foreign country held temptations all too easy to succumb to.

"Well, I go," she told them, making them gasp. "I swore to return home if there ever was a Return and I shall go."

Chava stared directly into her mother's eyes. "And I go with her," she said. "No one will stop me."

"Thank you, darling." Sarah kissed the top of the girl's head again.

Mirav glared at her mother-in-law, then turned to Nachum. "You're the girl's father—tell her she will not go!"

Instantly every eye at the table turned to Nachum, who shifted uncomfortably in his seat.

"If she wants to go so much…." he started.

Mirav let out a muffled grunt of exasperation. "You've always been a foolish and improvident husband," she exclaimed. "If it had not been for me, we would have all starved on that tiny piece of land…."

"You were happy enough to marry into it," Rahil snapped, roused for once to family loyalty. "It was much better than life in that stinking tanner's shop of your father's!"

Mirav turned a cold shoulder on her sister-in-law. "I won't stoop to argue with a woman who married outside the faith," she said. "Chava, you will *not* go!"

Sarah withdrew her hands from Chava's shoulders, where they had rested throughout the argument. "I cannot take you against your parents' wishes," she said, eyes clouding with regret.

"Nachum…." Uri said, slowly. But Zakiti put out a restraining hand and Uri subsided.

Nachum looked from his wife's clenched face to his daughter's beseeching one. A lone tear escaped Chava's eye and trickled down her cheek.

"She goes," Nachum said calmly—and put up a hand to halt his wife's quick protest. "And we will discuss it no further."

Mirav laughed bitterly. "We will—but clearly not here."

But Sarah knew her youngest son. He would not be dissuaded. From the rapt expression on Chava's face, her granddaughter knew it too.

"Thank you, Father," Chava whispered.

Sarah wiped the child's tears, putting an arm around her shoulder. "Thank you, son."

Uri looked at their transfigured faces. "You will not go alone," he said. "I come too."

Zakiti drew in a startled breath.

"But Papa," cried Irit, "how can you leave us? Leave Momma?"

"She is welcome to come, as are you all," Uri told them. "But your grandmother and cousin are right. I've been selfish thinking I would remain. The new Temple will need scribes. I'll go and serve in the land God promised us."

Irit and her husband whispered urgently. Asnat kicked her husband, but he shook his head. Atara simply went over to her mother and laid her head on her shoulder.

Zakiti sat, mute, looking at her husband's set face. Sarah knew well that look of resolve that settled over her eldest son's features. Both her sons were like their different fathers—once they'd made up their minds, there was no gainsaying them.

"Very well," Zakiti said, reaching over the table and taking Uri's hand. "I'll come with you, husband. But we will not travel as paupers. We'll equip ourselves and travel comfortably."

Uri kissed her, holding her to him. "What about it, girls?" he said. "Which of you have convinced these nice young boys of husbands to come with us?"

"We'll come," said Irit.

Asnat shook her head, face wet with sorrow. Atara looked pleadingly at her husband, her arm wrapped tightly about her mother's waist. But Jerah shook his head. "My father asked me to stay," he said. "Perhaps in a few years, we'll join you. But I cannot come now."

"You'll always be welcome," Uri told him.

"Chava is *not* going," Mirav said again, her face grim. "Nachum, you don't want to cross me in this."

But a look of finality passed between Nachum and his mother. The farmer turned to his wife, eyebrows raised. "No more discussion, I said," he replied. "We owe our livelihood to my parents. If Mother wants Chava with her, it is the least we can do."

Rahil still slouched in her seat, playing with her bangles. She looked at her mother's happy face and the pout on her own grew. She unfastened her gold necklace from around her throat and pushed several of her bracelets from her arms, dropping them before her mother.

"You will travel in style, then, Momma, you and little Chava," she said. "You won't repeat the horrors of your last trip across the desert."

Sarah looked into her daughter's eyes. "Thank you," she whispered. Her heart danced to see Rahil almost crack a smile.

Chava knelt before Mara, who was watching the family drama play out before her. Mara's eyes were hooded, longing buried deep inside them. "Aunt Mara, won't you reconsider?" Chava asked. "I'll pull another bracelet from Aunt Rahil's arm just for you. I'll take care of you on the journey. Please?"

But Mara shook her head, a hand creeping inside her shawl to clutch her breast as though it pained her. "No, child," she smiled. "You'll have to take care of our precious Sarah for me—for all of us. Promise, now?"

Chava nodded happily. "Yes, oh, yes. Oh, Mara, I can't believe it! We're going home!"

PART FOUR

The Return

538 BCE–Year 1 of the Return

50

Being Counted

CHAVA HUGGED HERSELF WITH EXCITEMENT. Thousands upon thousands of people crowded the great square, waiting to begin their journey to Judea. Families were crammed in with their livestock, camels who spit when you approached, bleating goats and sheep whose fur coats shimmered in the heat. Donkeys and horses panted under the weight of heavy bundles.

Having escaped Grandmother's watchful eye, Chava danced to and fro, introducing herself to the other youngsters in the caravan. "I'm Chava, of the house of Baruch," she said. "We're returning to our farm that overlooks the city of Jerusalem."

She met Adriel of Beth-El, Edan and Ketura of Zorah, Sharon of Tel Harsha, and Beula and Uziel of Jerusalem, before Grandmother called her back.

"Stay with me, child," Grandmother fretted. "What would happen if we left suddenly?"

"We won't leave today, Grandmama," Chava soothed the old woman. "Uncle Uri told us it would be at least a day before we depart. They must complete the counting first."

"That's right," Zakiti chimed in, shifting uncomfortably in her heavy gown.

Chava grinned to see her rich Babylonian aunt wearing modest Judean clothing. But Chava admitted that Zakiti was good-natured about it, even though the sun streamed down, causing the women's sweat to run in little rivers under their armpits and between their concealed breasts.

"You look hot, Aunt Zakiti," Chava teased her. "Should I bring you some fresh water?"

"That would be kind, child." Zakiti pushed out her lower lip to puff air into her face.

So Chava raced off again, running to the well where the young men lounged. As a modest maiden should, she covered her face with a scarf. But inside, she was skipping and prancing. It was a strange, giddy feeling, this freedom from the farm and all the routines of her life up to now.

After bringing her aunt water, Chava craned her neck to watch Uncle Uri inscribe the records of this auspicious day. She was proud to see her uncle and his friend Ezra on the platform with the dignitaries. Daniel was there—Chava grinned from ear to ear when the old soothsayer saluted her grandmother with a kiss and a blessing—along with Sheshbazzar, the High Priest of the temple, and Zerubbabel, a Hebrew prince who had been appointed governor of Judea by King Cyrus. Zerubbabel would lead the captives home.

A small procession in regal livery moved toward the platform. The people parted to make way for the delegation sent by King Cyrus, accompanied by his personal guard. Slaves carried heavy chests on massive, sweat-slick shoulders, grunting under the weight like the donkeys in the square. Bringing up the rear was a fussy little man who kept counting the chests, as though one of them might disappear in the bright sunshine.

The slaves laid the chests before Zerubbabel and bowed, giving him honor as a prince of the blood. Chava rejoiced to see Grandmama smile. A long time had elapsed since Judean royalty was accorded the dignity they were due. Chava squeezed her grandmother's arm gently. She put the old woman's wrinkled, brown-spotted hand to her lips.

"I am Mithredath, treasurer to His Majesty Cyrus the Great," proclaimed the fussy man, bowing before Zerubbabel. He had a penetrating voice for such a little fellow. "I return to the children's children of the

Judeans taken into captivity the sacred vessels that belong to their priests and their Temple."

A cry rose from the thousands of people in the square—a shout of exaltation. Cyrus's proclamation had been posted on every doorpost of Tel Abib, read over and over when the men gathered for prayers. Now this return of sacred vessels was concrete proof the Judeans would once again live in the land God had promised them. Chava jumped a little as she craned to watch slaves brandish the beautiful gold and silver cups and dishes before the excited crowd, then placing them in a pile before Zerubbabel.

In a corner, both Uncle Uri and his fellow scribe, Ezra, were writing quickly. The count began: thirty gold dishes, a thousand silver dishes, twenty-nine silver pans, thirty gold bowls, four hundred ten matching silver bowls, and thousands of other articles, such as candlesticks, incense burners, oil lamps, and gleaming silver knives.

"Back in Jerusalem," Grandmother told Chava, "I once saw the acolytes shining these items before the Passover Festival. It does my heart good to see them returned to us."

"In total," said Mithredath, after the lengthy pause of counting, "there are five thousand four hundred articles of gold and silver. His Majesty Cyrus the Great wishes they be returned to the great Temple of Jerusalem that your people are enjoined to rebuild, to bring further glory to His Majesty's kingdom."

"And glory to the Kingdom of God," said Sheshbazzar.

Mithredath shrugged, turning toward the High Priest in mild rebuke. "His Majesty honors your One God, Sheshbazzar," he declared, "as he honors the gods of all the nations."

The High Priest opened his mouth to retort, but Zerubbabel, trained at the court of Babylon, quickly forestalled him. "His gracious kindness and the honor he does my people in allowing us to sacrifice to our One God touches us all," Zerubbabel said, putting a hand on his chest. "Please convey my best wishes to His Majesty the King. We have a gift for him as well."

"A gift?" Mithredath's voice was fluted with surprise. "What can it be?"

Zerubbabel gestured to a servant, who brought over a collection of scrolls on a silver platter. "This is a record of my people's history, which we wrote during our exile in Babylon," the Judean prince said. "We present it to His Majesty and hope it will find an honored place in his library. When we return home to Judea, we will remember these writings as the best thing we did here in Babylon."

"A generous gift, one I know my king will treasure," said Mithredath, who, Chava thought, looked a little disappointed it wasn't a trinket of gold or a tribute of silver. But the king's treasurer bowed graciously and left, the palace slaves trailing behind him.

"We will begin the counting of the people now, so generations to come will have a record of this day," proclaimed Zerubbabel. "Uri and Ezra, my scribes, will record the numbers of those who plan to depart. I will send out my guards to count you. Please remain with your families and your clans, under the leadership of the man appointed as your group's leader, and we will accomplish this task quickly."

Chava sat at Grandmother's feet and waited. The groups were organized into some four or five thousand individuals, each led by one of the nobles—Zerubbabel, Jeshua, Nehemiah, Seraiah, Reelaiah, Mordecai, Bilshan, Mispar, Bigvai, Rehum, or Baanah. Sarah's family was in Mispar's group. The guards broke the groups into smaller family clans and began their counting. It was hard work for these men, as unused to number work as they were to carrying the spears they'd so recently been given. Judean exiles had not been encouraged to carry weapons.

"I have nine hundred forty-five descendants of Zattu here!" the cry went up.

"One thousand two hundred forty-five of the Elam family."

"Three hundred twenty-three of the clan of Bezai!"

"Two thousand eight hundred twelve members of the family of Pahath-Moab...who say they come from the line of Jeshua and Joab."

"Six hundred twenty-one of Ramah and Geba, traveling together because they have always formed an alliance."

"One hundred twenty-three men of Bethlehem."

"One thousand two hundred fifty-four of Elam!"

At that cry, Uri stopped the counting. "We've already heard from the men of Elam!" he said. "I have one thousand two hundred fifty-four men already marked down for Elam."

The guard conferred with the man in charge of the group. "This is the other Elam!" the guard finally called up.

Confused, Uri and Ezra conferred. The numbers were the same, leading the scribes to be sure this was a mistake.

"Are there two Elams?" Ezra cried out. "The leaders of the two Elam groups, please come up here."

It was finally established that there were, in fact, two Elams, who just happened to have the same number of people. Amid laughter, the counting went on.

Once the common men were counted, the Temple servants were brought forward. Chava watched Sarah's eyes brighten at the musicians and singers, and knew her grandmother was thinking that Uri's father, Seraf, would have been among their number.

The afternoon light was diminishing, and people setting up to sleep outside in the town square when the final proclamation was heard.

"Our company numbers forty-two thousand three hundred sixty who will take part in the Return," cried Ezra, consulting his records. "There are seven thousand three hundred thirty-seven menservants and maidservants and two hundred men and women singers. Altogether, we have also counted seven hundred thirty-six horses, two hundred forty-five mules, four hundred thirty-five camels, and six thousand seven hundred twenty donkeys."

Chava wondered at the numbers. Babylon was an enormous city, but how could so many people be gathered together? She felt dizzy at the thought of being a speck in such a mass of people.

"Do you think," she whispered to her cousin Irit as they prepared their bedrolls for the night, "that it felt like this on the evening after the Israelites crossed the Red Sea and were about to enter the desert?"

Her tired Uncle Uri, finally released from his long day's duties, overheard her, and gave her a kiss. "I think that's exactly what it feels like," he replied, and Chava saw the light that had been shining within her all day reflected back on his beaming face.

51

Departure

Only after the first of the caravans left the Babylon city square did Uri discover that Ezra was staying in Babylon. The two men leaned against the supports of the platform in the small pool of shade the dais provided, storing the records in goat-skin sacks sealed with wax to protect them during the long journey. As they worked, Uri wondered what their future in Jerusalem would be like. Ezra confessed, somewhat shamefaced, that he wouldn't be going.

"You're not...I don't believe that," Uri stammered, feeling oddly betrayed.

"There's so much to be done here," Ezra replied. "Baruch ben Neriah is too old to travel."

The cry went up for the next caravan. "Those going to Adonikam!"

As each group departed, the dust they left in their wake made everyone cough. It was as though a minor sandstorm struck the city square. A short distance from the foot of the platform where the two scribes stood, Uri could see Zakiti waiting patiently next to Sarah in the donkey cart. His daughter and son-in-law and niece were tying their sleeping mats onto the donkeys that Rahil's generosity had bought for them.

"First your father and now Baruch ben Neriah," Uri said, exasperated. "When will Ezra have a care for himself?"

A strange look flitted across Ezra's face. "I'm having a care for Ezra by staying here," he replied. "We've been so busy transcribing the Writings that we've only had a brief time to contemplate them. With all of you going to Judea, I'll have stretches of peace and solitude to study. I crave that."

"But...the Temple. What's more important than the Temple?"

Ezra smiled, picking up Uri's hand, as always encrusted with clay and stained with ink.

"The Temple is important. But the Law and the Writings set us apart. In years to come, Uri, people will have forgotten our names, or will confuse them with those of others. But what we have done here in exile, the words we compiled and the chronicles we wrote, you and I— that is the core of our faith. That is how we'll claim our covenant with the Almighty."

Uri stared into Ezra's blazing eyes. So many emotions assailed him at once—impatience at his friend's stubbornness, wonder at his absolute conviction—all overlaid with an awe that caused his fingers, lying limply in Ezra's grasp, to tremble. He drew them away, struggling to conceal a yearning to burst into tears.

"Still," Uri said, after a moment of choked reflection, "it is the Most High's Temple, isn't it? Shouldn't you be there for the rebuilding? Think what your father would have wanted. He was High Priest, after all!"

"Jeshua ben Jozadak—Sheshbazzar—will be High Priest. He doesn't need my father's son hovering in the wings, undermining his authority."

Another cry went up. "The men of Ramah! Come, let us sing as we depart the city of Babylon!"

The song they sang was one Uri had known from birth, one that his father had played often. The psalm's opening lines had become popular as a round, and the group sang it that way, splitting the company into three:

> By the waters, the waters of Babylon
> we lay down and wept
> and wept for thee, Zion
> we remember thee, remember thee, remember
> thee, Zion!

"My father the musician sang that to me." Uri turned back to Ezra. "But he sang the entire song. He had particular relish in singing the lines at the end."

"About the daughters of Babylon, doomed to destruction?" Ezra's slight smile lit up his typically dour face. "And look what came to pass!"

"I thought of that, the day the city priests opened the gates to the Persians," Uri confided. "Frankly I was glad we didn't see Babylonian babies dashed against the rocks, as described in the psalm's last line. But Seraf hated the Babylonians for what they did to him. Robbing him of everything that makes life worth living."

"He had you." Ezra lay a hand gently on his shoulder for a moment, then let it drop.

"The parties heading to Jerusalem! The parties heading to Jerusalem!" the cry went up. Suddenly, there was clamor as the bulk of the crowd readied themselves to leave.

"Aaron! Rachel! Where are you?" one woman cried, voice thin with frantic worry.

"We too will leave singing!" cried the leader of the Temple choristers. And they broke into another psalm of the captivity, their voices a peon of happiness:

> These things I remember
> as I pour out my soul:
> how I used to go
> with the multitude,
> leading the procession
> to the house of God,
> with shouts of joy and thanksgiving
> among the festive throng.

"That's your group, isn't it?" Ezra asked. He reached out and grasped Uri by the forearms with both hands. "Travel safe, my friend. Serve Zerubbabel and Sheshbazzar well. Send me news of all that happens!"

Uri grasped Ezra's arms in return, and the two stood there, clasping one another yet still maintaining distance between them. The stance was,

Uri realized, emblematic of their long relationship. "I still cannot believe you are not coming!" he said. "Change your mind."

Ezra shook his head. "Not now. I will come to Jerusalem one day, I am certain. But today is not that day."

They stood for a moment and the lifetime they'd spent together—squabbling, debating, annoyed with one another's choices—fell away. Ezra turned and walked off.

Little Chava—not so little any longer, Uri suddenly noticed—came running up.

"Uncle Uri! Hurry up! We're leaving!"

He took the girl by the hand, and the two of them ran to find Sarah and the family.

52

Ophir and the Secret Cache

AMITTAI WAS PITCHING FEED IN the hay loft, a job usually left for his son. Though he would never admit it, he was beginning to feel his age. But Ophir was still working with Hanun's men in the fields by the light of the evening's first stars, bustling to complete the harvest. Amittai, having eaten his own dinner, decided to do his son's evening chores for him.

He pulled away the hay for his beasts and his pitchfork rang out with a dull thick clang, striking something hard. "What's this?" Amittai said aloud, even though no one else was in the barn.

He brushed aside the covering of hay, finding a heavy wooden box with iron clasps, secured by oiled rope. He began to pull the small chest from its hiding place.

"Father! Stop!" Ophir cried, stepping into the barn at just that moment.

Amittai looked up. The look of abject fear on his son's face made him drop the oily rope.

"Ophir? What is this?"

Ophir ran in, thrust the chest back under the hay with one massive push, and started to cover it securely again.

"Help me," he muttered. "We don't want this found."

"What's in it?" Amittai wondered again, pushing hay from the other side of the rick over the wooden box. "Ophir?"

Ophir scrutinized the haystack with narrowed eyes. "Good," he said. "Go inside the house, Papa. I'll talk to you about this later."

"No." Amittai stood before his son with hands bunched at his waist. "Now."

Their eyes met, both steely with determination. Amittai rarely chastised his son. But when his ire was raised, he was ruthless. He might count on the fingers of one hand the times he'd whipped his son, but he knew those occasions had marked more than the boy's buttocks.

Ophir was remembering those beatings too, Amittai realized, as his son glanced at the wall where the horsewhips hung neatly.

"It's nothing." Ophir swallowed hard. "Go in the house. I'll come later."

Amittai took a step toward the horsewhips. But just then, one of Hanun's henchmen—Shobi, a man who always kept one or two paces behind his master—stuck his head in the barn.

"Ophir, join us in town after you finish, we're all going for a drink...." he started. But his voice trailed off as he saw the father and son facing one other. "What's going on?"

"Just tending to the beasts," Ophir said too loudly.

"Having a conversation with my boy," Amittai added to distract the henchman. "You don't mind, do you?"

"I don't mind...but this feels like a fight." Shobi sniffed the air. "Smells like one too."

"Get out, you fool," Amittai growled at him. "Ophir's still got an hour's work left."

"Want some help?" Shobi asked, eyes dancing at the idea of someone in trouble.

"No!" father and son yelled in unison.

Ophir added, "Go buy some beer for the boys. My treat. I'll pay you tomorrow."

"If you say so...." Shobi grinned. "How about you, Amittai? We did good work for you today. Want to buy the men a drink?"

"Sure, sure." Amittai waved him away. "Just go now."

They watched him stroll off. The sky darkened as clouds moved in and obscured the starlit night. A sliver of moon chased behind the thick clouds. Listening in the cool air, they heard Shobi gather the hired hands. Trooping down the hill toward the city, a ragged cheer rose for the two free drinks.

Ophir brushed by his father and grabbed two shovels. "If you insist on knowing what's inside, you have to help," he said, thrusting one toward his father. "Clearly the haystack's not a good enough hiding place."

Amittai accepted the shovel. "What's in there?"

But Ophir just walked past him, shouldering his own tool. Amittai followed.

"What's in the chest?" he repeated.

Ophir found a secluded spot in the bushes beyond the privy. "Here. No one would search here, would they?"

Amittai pinched his nose. "Not unless they had to. Ophir?"

"Dig, Father. I promise, I will tell you what's in the chest. But we must work fast. Hanun may be by later tonight."

Amittai looked at his son by the dim light of the partially hidden moon. Cold sweat stood on Ophir's forehead and a shadow of terror chased across his rapidly shifting eyes. Silently Amittai pushed his shovel's mouth into the soft ground.

It only took a few minutes to dig a hole deep enough for the wood box. They left their shovels and walked back to the barn. Amittai again tried to question his son, but Ophir just lengthened his steps and kept slightly ahead. They reached the barn and brushed aside the straw. Between them, they dragged the chest across the yard. It was heavy, Amittai realized, silently cursing his son for whatever danger he had exposed them to.

They lowered the chest into the hole. Ophir picked his shovel up and moved to the mound of dirt piled high beside it. But, quick as thought, Amittai blocked him.

"Tell me now." His voice grated with impatience.

Ophir looked at his father's set face and threw down his shovel. "I'll show you," he said, untying the rope that secured the chest. He cracked open the lid. Then raised it higher.

Amittai looked into a cache of daggers, piled high. He couldn't quite understand what he saw. He reached to pull one out, but Ophir let the lid slam shut.

Amittai pulled his hand away. "Why do you have this?"

Ophir picked up his shovel again and began scooping dirt into the hole. "Hanun," he said. "He gave it to me to hide. I don't want him to know you found it, all right?"

"Hanun?" Amittai, shoveling dirt, was more bewildered than ever. "Why are you hiding daggers for Hanun?"

"To fight the returning Judeans," Ophir said. "A secret cache, in case he needs it."

Amittai let his shovel drop out of lifeless fingers. "To do what?" he cried.

"To fight the returning Judeans," his son repeated, his voice soft, even.

Amittai's body shook. Almost without thought, his fingers curled into his palm, and he punched his son in the mouth.

Ophir staggered back, falling into the hole they'd dug. He hit his back against an edge of the wood box. "Moloch damn you!" the young man cried out in shock and pain.

The pagan curse made the blood rush to Amittai's head. His temples throbbing, he jumped into the hole and began beating his son. Ophir, younger and stronger, thrust him away, butting his father with a lowered head.

They stood there, inches from one another, panting, covered in dirt. The moon slid out from behind the clouds, and Amittai saw a trickle of blood seeping from his son's lips. Ophir spit into the gap and some of the blood from his saliva splattered Amittai's shirt.

After a moment of silent glaring, they climbed out of the hole. "I have to finish this," Ophir said thickly, mumbling around his swelling lip. "Either help or leave me to it."

Amittai edged away, moving so his back was propped against one of the trees that shaded the privy. Ophir glowered at him, then picked up his shovel. He finished the work swiftly, took both shovels and, ignoring his father, walked past him toward the barn.

He was halfway there when Amittai caught up with him. He fell into step beside his son, waiting until he had returned the shovels to their usual place. Then he grasped Ophir by both shoulders and demanded, "Why do this? Help Hanun against your own people?"

Ophir spit again. Amittai saw blood caking uncomfortably on his face.

"Because," his son burst out, "they aren't my people. Why should I think of them as my people? They don't consider us as part of their people, do they?"

Amittai felt his world turn black. He stammered, "What do you mean?"

"Who did the Babylonians exile? The royals, the nobles, the rich merchants, the freemen, the landed farmers. Who did they leave behind? The dregs."

"I am not...."

"The dregs," Ophir repeated. "The men who didn't matter. The women the soldiers raped, left pregnant, and widowed. The children whose parents the Chaldeans slaughtered."

"How can you say that?"

"Father." Ophir raised his arms and covered Amittai's hands with his own. "I love you. You've always been good to me. But you were born a nothing in Judea—a lowly shepherd boy. You only became what you are today because Hod stole this farm and gave it to you. And what will you do when the owners come back? They may already be on their way here. Will you give it back to them? Will you? Will you?"

"I...." Amittai found he had no answer.

"Well, I won't let you," Ophir said. "They think they're coming back to empty houses and empty streets. They think they can return after three generations and take what they used to have. But we won't let them. They might not have wanted to leave, but they left. We went on living in the shadows of their ruins. We scratched a living from this land. Why should we return to being the humble beggars of their generosity? Why can't we fight to keep our land safe?"

"This is Hanun speaking," Amittai realized. "Not you. Your father-in-law has been telling you this."

"And if he has?" Ophir said. "Does that make him wrong?"

"They're our own people," Amittai said, his voice rising in intensity and strength. "Do you think because you married an Amorite girl that makes you an Amorite? Do you think because the streets are crowded by Edomites and Samaritans that this land now belongs to them? No, Ophir. No. God gave our Father Abraham this land and promised it to us forever. When we left Egypt, He fed us manna in the desert and led us home. We are people of the mighty King David and the wise King Solomon. We are worshippers of the Most High, and this land—this land belongs to us!"

His shouting drew both Keren and Tobija to the barn. The two women stared at Ophir's wounded face but didn't dare question the men. They stood in the back of the building, waiting.

"We must protect what is now ours," Ophir said, stubbornly. "No one will take this farm from me."

"We don't need daggers to fight our own people!" cried Amittai. "We have judges and priests and laws to help decide who will go and who will stay."

"Ha!" Ophir said. "And do you think they'll grant you the use of this land when the nobles who used to own it return? They'll come in and pinch their noses at our smell and point their fingers toward the road and put us off the land. And all your great judges, father, will say it belongs to them, not to the rabble squatters who have been here only a scant three generations!"

"This land was bought by my...." Keren started.

Both men whirled on her.

"The man he bought it from stole the deed, Mother," Ophir cried. "Hanun told me so. The land is not ours."

"Hanun is a liar!" Keren spluttered.

Tobija's usually meek face flushed. "He's my father...!" she protested.

Amittai's energy was suddenly sapped from his bones. He wanted to go sit down somewhere, away from all these people, and let the cold night air clear his head.

"Tend to his wounds," he said, jutting his chin at Ophir's blood-encrusted face. "I'm going for a walk. I'll be back before dawn."

The wails and angry voices receded as he put distance between him and the farm. He walked to one of the hills surrounding Jerusalem, a place where he used to bring the flocks at night, where an outcropping of rocks protected them from a wind squall or a burst of winter rain. As a boy, he realized, his blood was thick enough to stay out all night with just a thin cloak. But now, despite the richness of his garments, he shivered in the cold.

The dregs of the country…. Ophir wasn't wrong. He thought of the men who'd sat at his table not long ago. Would any of them have a farm if it weren't for the exile? Or would they be the workers, sleeping in bunkhouses and drinking in the city taverns at night for warmth?

Amittai looked around him. The hillside, which had always been a refuge for him as a boy, was no longer enough. He closed his eyes and wished with all his heart that he'd be allowed, somehow, to keep the farm. Then he began the long tramp home.

53

On the Road

CHAVA WOULD ALWAYS THINK OF the four months on the road to Jerusalem as an adventure, the one time when no one scolded her to behave properly or loaded her down with chores.

Not that there wasn't work to do every day. The donkeys had to be watered and fed, their bodies combed of dust and desert mites. The meals they ate had to be prepared, a job she shared with Zakiti and Irit. Chava spent much of her day propping up her exhausted grandmother in the donkey cart, shielding her from the relentless glare of the sun and as many bumps in the road as possible. Sarah's eyes glowed bright as they drew closer and closer to Judea, but her face and frame became almost skeletal. She could not eat or sleep. Chava would wake in the middle of the night to find her grandmother clutching her thin bedclothes to her neck, her long white hair streaming down her back and her wizened face turned to the dark sky.

"Grandmama, you need your sleep," Chava whispered to her one night.

"The stars are still not the right stars," Sarah murmured. "I'll be home when I recognize the stars."

Chava could say nothing to that. She huddled under the pocket of warmth of her covers and fell back asleep.

During the day, Chava kept one eye out for Uziel, the young Judean she'd met in the market square in Babylon. She grew practiced in spotting his caramel-colored hair and his broad shoulders. Uziel would grin whenever he saw her. With the freedom of the road, he would walk alongside the donkey cart and talk with her for hours on end.

Uziel was a goldsmith's son, learning the trade. He showed her some pieces he had fashioned, and she marveled at their intricacy and beauty, turning them over in her palms. They felt warm, almost alive, to her.

"I hope I don't forget everything I know," he told her one day. "We've been so long on this journey."

"You couldn't possibly forget," Chava reassured him. "Believe me, when I get to the farm, I'll remember how to plant and sow and gather the crops." She laughed a little self-consciously, leaning forward, so Sarah wouldn't hear and feel hurt. "I'm not looking forward to it. It's such back-breaking work."

Uziel winked at her. "I'm sure you were good at it. But perhaps you'll marry a city man and won't be a farmer's wife."

Chava blushed. "Perhaps," she said, clasping her hands in her lap, so he wouldn't detect the sudden trembling of her limbs.

But Uziel didn't always approach her. He spoke to a lot of the girls—including Beula. While Chava was thin and wiry, her face flushed by the sun and brown skin roughened by years of work in the fields, Beula, the youngest daughter of a wealthy tradesman, had white skin and bright almond-shaped eyes. Her thick chestnut hair rippled down her back, covered with the thinnest of scarves. She was plump and curved, making Chava think of the goddess figure Zakiti had drawn into the sizzling pancake so many years ago. On the days Uziel lingered next to Beula's cart, making her laugh and throw her head back so that he could see the long white column of her throat, Chava wanted to curl up in a corner and cry. Only an innate sense of pride made her sit straighter in the cart, turning her attention completely to her grandmother.

"He's very handsome, child," Sarah once whispered to her, "but take care. He's looking for rich girls, the pampered pretty ones. Don't break your heart over him."

"Nonsense," Chava said, blinking back her hurt expression. "He's amusing, that's all."

Sarah smiled thinly and fell silent.

After the families ate, the young people would congregate around a fire built far from the disapproving eye of the priests. They sang songs of Israel's glories, of Jerusalem. One of the younger Temple singers taught them a clapping game to the tune of "David, King of Israel."

On the road to Jerusalem, even a child's song was charged with radiance. As much as Chava wished to reach the fabled city they all yearned for, she wished every day would last longer, so this strange, magical, unreal life could go on forever.

54

Mara and the Lions

WHEN MARA BEGAN TO COUGH blood, sharp pain radiating through her chest as though someone had knifed her, Mirav sent a messenger to Rahil. Mara watched from her narrow bed in a haze of agony as Rahil ordered her slaves to pack her sister's few belongings. They conveyed her, tenderly, in a horse-drawn cart away from the farm to Rahil's home.

Mara was made as comfortable as possible in a room overlooking the garden courtyard, next to the bubbling fountain. She swam in and out of consciousness, her feeble fingers groping for the mass inside of her that grew more painful and sore.

Rahil, lips pursed and hands on her hips, would enter the room at odd points in the day. Mara grew grateful for her care. Rahil never lifted a hand, but her voice sharpened when she saw Mara wince shifting on her low couch. Rahil harried her slaves into fetching softer cushions and cool unguents to place upon Mara's fevered brow. The cook boiled barley until the husks fell to the bottom of the pan, mixing the tenderest part of the stalks with cream and gentle spices, creating a flavorful gruel. She took meat bones and seared them until the juices ran, adding water and vegetables that bubbled for hours on the fire. Reaching for a fine cloth, she strained the soup, pouring a thin, savory broth into a bowl. It didn't matter. Mara could only manage the smallest of spoonfuls before her body rebelled, vomiting over the linen sheets. Rahil would edge away, shouting for someone to clean the mess. Rahil's raised voice pierced Mara's temples like a dagger. With only enough strength to murmur her thanks, she sunk back on fresh sheets, her befouled body laved clean with warm rosewater.

Lying in a daze, Mara had strange visions. She watched Uri and Zakiti sit under unfamiliar skies and speak of their lives in Babylon. She saw Chava talking with a handsome young man, their feet raising dust as they marched. She saw strangers walking the fields of the farm her father and mother had spoken of so often. And then one day she had a vision so clear, so peculiar, that she called for Rahil and told her to fetch Daniel from the palace.

Three days elapsed before Daniel came. Each time Mara drifted into unconsciousness, the vision grew brighter and more detailed. She nearly burst, wanting to tell him about it.

When Daniel finally arrived, Ezra the scribe accompanied him. Rahil greeted them effusively, saying how honored she was to have the foremost scribe of Babylon in her home, along with the noble who wielded so much authority in the Persian Empire. Daniel had been appointed one of Cyrus's commissioners, responsible for a third of his one hundred twenty satraps, or provinces. As such, he dressed in the purple and gold the murdered Prince Belshazzar had tried to bestow upon him the night before the city's surrender. Ezra, on the other hand, looked tired and dusty, his eyes red rimmed from days spent in study.

"Is there news from the travelers?" Rahil ushered the men inside the courtyard and offered them wine. Mara sat up in bed, watching from a window.

"Nothing of note," said Daniel, who would certainly know. "They are still on the road."

"I wish I could have gone...." Rahil moved her embroidered lambskin slipper out from beneath her skirts, etching a thoughtful pattern on the brick pavement. "But I am grateful to have financed my family's trip."

"You will be blessed for it, surely." Daniel looked around. "Your message said Mara was asking for me?"

"Of course." Rahil clapped her hands. A servant appeared. "Carry my sister out to the garden."

"If she's ill, should we not go in to see her?" Ezra asked.

Rahil shrugged. "You wouldn't find the rank-smelling sickroom pleasant. And it won't hurt Mara to sit in the fresh air. My servants will lay her on a divan, and she will be as comfortable here as she would be inside."

The two men looked at one another and shrugged.

In a few moments, a low couch draped with rugs was placed in the courtyard. A male body servant carried Mara out. Mara knew from the surprise on his face as he lifted her just how much weight she had lost. Her skin stretched over her bones. Self-consciously, with trembling fingers, she wrapped her shawl tighter around her shoulders.

The look on Daniel's face, which he quickly hid under a tight smile, confirmed Mara's suspicions. She was dying. As the manservant lowered her onto the divan, covering her with rich rugs, Mara closed her eyes and murmured, "Behold, they will all wear out like a garment; the moth will eat them."

Daniel sighed, then smiled wryly.

Ezra raised his eyebrows. "I've never heard that before. Who said it?"

"A young man who ate at my table for a while," said Daniel. "I should have introduced you. But Isaiah left Babylon soon after the proclamation. I do not know where he has gone, whether he accompanied those making the Return or traveled elsewhere."

"I spend my days thinking about what he said," Mara murmured. "While the Most High has seen fit to wither me, I no longer feel the burning hatred I once had for Him. When I feel it creeping in on me again, I remember that prophet's verses:

Whereas you have been forsaken and hated
With no one passing through,
I will make you an everlasting pride,
A joy from generation to generation.

Then you will know that I, the Lord, am your Savior
And your Redeemer, the Mighty One of Jacob.

Daniel sat back in his seat. "I wish Uri could hear you. He worried about you, Mara."

Mara smiled. "He is at peace. I see him in my dreams."

Daniel brought his stool closer to her, gesturing to Ezra to draw nearer as well. "Your sister sent me an intriguing message, that you dream strange dreams about me. I hope you don't mind my bringing Ezra to transcribe them."

Mara spread out her hands. "You will think it a child's tale, perhaps. I hate taking so much of your valuable time, Daniel, and yours, master scribe. But the dream burns my lips and compels me to speak."

"Then speak, child, and do not worry about our time. It is a joy and a good deed to sit here with you, in your sister's beautiful courtyard, and to console you as you lie in your sickbed."

Rahil, who had begun to pout as the two men ignored her, smiled at that.

Mara closed her eyes, as if summoning her vision. She spoke with them still closed. "Do you still pray by your open window three times a day, Daniel?"

Daniel nodded. "Of course."

"And is it true that Darius will replace Cyrus upon his death?" Mara opened her eyes, looking deep into Daniel's startled ones.

"Yes," he said slowly. "But very few people know that."

"In my dream, you are one of Darius' three commissioners, as you are today under Cyrus. And he wished to appoint you lead commissioner of the empire if you proved yourself worthy."

Daniel said nothing, but the intent glint in his eye showed how carefully he was listening.

"The other commissioners and the satraps are jealous and seek to dissuade the king from making this appointment. They encourage him to sign a law stating that all his subjects must pray only to him. If they refuse, the law states, they will be cast into a lion's den. And Darius, agreeing, signed the decree."

"A lion's den?" Daniel's voice was fluted with amusement.

Mara's lips turned up. "I know how bizarre that sounds. But every time I go to sleep, that's what I dream. And it becomes even more fantastic."

Ezra shook his head ruefully, writing quickly. "I wish Uri were here. He would do this story much more justice than I can."

"Once they entrapped the king into creating this new law, the satraps and commissioners tell him that you pray to the Almighty by your open window three times a day. And Darius comes and sees you, and he orders his soldiers to bring you to him.

"When you appear before him, he urges you to cast off the Almighty and to pray only to Darius and his gods. And you refuse."

Daniel's lips pursed together tightly, his amusement fading swiftly. "As I would."

"So Darius has no choice. He casts you into the lion's den."

Rahil rose hastily. "Mara, surely this is just a dream, a delirium…. Noble prince, I apologize for my sister…her illness must excuse it."

Daniel waved her protests away, looking annoyed at the interruption. "Let her tell her story, woman!"

"The king has his slaves roll a massive stone over the entrance to the cave and traps you inside, placing his royal seal upon the mouth of the cave so that no man could come to your aid. He orders soldiers to guard the cave. And then he departs, crying for the loss of you."

"At least he shows some genuine affection for me," Daniel commented dryly.

"And the night passes, slowly, and throughout the kingdom the news spreads, and those who believe in the Most High pray to Him and mourn you. But no one could save you.

"The next morning, Darius approaches the cave, fearful and trembling, calling your name in some wild hope you might have survived. He brings the royal physician to tend to your wounds, as well as ten men of our community to pray over your body and bury you if they find you dead.

"When he calls to you, he does not expect you to answer. But you do answer, saying in a clear and penetrating voice—'Oh King, live forever!

My Lord God protected me and sent an angel to lock the lions's mouths. The beasts and I spent a quiet night here together.'

"They roll the boulder away, and you emerge unscathed. Darius, amazed and delighted, orders that the men who implicated you be placed inside the cave to suffer the fate they conspired for you. They enter, together with their families, crying and afraid, for none have faith in the One True God. And sure enough, God's angel opens the lions's mouths and only torn flesh and bones are discovered the next morning."

Mara delivered the tale in a clear voice, but with the last sentence, she was beset with a coughing fit. As Daniel and Ezra watched, helpless, she coughed up thick blood and mucus, staining her bedclothes. Rahil clutched her sister to her bosom, trying to soothe her.

"I will send the king's physician," Daniel said.

Mara shook her head, gasping out, "No need. I've told you of my vision, and God is pleased. He will deliver me of my pain and suffering. I am ready."

Ezra backed away. Daniel bent and kissed her forehead. "Yes, God is pleased with you, my child. Go in peace."

Mara's coughing ceased, and Rahil turned away to bid farewell to the parting guests. Mara had felt a gentle warmth pervade her body as Daniel spoke his last words to her, knowing they were a benediction. When Rahil returned to her sister, Mara was gone, her lips turned upward in a tranquil smile.

55

Night Before Ascent

THEY CAMPED ON THE LAST night at the foot of the mountain. Above them was the City of Jerusalem. Delegates came down to greet them, bringing gifts and food. After speeches, prayers, and feasting, the night finished with wild dancing before the fire.

Amid the tumult and joy, Grandmother sat apart, suffused with elation, her face turned to the sky. Chava crept away from the feast to find her.

"The stars are my stars." The thin face was pallid and damp with her tears. "Oh child, I cannot believe it. I am home at last."

Chava hugged her grandmother's skeletal body. "I know, Grandmama. It's wonderful."

The old woman reluctantly withdrew her eyes from the stars to look at her granddaughter's face. "You are happy, little Chava?"

Chava looked away. Truth to tell, she wasn't happy. When the dancing started, she'd looked toward Uziel, but he was already in the middle of the circle, swaying together with Beula. The dancing had barely started when some clucking disapproval on the part of the matrons roused the priests from their feasting. They sent an officious acolyte out to halt the musicians.

"Men must dance in one circle, women in another," the acolyte proclaimed. "Anything else is an affront to the Most High here at the foot of His city."

Grumbling, the men and women drew apart. The musicians started the music again. Someone called, "Take joy in this miraculous night," and any lingering disappointment was swallowed up in the glory of dancing to God.

Chava had wanted Uziel to touch her arm and lead her into the circle, but now he never would. This was not a desire to confide in her grandmother though. "Of course I'm happy."

Grandmother looked satisfied. "Go then, child, and dance with the others. You are young. You should worship the Most High with your feet. Leave me to worship His creation with my failing eyes. Oh Chava, I cannot believe I lived to this day!"

Chava kissed her and left, content with her grandmother's bliss. Passing by their tent, she heard sounds inside that meant her uncle and aunt were enjoying a private celebration. The tent flap had been lowered and tied shut. Chava clapped a hand to her mouth, so she wouldn't giggle. In truth, she wished her own parents loved one another the way Uri and Zakiti still did. But even so, Chava blushed for them. At their age!

Her cousin Irit, dancing with the women, waved her long fingers. Chava wiggled through the crowd to reach her. Irit was flushed, droplets of sweat dotting her forehead. But she continued to bob and sway and, hanging onto her outstretched hand, Chava entered the spirit of the dance.

An hour later, Chava broke from the circle, exhausted and thirsty. She started toward a table set with pitchers of water and wine. The elders had gone to bed and the two circles were mingling at the darker corners. As Chava passed by, an arm reached out and grasped her waist.

"Where have you been, pretty Chava? I looked but couldn't find you," Uziel whispered in her ear.

"I've been dancing," Chava murmured, all thoughts of her parched throat forgotten.

"Come dance some more," Uziel urged her, moving with her into the shadowed corner.

Chava felt helpless to protest. She leaned against his strong body, his skilled fingers caressing her arm. Her head clouded, and she felt she might swoon.

"You are so darling," Uziel murmured, bringing his lips close to her ear, almost touching it with his mouth. "Will you make me happy tonight?"

Chava felt her knees buckle. As she considered what he was asking her to do, he shifted position to press his hips against hers. She felt his desire growing against her. Her lips parted, and he lowered his face down upon her, tongue snaking into her mouth, taking possession. She collapsed against him. He took her arm, drawing her away from the dancers into an area of thin scrub brush. Other couples panted there, each oblivious to anyone else. Uziel reached for her again, pulling her to the ground. His fingers untied the laces of her gown, opening her bodice to reveal her still slender body. He reached inside and cupped her narrow breasts.

He sighed. "Oh, Chava, I've longed for this."

The sensations flooding her body stopped any rational thought. She wanted him to continue touching her. Reaching between them, he adjusted his clothing. His hot male member burned against her exposed thigh. Her body was telling her to open her legs, to allow him in. Her hips moved of their own accord. He would possess her, and it was a sin, she knew, but she felt powerless to stop him.

"May I?" he murmured, and she buried her head in his shoulder in silent assent.

But instead of the piercing pain she expected, his body lifted off hers and cold night air woke her from her sensual dream. Shocked, she looked up and saw Uziel being dragged off her by an irate Uri. She flushed and quickly sat up, scrabbling to cover herself.

Irit knelt beside her. "Go to the tent," she told her. "My father will deal with Uziel."

Burning with shame, Chava ran crying through the camp, reaching the privacy of their tent. Flinging herself on her bedroll, she wept bitter tears of humiliation and unsatisfied desire.

Zakiti brought her a cup of tea. Grandmother, who was already in bed, sat up and patted her on the shoulder. Irit stood back, shaking her head, but a small smile grew on her face. "Oh, Chava, we should have watched over you better," she said. "But it will be all right. You'll see."

Chava's tears slowed, noticing that not one of the women in the tent was angry. Indeed Zakiti looked almost pleased. "Drink your tea," she said, "and tomorrow I'll tell you the story of your uncle and me."

"Did he—hurt you, child?" Sarah quavered.

Chava hung her head. "No."

"My father's gone to speak with his," Irit told Sarah. "It will be all right."

Chava suddenly understood what Irit was saying. "He's gone to Uziel's father?" she asked, hope flowering in her eyes.

But when Uri returned, his expression was sullen. "The boy is already betrothed, and I'm told there is not enough money for a second wife, even one of easy virtue," he said, throwing down his cloak in disgust. "Once his father knew nothing had happened, he refused to listen. He was insulting to Chava and to us. Chava, You'll have nothing more to do with the boy."

"He's already betrothed?" Chava gasped. "To whom?"

"Some merchant's daughter—Beula, I think her name is. In any case, you must not allow a man to touch you like that, not until marriage. If Uziel whispers your name to his friends…well, your reputation will suffer because of your carousing, that's all. I'm ashamed of you."

Blood pounding in her face, Chava glanced toward her grandmother, her aunt, and her cousin. All of them eyed Uri with scorn.

"Perhaps I should tell the child how we came to marry, Uri?" Zakiti asked, honeyed tones belying the underlying threat.

Uri thrust his chin outward. "Do you think because we sinned, I should encourage the child to do the same?" he retorted.

"Beula," Chava muttered. "He's marrying Beula."

"Shh, child," Grandmother said, worried eyes raking the girl's face. "Lie down and sleep. Tomorrow will be a wonderful day for us all. You need your rest."

Chava lay down and closed her eyes. Tears leaked out. Why couldn't they have left them alone for just a few minutes more, she thought? Once he had taken her, his father would have been forced to allow them to wed.

The family slept, but Chava remained awake, eyes burning and thoughts fixed hopelessly on the man who had wanted to take her virginity and then discard her.

56

Jerusalem

Jerusalem was a disappointment.

There was no other word for it, Uri thought, looking at the rubble of the small, narrow, winding stony streets, the hostile glares in the jostling marketplace, the smell of burning dung rising from the Temple ruins. It was unsettling, particularly after spending his entire life in Babylon. Uri had known Jerusalem would be smaller, but he'd pictured something like the great capital of the East—with its wide avenues and beautiful courtyard gardens. Here, feral dogs snapped at his heels and black-eyed boys, their olive skin marked with tattoos, begged for alms and tried to pick his pockets.

The climb to the city had been exhausting but exhilarating. The singers of the Temple gave voice to their feelings in songs of utter joy. The straggling olive trees lining the curving road to the mountaintop gave little respite from the sun, but Uri gloried in the glare of God's fiery creation. The priests headed the procession, bursting out in prayer as they scrambled from rock to rock up the sharp incline. Uri, as one of the royal scribes, followed behind, eyes taking in every detail of the day to transcribe later.

The city outskirts fooled him. He thought they'd arrived at a suburb like Tel Abib, a small satellite clinging to the skirts of her larger sister.

As they passed through these first streets, people hissed and spit at them. One had to only look at their immodest dress, the markings on their bodies and defiance in their eyes to know they were not Judeans.

"Samaritans," Uri said in a voice that mixed disgust and trepidation to Hevel, Irit's husband. The young man whom Uri had long ago adopted as his protégé walked beside him carrying his scribal instruments. "Or Ammonites."

The singers' voices hushed as they moved from one constricted street to the next. The priests were confused which way to turn. The city ruins were bewildering, even to the elders, who were forced to ask those who'd remained behind during the exile to lead them.

As they turned into the enormous public square that led to the Temple ruins, Uri fell back, looking for Sarah. His mother was sitting up straight in her donkey cart, eyes clouded.

"Does it look like you remember?" Uri asked.

Her voice was troubled. "Not in the slightest."

"You were so young, Grandmama," Chava tried to reassure her. "You've forgotten."

Sarah shook her head. "Would you forget Babylon—ever?" she asked her granddaughter. "I was your age when I was brought out of Jerusalem in chains. This is not the city I remember. This…." Sarah swallowed hard, once, twice, tears streaming down her wrinkled cheeks.

Uri wanted to cry himself. But Chava—who had reasons of her own for sadness—was already weeping with Sarah, the two of them huddled in the swaying cart. It would be unmanly to stay and weep with them. Besides he would be looked for in the Temple Square.

Nothing remained of the glory of the old Temple except a single altar stone, scarred and stained by sacrifices the Samaritans had given in their absence. As Uri drew up to Jeshua ben Jozadak, who had discarded his Babylonian name of Sheshbazzar the moment they left on their journey, Samaritan priests were haranguing the High Priest.

"We worship the One True God, as you do," one of them told Jeshua. "We kept His fires burning while you languished in Babylon."

"We are eager to help you in the rebuilding," said another, smiling broadly. "We hear Cyrus gave you gold and silver to build the Temple anew."

"Tell my scribe your names and where you are to be found," Jeshua told them. "We will speak with you before we commence the rebuilding."

"We could give sacrifice now, to welcome you home," urged a third priest. "I will send one of the acolytes to fetch wood to kindle the sacred flames."

"We thank you." Jeshua tilted his head so that his nose rose in the air. "But we must ritually prepare the altar first. Tell my scribe your names."

Uri took them apart and wrote their names on his traveling wax tablet. Then, curious, he asked, "How did you come to worship the One True God?"

Sadaqa, the chief Samaritan priest, responded, "We settled the land your fellow Hebrews, the Israelites, were forced from when the Assyrians exiled them. We lived in the city of Shomer, to the west, on a hill overlooking the valleys. A beautiful city, full of date palms and white stone. But it was overrun by lions and other wild creatures."

"Lions?" Uri asked, writing quickly.

"Savage beasts that carried off our young and made our lives a misery. So we knew we had offended the god of the country and sought to find out more about him and appease him with the proper rites.

"A priest of your faith lived among us. We implored him to show us how to appease the god who was angry with us. He taught us of the One True God."

"So you worshipped only Him ever after?" Uri asked.

The Samaritan priests looked at one another. "We are still loyal to the gods of our old country, of course," one of them said.

Uri said nothing, writing rapidly.

"But we want to worship with you," said Shimram, another of the priests. "We are earnest in this wish."

"Jeshua, our High Priest, and Zerubbabel, our prince and the governor appointed by Cyrus, will decide the matter," Uri replied, pocketing his small tablet.

The Samaritans looked at one another. "We will speak, then, with this Zerubbabel," Sadaqa said, drawing himself up. "Thank you, scribe."

Uri watched them move off, their long white robes and high turbans giving them an instinctive dignity. He returned to Jeshua and relayed what he had been told.

"They will not lift a finger here," the High Priest said, horrified that the altar of the Most High had been used to worship other gods.

"They'll be angry," Uri cautioned him.

But Jeshua looked at the scribe askance. "What does their anger have to do with us? You forget yourself. Do not presume to give me advice."

During the long journey to Jerusalem, Uri had learned that the new High Priest was not an easy master. He liked Prince Zerubbabel better, with his innate grace and royal courtesy. Jeshua was prickly and quick to decide when someone was not affording him proper respect. Even back in Babylon, Uri had found him difficult to talk to. Now that they were in Jerusalem, Uri sensed Jeshua would grow insufferable.

"If you don't need me, I would like to attend Zerubbabel now, to receive his instructions for settling the people for the night," Uri replied without apology.

Jeshua, his lips compressed and shoulders sagging as he turned to survey the wreck of the Temple, waved Uri off with a quick flick of his wrist.

57

Return to the Farm

SARAH LAY AWAKE WITH HER eyes closed. Chava shared her bedroll, pretending to sleep. But her body shuddered convulsively every once in a while. A few yards away, behind a screen created from a heavy piece of cloth, Zakiti hissed angrily at Uri.

"Why did you bring me to this desolate place?" she railed at him. "What kind of life will we have? Why did we come?"

Uri's calm, reassuring tones did not seem to comfort her. Beyond them, Sarah could just make out Irit and Hevel murmuring to one other in the dark. Sarah could not hear if they, too, shared the despair infecting the family, but she suspected they did.

Oh, would this night never end?

Tomorrow, Sarah told herself, they would go to the farm. Uri had been granted a day's grace from his scribal duties to find their ancestral home. He'd hugged Sarah and told her that everything would be better once they were safely settled. Sarah had smiled at him wanly and agreed.

Why did I bring them all here? The question buzzed around her like a black fly that insisted on flying in circles about her eyes and ears. *Why did I hurt them like this?*

Eyes closed, Sarah lay still and waited for dawn. In the hour before the sun was due to peek over the horizon, the tent settled down and slept.

Unable to relax into slumber, she rose, groping her way outside the tent, body shivering in the pre-dawn air.

The stars reassured her. Seated on a rock not far from the tent entrance, wrapped in a blanket, Sarah gazed at the familiar sky. Tears leaked from her swollen eyes, trailing down her cheeks. *Momma*, she thought. *Papa.* So long ago since they'd died. *Yoram, big brother.* She let herself remember them all under the gleam of the lightening sky. Remembered that brutal day. How had she and Reuven survived it?

The camp awoke as the sun rose. Chava staggered outside. She took her grandmother back into the tent, scolding her for sitting where the cold could seep into her old bones.

"Today's going to be a wonderful day," Chava said, combing Sarah's long white hair and pinning it onto her head. "Today we finally go home."

Sarah touched the girl's arm. "He isn't worthy of you, child," she said. "Put your longing for him aside."

Chava shook off her hand. "If he isn't worthy, let's not talk about it," she muttered through gritted teeth. "Please?"

Sarah nodded. "Let's prepare breakfast. Tomorrow we'll eat dates from our own trees! Today I'm afraid, all we have left is a little barley mash."

The family set out after breakfast, with their belongings packed on the donkey cart. As they ascended the hill leading to the farm, Sarah's heart pounded. The city might be a ruin, but here in the countryside, she recognized landmarks. There was the clump of trees—grown much taller now—where she and her brother used to play. There was the narrow riverbed which, in winter, filled with rainwater and there, around the bend, the tiny waterfall where she'd often been sent to wash the dishes or the family's clothes. Up around a hairpin bend in the road, they came upon the first terrace and a burst of olive trees, their gnarled roots greeting her like old friends.

"The trees look very well tended," Uri said in a low voice to Hevel.

Sarah heard the apprehension in his voice but made herself ignore it. This was too important a moment for doubt.

The house—a low flung, whitewashed, thick-walled building—stood precisely where Sarah had left it. Of course, she realized it couldn't be the same structure. The Chaldeans soldiers had burnt that one to the ground.

But someone had built a house remarkably like the one they'd been forced to leave. An extra wing extended off the back, and the entranceway was placed on the wrong side. But it was her home! She glanced at Chava, who was busy looking around, making new memories. *Oh, to be Chava's age again!*

The cart drew up before the house. A woman about the age of Sarah's children emerged. Peeking out of the windows were five heads, four children and a young mother.

"May I help you?" the woman asked, eyeing them warily.

"I am Sarah bat Baruch, returned home," Sarah said simply.

The woman drew herself up. "I am Keren bat Hod. My husband, Amittai ben Dotan, who owns this land, is in the fields. I'll send for him. You remain in the cart until he comes."

Her husband, who owns this land? Squatters! Sarah refused to be downcast. They would soon learn different. "My son, Uri ben Seraf, a scribe to the High Priest Jeshua ben Jozadak and to Governor Zerubbabel, speaks for us," Sarah told Keren. "He is a man of no small importance."

"Send for your husband," Uri said. "This is a matter for men."

Keren poked her head inside the door and a boy, perhaps six or seven years of age, ran out. He glared at the family in the cart with undisguised fear and loathing.

"Go get your grandfather," Keren instructed him.

He ran off, sandals slapping against his heels. Keren stood before them, arms folded across her chest, mouth pulled tight.

"From everything I've seen, you've done well preserving the farm," Sarah ventured.

Keren said nothing, looking off toward the fields.

"Look, Chava," Sarah said, pointing toward the barn, "that's where my father kept the animals. I would spend hours with them."

"My husband," Keren said to the ground, "built that barn when we first moved here after I was married. There was nothing left of the old house or barn except for charred embers."

"Mother," Uri murmured, "don't say anything more right now."

Sarah let out a pent-up breath. "I want to get out and walk around," she complained. "Why are we cooped up here? I want to show Chava the farm."

Sarah saw the impatience on Uri's face. She'd grown used to seeing that expression on the children's faces as she'd aged. But she'd also become skillful at ignoring it.

A tall muscular man strode up the hillside, followed by a younger man. Both men had olive complexions flushed by the early morning sunshine.

"I am Amittai ben Dotan," the elder of the two said. "This is my son, Ophir. Welcome to my farm."

"*My* farm," Sarah said firmly. "This land was taken from my family when we were exiled to Babylon. I've returned to claim it for my son and his family."

"The son is scribe to the High Priest and the new governor," Keren muttered.

As Amittai looked at the family in the cart, his face creased, looking uncertain. But he bowed low to Uri. "Then it is upon us. The day we have dreaded."

Keren and Ophir stared at him, wide mouthed. "What are you saying, father?" Ophir stammered.

"Please be my guests." Amittai ignored the horrified expressions on his son's and wife's faces. "My wife, Keren, and Tobija, my daughter-in-law, will fetch refreshment. You have come a long way to this poor strip of land. We welcome you as Abraham welcomed the angels."

Sarah was the first to clamber down. She stood, body bent and twisted, on the same land where she had once been a young, hopeful girl. She bent down, picked up a handful of dirt, and brought it to her nose. She sniffed deeply, closing her eyes. It was true. She was home.

She opened her eyes to find Amittai looking deeply into them, worried. A pang of doubt struck her. These people had lived on the land for three generations.

Keren and Tobija, Ophir's wife, set a table in the front yard, covering it with flat olive bread and dates.

"Break bread with us," Amittai invited them, "and then we will discuss how to proceed."

Sarah watched as Ophir pulled his father aside and whispered to him fiercely. Amittai shook his head and pushed the young man away.

Ophir went to his other side and pulled his head down, whispering again. Amittai swatted his son like a mosquito. Ophir, face mottled with fury, grabbed the boy who had run to the fields to fetch them. He hissed something in his son's ear and the boy went running off.

"Please sit," Amittai said.

The group sat uncomfortably around the table. Sarah tried to ignore the heavy tension as the family was served bread by one of young girls. Ophir stared defiantly at Hevel. Hevel, a scribe who lacked the heavy forearms and broad back of the farmer, eyed him warily. Tobija studied Zakiti's gold jewelry, which peeked out from under her heavy clothes. Despite being swathed in Judean dress, Sarah knew the Babylonian woman still liked a glint of gold on her ears and around her neck. Keren, face and neck red, refused to look at anyone. Only Amittai tried to be gracious.

Sarah couldn't eat, but she took some bread on her plate to be polite. "How soon can you leave the farm?" she demanded, her voice louder than she intended, breaking the bread into small pieces as she spoke.

Uri whirled on her. "Mother! Hush! This is a matter for men."

"And why is that, I wonder?" Keren demanded, picking up her flushed face to stare at him. "This farm was my dowry to my husband. I have a right to speak on this matter."

"You do not," Amittai snapped at her. "I am your husband and I speak for you."

"Then speak for me!" Keren shouted. "Inviting these strangers to our table as though they have a right to be here! Making me fetch food for them! Defend me, if you speak for me! Defend your son and your son's children!"

"He doesn't need to," came a voice from behind. "I'll do it for him."

Sarah whirled about to see a small, pointed-faced man surrounded by henchmen, holding the boy by the hand.

"And who are you?" Uri asked.

One side of the man's face rode up in a smirk as he ignored the question. "Ophir. Nadab here says you sent for me."

Uri turned back to look at Amittai and repeated, "And who is this?"

"My son's father-in-law," Amittai muttered. "Hanun."

Sarah couldn't help but notice that their host seemed ashamed to claim the man.

"Oh, Papa!" Tobija burst out. "They want to put us off the farm!"

"Do you think I'd let that happen?" Hanun said grimly.

"I am owner of this land," Amittai said. "This is a matter for me and the scribe alone."

"A scribe! Not a farmer, then. What about the other one? Boy! Are you a farmer?"

Hevel swallowed. "I too am a scribe."

"So what do we have here? Two scribes and four women—one of them a very old woman. If we hand the land over to you, what will happen? It will lapse into disrepair. No, no, that's just foolish. No one in their right mind—not the new priests or the new judges or the governor himself—would think that made any sense."

Uri flushed. "I can learn to farm the land," he stammered.

"You don't look like a fool, but you sound like one right now," Hanun taunted him. "You all appear like you've been suffering from some strange dream. But this is real, and it's time to wake up. Get off my son-in-law's land. Believe me, you don't want to fight me and my men."

Amittai rose from his chair. "You don't speak for me in this matter, Hanun," he said. "And you do me a disservice when you pretend you do."

"Oh, be a man for once in your life, Amittai," Hanun growled at him. "And if you can't—at least shut up while other men do your work for you."

Uri rose from the table. "We clearly will not settle this today. I will take the matter to the court and ask for a decision by the judges. Come, Mother. This is nothing more than a delay."

Sarah got up slowly. "We're leaving?" She couldn't believe Uri had given in so easily.

"Come on, Grandmama," Chava whispered. "We'll be back. It's just going to take a little more time than we thought."

Chava helped Sarah into the cart. Sarah looked around, feeling her heart would break anew. "This is my home. Why don't they believe me?" she wailed.

Chava turned to survey the land once more. Ophir stood close, watching them.

"We will return, you know," Chava told him. "You can't prevent us. This is my family's land. We waited for three generations to return, and no one will stop us."

Ophir looked the girl up and down. His expression changed from scorn to one of admiration. "Perhaps," he retorted. "But we've been here ever since. If you have rights, we do too."

Sarah watched as Chava's forehead puckered with sudden qualms. *No*, Sarah wanted to cry out. *No one has more right to the farm than I.*

As the donkey cart drew away, Sarah swiveled around to watch every landmark fade again into memory. *We'll be back*, she swore to herself. But for the first time since leaving the rivers of Babylon, Sarah felt doubt poison her mind.

58

The Scribe at Work

THE LINES STRETCHED OUT OF the governor's mansion into the streets of Jerusalem. The returned exiles found squatters on their land and demanded they be removed. The Judeans who had moved onto the deserted land complained they had nowhere to go. Before the first week ended, Uri and his fellow scribes filled hundreds of wax tablets—clay not as available in Jerusalem as in Babylon—with charges and countercharges.

Reports filtered in of violence in the streets. A rich merchant was stabbed in a dark alleyway, pockets emptied of gold coin. Some returnees reclaimed their land, only to find it under fire the next day. A Temple priest was found lying in the street, his severed tongue stuck into his robes. Whispers claimed he had encountered some Judeans heading to the sacrifices to Moloch and they hadn't taken well to his preaching.

Uri spent only half his day at Zerubbabel's mansion, for Jeshua claimed his time as well. The priests were supervising the cleaning of the Temple Square, readying it for the first sacrifice. Jeshua dictated dozens of lists to Uri—of the type of men needed for rebuilding, the amounts of timber and stone required. Jeshua, unfortunately, wasn't an organized manager.

"Has that order for cedar from Amon been sent already?" Jeshua asked one afternoon, bustling into the scribe's hastily constructed work-room, a dab and twig hut at the edge of the Temple's construction site.

"It has," Uri replied. "The messenger left yesterday."

"Well, send another man to retrieve him. We need more for the priests' annex."

Uri sighed. In recent days he had dispatched dozens of men, asking them to travel up and down the dangerous countryside. "Could we not just send a second message detailing the additional amount?" he asked.

Jeshua's lips thinned, an expression Uri had grown to dread and despise. "And confuse the foresters of Amon?" His splayed fingers played against one another fussily. "Just do what I bid, Uri."

So Uri sent a messenger to bring home the first, then sent him off again with an amended missive.

But despite Uri's frustration with the High Priest, he felt immense satisfaction as supplies began to arrive. The courtyard before the Temple grounds was cleared and cleansed, the construction foreman arranging neat piles of fragrant wood beams, hewn blocks of pink-veined marble, and basins of tile. Uri watched as the men measured the land, using sheep twine and sticks. As they marked out the Temple rooms, the priests blessed the space. From that moment on, it was considered holy ground.

As Uri made his way from the governor's mansion to the Temple grounds, he noticed men who had no business there, standing and watch-ing the preparations from the shadows of surrounding buildings. One afternoon, his curiosity got the better of him.

"What are you doing there, fellow?" he asked one of these lurkers.

"Just waiting for a friend," the man muttered. The tattoo stamped on his cheek meant he was either not Judean or had lapsed into idolatry.

"I'm Uri ben Seraf, a scribe to the governor," Uri told him. "Who are you?"

"I am Kemuel ben Eytan," the man replied. "I own farmland to the west of the city."

Uri's eyebrows rose. "I thought you were Amorite with that mark on your cheek."

Kemuel shrugged. "You high-class Judeans were gone a long time. Those of us left behind had to find ways to live with our neighbors."

"I recently wrote out a complaint by one of the grandsons of Eytan—Avi ben Baroch—that you and a man named Kenan were farming his land and refused to leave. Is that true?"

"We have more right to the land than Avi ben Baroch does," the man blustered. "Kenan and me, we're Eytan's sons."

Uri's head tilted to one side. "If you've a farm to tend, I'm surprised you're loitering here in the middle of the day."

"I told you—I'm waiting for a friend. We have business to transact. What concern is it of yours, anyway?"

"Just curious," Uri said, moving on.

As he left, two other men came up to the tattooed man. Uri glanced over his shoulder as Kemuel called, "Shobi! Over here."

Uri lingered, dropping to one knee and pretending to work a stone out of his sandal.

The man called Shobi looked like an Amorite. The second man was dressed in a soldier's light armor. "This is Rehum, an officer of the Persian forces," Shobi told Kemuel. "He'll take us to tell the secretary, Shimshai, what you've seen of the rebuilding."

Uri straightened and walked on.

During the next few days, Zerubbabel heard additional disputes over land. One of the first was that of Avi ben Baroch against the twin brothers, Kemuel and Kenan.

"These men," Avi told the court, held in a windowless room of stone lit by torches, where Zerubbabel sat on a seat carved from olive wood and Uri stood at a tall table, his stylus at the ready, "are idolaters and sinners. It is well known they sleep with the women of Moloch and—I blush to admit it—with boys and animals. They claim they were sired by my grandfather, but my grandfather was a pious man with three wives of his own. Why would he go to a whore for his bed pleasures?"

"Is the charge true?" Zerubbabel asked. "We see the tattoo on your cheek, Kemuel. Did one of the whores of Moloch stamp that on you?"

Kemuel's rueful hand covered his cheek. "I was a child when this was placed on me. I hate the mark. But it does not make me an evil man."

"And what of the charges of licentiousness?"

Kemuel shrugged. "What does that have to do with our claim to the farm?"

Uri leaned down and whispered in the governor's ear. The governor glanced at Uri in surprise, then turned back to the man on the stand.

"My scribe says he saw you a few days ago consorting with an Amorite and a Persian officer, just outside the Temple grounds. What business did you have there?"

Kemuel glared at Uri. "We were three friends meeting, that's all," he sputtered.

Avi ben Baroch told the court of his father's dream, that one of them would return to Judea and reclaim the farm. Avi wanted to wax poetic, but the governor—who had heard dozens of these stories in recent weeks—cut him off.

"Yes, yes, fine. This is a busy court. Avi, your petition to the governor is granted. Kemuel and Kenan, you and your wives and your children must leave the farm in two weeks' time. If you do not, we will send soldiers to help you move. Is that clear?"

"Where do you want us to go?" Kenan protested. "How will we feed our families?"

"Who's next, Uri?" Zerubbabel asked, turning away.

Kemuel glowered at them. "You haven't heard the last of us, Zerubbabel ben Shealtiel."

Zerubbabel sighed. "You're lucky I don't turn you over to the priests to be stoned. From the reports I hear, you deserve stoning. Get out of my sight. You disgust me."

Two days later, a fire broke out on Avi ben Baroch's land, laying most of the fertile ground to waste. One of the governor's men uncovered a copy of a missive dispatched to Persia, where Darius had just replaced Cyrus as king. Uri read it aloud to Zerubbabel, who called Jeshua to hear it as well.

"Read it again, Uri," the governor told him as the High Priest entered the room.

Uri read:

To King Darius:
Cordial greetings.

The king should know that we went to the district of
Judea, to the Temple of the great God. The people are
building it with large stones and placing the timbers in
the walls. The work is being carried on with diligence
and is progressing rapidly under their direction.

We questioned the elders and asked them, "Who
authorized you to rebuild this Temple and restore this
structure?" We also asked them their names, so that we
could write down the names of their leaders for your
information.

This is the answer they gave us:

"We are the servants of the God of Heaven and
Earth, and we are rebuilding the Temple that was built
many years ago, one that a great king of Israel built and
finished. But because our fathers angered the God of
Heaven, He handed them over to Nebuchadnezzar the
Chaldean, king of Babylon, who destroyed this Temple
and deported the people to Babylon.

"However, in the first year of Cyrus king of Babylon,
King Cyrus issued a decree to rebuild this House of
God. He even removed from the temple of Babylon
the gold and silver articles of the House of God, which
Nebuchadnezzar had taken from the Temple in Jerusalem
and brought to the temple in Babylon.

"Then King Cyrus gave them to a man named
Sheshbazzar, whom he had appointed governor, and he
told him, 'Take these articles and go and deposit them
in the Temple in Jerusalem. And rebuild the House of
God on its site.' So this Sheshbazzar came and laid the
foundations of the House of God in Jerusalem. From

that day to the present it has been under construction but is not yet finished."

Now if it pleases the king, let a search be made in the royal archives of Babylon to see if King Cyrus did in fact issue a decree to rebuild this House of God in Jerusalem. Then let the king send us his decision in this matter.

Zerubbabel and Jeshua took the letter from Uri and studied it together and separately, shaking their heads over it.

"We're going to have trouble," Zerubbabel said slowly.

"They can't stop us now," Jeshua responded, face brick-red with anger.

59

Chava at the Well

WHILE THEY WAITED TO PRESENT their request to the governor, Sarah's family made camp with other returned exiles in a desolate plain just inside the ruined city walls. Chava tried not to chime in when Aunt Zakiti and her cousin Irit carped and complained. But it was hard.

"Do you remember how we used to sit in the courtyard garden at sunset?" Zakiti moaned to her daughter as they prepared a midday meal. "The gardeners would leave you and your sisters a pile of reeds so you could make little houses. Remember?"

"I remember," Irit nodded. "They were sturdier houses than this tent. Momma, we must mend the back flap again. That rip keeps opening."

Zakiti sighed, looking at Chava who was grinding chickpeas in a clay bowl. "Don't you miss your parents, child? The farm? Walking the streets of Babylon?"

An image of the Great Ziggurat flashed upon Chava's memory. She looked at where Sarah was sitting, morose and flushed by the cooking fire. What would make her grandmother happy, with everything so unsettled? She thrust the clay bowl into Irit's hands. "I'm going to fetch water. Grandmama, you look hot and dirty. I'm going to give you a midday bath."

Sarah smiled wanly. "Do you think we're back in Babylon where we had time for such luxuries?"

Chava shrugged. "This is an easy luxury, Grandmother, one that costs only a little time and no money at all. Why not enjoy it?"

"I won't argue with you, child," Sarah sighed.

Chava grabbed the largest two buckets, stacked near the tent entrance. She had learned it was better to fill two buckets half-way than to try and fetch one full one. She walked off, deliberately warbling a tune that always made her grandmother smile, albeit wistfully: "And now our feet are standing within your gates, Jerusalem."

Chava's cheerful expression faded as she turned a corner where Grandmother could no longer see her. Unbidden, her thoughts turned again to that night when Uziel opened her gown and asked her to lie with him. Her mind was full of Uziel these days—his broad grin, the way he held a gold object to show her the detail on it, the glint in his eye as he picked her out of a crowd. She stumbled over some loose stones in the road. Pursing her lips and tossing her hair back, she recalled the task at hand. Some cool water would make Grandmother feel better.

The nearest well was close to the Temple courtyard. Chava wondered if she would see her Uncle Uri or Irit's husband, Hevel, following behind the priests, wax tablets at the ready. The family was much more fortunate, Chava thought, than many of the returned exiles. At least Uri's and Hevel's positions as scribes meant they had money to spend in the markets. Most of their neighbors had to dip into funds they'd planned to use to rebuild their homes. And others, who had come with only hope packed onto their backs, resorted to begging on the streets or lining up for charity outside the governor's stone mansion.

The line at the well was longer than Chava expected. She moved to the rear. She recognized the long chestnut curls of the girl who stood two people ahead of her. Beula. She was speaking animatedly with her companion. Chava winced, shutting her eyes. Why did Beula have to be there, of all people?

As if sensing her presence, Beula glanced over her shoulder. Chava watched, pained, as the girl handed her empty bucket to her friend and stepped out of line. She strolled back to Chava, standing over her, her nose nearly touching Chava's forehead. "You're a slut," she hissed.

Chava tried to take a step away, but a matron and her three sons had already taken places behind her, hemming her in.

"I had no idea...." Chava started to say, but Beula cut her off.

"He told me about it, how you begged him to lie with you. How you doused yourself in scent, uncovered your body, put your tongue in his ear. How you've slept with most of his friends."

More and more people turned to stare. The women's eyes narrowed, while the men studied her slender body with interest. Chava's skin crawled, as if with mites. She swallowed hard, stammering, "That's not true!"

"Whore!" came the cry from Beula's friend. A sharp rock hit Chava's elbow.

"She tried to seduce my betrothed," Beula cried. "She lay with him at the campfires before we ascended to Jerusalem, and her family tried to force him to marry her. She's a harlot!"

"The men all said they've had a turn with her," Beula's friend added.

"I didn't! They haven't!" Chava protested, but no one heeded her.

They pushed her out of line.

"Girls like that should be whipped," called one of the older women.

"Let's cut off her hair," cried another. "Skinny little thing. If we shave her head, there won't be anything to attract the men."

"Women like that have tricks," said a young wife bitterly. "My husband's second wife is like her, and he never leaves her couch. She's already having her third child. And me? Not one."

One of the little boys picked up a handful of stones and shied them at Chava. The other children in line, seeing the adults did nothing to stop them, followed suit. Chava dropped the buckets and put her hands up to her face. One of the sharp rocks struck the corner of her mouth, making her bleed. Another hit her shoulder, tearing her dress.

"Leave me alone!" she cried. Stumbling and falling, she backed away from them.

Another stone grazed her arm. She abandoned her buckets and fled, turning a corner, then another. Finally feeling safe, she sat on a rock and wept.

"Hello," came a voice above her. "Shh, now."

Strange arms curled around her body, pulling her up, holding her tight. Rocking on her heels, she looked into the stranger's face, his right cheekbone stamped with a heavy tattoo. She recoiled from him, but his arms held her fast.

"I heard what they said at the well," he whispered. "I think you're sweet."

Unbelieving, she felt the stranger's mouth moving in her tangled hair. She struggled against his arms. "Let me go! How dare you!"

"I'll take you home to my brother." The man laughed. "He likes them with spirit."

"No," Chava cried out, trying to push him away. "Stop it. Stop!"

Unexpectedly the man's arms released her. She staggered and nearly fell. A second man held the first in an arm lock.

"Ophir, what are you doing?" Chava's attacker grunted in pain.

"The girl doesn't seem to care for you, Kemuel," Ophir retorted. Chava realized with shock that he was the young husband from Grandmother's farm. "She asked you to stop."

"She's just being playful—ow!" Kemuel cried, as Ophir viciously twisted his arm up behind his back.

"Were you just being playful?" Ophir asked her.

Chava saw the sudden spark of recognition in his eyes when she lifted her bloodied face and pulled her hair out of her eyes. "No!"

"They said she lay with another man. With his friends. She's a slut—let me go!" Kemuel cried.

Some of the light seemed to fade from Ophir's eyes. He looked her over. "Is that true?"

"I'm not a whore," Chava retorted, stumbling over the words. "But yes, I nearly lay with another man, a man I loved and whom I thought wanted me as his wife."

Ophir sent Kemuel spinning. He staggered across the alleyway, slamming into a stone wall.

"Go home, Kemuel," Ophir said, "wherever it is you make your home these days."

"Think it won't happen to you, Ophir? That you won't lose your farm? Despite having Hanun to protect you?"

"Be quiet," Ophir hissed. "Leave before I beat you to a pulp."

Kemuel slunk away. Ophir turned to Chava. "They stoned you?" he asked, gently.

Chava hung her head. "Yes. I left my buckets at the well," she said. "I don't know what I'll tell them, back at home. They'll be worried."

"We'll go get your buckets, and I'll walk you home."

"You don't have to...."

Ophir smiled grimly. "I think I do."

"I'm so ashamed." Chava sank back on the rock. "How could he treat me that way?"

Ophir stared down at her. Chava wrapped her arms around her body and shut her eyes. When she opened them again, she was surprised by the warmth in Ophir's expression.

"We're wasting time," he said, reaching out a hand to pull her up.

She let him lead her back toward the well. The women and children who had threatened her had moved on. Her two buckets were still lying where she had abandoned them. Ophir silently picked them up, filled them both close to the brim, and looked to her to start walking back to the tent. She noticed how strong he was. If she had filled the buckets that full, she would have staggered under their weight.

They walked in silence. Chava licked blood from the corner of her lip and pulled her torn dress, so the tear was no longer visible.

"You must hate me," Chava said, finally. "Hate my family."

"A little," Ophir admitted.

She wanted to cry again. "We're nearly there. I can manage from here." She reached for the buckets.

He let her take them. She steeled herself not to show him heavy they felt. Walking stiffly forward, she willed herself not to look around. But just as she was about to turn the corner toward the tents, the impulse grew too strong.

There he was, standing still, watching her, an unreadable expression on his face. She hitched the buckets up and walked on.

60

Zakiti in the Market

535 BCE–Year 5 of the Return

ZAKITI, TOGETHER WITH DAUGHTER IRIT and niece Chava, walked the stalls of the main market in the center of the city. Zakiti frowned at the rubbish left strewn on the ground, the vermin that skittered away whenever someone drew too close. In Babylon, the merchants took pride in their clean boulevards, sending out slaves every dawn to sweep away any refuse from the day before. Jerusalem's narrower alleyways were shielded from the sun by cloth draped from one side of the street to the other, bathing the market in a half-light that made it easy for the tradesmen to conceal less-than-fresh produce. Zakiti had learned to be vigilant in the dimness.

"Do you remember the markets in Babylon?" Irit sighed, picking up a lemon from a stand. She asked the question every time they shopped the marketplace.

"I do, but I don't know why you would." Chava giggled. "You sent your slaves out to do your daily shopping, didn't you?"

Zakiti grimaced. Five years had passed since they'd arrived in Jerusalem. Uri was doing well enough now to buy a slave girl, but some odd scruple made him deny her that luxury. Though she had to admit that these trips to the market were one of the few pleasures she had in this terrible city.

She snapped a finger at the man standing behind the lemon stand, the bangles she hid beneath her long sleeves jangling lightly. "Ephraim. Last time I found a rotten lemon in the batch you sold me. Don't make me check every piece of fruit this time—because I will."

The merchant bowed low. Zakiti suspected him of mockery. Her suspicion was confirmed when he replied with a swagger, a hand resting on his chest, "Give me your basket, and I'll personally inspect each and every lemon. You will have the best lemons in all of Jerusalem. I swear it!"

She ignored the sarcasm, handing her basket over the pile of fruit. "See that you do."

As the man made a show of picking through the lemons, discarding some, placing others into Zakiti's basket as delicately as if they were blown glass, he asked, "I hear the Temple will be finished in time for the Passover sacrifice. Is it true?"

Another rare pleasure. While these Judeans might frown upon her for being Babylonian, they did accord her the respect she deserved for being married to the foremost scribe in all Judea. They often asked her to confirm or deny rumors, because everyone knew that, as Uri's wife, she was privy to the truth. "It is," she said graciously, letting Irit take the basket from him and handing him a siglos. She watched the merchant as he ran his thumb over the thick silver coin to feel the embossed portrait of the kingly Darius holding a bow and arrow, and hoped it wasn't a sign of distrust. "My husband tells me that every available workman has been assigned to finish construction."

But instead of the smile she expected, the lemon seller suddenly frowned, leaning closer. "While we're left vulnerable to attacks, while the city walls cry out to be rebuilt. Have you heard the latest? That Amorite henchmen put Gedaliah's fields to the torch and murdered the man and his family? I heard they stabbed the poor man several times, leaving him to die a slow, cruel death."

"Isn't that the farm Ladan claimed during the exile?" Irit asked.

"The very one," the merchant replied, shaking his head. "And now Ladan's back in court, asking to return."

Zakiti, tiring of the gossip, turned to see Chava had crossed the alleyway and was looking wistfully at the gold and silver items in the goldsmith's stall. Was she hoping to catch a peek of Uziel? Still?

"Come away from there," Zakiti called. Would the girl ever learn not to make herself an object of scorn by such obvious longing?

The lemon merchant sniffed. "You're lucky Beula is not serving behind the counter today. The things she says about your niece…."

Zakiti, almost all the small pleasure the market gave her destroyed, crossed the alleyway and took Chava by the hand. "Perhaps you should go home," she told the girl tenderly. "We've left Sarah on her own for too long."

Chava nodded and Zakiti watched her walk away, noticing several of the merchants sniggering behind her back. Despite Chava's growing beauty, it seemed increasingly possible she might remain unwed. Beula, long married to the goldsmith, continued to hint how Sarah and Zakiti herself had been Babylonian prostitutes, so of course Chava was well trained in the art of seduction. Beula, spreading these lies in whispers behind cupped hands, was heeded avidly by the shocked Jerusalem housewives. Kemuel, too, implicated the young girl in boasting tales of his orgies, which he related to wide-eyed young men in the wine shops.

The only remedy, it seemed, was to keep Chava at home, in the little stone house Uri had been able to purchase with his salary as a scribe. The house was tiny compared to their spacious home in Babylon, and with everyone living there—Zakiti and Uri, Irit and Hevel, Sarah and Chava—it was cramped and crowded. But it was far better than the camp where many of the returned Judeans still lived in tattered tents.

That evening, after settling Uri with a cool drink and proudly showing him the basket of lustrous lemons and the skein of embroidered cloth she had bargained down to less than half of the merchant's opening bid, Zakiti broached the subject of Chava yet again, telling her husband how the child had made herself a spectacle at the goldsmith's stall. "What will we do if she remains unwed?"

Uri sighed. "If all she does is remain chastely at home, the false rumors of her loose behavior must die down someday. Then someone will offer for her. She's a sweet girl. Someone will see that."

"That may be," Zakiti said. "But still…."

Uri put up a hand. "All we can do is wait."

Zakiti gave up, sitting next to him on the cushioned divan she'd found in the market and refurbished for his comfort. She leaned her head against his shoulder, nestling into his side. He put an arm about her waist. "I hope you're right. But then, there's Sarah…."

Uri sighed again. Just then, Zakiti's mother-in-law came into the room and sat at the table, almost as if she'd overheard them talking about her. "I know how busy you are…." she began, addressing her son.

Zakiti closed her eyes. While everyone else thought Sarah's patience was admirable—it had been five years, after all, while the farm still remained in the hands of the squatters who'd seized it—Zakiti often thought the old woman had no right to make her husband feel guilty. After all, Sarah was the reason they were here and not back in Babylon, living in comfort and luxury.

Uri rose and walked over to his mother. "I'm sorry. With everything going on at the Temple, I haven't had an opportunity to approach Zerubbabel about the farm. I'll talk to him after the Passover feast," he assured her.

Sarah, whose face had grown even more chiseled over the long years, nodded slowly. "Your work on the Temple comes first, of course," she said.

Zakiti watched as Sarah gamely tried to hide her impatience, but the tapping of her fingers on the tabletop gave her away. Uri leaned down and kissed the top of her white hair. "The moment the Passover feast is complete, Mother, I promise," he said. "Are you excited about seeing the Temple again?"

Sarah's face creased into a smile. "It seems like I've spent a lifetime waiting for this Passover," she agreed. "It's going to be a glorious day."

Passover. That dreadful week of eating tasteless, unleavened bread. Zakiti bit back a sigh. Why did no one understand how hard this life was for her? How much she had sacrificed for her family?

61

Rededication

THE BUILDING OF THE TEMPLE had temporarily halted while King Darius's scribes sought the scroll that contained King Cyrus's instructions. The last five years had been frustrating ones, years in which Uri penned missive after missive recalling Cyrus's declaration and how the return of the Temple vessels showed the Persian king's intentions. The unremitting calls on his time made these years pass by in a blink of an eye for Uri—though, he often reflected, especially when looking at his mother's strained face, they must be dragging for her and the rest of the family.

But fast or slow, pass they did. On a fall day with gray and cloudy skies, Uri finally transcribed a copy of the king's scathing response to those who would halt the construction:

> ...stay away from there. Do not interfere with the work on this Temple of God. Let the governor of the Jews and the Jewish elders rebuild this House of God on its site.... I decree that if anyone changes this edict, a beam is to be pulled from his house, and he is to be lifted up and impaled on it. And for this crime, his house is to be reduced to a pile of rubble. May God, who has caused his Name to dwell there, overthrow any king or person

who lifts a hand to change this decree or to destroy this
Temple in Jerusalem.... I Darius have decreed it. Let it
be carried out with diligence.

"Excellent, excellent," Jeshua exulted, taking the paper from Uri's
hands and waving it. "This puts an end to their interfering!"

"I only wish the king would issue a similar decree about the city
walls," Zerubbabel fretted, face worn and creased with constant worry.
"Without them, we cannot protect our people from being harassed by the
foreigners in our land—or from associating with them, either!"

"Tell the men to continue their work on the Temple," Jeshua told Uri,
ignoring the governor's concerns with a dismissive wave of his hand. "We
should complete the construction by spring, God willing!"

Zerubbabel's concerns about the safety of the city streets were well
founded. Rumors circulated that a certain Amorite, a man named
Hanun, was organizing acts of terror. A merchant's house was burned
to the ground because he refused to pay protection money. Avi ben
Baroch—who had wrested the farm from those licentious twin brothers,
the bastards Kemuel and Kenan—found his crops uprooted and his
livestock missing.

"We must complete the wall around the city and expel the foreigners," Zerubbabel declared on countless occasions. But after Darius's decree to finish the Temple, most of the city's carpenters and masons were
already hard at work. When Zerubbabel succeeded in sending a small
crew of workers to rebuild even a portion of the walls, they were attacked
by men with heavy scarves tied around their faces and a ready supply of
daggers in their hands.

"Let's keep our swords next to us while we build," the head of the
masons suggested to Zerubbabel after one such attack. Uri made a note of
the idea. But then the winter rains came, and all building stopped anyway.

Spring was early that year, a beautiful season of wildflowers and
pleasant days. The pace of building at the Temple intensified and Jeshua
planned that the rededication take place before the Passover celebration.
Uri had to remain on the construction site all day long.

On the fourteenth day of Adar, Uri woke from a restless sleep. The
dawn sun stained the eastern sky a bright red, small clouds chasing across

it in fluffy gold and saffron. Uri wondered for a moment if Daniel were still alive and perhaps lying on his luxurious couch, longing for a glimpse of the Temple. He knew Ezra still lived, for they exchanged letters as often as messengers traveled between Babylon and Jerusalem. Ezra must find it hard, Uri thought, to be so far away today. For all his belief that study and the Writings were more important than the Temple, Ezra would have been ecstatic to be present for the sacrifices.

The family rose and Chava laid out breakfast for them in the back courtyard. The day before, she had chased through the house, making sure every crumb of bread had been swept away. She worried in case a speck fell from someone's fingers, undoing all her hard work. Irit had spent yesterday at the city bakery, preparing the family's store of unleavened bread. Zakiti, used to escaping to her father's home to dine when she tired of matzo during the fast, eyed the stack of round, flat cakes with misgiving.

"Are you worried, Aunt Zakiti?" Chava teased her. "Surely the idea of the Passover fast isn't new to you? After all these years living in Judea?"

Zakiti sighed. "I'm looking forward to it, foolish child."

Uri smiled, inwardly saluting his wife's attempts to conceal her true feelings.

The excitement rose in the hours just before sunset when, washed and arrayed in their best clothing, the family joined the rest of the city in their trek to the Temple grounds. Hundreds of tables were set up, all laden with the ceremonial food—the apple, honey and nut mixture, the roasted egg, the fresh herbs and the salt water. The Pascal lamb, of course, was still missing. It would be sacrificed before the multitude and offered to the Most High before every table received its share.

A week ago, Uri had attended the ceremonial dedication of the Temple, where a hundred bulls, two hundred rams, four hundred male lambs and, as a sin offering for all Israel, twelve male goats, one for each of the tribes of Israel, had been sacrificed. During this ceremony, the Levites and priests were installed in their offices. As the animals were slaughtered, with blood running down the Temple altar and the smoke rising to Heaven, Uri closed his eyes and thought of his father and mother, both of whom had seen sacrifices in King Solomon's Temple.

This Passover ceremony would be the first time his mother, Uri's only living connection to that original building, would see it rise from ruin. He eagerly watched her face as she turned into the massive gates and saw the new building for the first time.

"What do you think?" he asked.

Sarah looked around eagerly. "It's smaller."

"Smaller?" Uri's face fell. "Is it really?"

"And perhaps—more modest? I remember pure white marble that was blinding in the sun and columns that seemed to reach toward the sky. Gold lining the inner sanctuary, the smell of fir and cedar from the floors and walls. This building...." Sarah hesitated, looking into Uri's face. "Well, it's a miracle we have our Temple back at all, isn't it?"

Uri tried not to let his disappointment show. He ushered Sarah to the table where the family sat. They watched as Jeshua, wearing a sparkling white robe and a high white hat, with the jewels of the High Priest glittering on his chest plate and on a heavy chain around his neck, raised a silver knife and plunged it into the first Pascal lamb, being careful to ensure that the slaughter was painless. A haunch of the slaughtered lamb was burned completely in the altar, while the rest was removed to be prepared for the priests. Each table dispatched a representative to the altar to make an offering to God. Uri and Hevel took their turn for the family. The lamb carcass that remained was cooked in a huge pit outside the Temple grounds, turning on a spit the workers had recently erected.

Then the assembled Hebrews retold the age-old tale of the Return from Egypt. The exiles, who had experienced their own Return, sat with tears streaming down their faces, weeping for family and friends lost upon the way. Sarah was both exultant and saddened by the story of the Exodus. Uri and Chava, who sat on either side of her, held her hands and wiped away the tears that persisted in rolling down her elderly cheeks.

Feasting followed. The clash of timbrels recalled Miriam on the shores of the great Reed Sea when it parted to allow the Israelites to escape from Pharaoh. Chava's feet tapped but, perhaps remembering what happened when she rose to dance years ago, she remained in her seat, resting against her grandmother's side, talking to her softly of the family back in Babylon.

Uri, sated after the feast, happy at the magnificent conclusion of their hard work in rebuilding the Temple, rose to dance. He led his wife onto the floor, and the two of them laughed and swayed to the music. When Zakiti tired and wanted to return to the table, Uri was stopped by various petitioners who wished him to relay a message to the court or the Temple.

"Would you ask the governor...?"

"Would Jeshua consider...?"

"Uri, my good friend! How fortunate we meet like this!"

Zakiti wearied of the halting motion toward the table and left her husband behind to contend with the press of claimants. Uri smiled and nodded and jotted down names on the wax tablet that he always carried. Finally, nearly back at the table where Chava was propping a now drowsing Sarah against her shoulder, someone reached out and clutched his arm.

"Uri ben Seraf?" came a voice. "I have a proposition for you."

Uri turned, not recognizing the voice. He was startled when he realized it was Amittai ben Dotan, accompanied by his son, Ophir, and an old man whom Uri had never seen before.

62

Hod's Idea

IT WAS HOD'S IDEA.

So Amittai told Uri, after introducing him to his father-in-law. Amittai and Hod had spent the past years waiting with apprehension for the summons to court, while watching friend after friend lose their property to the returnees. Every morning, Amittai told Uri, he woke with dread lingering about his heart. His wife indulged in day-long fits of crying. And his son....

Amittai broke off, looking at Ophir gravely. Uri didn't understand the glance that passed between them. He wasn't sure he wanted to.

"So what do you want of me?" he said brusquely. "What's your proposition?"

Amittai looked toward the table at Chava. The girl looked lovely in the moonlight, Uri realized. Where before she had been a skinny thin-chested child, now her figure had filled out. Years of living in town had whitened her skin, and her hazel eyes often took on the green glint of her grandmother. She was older than his own girls when they had wed.

Uri's measuring glance went from his niece to the man who was squatting on his family's farm. "You want your son to marry my niece?" he asked. "To become his second wife?"

"Hear me out," Amittai said, gesturing to both Hod and Ophir to stop them from saying anything. "This way, no one loses."

Uri grasped the simplicity of the plan. "You would continue to farm," he said to Amittai, "and Sarah and Chava would move in with you."

"She is unmarried," Hod said. "From what I hear, she is unlikely to have a better offer."

Uri frowned. "There's no reason to say that," he replied. "What you've heard is gossip, not truth."

Hod shrugged. "Gossip or not, she is damaged in the eyes of Jerusalem's pious families."

"This is not the way to convince me," Uri said, starting to turn away. Out of the corner of one eye, he was gratified when a twinge of panic crossed Ophir and Amittai's faces.

"We mean no disrespect," Amittai hastened to say, grasping Uri's elbow. "But think what it would mean to your family to have her live on the farm. And the old woman too, of course."

"You have your own home now, after all," Ophir interposed. "You're a man of standing in the community, a man who serves both governor and Temple priests."

"This could work," Uri mused. "If Chava is willing." He turned to Ophir. "You wish this?"

Ophir shrugged. "My first wife is well enough. But she has certain... problem relatives."

Uri squinted at him. "Problem relatives?"

"Her father," the old man explained, "is Hanun the Amorite. You met him, I understand."

"When we first visited the farm," Uri recalled. "I'd forgotten. The governor's guards are on the watch for Hanun the Amorite, you realize."

Ophir shrugged. "They won't find him. He's lived in the hills beyond Jerusalem all his life. He's like the fox everyone calls him."

"And we Judeans are the chickens in the henhouse?" Uri mused dryly. "I wonder if that will always be the case."

"So what do you think?" Amittai broke in impatiently. "Would your niece be willing?"

Uri looked again toward the table. Chava was pulling her grand-mother to her feet. "Go help her," he said to Ophir.

Ophir approached the table. He said a few words to Chava, making her blush. She stepped aside, letting Ophir take Sarah's arm. Sarah stared at the young man, as though trying to remember who he was. But her current state of sleepiness mixed with the fog of old age, Uri realized, stopped her from placing him as the young man who now occupied her ancestral home.

Uri had seen enough. "I'll talk with Chava tonight. I will be glad if we can arrange this."

"You are a generous man," Amittai said, putting out his hand.

Uri grasped it. "We'll see," he cautioned. "She has to be willing."

When Uri finally reached home that night, the stars shone brilliantly overhead. He breathed in the sharp mountain air. He felt content with his wife on his arm, his daughter and her husband walking behind them. Jerusalem, Uri realized, still felt small and confined after the glories of Babylon. But it was home, now, and he was glad he had come.

He turned a corner into the quiet back street where he had built his home. Chava was sitting on the flat stone that formed a step to the house, Ophir by her side. Uri saw tears glistening on her cheeks in the moonlight.

"Chava?" Zakiti said, coming forward quickly. "What's wrong?"

Ophir rose and, with a quiet nod toward Uri, disappeared into the night.

Zakiti looked from Chava toward Uri, bewildered.

Chava, still weeping, rose and cast herself onto her uncle's shirt. "He was kind to me once," she said, almost incoherently. "He says he will always be kind. I believe him."

"Then why are you crying?" Uri asked. He would never under-stand women.

Chava reached up and, with both hands, wiped away her tears. "I'm not sure," she admitted, half laughing.

The wedding blessing of Ophir and Chava took place on the thirty-third day of the counting of the Omer, the only day weddings were allowed before the holiday of Shavuot. It was a simple ceremony, held just outside the back steps of the farm. Keren had set up a small *chuppah* of embroidered cloth, strewing the path leading up to it with rose petals. Just beyond, she placed a long table and covered it with a simple but abundant meal. Ophir's first wife, Tobija, stood to one side, her oldest boy, Nadab, eyeing Chava warily. Sarah stood on the other, her face wreathed in smiles. Keren had been careful to make sure the old woman was comfortable, recognizing that Sarah's wishes were now paramount. Sarah would sleep in the farmhouse that night and every night following. Sarah had blessed Chava for restoring her home to her, had kissed the child's hands and forehead.

And Chava? Uri hadn't been able to read the girl's emotions since the night he pulled the young goldsmith from her willing young body. Having lived with Sarah's stories her entire life, Chava seemed to glow at the thought giving her grandmother this happy ending. Uri didn't think Chava felt the marriage was a sacrifice, but of course, girls rarely had a say in whom they wed.

Zakiti and Irit dressed the bride in a soft white robe, belted with a wide blue embroidered sash. They covered her hair in flowers and swathed it with a transparent white veil. On her feet were sandals of Babylonian make, softer and more expensive than anything that could be obtained in Jerusalem. She wore bangles of gold and silver under her short sleeves and a heavy jewel diadem rested on her forehead.

"She looks more like a Babylonian bride than a Judean one," Uri whispered to his wife.

Zakiti grinned. "You Judeans—always so modest in your dress," she replied. "Chava can cover herself up from head to toe after today. But a bride should be beautiful for her husband."

Her dress didn't seem to do her any harm in Ophir's eyes. Ophir watched as she circled him seven times, his face suffused with her grace. Tobija, in the back, sobbed loudly as he placed a ring onto her finger and kissed her in front of the small gathering. He led Chava into the house, where they would sit alone for a few minutes before rejoining their guests.

Hanun, Uri thought, couldn't interfere with the festivities. A small contingent of the governor's guard stood ready to capture the Amorite if he dared show his face and protest the wedding. Hanun had openly threatened Ophir if he married Chava during a night of curses, a dagger flung into the wood of the tabletop, a toppled cup of beer. But, Amittai boasted, for once in his life, both he and his son had ignored the Amorite.

"Ophir was not always happy to be thought of as Judean," Amittai admitted to Uri when they were negotiating the wedding terms. "But he's been shocked by his father-in-law's actions, by the senseless violence. Before, he was a young boy eager to fight for what was his. Since his betrothal to Chava, I know that he wishes to be considered Judean."

"He attended the sacrifices, you say?"

"The act of a young man seeking truth." Amittai glossed over the sin. "I did the same before I married my Keren. Chava will redeem him just as Keren brought me back into the fold."

In the end, Sarah had decided it all. "We'll be back on the farm?" she asked breathlessly when Chava and Uri broke the news to her. "We'll live there?"

"Yes, Grandmama. We'll live there."

"Amittai and Ophir will continue to farm the land," Uri said. "I will remain in my house. You're welcome to stay with me...."

"Or to come with me, Grandmama."

"I'll live at the farm again!" Sarah's face was alight with joy.

Sarah really should have been the bride today, Uri thought, watching Keren settle the old woman into a place of honor at the table. Sarah had already walked over the grounds, a long, exultant, halting walk where she seemed to caress every bush and tree, to embrace the very sky above them. After coming to Jerusalem to talk to her, Keren made Sarah's new room resemble her childhood quarters as much as possible, down to the sheepskin rug on the sleeping couch, the stool at the window, and the light blue tinge to the wall's whitewash. When Sarah stood at the threshold, she couldn't hold back the tears that slipped down her wrinkled cheeks, nor did she excuse them away. Sarah, Uri thought, resembled nothing as much during this halcyon day as a vessel for bliss. A new light shone in her eyes, as though something broken had at long last been repaired.

Chava and her husband emerged. As was traditional, Tobija offered her husband's new wife the first morsel of food. Chava took the bread dipped in honey from the Amorite girl's extended hand and kneeled before her.

"I hope to serve our husband well," Chava murmured. "Will you teach me what he likes best?"

Tobija looked down at her, a cold look marring her usually meek, complacent face. "You have already given him what he likes best," she muttered. "This farm."

Chava kept her head ducked low. "He gave me my farm as well," she replied softly. "My grandmother and family and I are grateful to him and to our father-in-law."

Tobija turned away, taking her children into the house, to the back hearth Amittai had built for her all those years ago. The wedding feast continued without them.

It was dark when Ophir drew Chava inside. Sodden with wine, Uri watched them go. Amittai, seeing him stagger as he rose, hastened over.

"Sleep here tonight," he said. "It is late, and you and your family are welcome to spend the night under my roof. There is room for all."

Relieved not to have to stumble down the mountainside in the black night, Uri agreed. He and Zakiti were bedded down in the farmhouse's spare room. Uri slept deeply, his wife's head resting on his shoulder. Toward morning, he awoke to hear the house stirring.

"It's a farm," he whispered to Zakiti, who stretched and slid open one reluctant eyelid, "farms wake early. We can go back to sleep."

But while Zakiti dozed, Uri found it impossible to stay abed. He rose, dressed, and made his way soundlessly outside. The ground crunched under his feet. Looking at the farmhouse in the soft morning light, he saw Sarah's face pressed against the side of her open window shutter. She must have woken early to see the dawn in her old home, he thought. The morning cold made him shiver. He crept back inside, up to her room. In the hallway, he encountered his niece, already dressed for the day.

"I heard Grandmama stirring and came to see if she needed anything," Chava whispered.

"She's at the window, looking blissfully out on the farm. Child, do you know what a wonderful gift you've given her?"

Chava smiled. "I do know. I'm happy to have done it."

Uri put an arm about her shoulder and together they moved into Sarah's room. He could see that the old woman had barely slept—her bed looked only gently tousled.

"Grandmama," Chava murmured. "Come away from the window. You'll catch cold."

Sarah didn't stir. A sudden prickle ran up Uri's spine.

"Grandmama?" Chava asked, fear touching her tones.

Uri took three steps forward and put out hesitant fingers to feel his mother's cheek. It was ice cold. He felt her neck, then bent down to listen to her heartbeat.

"She's not…. She can't be…."

"She's gone, Chava. She waited to return home to die," Uri said, tears welling up inside him.

Chava flung herself onto her grandmother's rigid lap and wept. Uri looked out at the farm spread beneath the window. "She's home now."

PART FIVE

Expulsion

525 BCE–Year 15 of the Return

63

Ezra's Return

URI FIRST NOTICED THAT HE had difficulty in holding the stylus during the chill winter mornings. His fingers, strong and muscled from years of writing, would suddenly curl inward and throb with pain. He had to stop to flex and blow on them. It grew more and more difficult to write. Even now, with a new spring approaching, the stiffness remained.

His son-in-law, Hevel, noticed. "What ails you, Father?" he asked. "Here, I'll write out the account for you. You're so slow this morning!"

Surrendering his stylus to the young man, Uri stepped outside into the balcony overlooking the courtyard. The scribes now had their own offices in the governor's palace, just off his beautiful gardens. As their work increased, Uri began to teach new apprentices how to transcribe the hundreds of missives the governor needed. Uri had stopped serving in the Temple many years ago. As he'd predicted, Jeshua grew more and more insufferable as High Priest. Uri could still remember the joy he'd felt the first morning he dispatched other scribes to the Temple, fixing them there permanently, leaving a small group, including Hevel and himself, to serve the governor.

The morning coolness held a hint of humidity, a harbinger of the springtime to come. After years of living in the arid, hot climes of Babylon, Uri often shivered on mountain mornings, reaching for Zakiti at night when the cold of the hills seeped into their stone house and into their bones. Jerusalem weather! The winters were the worst. Uri had seen his first snowfall a year ago, watching as the surrounding hills covered over with a thin frost. His grandchildren had tumbled out of the house, laughing with open mouths to catch the icy flakes.

The heat of Babylon was kinder on aging scribes, Uri thought with a thin laugh. He glanced at the terraced garden wall to the city beneath them, longing for warmer days to come.

More than a decade had passed since the day Sarah had died and they'd left Chava on the farm, captive to her grandmother's lifetime of dreams. Uri wondered if his niece was ever unhappy as the second wife of a Judean farmer, but if she were, she never let it show. Instead she took pride in her crops and in her three children, Yoram, Sarah, and Reuven, named for the three youngsters who'd grown up on the farm two generations earlier.

As Uri watched from his balcony perch, a scuffle broke out in the streets. It remained difficult to police the city while its encircling walls were no more than rubble. Every time a small portion of the wall was reconstructed, its gates were burnt, and stones broken. Once, the masons were even stabbed as they slept. It was whispered that Hanun the Amorite, still at large after all these years, was the chief instigator of the city's troubles.

Uri frowned as he remembered his conversation with Ophir when the family had gathered at the farm just last month.

"I've told you, he's a fox," Ophir said. "You'll never catch him. He'll die in the hills."

"Your first wife never sees him?" Uri slanted a glance toward Tobija, bouncing little Reuven on her knee while Chava fed the two older children. The Amorite woman seemed resigned to helping to care for Ophir's newest brood of children—or else she was able to conceal her resentment.

"If she does, she doesn't tell me," Ophir replied, shaking his head.

Uri wondered if Ophir knew more than he would admit. But he was the boy's guest, so he turned to other subjects.

Later though, he asked Amittai the same question and watched as the man's face closed in. "Hanun is not welcome here, so he doesn't come," was all Amittai would say.

Uri forbear to question Chava. A wife should not be asked to contradict her husband.

Shaking himself out of his reverie, he watched a pack of brash young Hittites swarm a Judean trader, taunting him. The Judean, arms full of the cloth he was bringing to market, could do nothing but walk steadily onward, head bent in shame.

Uri flushed in anger. *This is our land,* he thought, *promised us by the Covenant. Why do they not let us be? Canaanites, Hittites, Perizzites, Jebusites, Ammonites, Moabites, Egyptians, and Amorites,* Uri thought, ticking them off on his fingers as the Judean slunk his way through the small knot of bullies, *bedeviling us in this city where we should be most at peace.*

Turning back to work, he heard another cry and craned his neck to see the source of this fresh outburst. What now?

An old man strode into the city square with quickened step at the head of a mass of pilgrims: hundreds of men, women, and children, together with animals—sheep and camels, braying donkeys, and a long row of carts. Despite appearing travel-stained and weary, they shouted in joy and sang loud hymns of praise.

Newcomers to Judea? Come from where? Uri wondered.

Hevel and the other scribes hustled onto the balcony to see the reason for the hubbub.

"Send someone down to discover who they are," Uri commanded, but a second later he threw up a hand, gesturing them to wait. He'd caught a sudden movement by the leader, a toss of the head and straightening of the shoulders that could mean only one person.

Ezra! Ezra finally here in Jerusalem!

"Never mind," Uri said, "I'll go myself."

He pushed his way past the younger scribes, running down three flights of stone steps and out a side door, past the palace pillars and into the street.

"Ezra ben Seraiah!" Uri called loudly to be heard over the shouting and singing, elbowing his way through the crowd. "Ezra!"

Ezra turned at the familiar voice and extended his arms. In an instant, a pathway cleared between them. "Uri ben Seraf! Fellow scribe!" he called, his round, rich tones the voice of a much younger man.

The two men embraced, to the loud cheers of the throng, now augmented by curious onlookers. Joy surged through Uri's veins at being reunited with his old friend, who, despite his brittle limbs and parchment-white skin, wore his exaltation like a shining halo.

"How do you come to be here?" Uri asked.

"By the grace of the Most High, we left Babylon on the first day of the first month of the year," Ezra said, bright blue eyes glistening with emotion. "Oh, Uri, is it true? Am I truly standing on Jerusalem's sacred soil?"

"It's true," Uri admitted, "and I welcome you with all my heart. Who is in your party? How many are you?"

Ezra let his hand sweep over his followers. "Almost too many to count—though count I did," he chuckled. "Zacheria of the house of Parosh and his one hundred fifty men. Shecaniah, son of Jahaziel, and with him three hundred men. Joab, Obadiah son of Jehiel, and with him two hundred eighteen men...."

"Stop, stop!" Uri laughed. "You make me remember the day of counting before we left Babylon. Come, direct your people to a campground on the outskirts of the city—I will show you where we camped when we first returned. Just make sure your leaders set a stout guard, for the foreign peoples of Jerusalem will not welcome you as we Judeans do."

"Foreign peoples?" Ezra asked, voice sharp. "What do you mean?"

Uri sighed. "Later. We'll talk later. Let me bring you to the governor."

Ezra nodded. "Shelomith ben Josiphiah! Johanan ben Hakkatan!" he cried. "Attend me with the treasure carts."

"Treasure?" Uri wondered.

"King Xerxes opened his treasure house and commanded its keepers to allow us to take gifts for the Temple from its store," he said. "There are a hundred talents of silver, a hundred sheaves of wheat, a hundred barrels of wine, a hundred barrels of olive oil, as well as five hundred barrels of salt."

Uri shook his head. "Living here, in this poor land, I'd forgotten about the excesses of Persian royalty."

Ezra looked him over from head to foot. "And yet, you appear to have prospered here, my friend. You seem well fed and well gowned."

Uri put a wistful hand to his paunch. *Ezra's sharp tongue had not dulled over the years.* "I serve the governor as head scribe," he explained. "It behooves me to dress properly for my office."

Ezra wrapped his own tattered mantle about his thin shoulders and smiled.

After a moment, Uri spoke again. "Have your men take the treasure to the Temple. They'll welcome you with open arms."

"I will see them bestowed myself," Ezra said. "But I've a letter for the governor as well."

"A letter?" Uri asked, curious.

Ezra nodded. "I was disturbed by what I heard of our people here," he explained. "When I shared my fears with Xerxes, he gave me the authority to make some changes."

Uri's eyebrows shot up, a frisson of irritation racing through him. "Surely that is ill advised!" he cried. "As a stranger, you cannot know the troubles we face."

Ezra smiled wryly. "It feels like old times, to be arguing with you like this," he said. "But we have much to do, and I am tired."

Uri led the party to the Temple, where their gifts were indeed welcome. After Ezra kissed the hem of Jeshua's garment, the High Priest fawned over him. "We hear nothing but wonders of your scholarship," he told Ezra. "It will be a pleasure to sit together and discuss the Writings."

"A pleasure indeed," Ezra agreed.

Uri bit his lip. Were his years of service considered paltry when compared with Ezra's erudition? But he chided himself, recalling that he and the High Priest never managed to agree. The last thing he would have wanted would be to sit down with the man for a long talk of any kind.

"Come," Uri said to Ezra. "The governor will have heard of your arrival by now. It won't do to keep him waiting."

As they walked back through the streets, Uri noticed how Ezra's sharp eyes took in every foreign face, every maiden arrayed less than modestly, every idol in the shop windows.

"The city is indeed in a sorry state," he murmured, face stony with disappointment.

Uri said nothing. Ezra would learn soon enough how hopeless the situation was.

Sitting on his carved olive-wood chair in his antechamber, Zerubbabel greeted the scribe from Babylon much less warmly than Jeshua had done. After the initial greetings, he turned to Ezra and said, "We hear you have a missive for us from our brother in Persia."

Ezra's eyes widened, apparently not pleased to see Zerubbabel taking on the airs of royalty. "I have a letter from the great King of Persia to the Judean governor," he replied, pulling the scroll from his tunic. "Here it is."

Zerubbabel indicated with a careless wave that Uri should read the scroll aloud:

From Xerxes, king of kings,

To Ezra the priest, a teacher of the Law of the God of Heaven: Greetings.

I decree that any of the Israelites in my kingdom, including priests and Levites, who wish to go to Jerusalem with you, may go. You are sent by the king and his seven advisers to inquire in Judea and Jerusalem about the Law of your God, which is in your hand. Moreover, you are to take with you the silver and gold that the king and his advisers have freely given to the God of Israel, whose dwelling is in Jerusalem, together with all the silver and gold you may obtain from the province of Babylon, as well as the freewill offerings of the people and priests for the Temple of their God in Jerusalem. With this money be sure to buy bulls, rams, and male lambs, together with their grain offerings and drink offerings, and sacrifice them on the altar of the Temple of your God in Jerusalem.

Now I, King Xerxes, order all the treasurers of Trans-Euphrates to provide with diligence whatever Ezra the priest, a teacher of the Law of the God of Heaven, may ask of you. You are also to know that you have no authority to impose taxes, tribute, or duty on any of the priests, Levites, singers, gatekeepers, Temple servants, or other workers at this House of God.

And you, Ezra, in accordance with the wisdom of your God, which you possess, appoint magistrates and judges to administer justice to all the people of Trans-Euphrates—all who know the laws of your God. And you are to teach any who do not know them. Whoever does not obey the Law of your God and the law of the king must surely be punished by death, banishment, confiscation of property, or imprisonment.

Uri faltered over the last paragraph. Looking up, he was not surprised to see Zerubbabel's face purpling with rage.

"What does this mean, you should appoint magistrates and judges and are given the authority to decide death or banishment?" the governor hissed.

"It is as Xerxes, the king of Persia and Babylon, decrees," Ezra said coolly. "And from what I see in the streets, it will be a welcome change."

64

Amittai and the Fox

A FOX MUST BE SKULKING about the farm, Amittai realized, as he woke in the predawn to the sound of chickens squawking.

Beside him, Keren sighed in her sleep and rolled over. The blankets slipped off him as she pulled them to her. Shivering in the cold air, he gently eased part of the blankets back. Keren moaned softly and lapsed into even breathing, while he lay quietly and listened.

The chickens were still squawking. Something must be wrong.

Amittai rose, reaching for his sandals. He put a mantle on his shoulders and started down the hallway. Entering the storeroom, heading for the back door, he was brought up short by the sight of Tobija entering the house.

She carried a small torch, the flax still smoking as though she'd hastily extinguished it. Her cheeks, Amittai realized, were wet. Noticing him, she startled, hunching her shoulders. Muttering a strangled greeting, she tried to ease by him. But he caught hold of her arm.

"Is he still out there?" Amittai demanded.

"He who?" she retorted. "I heard a noise, that's all."

Amittai's fingers bit into her flesh. "So you went out to have a look all by yourself?"

She tried to yank her arm away, lips twisting in a grimace. "I had no husband in my bed I could dispatch."

He let her go. It was true Ophir rarely spent his nights with his first wife, preferring Chava's younger caresses. Amittai supposed the Amorite woman was to be pitied in a way. He thought of what Keren might do, had he been tempted to take a second wife. The notion made him chuckle. Tobija, slinking past him, cast him a look of aggrieved fury.

"I know you're happy your son has at least one Judean wife," she accused him. "But I promise, you won't always be."

"What do you mean?"

She stared at him from the threshold of the door that led to the rest of the house. A rooster crowed. Amittai glanced through a window. The sky, while still dark, was lightening. It was nearly morning and soon the house would be stirring.

"What do you mean?" Amittai repeated.

Tobija's only answer was her level, contemptuous glare. Amittai's eyes narrowed. "If I find your father on my farm…." he began.

"You'll what? Cower before him as you have always done before?"

Amittai closed the distance between them with two hasty steps and slapped her. The force of the blow snapped her head around. Amittai was shocked at how good it felt to hurt her. But just as he pulled his hand back to do it again, Ophir burst into the hallway.

"I heard…what's going on?" he demanded.

Tobija clutched her reddened face. The impression Amittai's fingers made reached up her cheeks toward her eyes.

Ophir placed himself between his father and his now sobbing wife. "What's going on?"

"Ask her," Amittai retorted. "There's a fox out there. I'm going to make sure he's gone."

He stalked out into the cool morning air. The palm of his hand stung. He flexed it, shame mixing with his exaltation. *But she has to learn*, he told himself. This was his farm, Ophir's farm, no matter what her father told her.

The henhouse seemed untouched. Amittai counted the chickens. They were all there. What had spooked them, if not a fox? Amittai approached one of the hens and was taken aback when the entire peep of chickens began squawking again.

He reached into the nest beneath the chicken, groping around, ignoring the hen's frantic pecking of his hand. His fingers touched the hilt of a dagger. He pulled it out and fumbled some more, drawing out two more daggers.

He checked the rest of the henhouse. Each of the chickens had two or three daggers buried deep in the pile of straw beneath them. Amittai put them back, all but one, which he stood contemplating in cold fury.

Ophir burst into the henhouse, face red with fury. Amittai, still holding the dagger, whirled to face him. The chickens started to squawk again, their protests rising to the rafters.

"Why did you strike my wife?" Ophir demanded.

"Why do you permit your father-in-law to hide his weapons on my property?" Amittai snapped back. "Didn't we deal with this matter years ago, when we returned the chest you were fool enough to bury near the privy?"

Ophir glared at the weapon in his father's hand. Like most Amorite daggers, the tang was made of copper smelted with tin and hammered to a deadly edge, a thick layer of twine neatly covering the grip. A weapon for close quarters fighting, for plunging into a heart at near range. There had been more than fifteen years of such attacks, intimidating the returning Judeans.

Amittai flipped the dagger neatly and thrust the handle into his son's stomach, making him flinch. "Get them out of here," he commanded. "Tobija should tell Hanun not to come here any longer. And she should treat her father-in-law with greater respect."

"I didn't know he hid them here," Ophir stammered.

Amittai turned away. "I'm sure you didn't," he said. "But if they're discovered, it won't just be Hanun who is hanged in the market square. You're lucky Chava didn't find them."

"Chava would never…."

"Wouldn't she?" Amittai threw the question over his shoulder, stalking toward the farmhouse. "Niece of the head scribe? Returned from Babylon to repossess her family's farm? Are you so certain where her loyalties lie?"

65

Chava on the Farm

"TELL ME AGAIN ABOUT THE gardens of Babylon, Momma," little Sarah wheedled.

Chava paused, hands full of bread dough. She looked at her daughter. Sarah was nearly five years old now, the age Chava had been when Grandmother Sarah had told her all the stories about Judea. *It's funny how things transpire*, Chava thought. Sarah had told Chava stories and shaped her future that way. Would telling little Sarah of Babylon make her dissatisfied with the simple life on the farm?

"Not now, child," Chava replied. "Go pick some fresh dates for dinner. Your Uncle Uri likes them."

Sarah balanced on one foot, holding the table for support. She experimented twirling from one side of her bare foot to another. "Why does Aunt Zakiti have funny lines around her eyes?" she asked.

"It's kohl, sweetie—she uses kohl to make herself beautiful," Chava explained. "That's how women decorate their faces in Babylon where Aunt Zakiti was born."

"You were born in Babylon," the girl persisted, twisting faster on one toe. "But you don't decorate your face."

In a moment Sarah might topple over. Chava put out one dough-encrusted hand and steadied the child's elbow. "No, I don't," she said.

"Judean women are taught to be modest. To dress so that men aren't tempted to look at them, especially after they are married. Other people—Babylonians, Persians, Hittites, Amorites—don't believe that."

"Mother Tobija is Amorite, and she dresses like you," Sarah said thoughtfully, coming down flat on both feet. "Look, Momma, you got dough on me."

"Go get the dates," Chava sighed. "Brush off the dough outside the chicken coop. The hens will eat the scraps."

Sarah took a straw basket and left, humming a song under her breath. Chava smiled as she finished kneading the loaves, putting them into a large, tightly woven basket to prove. These weekly visits by Uncle Uri and his family gladdened her heart, keeping her connected with her past. But recently, undercurrents of tension had become palpable, strain between Uncle Uri and Amittai, her father-in-law. Between Amittai and Ophir. Between Ophir and his first wife.

And between Tobija and herself. But that enmity was so long lived, it almost didn't bear mentioning. Tobija hated her, had hated her from the first moment she wed Ophir. She masked it under a coating of sweetness. No one could have been nicer than Tobija when Chava first became pregnant. And no one could have acted more maliciously when Yoram was born, pointing out that the shape of his face and the color of his eyes were just like that of the young goldsmith's. "What's his name?" she'd wondered sweetly. "Uziel?"

Lucky for Chava, Ophir was impervious to his first wife's taunting. Over the years, Chava had grown fond of him. The good heart that had prompted him to help her that day at the well meant he was a loving father to all his children, a kind husband to both his wives. But she had to admit that he favored her company and, of course, her bed. Because Chava disapproved, he stopped attending the sacrifice. It was because she too had borne Ophir sons, Chava thought, pulling out a basket of fava beans to prepare, and because he preferred her bed, that Tobija couldn't accept her.

She remembered an evening not long ago, standing in the kitchen garden, when Keren spoke to Chava about what her children could expect in the future. "It's fortunate that we have ample room for all of your sons to stay on the farm," she said.

"That's not always possible, I know," Chava responded. "Only my eldest brother could inherit our farm in Babylon. The other two were apprenticed out."

Tobija, who had been preparing the evening meal for herself and her children in her little kitchen, walked out just then and must have overheard. She glared at both women but said nothing until Ophir came in from the fields, young Yoram perched on his shoulders.

"Nadab is your first born," she shrilled at her husband. "He deserves a first-born's portion. The children of your second wife should receive less. Or nothing at all."

Chava took Yoram from his father and backed away, but not quickly enough. Tobija whirled on her.

"Don't think I don't know whose doing this is! You've poisoned my husband against me, against my children. You're a witch, a scrawny black-eyed daughter of a pig! A whore!"

Amittai came up from behind them. "Shut up, woman!" he cried. "There will be no shrieking and screaming in my house."

"Hah! In your house? *Your* house? It's her house! She owns you all, body and soul. And you all know it and pretend it isn't so!"

Keren, who had moved inside, stood at the door, her face grave. "Chava. Bring the children. Dinner is ready."

Chava went, head lowered as she brushed past Tobija. Tobija spat on the ground at her feet, splattering her toes. Chava kept walking.

Remembering that now, she shelled the beans mechanically. She had much to do before Uncle Uri and Aunt Zakiti arrived for the evening meal, together with her cousins and their children. Tonight was special because Ezra the scribe was coming with them. Chava knew that Ezra had been at Aunt Rahil's home when Aunt Mara had died, that the scribe would have news of the rest of the family. Chava pushed a sudden wave of homesickness aside as she put the shelled beans down on the table and started to dress the meat. Was she sorry she had married Ophir now that Grandmama was dead? Despite Tobija's poisonous tongue, she found she couldn't regret it. Ophir was a good husband and father. And her memory of her grandmother's joy at returning to the farm would be with her always.

It was a beautiful evening, so Keren suggested they eat outside beneath the stars. She and Tobija set a table under the thick grape leaves of the arbor. The sky was a deep indigo blue, a line of orange thinning at the horizon, when Ezra intoned the prayer over bread.

"It is an honor to have you in our home," Amittai said, for the third or fourth time that evening. "We welcome you, Ezra ben Seraiah."

Ezra merely nodded. Chava took the broken bread from his hand and passed it around the table. Half the meal passed as Ezra told Uri, Chava, and the rest of the family the news from Babylon—how Rahil's husband had taken a third wife, how Mirav's quick tongue had gotten her into trouble in the marketplace, how Uri's daughter Asnat had given birth to another son.

"That's all I know," Ezra finally said, as young Sarah, bidden by her mother's sharp eyes, bustled around the table with the clay bowl of dates.

"And what of Daniel?" Chava asked. "Does he live still?"

"Daniel? No. Daniel is no longer with us." Ezra shook his head regretfully. "Toward the end of his life, I began to doubt Daniel's visions."

"Doubt them? Why?" Uri asked.

"Oh, he always had odd dreams. You know that. But before his death, he stood on the banks of the River Tigris and claimed to see a man whose face flashed like lightning, who was sumptuously dressed in linen and gold.

"Daniel claimed this man told him of the end of the world—a strange, contorted tale of kings of the north and the south, of a time when the daily sacrifice would be broken. When he called me to him and told me this tale, bidding me write it down, I admit I was loath."

"But you did anyway." Uri nodded. "A scribe writes what he is bid, without question."

"I did, of course. Daniel died content, knowing his last vision would live on."

Uri and Chava sat in silence. The rest of the family shifted restively in their seats. Finally young Nadab spoke up. "Could you tell another story of the beginning of the world, scribe Uri?"

Ezra laughed. "Uri and his tales of the world's origins! It was ever so, boy—Uri the scribe, fascinated by our earliest roots. Tell the lad a tale, my friend, so I can imagine the two of us as young men again, with Baruch parceling out the next day's tasks."

Uri smiled. "Very well, how about the story of the flood? You and your mother and your sisters might enjoy that, for Ham, Noah's son, had a grandson of the Amorite people, whom it is said lived between the mighty rivers of Egypt and the Euphrates."

Chava was watching Ezra when Uri spoke, and she noticed how his glance instantly shifted toward Tobija and her son and daughters, eyes narrowing. *Did he not know that Ophir had taken an Amorite as his first wife?*

"Once upon a time," Uri started, "before our Father, Abraham, was born, there was a righteous man who lived in an evil age. And the name of the righteous man...."

"Was Atrahasis," Zakiti interrupted.

"Was Noah," Uri continued, shaking a finger at his wife to hush her.

But Zakiti, perhaps having drunk too generously from the wine that Chava had served with the meal, would not be stopped. Every time the two stories differed—Noah being commanded to build the ark directly from God, while Atrahasis received his instructions in a dream, the flood taking only six days in the Babylonian version versus forty in the Hebrew—Zakiti interrupted her husband's tale to amend his account.

Chava watched as Ezra grew more and more indignant. Finally as Zakiti said, "You forgot the swallow, husband—there were three birds released, not just two, not just a raven and a dove," he apparently could stand it no longer.

"Be quiet, woman!" Ezra burst, bringing his fist down on the table with an emphatic bang. "Do not defile our truth with your warped myth!"

Zakiti's eyes flashed. Under her long-sleeved gown, she twisted her forearms, so her gold bangles jangled.

"Judeans!" she muttered. "Always so convinced your truth is the only truth!"

Chava watched as Tobija, who had listened to the story of the flood almost wistfully, eyes on her lap, sent a sympathetic gleam over the table at the Babylonian woman.

"Zakiti!" Uri cried furiously. "Be quiet! You shame me!"

"Tell the truth, now! You had that story from me, husband," Zakiti retorted. "It comes from our history tablets, our story of Gilgamesh. Someday you will admit that."

Ezra stood, pushing his stool out from under him. "I will not stay here a moment longer," he cried. "Uri, you who are supposed to be a holy man, writing of holy things: You have defiled your own home and garden. I come here at your invitation and what do I find? A Babylonian wife—whom I always objected to—and an Amorite wife—both allowed to sit among us and sneer. Our bloodline is being polluted with their children and their children's children. I have felt this ever since coming to Jerusalem, but never more so than tonight!"

"This is our land, too!" Tobija cried, high patches of red on her burnished cheeks. "You Judeans want to push us out, but we won't let you!"

"You won't? How do you propose to stop us?" Ezra shouted, his voice thick with anger.

"My father will stop you! My father will not cease his attacks in the marketplace or the quiet corners of Jerusalem's night city, until you accept us!" Tobija retorted.

Amittai pushed his seat back and rose hastily. Taking three steps toward his daughter-in-law, he grabbed Tobija's sleeve. She shook him off.

"And exactly who is your father, woman?" Ezra demanded.

"Come, Nadab." Tobija rose, pushing past Amittai, ignoring Ezra as she took her wide-eyed daughters by the hand. "Let us leave your father's table where we are no longer welcome!"

"Who is your father?" Ezra insisted again.

"I am Tobija, daughter of Hanun the Amorite," Tobija cried, her head erect. "And we will fight you Judeans to the death!"

"Leave my house this instant!" Amittai screamed.

But Ophir stepped between her and his father, looking disdainfully at Amittai. "She is still my wife," Ophir said. "These are still my children."

Ezra had turned white at the mention of Hanun. He whirled on Uri. "You had me eat here, at the table of Hanun's offspring?" he cried. "How could you?"

Uri stood, speaking in measured tones. "Ezra. Be calm and listen. We've never seen this matter in the same light...."

"No—because your household is defiled by the blood of strangers," Ezra retorted, giving a quick shake of his head.

"Believe me, there was no attempt to insult you!" Amittai cried. "You have honored us!"

Ezra ignored him, staring at Uri. His breath rasped in his throat, and he put a hand over his chest, as though to quiet his heart. "I never thought you deserved to be made a scribe." He spoke slowly, sounding more sad than angry. "Do you remember the day I took you to be purified in the mikveh and you told me you were the son of a gelding?"

Uri blushed. Chava knew her uncle was shamed by his father, even after all these years.

"I had some hope for you—but then you married out of the faith. Baruch should have listened to me then and made you leave your post. But he refused."

"You wanted Baruch to discard me because I wed the woman I made pregnant?"

Chava saw the mixed mortification and resentment on Uri's face. Zakiti sat rigidly upright, face hard as iron.

"I will take my leave of you all. Uri, you and I will discuss this another time." Ezra rose and left, his footfalls echoing in the night.

Zakiti snatched at the heavy scarf that hid her still-dark hair, letting it drop on the tabletop. "We don't need him," she said defiantly.

Chava looked at the ruin of her dinner party. Tobija and her children had already skulked off. Amittai and Ophir were arguing in a corner. Aunt Zakiti stood straight in the evening night, eyes dark and sparkling, gold bangles dancing on her restless arms. "Let's go home, Uri," she wheedled. "Ezra always hated me. You know that."

Uri looked at his niece and opened his mouth. But then he shut it again—wisely, Chava thought. After all, any more words could only do harm. "Good night, Chava," he said after a long moment. "We will see you again next week, God willing."

66

Ezra Tears His Cloak

THE SPRING AND SUMMER PASSED. Uri, busy with work for the governor, wearied by constant cares, did not reconcile his differences with Ezra. Ezra was too occupied for such small matters anyway. He sat on judicial proceedings and declared his opinions as if they were law. The priests, noting how this infuriated Zerubbabel, maliciously backed Ezra. When Zerubbabel or his officials protested, the priests cited Xerxes's letter giving the scribe the authority to appoint magistrates and judges and decide between life and death.

At such times, Uri sat thin-lipped as he wrote out the proceedings. He was just a scribe, he reminded himself, not a magistrate, not the governor, not a priest of the Temple. Uri's job, just as Baruch used to tell him, was to write. Judgment was for others.

Acting in his new capacity of—Uri wasn't quite sure what to call it—Ezra would often snap his fingers to demand Uri's notations. His stylus flying, he swiftly changed the record if it did not satisfy him. "This is how it was," Ezra said, handing the tablet back to the glaring scribe. "This is how history should remember it."

Throughout the summer, Uri heard rumors of Ezra's mounting frustration with the Judeans' foreign wives and children. Before a meeting with the governor one morning, High Priest Jeshua gave the whispers shape.

"We miss seeing you at the Temple, Uri," he said, seating himself in the carved olivewood chair and taking the cup of wine a servant handed him. "We are well-served by the young scribes you send our way, of course."

"I am glad to hear it," Uri said, checking his wax tablets to make sure he had enough.

"All but Hananiah ben Kelal," Jeshua added.

Uri frowned, looking up from his counting. The scribe named had always been diligent and particularly apt at capturing complicated procedures. "What ails Hananiah?"

"Oh, the boy is well enough in himself," Jeshua said. "His parentage is the problem."

"His...parentage?"

"Kelal took a wife from among the Jebusites, you know. Ezra tells us...."

A wave of exhaustion nearly overpowered Uri. "Send the boy back to the palace. I can put him to good use."

"The Temple, you know, should remain pure. We've noticed—and were glad to see—that you never dispatched your own son-in-law to us."

"My son-in-law? Hevel? Hevel is born of two Judean parents," Uri stammered.

"Yes, but he is married to a woman who is not," Jeshua said, looking toward the door. "Ah, here is Zerubbabel now."

It took all of Uri's scribal training to remain seated. He knew what was unspoken: the fact that he, too, had married outside the faith. That his own daughter, being the child of a Babylonian, was not considered pure. He picked up his stylus with a shaking hand.

With the fall came the rains. The first of them had the city dancing in the streets, for it had been a long, hot summer and the fields were parched. It was nearly time for the most holy days of the year. The people gathered in Jerusalem, coming from all corners of Judea.

Uri woke early that fateful morning. He was tempted to stay in bed, for Zakiti stirred and smiled suggestively at him. After all these years, she still had the power to fire his blood. But there was too much to do. He and one of the governor's aides were expected at the Temple to discuss the coming holidays, how they would house the city visitors and make ready the provisions they would need. How much grain and how much barley, how many barrels of water, where to arrange the communal privies—the details were endless.

So Uri rose and washed and walked to the Temple. On the way, he saw one of his neighbors. "Shimei! Good morning!" Uri called. "Where are you going? Why aren't you in your shop?"

"Have you not heard?" Shimei replied. "They say Ezra is to address us this morning."

"No, I hadn't heard." An unexpected whisper of fear chased up Uri's spine. "What about?"

"I am not sure," Shimei said. "But I heard it would be important."

Uri made his way through the crowds, surprised by the throng standing in the Temple yard. The enormous outer courtyard, built to house the mass of people who came for the sacrificial holidays, was packed. As Uri pushed through to find Zerubbabel, he heard a commotion on the broad white marble stairs leading to the outer Temple entranceway.

"This is what I feared to tell you, oh Ezra, son of the exiled High Priest, wise scribe, and extraordinary scholar of the Writings," Jeshua cried out, his trained priest's voice carrying into the far reaches of the crowd. Jeshua was dressed in a flowing garment of white, and wore the jeweled breastplate of the High Priest, which he generally only donned on important holidays. His balding head was covered by a white turban. "The people of Israel—even the priests, I am sorry to say, even the Levites—have not kept themselves aloof from the neighboring peoples. Many have married those who practice idol worship and human sacrifice. They allied themselves with the Canaanites, the Hittites, Perizzites, Jebusites, Ammonites, Moabites, Egyptians, and Amorites. They took their daughters as wives for themselves and their sons, mingling our holy race with the impure pagans around them. And I tremble to tell you, even some of our most trusted leaders and officials have played a role in this unfaithfulness to the Most High."

Uri flinched as he heard this. But then his eyes, like everyone else's, were inexorably drawn to the figure of Ezra, who rose and wailed. Unlike the High Priest, Ezra's clothes were modest, even slightly ragged, falling off his skeletal frame. But his poor clothing could not detract from his commanding presence, the imposing aura of his strong and certain faith.

"Tell me this is not so!" Ezra cried. "The God of Israel would not have this be so, after our many generations of suffering and our long journey back to our homeland!"

Jeshua turned away, as though he were weeping in shame.

Ezra took hold of his tunic and cloak with both hands. He pulled, tearing them with a rip that echoed through the silent, tense crowd. He left the rent garment hanging on him and reached into his hair and beard, pulling out huge handfuls. Then, with a gasp of pain and sorrow that reverberated through the people's hearts, he collapsed on the top of the Temple steps and crouched there, praying and wailing loudly, as though in mourning.

The people stood, frozen, unable to move. Many joined his weeping, crying out to God to forgive their sins. Uri watched as the crowd swelled, newcomers swiftly told of Ezra's sorrow from the eager lips of their friends and neighbors. Hours passed, but no one dared leave. Ezra sat on the steps of the Temple, perched where all could see him, for an entire day. The crowd grew restive. The evening sacrifice took place a little early that evening, the priests hurrying through it. When it was complete, Ezra rose, walked a few steps forward and lay flat on the top of the stairs, facing the open portal to the Temple's interior.

"O my God! I am too ashamed and disgraced to lift my face to you, my God, because our sins are higher than our heads and our guilt has reached the heavens!" he cried. He pulled himself up, staggering a little from his day's fast, calling, "From the days of our forefathers until now, our guilt has been great. Because of our sins, we and our kings and our priests were subjected to the sword and captivity, to humiliation at the hand of foreign kings. So too, today."

Around him, Uri saw heads nodding. All of them knew, knew in every fiber of their being, what it meant to be a subject people. He could not help but wonder: Had they truly brought this on themselves? Had he, by his marriage to Zakiti, contributed to his people's sin?

Ezra continued, "But now, for a brief moment, the Lord our God has been gracious in allowing us a remnant of former glory, giving us a firm place in his sanctuary, giving light to our eyes and a measure of relief from bondage. Slaves though we might be, the Most High has not deserted us. He has shown us kindness in the sight of the kings of Persia: He has granted us new life to rebuild the house of our God and repair its ruins."

The crowd murmured and whispered to one another. Uri felt their deep relief. Perhaps Ezra's one-day fast was enough to expiate their sins. Perhaps this date would be marked out as a new fast day, a day to regret their past and resolve to do better in the future.

But Ezra was not done. Loudly, to be heard over the rustling of the throng, he cried, "But now, O our God, what can we say to you? For we have disregarded the commands You gave through Your servants the prophets when You said: 'The land you will enter and possess is a land polluted by the corruption of its peoples. By their detestable practices, they have filled it with their impurity from one end to the other. Therefore, do not give your daughters in marriage to their sons or take their daughters for your sons. Do not seek a treaty of friendship with them, so you may be strong and eat the good things of the land and leave them to your children as an everlasting inheritance.' This You told us."

Ezra paused before continuing. "The punishments we have endured were the result of our great guilt. Yet, God punished us less than our sins have deserved and gave us our home and Temple again, even though it is only a remnant of its former glory. Shall we again break Your commands and marry foreigners who commit sin? Would You not be angry with us if we do so, angry enough to destroy us? O Lord, God of Israel, You are righteous! We stand before You in our guilt, even if because of our sins not one of us can stand in Your presence."

Ezra said no more, sagging against a pillar under the weight of his confession. The people around Uri wept and moaned. But then came a shout from the crowd.

"I am Shecaniah son of Jehiel, one of the descendants of Elam!"

Uri recognized the man as a servant to the priests.

"We have been unfaithful to our God by marrying foreign women from the peoples who surround us. But there is still hope for Israel!"

"Hope!" the call went up from the crowd. "Still hope for us!"

Shecaniah continued. "Now we should make a covenant before God to send away all these women and their children, according to Ezra's counsel. Let it be done!"

"Yes!" the people cried. "Let it be done!"

Shecaniah was pushed forward to the steps where Ezra stood, a look of joy transforming his tear-drenched face. Shecaniah took both of Ezra's hands and called out, "Rise up; this matter is in your hands. We support you! Take courage. Do what must be done."

"We love you, Ezra," came a cry from the crowd.

"We support you!"

"We will do what you require!"

Uri looked around him, suspecting that Shecaniah's words were rehearsed. Regardless, the people were afire with a new sense of joy, the transcendent glory of resolving to set aside their sins. There was nothing, Uri realized with a sinking heart, nothing that Ezra could not tell them now that would not be accepted by his fellow Judeans.

Ezra stood erect, pushing himself off the pillar. "You give me heart, People of Israel! You give me strength! Do you swear to do what has been suggested here today? Do you swear to send away these women and these children?"

"We swear!" the crowd called in one voice.

"And you, you Levites and you priests of the Temple, you who should be the shining example to our people. Do you swear?"

"We swear!" came the cry from the line of priests behind Ezra, intoned as though in a sacred rite.

"Then it shall be so!"

A shout of exaltation rose from the crowd, wave after wave of wordless cheering. It beat a merciless tattoo on Uri's heart.

Ezra turned and left the Temple courtyard. Uri was called for, to attend him in his capacity as lead scribe. He was led to the house of Jehohanan ben Eliashiv, following in the wake of those who chose to accompany Ezra there, continuing to cheer and shout praises to the Lord God. When they arrived at the house, Uri had to push his way once more through the crowd.

As he was ushered inside, he pulled his tablets out of his goatskin satchel. Ezra sat in Jehohanan's spacious antechamber, surrounded by priests, his poor clothing contrasting vividly with the rich wall hangings and sheepskin rugs of the merchant's home.

"Let the servants fetch you something to eat, Ezra," Jehohanan's wife was saying as Uri entered the room and went silently to a table set off to one side.

"No, no, thank you, Aliza," Ezra told her. "I am still in mourning. I will eat nothing."

"Something to drink then?" she pleaded, gesturing toward a young servant girl who held up a silver ewer.

"No, nothing. Not so long as the exiles," here Ezra fixed Uri with a baleful glare, "continue to be unfaithful. The crowd has heartened me, but until the foreigners are expelled from our midst, I will not eat or drink for my own pleasure."

Uri swallowed hard, wishing Aliza would offer him some wine or water. A lump lodged in his throat. He swallowed again, wistfully watching the pitcher of wine as it was covered by a cloth and removed from the room.

"Take this down, scribe," Ezra said to him sternly. "It is for this day you learned to write."

He dictated: "I, Ezra, given my authority by Xerxes, King of Persia, and by the hand of the Lord, do proclaim throughout Judea and Jerusalem the Holy City that all exiles are required to assemble in Jerusalem in three days. Anyone who fails to appear within this set period of time shall lose their lands and property, forfeiting all in accordance with the decisions of the officials and the elders. They will be expelled from our people by the Assembly of Exiles, which was founded to keep our faith and people alive while in captivity."

Uri wrote, then stood waiting, his stylus at the ready.

"That's all," Ezra said. "Make sure that is sent out to all the corners of the land."

"Three days?" Uri could not help but question him. "It hardly seems long enough."

"Three days," Ezra snapped, tilting his head so his jaw thrust upward. "I can wait no longer than that."

67

The Rains

THE RAIN PELTED DOWN, A sheet of water bouncing off the arid land and running, in great rivulets, to flood the roads. The fields were sodden in standing pools. It would take days for the runoff to seep into the hard-packed earth. Amittai stood under the overhanging roof of his barn, watching the rain grimly.

He'd fled his house, where Tobija's voice was raised in relent-less protest.

"My father will not permit this!" she cried as Keren stood over her and bid her pack her things. "You'll see! He'll come with his men and take this farm away from you."

If Hanun were to come, thought Amittai, he would finally have to do something about it. The judges and the magistrates of Judea would pay him well for delivering the scourge of Jerusalem. And he'd attain great honor for it, besides. Standing idly watching the fields fill with rainwater, Amittai allowed himself the rare luxury of a daydream. He would cut Hanun's head off and bring it into the city, where the crowds, obedient to Ezra's proclamation, were searching out a dry place to await the end of the three-day period. He'd put the head into a basket and bring it to Ezra as he stood on the podium erected for the ceremonies and pull it out. His friends and neighbors would be the first to recognize the severed skull, whispering to the newcomers to the city, until Amittai was buffeted by the force of their cheering. Ezra would come down the Temple steps and put a hand on his shoulder and tell the governor to grant him and his family the farm in perpetuity as a reward for his service that day. All those years of scraping and bowing to Hanun's will would be more than rectified. And no one would ever question his allegiance to the Judean people again.

"Father?" came Ophir's strained voice behind him, making Amittai jump. "Should we take the milk cows and the sheep to higher ground to feed?"

Amittai turned slowly, unwilling to face his son's grim face. Under Ophir's eyes were dark shadows. It was clear that the boy had gotten no sleep at all for the last couple of days.

"But she's my wife!" Ophir had cried when the news was first brought to the farm. "They're my children!"

Chava, Amittai noticed, took one look at her husband's tortured face and turned away, seating herself at the table and cradling her head on her arms. Tobija let out a wail that cut through the air like a knife. It came as no surprise to Amittai that Keren was quickest to act upon the proclamation. Implacable, his wife put a hand on their son's shoulder and whispered into his ear. Ophir looked at his mother with an expression of disbelief and contempt. But he controlled himself, merely pushing her hand away and walking off.

"You are glad of it!" Tobija cried out, as Ophir left the room. "You revel in my misery!"

Chava hunched her shoulders in denial. Keren, however, merely raised her eyebrows, watching her daughter-in-law with open scorn. It took Nadab to touch Keren's heart.

"Grandmama?" the boy asked. Nearly a man, tall and lanky, his soft brown eyes looked at her pleadingly. "Grandmama, do you really want us to leave?"

Keren looked at the boy, her face softening. "No, Nadab, but it will be better this way."

"Better? Better for whom? For that donkey over there, pretending to cry?" Tobija shouted, pointing at Chava. "For you, who always hated me and my children? For your coward of a husband?"

Amittai felt his palms itch. But he saw the uncertainty that crossed Keren's face as her grandson asked her another question. He walked over and cupped his wife's shoulder with his hand.

"Do you hate us so much, Grandmother?" Nadab asked, eyes wide with betrayal.

"I don't hate you, child," Keren stammered.

"But you wish he had never been born," Tobija shrieked. "Admit it! You wish my children had never been born!"

Keren turned away. But Nadab saw the answer in her face. He took two steps over and put his arms around his sobbing mother.

"It will be all right," he told her, trying to pat her shaking shoulders. "I'll take care of you, Mother."

He led her out. Amittai was left in the silent room with Keren and Chava. Chava's head rose. Amittai was surprised to see her face was damp with tears.

"I need to go see Uncle Uri," Chava said. "My aunt...they must be in agony there too." She rose, put a shawl over her head, and turned to Keren. "Watch the children for me?"

Keren nodded and Chava slipped out the kitchen door.

Chava returned home before nightfall, soaked through. She changed her clothes and sat wearily at the table, eating a crust of bread.

"What will Uri do about Zakiti and Irit and his grandchildren?" Amittai asked, curious. "Will he send them off?"

Chava drank some water, looking off into the distance. Amittai didn't dare repeat the question, which hung in the air, unanswered.

"Father? The animals?" Ophir's voice cut into his reminisces. "Should I lead them to higher ground?"

"Yes, of course. Go ahead."

He watched Ophir's receding back, then turned to contemplate his soaked fields again. *Hanun*, he thought. *You're out there somewhere, still a threat to me and mine. What will you do when we send your daughter from us? And what will we all do when Nadab—the first grandchild I cradled against my breast—realizes he is old enough to wield a dagger himself?*

68

In the Temple Square

URI WALKED TO THE TEMPLE Square each day, feet dragging. He could smell the people long before he reached them—the tang of drenched clothing, of smoky fires kindled under a tent awning to make a hot cup of soup, of sweat, human waste, and fear. The pungent odors assailed his nose, tempting him to turn and flee.

But no place on Earth contained peace for him. His wife cried and wailed and tore at her clothing, resolving to put aside the modest garb she had endured ever since embarking on the long journey of Return. His daughter—brought up as a Judean woman, married to a Judean man—sat in a darkened corner of their home and wept. How would Ezra deal with her and her children? Would her husband, her beloved Hevel, cast them off?

When Uri had a moment to reflect, he shuddered at the thought of the drama taking place at the farm as well. Chava came the first day, to sit silently with a wailing Zakiti, holding her hand. She hadn't appeared after that.

The three days had flown by for Uri, in a kind of limbo of details that bedeviled him. The crowds of people, obedient to Ezra's commands, had to be housed. There had to be enough barley to feed those with money as well as those without. When fights broke out, as they so inevitably did when tempers were frayed this thin, Uri had to dispatch a scribe to serve the hastily convened tribunal as it heard the complaints from both sides and meted out punishment. He had no time to sit and ponder. But the thought was always in the background, pounding at his skull, demanding attention. *What should he do?*

Zakiti is my wife, he thought now, turning the corner, flinching at the sight of the Temple Square packed with humanity. *I took her hand just as Adam did Eve, or Moses his wife Zippora. How can I send her from me?*

Uri shoved his way to the Temple steps, where an impatient Ezra waited with the priests. From the look of the clouds scudding past the sun, another downpour threatened.

"We should address the people before the rains come," one of the priests was saying, peering into the darkening skies.

"There have been more complaints," another added.

"We will address them soon," Ezra replied, smoothing down his tunic. "Send the men out again to count heads."

"Anyone who is coming is here." Jeshua looked impatient. "Any stragglers will hear the news from their neighbors."

"We don't have provisions for another day," the first priest said. "We must speak now."

Uri took his place beside Ezra, silently picking up his tablet of wax. Ezra looked at him with a stony glance. "You do not look well, my friend," Ezra badgered him. "Are you not rejoiced at the sight of so many people of Judea ready to right the wrongs they have committed?"

"I am rejoiced," Uri said mechanically, knowing he had no choice but to placate the man. "I am here to write at your command."

Ezra frowned. "You think I do this lightly. You think I wish you harm."

Uri thought back to the day he had pulled Ezra's leg in the mikveh, forcing him under the water. "My feelings do not matter," he said now. "Our former master, of blessed memory, Baruch ben Neriah, would have told me my job as scribe is just to write down what I witness."

"And so you must." Ezra nodded. "And so you shall."

He stepped forward and raised his arms. "People of Zion! People of the Return! You please my heart, for you were faithful to my summons, despite the hardship of leaving your homes in this season and camping here in the rain. I bid you welcome!"

A wordless roar rose up. Ezra turned to all corners of the square, arms still raised, as though he were a priest with the power to send forth a benediction.

"You have been unfaithful!" were his next words, and they reverberated through the crowd like a breaking wave.

"We have been unfaithful!" they responded. "We have sinned!"

"You have married foreign women, adding to Israel's guilt!"

A moan of contrition rose from the crowd. Uri felt the weight of his own marriage assailing him. His shoulders sagged.

"You must make confession to the Most High, the God of your fathers, and do His will!"

"Tell us how!" came the shout.

"Yes, Ezra, tell us how to make amends to the Lord!"

"Ezra, what should we do?"

"What should you do? The answer is simple. You must separate yourselves from the peoples around you and from your foreign wives."

"Yes! Ezra is right!" the crowd cried. "We must do as he says!"

But not everyone was so quickly convinced. Uri felt his fingers flying over the tablet, trying to capture all of the responses.

"You tell us we must do this. But it is not something so easily done!"

"They are our wives, Ezra! Our children! You would have us wrench apart our families!"

One man rose from the crowd, standing on a broad stone so he could be seen as well as heard. "I am Jonathan ben Asahel! Have I done otherwise than our forefathers, by taking a bride from the peoples who surround us? Think of Isaac and of Jacob! Think of King David, who married the wife of a Hittite! Is my sin worse than theirs? Think of Moses, who married a Midianite! Who is more holy than our blessed Moses?"

"He is right," cried another man. "I am Shabbethai the Levite who says so!"

"No!" protested several voices. "Ezra is the one who is right! We have sinned. We must make amends!"

Ezra raised his arms again, to signal for silence. "Our history is full of marriages to foreign women, to alliances with foreign people. But look how the Lord has treated us each time we defiled our homes and our families in this way! Think of your friends and neighbors who compound their sin by attending the sacrifices, by allowing idols in their homes! Think of how our people have just survived exile by remaining true to our faith and the word of the Most High! Think of our brethren to the north, the Israelites, who have vanished amid the nations, dispersed and disintegrated into the sands of time! Would you be like them? Would you allow the covenant with the Most High be squandered upon foreign couches, where these women deprive us of our strength as Delilah did Samson?"

Another man rose from the crowd, three others standing with him. "I am Maaseiah ben Jozadak, brother of Jeshua the High Priest. I and my brothers—Eliezer, Jarib, and Gedaliah—have all wed foreign women, taken many wives, none of them Judean. But we put our hands together here, in pledge that we will put these women aside, and do the will of the Lord God!"

A cheer rose and his brother, Gedaliah, cried above it, "Further, we will each give a ram from our flocks in sacrifice, to expiate our great sin against the Lord."

"No!" came another cry. Heads craned to find the speaker. A small, wiry man rose reluctantly. "I will not do this! I am Jahzeiah ben Tikvah, a shepherd. My beloved Isnat has given me strong sons. She suffered when one of them died as a child and nearly died herself giving birth to three of them. She endured without complaint years of hunger at my table when my flock sickened. She has no family to return to. How should the Lord treat me should I forget her sacrifices for love of me? He would strike me dead, and I would deserve His wrath!"

Uri looked at Ezra as Jahzeiah spoke. Such a declaration would move all but the most implacable of men. And he thought he saw even Ezra flinch under the man's touching words.

But then Ezra spoke, and Uri's sudden flash of hope died. "We honor you for the strength of your vows, and were she only of our faith, we would honor her as a woman of valor. But she, and her sons, beloved though they may be, cannot remain here any longer, not if we would keep our people intact.

"This is not something I ask you to do without recognizing how it will tear at the fabric of your families. We know you have lived with these women, some of you, for an entire lifetime. They have grown around your hearts like ivy around a strong tree limb. But left untouched, ivy chokes the life from a tree. And your beloved wives will choke the life from our people, will leave us nothing more than a memory in the world."

Jahzeiah's face darkened and he sat down, sheltering his face in his hands as he wept. Uri watched as his neighbor, Meshullam, tried to comfort him. But Jahzeiah shrugged him off.

Uri reached up, flicking away the tears welling in his eyes, wishing he had the strength of mind to oppose Ezra. His hands hurt and he found it difficult to curve his fingers around the stylus. But he forced himself through the pain, focusing on the task at hand.

"We must determine who has taken a foreign wife," Ezra said slowly. "But how?"

Uri saw that the enormity of the task suddenly overwhelmed his fellow scribe.

One of the men in the crowd rose. "It is the rainy season, and we cannot settle this matter in just a day or so. You've gathered us here when we've work to do in our fields and in our places of business. Let us go home and each man will act according to his own conscience."

"No!" Ezra cried. "I cannot trust your consciences any longer. This is something you must do or be forever lost to our people, expelled as thoroughly as if I were another Nebuchadnezzar!"

"But we can't stay here," someone else whined. "It's about to pour again!"

Ezra thought for a moment. "Return home now. Only the leaders must remain, one from each family. My scribe will enter your names on his tablets and assign you a time to return, bringing your people back with you. On the first day of the tenth month, we will investigate these matters and decide who must put aside their wives and children. When we are finished, we'll have cleansed ourselves of these foreigners and will be strong and pure."

There were more protests, but Uri, his hands aching and heart sore, put down his stylus. Men began to leave. After some confusion as to how the family heads would present themselves, they finally made a long, snaking line, waiting miserably in the pouring rain. Ezra and Uri, sheltered in the Temple entranceway, gave them each a date to return.

Uri saw it would take them into the first month of the next year to hear all of the cases. *I still have two months*, he thought, snatching at the extra time as though it might save him.

69

The Missing Child

"Ophir?" Chava peered around the door of the barn, where her husband was hanging his tools on the hooks to one side. "Have you seen little Sarah?"

Ophir finished hanging the hoe, then looked around. He looked worn out from the long afternoon in the fields. She knew he wasn't sleeping well these days.

"No. I haven't seen her since the midday meal. Isn't she with you?"

"I sent her to the well two hours ago."

Ophir's lips tightened. "Perhaps she's playing a trick on you."

Chava shook her head. "Maybe. But I'm worried. Can Yoram help me look?"

"Why don't I just send the soldiers who guard the farm day and night?" Ophir asked caustically.

One corner of Chava's mouth twitched. She choked back her involuntary chuckle. "I asked them. They said they hadn't seen her, so she must still be on the farm."

After Ezra declared he would decide who could stay and who must be cast aside, attacks on the city intensified. Whispers circulated that Hanun the Amorite was revenging himself on the Judeans because his daughters were sure to be expelled from their homes. The assaults grew so vicious that Hanun earned the title of the Scourge of Jerusalem. Frantic meetings took place in the governor's offices to decide how to deal with the threat. Soldiers dispatched to each of his daughter's homes were instructed to dog the women's footsteps. One of Hanun's daughters would betray him, a smug magistrate told a horrified Tobija, with an equally appalled Chava and Ophir standing handfast behind her. It would not be long, the magistrate added, before they'd apprehend the outlaw and hang him for his crimes.

"You're crazy if you expect me to lead you to my father!" Tobija screeched. "Oh, gods, that this nightmare would ever end!"

"Tell us where he is and we will trouble you no more," the magistrate urged.

"So you can kill him?" Tobija cried. "Do you really expect me to betray him?"

"Then the soldiers stay," she was told. "Here and in your sisters' houses. One of you will bring Hanun to us."

"I'll send Yoram out to look for Sarah," Ophir said now. "If she's playing a trick, though, Chava, I'll punish her. It's a bad time for her to worry us."

Chava bit the inside of her cheek. Her husband was right, but she wanted to protect the little girl from too harsh a reprimand. "She's just a child, Ophir. She doesn't think."

"She has to be taught to think!" he retorted, turning to hang the scythe in his hands on another hook.

"Let's just find her first," Chava pleaded. "I'm going back to the well."

Chava walked quickly away. She was more worried than she wanted Ophir to see. *I'll punish her myself*, she thought, crouching over the well and looking into the gloomy shadows below. "Sarah!" she cried. "Sarah!"

The only answer was the slight, mocking echo of her own voice.

Yoram ran up to her, panting slightly. "Papa said to come help you find Sarah," he cried, small fists balled at his waist. Chava had to smile at his determined stance, which reminded her of her father. But at Yoram's next question, her smile faded.

"Where should I look?"

"Where does she play?" Chava asked. "Try all her favorite spots."

At dinner there was still no sign of her. The meal went uneaten as the entire family—all but Tobija and her children—trekked through the farm, looking for the missing child.

As night fell, hope waned. *Had she managed to slip off the farm? Had something happened? Was she lying hurt somewhere?* The thoughts chased around Chava's head like small demons, terrifying her.

"We have to wait until morning," Ophir said, coming in to find Chava tearing through the farmhouse once. He put his arms around her. "She'll survive a night outside."

"No!" Chava cried, pulling away. "I couldn't possibly sleep while she's missing!"

Chava ran from the house, grabbing a torch from the hearth. With a shaking hand, she kindled the flax head. *As long as the torch lasts, I'll keep looking,* she promised herself. She went back out, determined to walk the perimeter of the farm. "Sarah!" she cried. "Sarah!"

The soldiers waved her on, sympathetic. "You'll find her," one of them called encouragingly. "Don't worry!"

Oh God, thought Chava. Fear chased through her, the feelings of guilt pervading Jerusalem affecting her. Was this God's punishment for sympathizing with Aunt Zakiti and Irit and Irit's family? For feeling sorry for her husband's pain in having to put aside his first wife and his children? For wishing Ezra had never returned to Jerusalem?

I will repent, Chava pleaded with God. *Just restore my child to me. Oh, please. Please!*

She walked and walked, crying out the child's name, her voice thickening, growing hoarse. The torch began to sputter. She would have to return home soon.

"Chava," hissed a man's voice from the thicket bordering their land. "Hist! Chava!"

A hand reached out and pulled her through the bushes into the tall border grass Ophir hadn't bothered to scythe. Chava shrieked. A hand quickly stifled her mouth.

"Not a sound!" came the harsh voice.

Her heart beating so hard she could barely breathe, Chava saw a tattooed face, a sharp chin, red-rimmed eyes glinting at her. *The man looked like a fox*, she thought, crazily. *Who…?*

"You've lived with my daughter for years, but I was banished from visiting your farm because of your marriage," he said, his voice now turned silky, taking the torch from her hand and extinguishing it, plunging them into the dim half-light of the cloudy evening. "I am certain you know me by reputation, however. My name is Hanun. And I have your daughter."

"Sarah!" Chava moaned, struggling to free herself from Hanun's iron grip. "Where is she? Is she safe?"

"Safe for now." Hanun leaned closer to Chava's ear. "But for how long? That's the question you must ask yourself. How long will your daughter be safe with the Scourge of Jerusalem?"

"She's only a child!" Chava whimpered. "Let her go!"

"My daughter was only a child once," Hanun growled. "My grandchildren are children still. And how do you treat them, you Judeans? You spit on them and turn them away. And my girls, all my girls, are being used as bait to trap me!"

"Give me back my daughter!" Chava pleaded. "She's done nothing to you."

"Give you back your daughter? Certainly. First give me back mine!"

"What?"

"I want my daughter and grandchildren led to me, to a place where I can keep them safe. Someone must guide them past the soldiers, southward, to Moab. There I'll make a life for them."

"But the soldiers…." Chava moaned. "How?"

Hanun thrust Chava into a crouching position, leaning over her threateningly. His hot, menacing breath scorched her hair and face.

"Listen. Your father-in-law was a shepherd once. He knows his way through the mountains, knows pathways and ravines the soldiers aren't aware of. He must lead my family to escape. I'll meet them in Dibon. Tell Amittai I'll meet him at the Sheep Gate into the city. He knows the Sheep Gate. And I'll hand him the child then. A daughter in return for a daughter."

"Tobija will not go," Chava said. "She won't believe me. She hates me."

"Do you blame her?" Hanun sneered. "She has done nothing but love your husband, make a home for him, give him children. Until you returned from Babylon, she was a happy woman. But then...!"

"I never did her harm," Chava protested.

"You did her nothing but harm."

"Still—she will not listen to me. Please, oh, please, just give me back my little girl!"

Hanun reached into the pouch he wore draped over his belt. He yanked her to her feet. "Here," he said, thrusting something into her hand. "Give her this. It's my sign. She'll recognize it."

Chava took the small clay plaque, with an impression of a small fox head stamped onto it. She stood, stupidly staring down at it.

"Don't let the soldiers see that," Hanun warned. "You'll be hanged if they suspect you're in league with me."

"I can't do it," Chava gasped, holding the plaque out in her upturned palm so he would take it back. "I can't betray my people."

He ignored her outstretched hand. "If I am captured, more than I will hang for it. I will tell your magistrates how your beloved Ophir hid weapons for me. How I even took him on a raid or two. How will you like that?"

Chava swallowed hard. *Was it possible?* But she hid her consternation and curled her lip. "I don't believe you."

"And if you do not help me, I'll kill your daughter tonight. I'll rend her limb from limb and leave her body in pieces around your farm."

Looking into his implacable face, Chava knew he would do it. She knew she had no choice. Not if she wanted her child to live. Or her husband.

Strange thoughts assailed her as she closed her fingers around the clay plaque: *I wonder if this is what Grandmama felt when the Captain of the Guard forced her to lie with him. Or what Uri's father felt when they took his manhood. This helplessness.*

"I'll do as you say," she muttered.

"Good. In three days, Amittai's uncle will be summoned to give his testimony as the head of the family. No one would suspect that Amittai would leave Jerusalem on that day. If he leaves that morning, he can be in Dibon in two days of hard walking. Tobija and the children are strong, they can keep up that pace."

"So can I," Chava nodded.

"You?" Hanun looked at Chava calculatingly. "If you are caught...."

Chava glared at him.

"Fine. I will see you and my daughter five days from now in Dibon."

Hanun was about to walk off when Chava caught his arm. "Sarah is unharmed, is she not? Is she frightened? Hungry? Can I give you some warm clothes for her? Food?"

Hanun laughed, yellow teeth bared in a malicious grin. "She'll survive. Think what tales she'll have to tell her own grandchildren if you keep your word."

70

Uri's Choice

"But I thought...in light of my long service...." Uri pleaded.

"Don't you see? If we made an exception for you, we'd have to do so for others," Ezra responded.

They were in one of the antechambers of the Temple, where Ezra met with each head of family, forcing them to agree to cast off their foreign wives and children. The room was lined with fragrant planks of cedar. Ezra sat upright in a seat of state, fashioned from olivewood inlaid with mother of pearl, one of the Temple treasures. In the past weeks, men had lined up outside this room. Uri watched as each one was ushered inside, the slightest flicker of hope in their eyes, a hope extinguished almost immediately.

Now it was Uri's turn to despair. His head dropped as he felt the full weight of Ezra's cruel and implacable ruling. He'd hoped against hope that a personal appeal to Ezra might move the man who held so many thousands of lives in his hands. Helplessly Uri spread his own hands wide, signifying that he had finished speaking. He looked up, to find Ezra staring at him quizzically.

"What will you do?" Ezra asked.

"Without my wife and daughter? I don't know," Uri responded. "They're my entire life."

"Hevel does not feel the same," Ezra said. "Your son-in-law has already found a new bride among the Judean women."

Uri sighed. It was true. Just last week Irit and the children watched as Hevel came home, packed his belongings into bundles and left, ignoring their pleading.

"He didn't even wait until you went before the council," Irit sobbed. "There's this woman...."

She broke down, and Zakiti took her in her arms. "Come, come," she told their daughter. "We don't need these men, do we? What do they do for us besides trouble us and cause us pain? Shush, little one. Shush."

The next time Uri saw Hevel, the younger scribe turned his back on the elder with a shocking lack of respect. Uri, body shaking in rage, wanted to strike him. Clenching his jaw, he ordered, "Go serve in the Temple. Remove yourself from my sight."

Hevel took one look at Uri's snapping black eyes and slunk off. But the younger man had a way to take his revenge. Uri began to overhear whispers that he was no longer capable of doing his work—because his hands, crippled by age and pain, could not write swiftly any longer. *It could only be Hevel spreading these rumors*, Uri realized.

Not that they were untrue. Uri woke barely able to move his hands. Only after plunging them into water that his wife heated over the hearth stones, soaking them for several minutes, did he regain use of them. Zakiti brewed a potion that kept the pain at bay. But the drink made him dizzy at odd times, out of touch with what was going on about him.

He had not drunk the potion this morning, needing his mind clear to speak with Ezra. But his abstinence hadn't helped and his hands, as well as his heart, ached. Ezra, eyes shining with the zeal of the fanatic, remained unmoved.

"You and I were always friends," Ezra said now, rising from his seat and putting out a hand to clap Uri's shoulder. Uri flinched at his touch, stepping back.

"You and I were never friends," Uri retorted. "Let's not pretend otherwise."

"We tried to be," Ezra persisted.

"We tried, that's true. When you were not busy telling me that the choices I made were wrong, we tried." Ezra didn't understand; he had never understood. Bitterness lodged like a heavy stone in Uri's chest.

"What will you do?" Ezra asked again. Pity lurked deep in his eyes, but Uri knew it was useless to appeal to it.

"I don't know," Uri replied, weary to his core. "Zakiti wants to return to Babylon. Her father is dead now, but she thinks her brother will take her in. Perhaps I'll go with her."

"I would miss you," Ezra said. "No one else dares contradict me the way you do."

Uri smiled despite himself. "We always did irritate one another. I wish you well, Ezra. I'm going home now."

Ezra reached out, as though to hug him. But Uri turned away. "Farewell."

He felt the prophet's eyes—for prophet was what the people were beginning to call Ezra—burning his back as he slowly made his way out of the palace.

The idea of a journey back to Babylon exhausted Uri. He dreaded going home to tell an anxious Zakiti and Irit that he hadn't been successful in his plea. Too tired to face them right now, he entered a wine shop just off the main thoroughfare. Early as it was to indulge in a drink, the small tables of the shop were crowded with men who spent their days sitting about imbibing.

"Some wine and a quiet corner," he told the proprietor, who silently accepted his coins and bowed him into a secluded spot.

Uri poured out the wine and sat looking at it. The murky red liquid held no answers, he knew. But he felt his bones had melted, leaving him helpless to move from his seat. He took a drink, then another. He closed his eyes.

"What will you do, Manasseh?" the question from one of the noisier tables filtered back toward Uri's corner.

"I won't stay here and let them rip me from my family, that's certain," the first-born son of the High Priest boomed, his voice overloud.

He sounds as though he's been drinking a long time, Uri thought.

"But won't your father help you?" someone else asked.

"My father? My father does everything Ezra tells him to do. It's as if the man has mesmerized him, along with half the country."

"So where will you go?"

There was a moment of silence, then a clink of cups. "To Mount Gerizim and the Samaritans!" toasted Manasseh.

Uri took another sip. The wine wasn't helping, he realized, rising from his corner. The son of the High Priest caught his eye and waved. "Uri ben Seraf!" he called. "Just the man! Come join us!"

"Me?" Uri asked. Manasseh—the pampered son of the high priest he despised—had never sought him out before.

"You're in the same predicament I am," Manasseh said. "I hear you won't cast off your wife or daughter either."

Uri recalled now that Manasseh had married the daughter of Sanballat, a leader of the Samaritan people, against his father's wishes.

"Like you, I'll seek refuge in the homeland of my wife's family," said Uri. "You'll excuse me, I know. I'm going home now to tell them."

"No, sit a moment! I have something to ask you," insisted Manasseh. "The rest of you—go have another drink on me!"

The others rose, laughing and cheering. Uri sat down unwillingly. Manasseh looked into his eyes with bloodshot pupils. "You hate what is happening here as much as I do," he whispered. "Why else would Uri the diligent scribe be in a wineshop before the midday meal?"

"I had a shock this morning," Uri said. "That's all. I'm going home now."

"But I have a proposition for you," Manasseh said. "The Samaritans want me to show them the proper way to sacrifice to the Most High. I am enough my father's son to do so. And they want someone who knows the Writings to act as scribe. Who better than you, Uri?"

"They mix their worship of the Lord with their other gods," Uri protested. "That's why they weren't allowed to help us build the Temple."

"Exactly!" Manasseh took a hearty sip from his wine cup. "They need someone to lead them away from their pagan gods. You and I, Uri ben Seraf—we could do that."

"Ezra thinks…. And your father…."

"Don't quote either one to me!" Manasseh said. "I'm disgusted with them both."

"They're only doing what they think is right," Uri said, suddenly realizing it himself. "They do this so we Judeans will survive as a people. So many other ancient peoples have already dissolved into the mists of time, vanished forever."

"I know the reasons." Manasseh nodded. "But the pain they inflict is too great. The Samaritans—because they worship other gods—will allow us our pagan wives. And their desire to serve the Lord is great. Together we'll bring them to the true worship of the Most High."

"It's tempting," Uri said. "A much shorter journey."

"And all honor to you, as my scribe," Manasseh said. "Consider it!"

Uri shrugged and nodded. "I'll consider it," he said after a pause. "It is, at least, another choice."

71

A Daughter for a Daughter

IN THE END, AMITTAI AND Ophir wouldn't permit Chava to go with them. "It is too dangerous," Amittai told her. "And your sons need you."

"I've noticed you haven't removed yourself to another couch for more than two months, which you would have done if you weren't pregnant," Ophir added.

Amittai sent a swift glance in her direction, noting her blush. Despite his fears for the missing child, he felt a twinge of deep satisfaction. Another grandchild on the way.

He looked at Keren, who was all concern. "Chava, you cannot go," Keren insisted. "Not if you carry another child. We women will stay here together and keep the farm going."

Chava did not yield without tears and arguments. Deep in the night, Amittai was startled from a restless sleep to hear her and his son yelling at one another.

"You hid weapons for him? I told him I didn't believe him…. Ophir, how could you?"

"How would you feel if you were thought unworthy because you were not exiled with your people?" Ophir flung back. "At the time, Hanun convinced me that he was right to oppose the returned Judeans. But I saw how wrong I was when I married you."

"Had I known I would never have married you!"

"And that's why I never told you!"

"Get out of my bed! Go! I can't look at you!"

There was a loud thud, as though both of Ophir's feet hit the ground at the same instant. Amittai heard his son stalking out of her bedchamber. Amittai turned fretfully on his couch, shifting to look into Keren's open eyes. He shook his head sadly.

"After Tobija leaves and the little one is returned to us, all will be well," Keren whispered. "Chava is worried for her daughter."

Amittai wasn't convinced, but he didn't want to start an argument. They were to start the journey to Dibon tomorrow before cock's crow. He turned again, trying to find a comfortable corner where he could lapse into rest for the few hours left of the night.

He woke to find Keren moving about their chamber in the dark, gathering warm clothing for him. He lay in bed, listening to the household. In Tobija's chambers, she and the children talked quietly about their grandfather and what life would be like in the hills around Dibon. Ophir was with them, Amittai realized, hearing him instruct Nadab how to roll his belongings into a pack he could wear comfortably on his back. Listening carefully, Amittai heard someone sobbing in Chava's room. *Had the girl gotten any sleep last night at all?* he wondered.

He rose, unwillingly. They had to be long gone before the soldiers awoke. Just before bedtime yesterday, Keren had prepared a large meal for the soldier on guard, dropping some poppy seeds into a warm cup of wine. With luck, he was still sleeping at his post. But even awake, Amittai knew this guard rarely stirred from his seat on the fence. They would slip out through the barn and leave the farm through the terraced olive groves.

He joined Ophir and Tobija and the children, standing around the hearth. Amittai's heart went out to his two grandsons and three granddaughters. Tobija turned her face away. They had not spoken for weeks. Nadab, the eldest, glared at him. Amittai wished Ophir knew the way to Dibon without him. This would not be pleasant.

Chava slunk into the room, eyes red-rimmed. "I want...." she started.

But Ophir, putting his arms around her, stopped her. "You carry my child," he told her. "You'll stay here."

Tobija, who had not been told of Chava's pregnancy, raked the second wife's stomach with piercing eyes. "You won't miss me or the children at all, will you, Ophir?" she hissed.

But one look at Ophir's face showed Amittai how untrue that was. His son looked tortured. Nadab saw his expression and his face puckered.

"I cannot believe you want us to leave, Father," he said.

Ophir shut his eyes in agony. "We must go now."

"Come," Amittai nodded, cracking open the kitchen door and looking into the darkness. "Not a word once we leave the house until I say it is safe."

"Ophir!" Chava mouthed. "Bring my daughter back to me!"

Tobija took one last, searing look around the house where she'd lived for so many years. Keren stood in the background, arms folded over her chest, eyes dark and hard as stones. None of the grandchildren approached her, Amittai noticed. They filed out of the house silently. Nadab's wet cheeks glistened in the moonlight. So did Ophir's.

They left the farm undetected, wending their way through the rocky terraces to higher ground. They walked swiftly, silently. Amittai and Ophir carried most of the belongings tied to their backs, allowing the slower Tobija and children greater freedom of movement. They left the farm behind, clambering over a fence to a neighbor's land. They slunk low, keeping out of sight. This farm belonged to one of the Judean returnees whom Hanun had once attacked. Amittai knew their flight would win no sympathy here or anywhere in Judea.

By the time the sun rose, they were far from Jerusalem, in the woody hills surrounding the city. Amittai unerringly moved the group down the slope of a hill to a rocky ravine. In the summer, this dry riverbed provided a secluded roadway, used mainly by shepherds. The recent rains had made the ground muddy, hard to traverse, but at least they could still walk through it. Amittai strained to hear the sound of bells, making sure they kept out of sight of the flocks being led out from their night's safe enclosure into the wild, to graze throughout the day.

At midday they rested in the dank coolness of a cave mouth. Tobija and her children sat apart from Amittai, who opened his pack and brought out bread and cheese. Tobija nearly snatched the food from his hands, breaking it into pieces. Ophir looked at the small group, shoulders drooping. He opened his mouth to speak.

"Will Chava soon forgive you, do you think?" Amittai whispered to his son.

Tobija, overhearing, turned her back on them. Ophir glared at his father and shook his head, taking his own portion of bread and moving aside to eat by himself.

Amittai sighed and ate alone.

As they moved farther from the city, Amittai saw the tension begin to drain from Tobija. She talked to her children about life in her father's caravans, how they would be surrounded by riches unlike any they experienced on the farm. She didn't bother to mention how Hanun attained those riches, Amittai thought wryly. Because they so clearly did not want to hear his voice, he spoke in a series of grunts, leading the party through gestures and by tossing his head in one direction or the other.

Ophir, too, remained largely silent. Once in a while, he approached one of the children and lay a hand on his arm or her hair. But Tobija's poison had seeped into them all. Amittai watched as they steeled their young eyes from softening at their father's touch, how after Nadab spit on the ground when Ophir tried to touch him, the others did the same.

They passed a sleepless night out in the open, lying next to a small fire, listening to the desert beasts howl. "As long as we have a fire, the animals won't approach," Amittai told them, relieving the strained fear in their eyes. He sat up, watching where the light of the fire melted into darkness, wishing he had his old shepherd's stick with its sharpened end. Where had that stick disappeared to?

The next morning, the bustling city of Dibon could be seen an hour's journey away, rising from the fragrant orange groves of Moab. Amittai knew a place where a man could pass unquestioned into the foreign land. He led them through it, cautioning them to keep their heads down if they met anyone. *It was market day*, he realized with a start, as they joined dozens of people on the road making their way to the Sheep Gate. Hanun, that sly old fox, had deliberately chosen a day when strangers would go undetected in the crowds.

They reached the Sheep Gate by mid-afternoon. Exhausted by the stiff pace of their journey, the children collapsed by the roadway. Tobija sent one of her daughters to fetch water from the well. They drank thirstily, then sat stolidly for close to an hour, waiting.

"Daughter!" came the loud cry, waking them from their stupor.

Tobija rose and ran to her father. She flung herself on his chest, laughing and crying. The children gathered around him, a little shy. In recent years, banished because of Ophir's marriage to Chava, Hanun had visited only infrequently and in secret. Nadab, however, picked up his grandfather's hand and kissed it.

Ophir looked past his family, to the little girl held by one of Hanun's henchmen. "Sarah!" he cried, taking a few steps and seizing the child. He held her tightly cradled to his breast.

"Father!" Sarah clung to him, face wet with tears, small hands pulling at his shirt.

Hanun looked around. "Your other wife said she'd be here," he sneered. "I thought she meant it...."

Tobija, head still snuggled against her father's chest, looked up. "She's with child," she said, bitterly. "The Judean farmer you bought me is busy planting his seed elsewhere."

"I see," Hanun nodded. "Oh, well. Amittai of Judea! We'll not meet again, you and I."

"I am glad of it," Amittai said, his heart beating rapidly.

Ophir seemed to sense his father's fear and a look of disdain crossed his face. He turned to his father-in-law. "I return your daughter to you, Hanun," he said calmly. "And no matter what she or you think of me, I am sorry to be forced to do it."

"You were always a good boy, Ophir," Hanun grinned. "I'll miss you."

"Tobija!" Ophir cried. "Take care of our children. Raise them not to hate their father or his people."

Tobija pursed her lips. "You ask too much of me, husband," she said. "But I will have a care for them, at least."

"You have your daughter, and I have mine," Hanun said. "We'll leave you now."

Ophir handed Sarah to Amittai and gave each of his children a parting kiss. Amittai saw how their eyes melted a little as their father embraced them.

The little girl clung to her grandfather. "I was scared," she whispered. "Grandfather, I was so scared."

"Shh," he murmured into her sun-hot hair. "Don't be scared any more. I'll protect you."

Her limbs relaxed. *She must have been terrified*, he realized, his thoughts lighting upon the day Chaldean soldiers slaughtered his mother. *Sarah was just a little older than me*, he realized, when their lives were turned upside down, frightened almost past enduring.

But at least little Sarah was luckier than he had been, than so many of them had been. She at least would return—to her home and to her mother.

72

Harvest Festival

500 BCE–Year 25 of the Return

TEN YEARS PASSED. THE HARVEST was gathered, and the people came to the Water Gate to celebrate. The High Priest had blown the shofar just a few days ago on the world's most solemn of days, and the people who gathered before the recently rebuilt walls were in a celebratory mood.

"Bring out the Writings," someone called. "Ezra! You promised us the Writings of the Lord!"

There was a pause. Chava looked around. The mass of people—husbands, wives, children, servants, slaves—were dressed in their holiday best, smiling under the high clouds of the azure blue autumn morning.

"Ezra! We want to hear the Writings!" someone else called.

There was a stir and the crowd parted, allowing Ezra to pass, the Levites at his heels. They carried the heavy scrolls of the Writings. All those hundreds of clay tablets, Chava thought, the tablets she'd seen stacked in niches in the Academy of Sages in Babylon, had been transferred to lambskin and rolled about the gold-encrusted wooden dowels, covered with embroidered cloths.

The people sprang to their feet, cheering as the Writings were carried though their midst. "Sing praises to the Lord!" someone cried, and the voices of the Temple singers rang out: "Let Israel rejoice in their Maker; let the people of Zion be glad in their King!"

Ezra's progress toward the high platform was halting, blocked time and again as people clapped him on the back, dancing and singing praises to the Lord. "It is like Miriam and her women," Chava said to her daughters, who tapped their feet in excitement. "We dance just like they did, with their timbrels and bare feet upon the shores of the Reed Sea!"

The people reached to touch the sacred scrolls, kissing their fingers in ecstasy.

Finally Ezra reached the wooden platform, climbing the steps. Some of the people had sat back down again, but as Ezra picked up the scroll and held it high over his head, they jumped to their feet, crying out in exultation.

"We are here today," Ezra's voice rang out. "Here in a secure and walled Jerusalem, because of your sacrifices, my people. You gave of your time and money to rebuild the walls. Some of you gave your lives. Though he's returned to the king of Persia's service, we must offer huzzahs in the name of Nehemiah, he who armed the builders of the walls of Jerusalem and made the city safe!"

"Huzzah!" called the people. "Praise Nehemiah!"

Chava's two grown boys, Yoram and Reuven, grinned at that. They, along with their father, had been pressed into service at the Fish Gate, under the direction of the sons of Hassenaah. It had been a long and weary time, Chava remembered, as every morning her husband and sons placed daggers in their belts and lay beside them the long swords Nehemiah had provided every builder of the wall. They were more fortunate than many of the others, for only once did the followers of Tobiah the Ammonite and Sanballat the Horonite harry them—and they'd been able to grab their weapons and repel their attackers in short order.

"Nehemiah has returned to the king's service as his cupbearer, but he left behind his brother, Hanani. Moreover, the commander Hananiah, so ably trained in the Persian forces, stands steadfast at the citadel and keeps those who would lay claim to our lands outside the gates through his strong sword and devout heart. All praise Hanani and Hananiah!"

Once again the people shouted in praise. Chava felt one of her children tugging on her dress and looked down to see little Mara looking up at her, wide eyed.

"Aren't they ever going to start the stories, Momma?" she whispered.

"Soon." Chava smoothed down her ten-year-old's black hair. She looked at Mara's twin, Seraf, who was tussling with his two older brothers. "Don't hurt him," Chava called.

Yoram picked up the little boy and held him high in the air. "Hurt him? Why, we couldn't do that. Mighty Seraf here is a lion of Judea!"

Seraf grinned and let out a pretend roar. Chava smiled at Ophir, who looked proudly at the oldest of the sons still left to him. She wondered if he missed his parents, both of whom had passed on in the last year— Keren first, of a sudden chill, Amittai soon afterward. While Ophir always laughed when she mentioned it, she was certain her father-in-law had died of a broken heart. Amittai might have been a weak man, she thought, but he had loved his farm and his wife. She honored him for that, at least.

Suddenly the crowd hushed. Ezra unrolled the first scroll. "In the beginning," he read, "God created the Heavens and the Earth. Now the Earth was formless and empty, darkness over the surface of the deep, and the Spirit of God hovered over the waters...."

Chava was plunged back into memory. She was a little girl again, bringing her uncle lunch at the Academy of Sages in Babylon. "A good story, I find, holds most people's attention for as long as you tell it and for just as long again," Uri had said. And Ezra the scribe had considered his words and said, "I must remember this...."

"These are Great Uncle Uri's stories," Chava's son Reuven exclaimed, as Ezra captured everyone's attention with the story of the Flood.

Chava nodded, closing her eyes. How fared her Uncle Uri, she wondered? He, Zakiti, and Irit had gone to Samaria as members of Manasseh's household. Had his been the hand that transcribed the dozens of letters Sanballat and Tobiah wrote King Xerxes from the Samaritan hills, harassing the Judeans? Chava couldn't believe that. No, Uri must be in the temple of the Samaritans, teaching them the stories of the Torah, the same origins of time that Ezra now was reading aloud to a rapt people.

"Aunt Zakiti always got angry when Uri told the story of the Flood," Chava whispered to Reuven. "She always claimed it was first a Babylonian tale."

"Chava! Quiet! You'll scandalize the neighbors," Ophir hissed. But then he shrugged, grinning.

Chava smiled at her husband. She took Mara onto her lap. Seraf looked wistful, but he was too old to cuddle—at least in public. Sarah and Reuven and Yoram, all grown and starting their own families, sat close by. Chava put out a hand and touched Sarah softly on her protruding belly. *Grandmama, your namesake does you proud*, she thought. Chava blinked back tears, glad to remember how she'd given her grandmother one day of joy in her old home, at least.

Ezra read the stories of their people until noon that day. He continued to read them on the next, and then the next. Like the Israelite tribes who wandered the arid deserts to reach their long-lost home, the people gathered branches from wild olive trees, from myrtles, palms, and shade trees, making themselves booths to live in during the reading. For seven days Ezra read to the people their story. On the eighth day, they rejoiced with a great festival. And Chava and Ophir, handfast, kissed their children and called down the blessings of the Lord to grace their homes and their hearts.

Author's Note

Why did the Jews survive as a people when so many ancient communities did not? This is the question that captivated me when I began researching the Babylonian exile. After all, how easy it would have been for the Judeans—conquered, their Temple burned, their God seemingly vanquished, tempted by the opulence of Babylon—to simply surrender their beliefs and traditions, disappearing into the mists of time.

Obviously, many Judeans succumbed. They adopted Marduk and the entire pantheon of Babylonian idols, put aside their old beliefs, and assimilated into the empire. Still, others clung to their faith, recording the stories of their people, turning inwardly to prayer and charity, and created a new form of religion that eventually superseded Temple sacrifice.

When I started writing *Babylon* some fifteen years ago, I was waiting for *The Fruit of Her Hands*, my medieval historical novel, to find a home. I had touched upon the idea of assimilation in that novel and felt called upon to explore it more fully. I was drawn to this ancient episode by a nearly forgotten short story in a Sunday School text. It related how some Judeans returned home when Cyrus freed them, while others remained in Babylon, unwilling to sacrifice the comfort of their new lives.

I was also fascinated by the idea of our Biblical stories first being written down in Babylon as a way to preserve our faith. I've allowed myself considerable artistic liberty in how these stories might have been recorded, passed down orally from generation to generation, before finally being captured in clay and on the page.

While planning the novel, I read the Biblical story of Ezra the Prophet. Ezra's requirement that non-Judean wives and children be expelled from Judea to preserve the purity of the Hebrew people both fascinated and repelled me. How could anyone be so cruel, so obdurate? And yet I asked myself: Would the Jewish people have survived otherwise? Even though this event occurred approximately more than eighty years after the Return from Babylon, I felt that it was the necessary dramatic curtain for my novel. By radically compressing my timeline, the Judeans had come full circle: once exiled, now compelled to banish others.

As I did my research, I came across many ancient names, particularly Babylonian ones, that may appear long and unfamiliar to the Western reader. Babylonian men all seem to incorporate the prefixes of Neb- or Bel- or the suffixes -Marduk or -shezzar in their names. For instance, Daniel's Babylonian name, Belteshazzar, is easily confused with that of Belshazzar, Amel-Marduk's favorite courtier, whose name would crop up again when Nitocris's stepson appeared on the scene. I hope the family trees provided help clarify the various relationships in the novel.

Acknowledgments

IT IS DIFFICULT, AT A space of some fifteen years, to recall all the people I should thank for their contributions to *Babylon*. If I have forgotten anyone, please do forgive me. My sister, Sipora Coffelt, was the first reader of the "snippets" I wrote, out-of-sequence scenes that eventually converged into the novel. My business partner in The Writers Circle, Judith Lindbergh, graciously opted not to write what would have been a very different book about Babylon upon learning that I was engaged on mine. Judith, Stephanie Cowell, Caprice Garvin, Mally Becker, and Alex Cameron were all early beta readers. Maggie Crawford, my editor for *The Fruit of Her Hands*, was kind enough to read the novel and suggest some radical changes. Vinessa diSousa and Alex Cameron were my editors prior to submitting a final copy to my publisher, and I am grateful for their thoughtful comments. My brother, Matthew Kreps, helped me with the final proofread of the novel. Elizabeth Schoenfeld created the map and family trees, while Beth Forester took the author photo. I also want to thank the Jew(ish) Binder group on Facebook, especially Zeeva Bukai, for telling me about the Wicked Son imprint. And of course, my gratitude goes to everyone at Wicked Son, including publisher Adam Bellow, managing editor Aleigha Kely, copy editor Mal Windsor, proofreader Neha Patel, and artist Hampton Lamoureux.

Finally, I am thankful for my husband Steve's patience and understanding when I am consumed by the writer's drive: that irresistible impulse that moves me to sit for hours before the computer, trying to bring historical worlds, peopled by real and imaginary characters, to life.

Photo by Beth Forester

Michelle Cameron is the author of historical fiction, including the award-winning *Beyond the Ghetto Gates* and *The Fruit of Her Hands*. She has also published a verse novel, *In the Shadow of the Globe*. *Napoleon's Mirage*, the sequel to *Beyond the Ghetto Gates*, is forthcoming.

Michelle is a director of The Writers Circle, a NJ-based creative writing program serving children, teens, and adults. She lives in Chatham, NJ, with her husband and has two grown sons of whom she is inordinately proud.

https://michelle-cameron.com/
Facebook: https://www.facebook.com/michelle.cameron1
Instagram: michellecameronwriter
Twitter: mcameron_writer